THIRTY DAYS HAS NOVEMBER...

CRONUS: TEAM ZEUS
BOOK 1

ASHER ZANDS

30 Days Has November - CRONUS: TEAM ZEUS

Printed in Australia

First Printing, 2024

To friends and family lost too soon.
Gone but not forgotten.

The FAMILY TREE

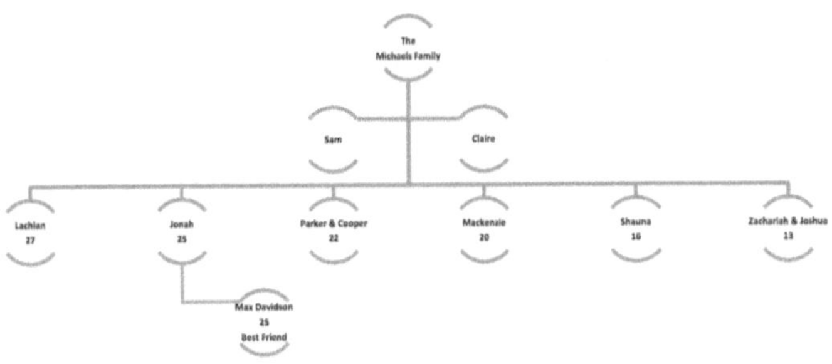

The CRONUS TREE

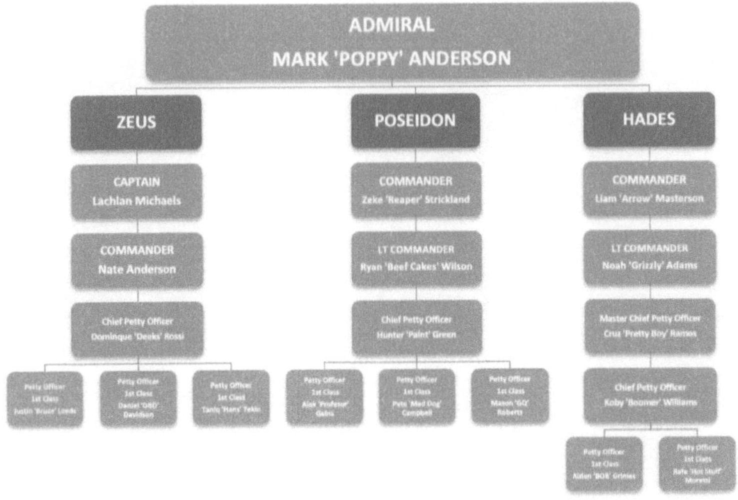

PROLOGUE

Six Years Ago

Something wasn't right. A cold chill ran down his spine as every hair on his body stood on its end. Alert, Lachlan tuned out his brothers and fiancée and searched the small bar, finally landing on the bartender. He didn't trust the guy. If you looked, it was obvious he hated the patrons in his establishment. Why he worked there confounded Lachlan.

This was the one place, soldiers, airmen, marines and seamen alike felt safe enough to attend on their downtime. Although Lachlan didn't know why. Being located just off base didn't mean it was safer than any other bar in Iraq, but it had long become the place to go.

Word was that the US would leave Iraq by the end of the year and most of them would be sent to join their comrades in Afghanistan. Rumours circulated that they had fresh intel and were closer than ever to finding the infamous Al-Qaeda leader.

The opening of the main door drew the bartender's gaze, but no one entered. A slight tilt of the head was the only acknowledgement of any interaction before the door closed again but it was enough. Although, Lachlan would have missed it had he not been looking straight at the man. Without hesitation the barkeep dropped his cleaning rag and headed for the back exit.

Fuck!

Lachlan's heart raced. His instincts were screaming 'get out!'

A quick glance estimated about eighty people inside, mostly American military personnel, many drunk off their asses. Lachlan's gut churned. War was nothing new to him but normally he was armed for an apocalypse and his fiancée wasn't sitting right next to him.

With no time to overthink, Lachlan scrambled from the booth pulling his fiancée out behind him while barking out blanket orders. His team followed without hesitation.

"Out. Everyone, get out! Head for the side door. Now! MOVE!"

Spinning to face his 2IC, Lachlan first kissed his fiancée and then pushed her into her twin brother's arms. People were hurrying around them, but the process still seemed somewhat orderly.

A shouted 'It's locked!' was accompanied by three gunshots. The door flung open, and people started filing out into the night.

"Go. Get out fast and keep alert. I expect they're going to blow this place but that doesn't mean they're not outside waiting to shoot everyone exiting."

"Awesome, that sounds like fun. We'll see you soon. Don't get dead, asshole." With that, Nate grabbed his sister's hand and started navigating a pathway to the side of the building, most of his team followed helping corral others along the way.

Lachlan headed toward the bar, DBD was already steps ahead of him. If there was a bomb inside, that's where it would likely be. If they found it in time, his demolitions man would hopefully be able to disable it.

Shit, he hoped he was right.

It would be faster to leave by the front or back but after the Bali bombing, valuable lessons had been learned. People were habitual, they wanted to leave, the same way they entered. The only reason anyone was listening to him now was because they were military personnel, and they were used to following orders. If they started to panic, then all bets were off. Plus, there were also many non-combatant personnel in attendance tonight who for the moment were just following the group.

As the crowd huddled together and moved toward the side of the building, the area around the front entrance, the bar and the back exit was becoming less congested but not fast enough.

It was too slow.

Getting everyone out the side door was taking too long. Others were realizing it too. Lachlan turned when he heard orders being shouted out contradicting his. A Marine Colonel had decided to take control. Toward the back of the building, the man redirected those closest to run for the rear exit.

Lachlan winced moments later when rapid gunfire echoed back though the opening, along with the screams. A large explosion shook the building and took out a good chunk of the back wall. Sometimes it sucked to be right. Those who hadn't been killed or trapped under the debris, turned and started pushing back in, redirecting themselves towards the side door, but it was too late. Panic had taken hold and the somewhat orderly exit had turned into that of an unruly mob.

Lachlan yelled for DBD to get out, there wasn't going to be time to disable any other IED's even if they did find them.

A few feet in front of him, Lachlan watched an army second lieutenant fall, tripped among the fleeing crowd. He started her way, but movement caught his eye when the front door opened once more.

Time was up.

"GRENADE!"

Everything slowed. A decent sized clearing had been made around the entrance, but Lachlan was still too far away. Pushing against the flow, Lachlan fought to get through, eyes focused solely on the grenade and as it started its descent, he launched himself

toward the flying object. Arm outstretched; his body extended…
He wasn't going to make it.

Fuck!

Still in the air, his view was abruptly blocked. It took milliseconds to realize his teammate, had also dived for the grenade, only he was closer. Falling, Lachlan watched DBD catch the device and pitch it back toward the door as the floor rushed up to meet him.

The resulting explosion was loud, the secondary boom that it triggered was deafening, that was then followed by a third explosion from somewhere behind the bar. Pain tour through his body as the ceiling and other debris rained down, the building collapsing quicker than a frog snapping up a tasty fly. Lachlan could only hope that his fiancée and the rest of his team had made it out safely and that DBD was alive under the rubble that now covered them.

A sudden eerie silence surrounded the space as darkness settled in. For long moments, his own labored breath and a low ringing in his ears, the only sounds he heard. He didn't know if he lost consciousness, but suddenly his body jolted sending sharp stabbing sensations throughout his brain when without warning, noise flooded his senses in a rapid ambush.

Breathing through the pain, something thick and wet trickled down his cheek. Slowly the noise became more distinguishable. The sounds of rubble being cleared and muffled yells filtered down. Pinpricks of light started peeking through. With each ray, the voices got clearer and louder.

"Lachlan! Lachlan, answer me damn it."

Huh? Nate?

"Lieutenant Commander Michaels!"

Lachlan groaned, squinting when more and more light poured in. Turning his head away, he closed his eyes and felt the substance on his cheek trickle into his mouth. The copper twang, a poor substitute for the water he craved.

Then he was being yanked and pulled from different directions. Floating, he felt himself being lifted into the air, the remaining rubble that had pinned him down falling away. Soft hands cupping his cheeks encouraged him to open his eyes. The beautiful tear-stained face of his fiancée filled his view. She was alive and safe. Thank Mary!

His team?

Lachlan opened his mouth to speak but she shook her head.

"No, don't waste your energy. Please honey, just rest. They're getting to DBD now, unlike you he's been communicating with everyone. He thinks he's fractured a few bones, but a fallen beam provided a safe pocket for him."

Letting his eyes fall closed, he sighed as his fiancée's warm lips brushed his forehead. Her quiet tear laced words, the last thing he heard.

"I love you Lachlan. Fight for me!"

ONE

MONDAY 30TH OCTOBER

Consciousness came slowly as she struggled to focus through blurred vision. Dread surrounded her, a heavy cloak of despair. Sprawled on a hard, cold floor. Body aching. Thoughts incoherent. A memory just out of reach. *Where the hell was she?* Her pulse spiked. Her stomach churned. As panic took hold, the darkness reclaimed her.

"Shoot me, anyone! For the mother of loving Mary, please shoot me!" Sheriff Lachlan Michaels groaned into his hands as half the town board argued around him like they were fighting for world peace. Principal Mullins, the town gossip Mrs. Hayworth, and Mayor Lewinski flung barbed words at each other with the zeal of teenagers in a food fight. All with superior righteousness. The ridiculousness was the argument itself. What time should they dismiss school on Halloween – 12 p.m. or 1 p.m.? Like it bloody mattered!

Why the hell was he even here? He was the damn captain of a special ops team for Mary's sake and here he was playing sheriff. These people were draining the life out of him. He needed explosions, gun fire, just some damn fun with his team. Three more months, he just had to survive this boredom for another ninety-three days and then he could go back to doing what he did best.

More importantly there'd be no more secrets. For better or worse the truth would be out there.

The biggest question was whether he could really go another three months without killing anyone? Some would consider it a public service. War zones were so much easier. Idiots tended to end up dead by their own actions, sometimes taking others with them, while no one raised an eyebrow if you took out the enemy as long as they were pointing a gun at you with intent. Simple.

What wasn't simple was small town politics filled will egotistical, overestimated small town minds, with visions of taking over their small worlds.

Pulled from his sulking, Lachlan clocked movement from his left before a hand squeezed his shoulder in a show of comfort and solidarity. Fire chief Sanders smirked as he whispered, "Be thankful you missed the last meeting, son."

Lachlan scoffed as he turned to face the older man, still to this day one of his dad's closest friends. Sanders big brown eyes were currently shining brightly as the surrounding lines tightened in his effort not to laugh out loud.

"Sanders, it's been twelve months, six days, and around twenty hours since I was last shot. I know this because my asshole teammates made a damn website for me. Other websites count the days between trucks running into low bridges. My team calculates the time between bullet holes. By my standards, I'm overdue. You'd be doing me a favor." Lachlan pointed his index finger at Sanders to emphasize his point.

"Just one little controlled shot. It doesn't need to do much damage. Just enough to get me out of any official town business for the next month would be awesome. Because I promise, I'd rather be lying on my ass in hospital nursing a bullet wound with doctors bitching at me than sitting here listening to this shit. And to be clear, the only reason I am here is because the last meeting I missed, this committee thought it'd be a brilliant idea, not only to give all the little shits Halloween afternoon off, but the whole rest of this week and the start of next, until the winter fair is over!" Huffing in disgust, Lachlan continued working up more steam. What the hell was wrong with this town?

"What? We didn't think a few hours after school was enough time to terrorize the town, we had to prolong it for an entire week! Have you seen what they've done outside? Seriously, it looks like the town drunks went on a rampage vomiting pumpkins and carrots all over the place after their latest bender. Wherever you look, it's damn orange! Someone has even painted parts of the sidewalk. The sidewalk, Sanders! What the hell is the point in painting the damn sidewalk? And what's going to happen for the winter fair next week? Are they painting the sidewalks winter cloud white for that? This town has lost its fucking mind!"

Another choked laugh came from his right before cutting off. Doc Stevens whispered behind his hand, "Shit, I think that's the most words I've ever heard out of your mouth in one conversation, let alone one breath. The whole damn town has been worried sick about how withdrawn you've been, and all we needed to do was give the kids some time off school and paint the sidewalks."

Doc Stevens had only been in town a few years and had become partners in Lachlan's mother's medical practice, but the man was kind and had inserted himself into the community without effort, quickly gaining the respect of all who met him. That didn't mean Lachlan wouldn't strangle the smart ass.

"So true. Oh, and Lachlan, they're looking to go with a combination of dark blue and gray with touches of white for the sidewalk next week!" Sanders whispered back.

"Fuck you." Lachlan shook his head before chuckling along

with them. Their mirth cut short as silence descended around them. Sure enough, as Lachlan lifted his head from his hands, the three members of the board who had been arguing were now glaring at them.

"Anything you'd like to add to this, gentlemen? Or are you all happy to sit there and giggle like little children?" Principal Mullins demanded in her gruff, I've smoked three packs of smokes a day for fifty years' voice.

Under torture, Lachlan might admit he tended to avoid the intimidating woman who was the town's school principal. Lachlan had only been back in town a few months, but every time he'd seen her, she had a damn ugly scarf around her neck. This one, a disgusting bright yellow with brown spots. Even with the scarf he thought she would make an excellent linebacker for the San Francisco 49ers. He was thankful she hadn't been the principal when he was in school. She was terrifying.

In contrast, Mrs. Hayworth looked like any perfect storybook Fairy Godmother. If only she could stop talking for a few moments to give others a chance to voice their wishes, and then didn't venomously oppose them for no damn reason.

"I think," Lachlan cleared his throat, "this is asinine. Twelve p.m. is lunchtime. We're sitting here while you argue over whether we should run the cafeteria for both breakfast and lunch, or only breakfast. None of the kids living here go without food. As a town, we'd know if anyone was struggling, and we'd help. So, no, I have nothing to add, and if this is seriously all that's on the agenda for today, I will happily take my leave."

"Right, right you are, Lachlan, son," Mayor Lewinski boomed out. "Let's give the cafeteria staff half the day off, too. Twelve p.m. it is then. Are we all agreed?"

Murmurs of agreement sounded around the table. Lachlan received a nod from Principal Mullins, who had been on the winning side of the argument. Mrs. Hayworth looked slightly put out, but that was likely because Principal Mullins had got her way.

The two women always being on opposing sides was the main reason these meetings dragged into eternity.

Mayor Lewinski just loved hearing his own voice, a true politician. Lachlan wasn't sure he entirely trusted the man. He garnered a lot of enjoyment from egging the two women on. Thankfully, there was nothing else to discuss. So, the mayor adjourned the meeting, and Lachlan was finally free to leave.

Walking back to the station, Lachlan shook his head when his pup dashed two shops ahead and disappeared into the butcher's. Chuckles rang out from several locals when only moments later his husky reappeared, prancing back towards him, proudly displaying his prize. The bone hanging from the pup's mouth was nearly as big as one of Lachlan's thighs. Somehow the rascal kept conning people into giving him food. You'd think Lachlan didn't feed him or something.

Deciding to save his breath, Lachlan waved a hand in thanks as he passed the store and continued heading toward the station. It didn't matter how many times he told the townsfolk to stop or if not, tried to give them money for the treats, they always ignored him or just flat out refused.

Being a small town, most of the older residents had watched Lachlan grow up. That he was back after nine years in the navy made him a bit of a novelty. If only they knew how much change he was about to be the catalyst for...

Stepping into the sheriff's role was always meant to be temporary. Just for six months, while his dad recovered from a torn tendon. Not that he really needed that much time, the man seemed to be walking just fine now, but the doc was adamant his dad didn't return to work too early. Something about relapsing.

Or so they said. Yeah, Lachlan saw through their ulterior motives. His parents wanted him home and thought if he came back for six months, he might just stay. What they didn't know was that he'd already been headed back.

He just wasn't coming alone.

Lachlan had to wonder how accepting everyone would be to the coming changes. That Forest Haven sat nestled in a small valley surrounded by mountains and flanked by a massive river, helped keep big business out. Too far for most to invest in the logistics of setting up, even if long-term it would pay off.

The town was technically close to the Canadian border. If one wanted to hike eighty miles through the mountainous terrain. From there, it was another fifty miles to clear the ranges completely and get to the nearest town. So, no, before now they'd been safe from franchises and mass migrations.

But Lachlan had money and he was happy to invest in the future of this town for everyone that stayed. A small corner of the world where Lachlan could protect and keep his family and friends safe, while still encouraging everyone to prosper. His siblings might leave for college, but he wanted to give them a reason to want to come back here to live.

Flinching, Lachlan did his best to ignore the gaudy Halloween decorations that had taken over Main Street. It wasn't that he didn't like Halloween; he did. He was especially looking forward to it this year, but this was nuts. The town had gone overboard to the extreme.

But maybe it had more to do with him than the town. For as much as Lachlan was looking forward to Halloween the next day, he was also dreading it at the same time. To get to the candy part of the day, Lachlan was going to have to face his family and come clean. Fun. Not!

It's not like they didn't love him. And, yeah, he knew everything would work out fine, but that didn't mean it would go smoothly. There would no doubt be hurt feelings and lots of questions. On the bright side, at least he'd be able to stop sneaking out of town most nights.

Both his deputies, one of which was his younger brother, were due back this morning. His family—like several others in town—had a small cabin up the mountain. The only condition he'd set when they asked for time off together was that they be back before Halloween. Especially since all the little shits had free rein. Okay, so 'maybe' he shouldn't have skipped the last meeting—stupid council meetings. But, if ensuring they were back before Halloween was also because Lachlan didn't want to confess everything twice, well, they didn't need to know that.

Lachlan would have liked to go hide out at the cabin himself—literally. He'd happily leave it to someone else to explain the events of the last few years to his family, but he knew no one would allow that. His team would eagerly hunt him down and drag his ass back. Assholes.

Besides, winter was fast approaching which meant snow. And once the snow hit, it would be difficult to make it in or out of town for weeks, unless it involved a helicopter. Luckily, that wasn't a problem for him, not that anyone in town knew that.

A man needed some secrets.

Being able to escape was paramount to Lachlan's survival. People being snowed in tended to result in raging tempers and the stupidest arguments known to man. It sucked that they expected Lachlan to calm and settle said stupid arguments, instead of just shooting the protagonist. His way would be a hell of a lot more effective.

Hmmm, maybe if Lachlan accidentally shot one of the town idiots, his dad would come back to work early and end Lachlan's suffering.

Hearing the nectar of the gods call out to him, Lachlan unlocked the station door and headed straight toward the small kitchenette. He made it halfway to the lifesaving liquid, only to stop short when the station door flew open, banging into the wall before slamming shut again. The sound of pounding feet loud on the vinyl floors. Dammit! He needed coffee to deal with this.

Turning to confront the intrusion, he watched the two young boys speed past him. Lachlan didn't bother reacting to the sound of the station door again, hitting the wall and closing with force. If things were serious, the twins would have aimed for Lachlan, not run past him. The brats made it into the safety of the first cell—again with the slamming—the cell door automatically locking them in and collapsed onto one of the two small cots. Their chests were heaving, but their eyes were locked on the dangerous predator that, while behind Lachlan now, no doubt wouldn't be for long.

Fuck! Lachlan pinched the bridge of his nose between his thumb and forefinger. He was too old for this. A flash of black streaked past him, headed straight for the cell that contained the boys. The older teenager unsuccessfully tried to shake the bars loose, all the while screaming at the twins, her whole body vibrating in anger. Man! Was she pissed and loud.

"Come out here and face me! You had no right to interfere, you insufferable, nosy little twerps!"

"Come on, Shauna, calm down," the youngest twin whined. "We didn't mean anything."

Calm down? Shit! Even Lachlan knew not to say those words to an irate female. Since the yelling only escalated, Lachlan figured he should settle in for the long haul and that required coffee. Lots and lots of coffee. All the coffee! Hmmm, an Advil chaser sounded good, too.

Coffee in hand, Lachlan positioned himself to lean back against Jonah's desk, legs crossed at his ankles, to watch the rest of the show. Moments later, he heard the door open and then close normally—no slamming involved. Lachlan didn't bother taking his eyes off the commotion in front of him as his deputies entered the fray.

"Hey, Lachie."

"Morning, good trip?"

"Yeah, was nice to get away for a bit. Kinda wished I had stayed another couple of hours." Jonah half gestured toward the cells, but he sounded like he was hoping Lachlan didn't answer his question. "Do I want to know?"

Lachie shrugged. "Like I have a clue. They're closer to your mentality than mine."

Jonah, two years younger than Lachlan, rolled his eyes and stalked off to the kitchen. Smirking, Max shook his head at Lachlan for baiting his brother and commandeered a portion of the desk next to him.

Max Davidson was also Jonah's best friend, the two of them had been stuck together from the moment they met. Lachlan liked knowing they had each other's back, although it also meant they often tried to gang up on him. Not that it ever worked. Lachlan won, he always won. He would always win. That's just how it was. Things might suck getting there, but would always result in him winning. It was a gift.

"So, Lachie …" Jonah said, handing Max a coffee. "Are you planning to do anything about this? Not sure mama would be too happy if we all sat back and watched our baby sister scream her head off at our baby brothers all morning."

"Meh, I figure they deserve it. Besides, I have coffee." Lachlan paused to take a sip. "And I took some Advil. Guessing she'll lose steam soon but feel free to step in, I ain't stopping you."

A few minutes later, since the yelling continued and didn't appear to be subsiding, Lachlan conceded he didn't have enough Advil for this and decided it was time to intervene. This shit, on top of the town board meeting, was too much crap to deal with so early in one morning.

"Shauna. Enough!"

There was a frustrated growl as Shauna spun to face them. If they'd been too dumb to work it out, from all the screaming. Her hands fisted at her side highlighted how angry their little sister was.

Cocky little smirks took pride of place as Zac and Josh finally stood. Their pretty, blue-eyed sister had a hell of a temper, but once

Lachlan stepped in, everyone knew she wouldn't start in on the brats again. Well, not in front of him at any rate.

"So …" Eyebrows raised, Lachie looked at his youngest sister. "What did they do?"

"Hey!" Zac rolled his shoulders before aiming a dirty look his way. "Who said we did anything?"

"Shut it! Nobody was talking to you." Jonah had obviously reached his end point, too. "What did they do, Shauna?"

With folded arms, her right foot tapped an uncoordinated jerky beat while Shauna glared at them. Her straight brown hair, wind-blown from her pursuit of the twins, made her look even angrier. Although that might have also been the 'all black' look she had going on. If Lachlan didn't know better, he'd figure she had a heist planned after this. Black jeans, black long-sleeved shirt and black boots completing the outfit. But instead of getting some answers. Shauna growled, spun, and stormed straight out of the station, the door once again slamming behind her.

"Well, that went well." Jonah refocused his attention on their baby brothers.

Only thirteen, these two got into more shit than the rest of the town put together. They were cute. With their deep-brown eyes, they'd perfected the sad puppy dog look, not that it always worked to con their way out of trouble.

"Explain!"

Zac huffed in disgust and ignored Jonah. His calculated eyes instead zeroed in on Lachlan. The boys didn't often get much past them. Especially Lachlan, but for some reason, Lachlan's gut told him they might be on the twin's side—this time…

"You see it's like this." Josh broke first. "Shauna's got a new boyfriend. He's older. Much, much older! We were trying to watch out for her." A quick glance at Zac had him taking over.

"Look, we just introduced ourselves and had a friendly chat. That's all. Simples. Shauna overreacted as per normal."

Lachlan raised his left eyebrow at Zac and folded his arms

across his chest. It was amazing how effective that little move was on grown men, let alone teenagers.

"Geez, okay, fine. It's possible we let it slip that one of Mackenzie's former boyfriends disappeared and joined the marines all sudden like." Zac conceded with a smug smirk, "and that it wasn't his idea. That if he didn't join, you were going to have him put away for life in ADX Florence on some trumped-up charge. Then we pointed out the age difference between Shauna and him was much bigger than Mackenzie, and her boyfriend was back then, and that you had even less patience now and bigger muscles than ever before."

Shit! That there said everything about small town gossip. The twins had only been four at the time. Lachlan fought to keep any emotion off his face, just remembering that piece of shit anywhere near his then eleven-year-old little sister was anger inducing. Now twenty, Mackenzie was in college with their other two brothers, but Lachlan still kept an eye on them.

"Oh, boy." Jonah ran both hands through his hair. Unlike Lachlan, Jonah didn't have a buzz cut. "I appreciate you had good intentions, but I can see why Shauna wanted to pummel you into the ground."

It also explained why she stormed out. No way would she want to face Lachlan if the age difference was that large, considering Shauna wasn't anywhere near eighteen yet.

"Best you stay out of Shauna's way until she runs out of steam."

"Yeah okay, fine. Can you open the door now?" Zac tried pulling his puppy dog eye look.

Like that was going to work on him. Instead, Lachlan raised another eyebrow, scoffed, and headed for his office. A few minutes of cajoling later, Lachlan heard the cell door opening and watched from behind his desk as the twins trudged out, slamming the door behind them. Lachlan shook his head and sighed as Jonah and Max chuckles grew closer.

"Crap, we should have got his name. She hid that from us well," Jonah groaned as he and Max came into view.

"Yeah, well, I'm more interested in how much older he is." Lachlan sighed. "Let's give it a couple of days. Besides, the twins might have scared him off—which would have accounted for Shauna's mood," he added thoughtfully.

It wasn't like this was a big town. They either knew the guy, or he was newly relocated and hiding from everyone, which would raise the bigger question of why. Visitors and tourists never really stayed long so strangers hanging around town accumulated gossip that spread like wildfire. Lachlan wasn't sure if he should take comfort in that or be terrified. Only time would tell.

"You gotta admit, it was a damn excellent strategy," Max continued when both he and Jonah turned to him with questioning looks. "Well, considering the fact one of Mac's boyfriends did indeed join the marines, their story will holdup if he asks around."

"Yeah, well, no one can prove he didn't join of his own free will," Lachlan smirked dismissing them, before he turned back to his monitor, ignoring Max and Jonah as they headed to their own desks. Although Lachlan didn't miss Max's whispered words to Jonah. "He's joking, right?"

"Yeah, he's kidding," Jonah said with a shake of his head. "Lachlan was only like seventeen or eighteen when that guy left."

Since neither Jonah nor Max sounded confident, Lachlan kept his smile to himself and went back to work. His one regret was not putting a bullet in that asshole's brain.

As her eyes slowly adjusted to the dark, she tried to take in her surroundings. A near blinding headache making the task all the harder. Pins and needles prickled her limbs, adding to her discomfort. The room was small. There were no windows, no natural light penetrated through into her makeshift cell. Cell? Or dungeon? Jesus, why was she focused on the damn descriptor?

A toilet with a simple, old-fashioned basin sat in one corner next to a mound of blankets. Nothing was familiar.

Where was she?

How did she get here?

She had no answers, but for now, she was alone.

Shivers of fear racked her body as she pulled her knees to her chest. Resting her head on top, she let her silent tears fall, wondering if in this situation, not knowing was better or worse.

TWO

HALF AN HOUR after Shauna and the boys had left to get their asses to school, the station phone rang. Not known for being stupid, Lachlan pulled the cable out of his desk phone and continued with what he was doing. His only regret was not shutting his door when moments later, Jonah's voice replaced the annoying call tone.

"Sheriff's office, Jonah speaking … Oh, hi, Ma. How's things? … Yeah, about an hour ago … Yep, we had a great trip, wish we could have stayed longer … Cool. So, what's going on?"

Lachlan jerked and threw his arm up when a rush of movement caught his eye, snatching the object out of the air. Luckily his reflexes were good although he wasn't fast enough to hide his smirk once he read the five words written in permanent marker on the back of the yellow happy face stress ball.

'I KNOW WHAT YOU DID! ASSHOLE!'

"Hmmm, you've been speaking to Shauna, huh? So, how is she?" Jonah grimaced and threw Lachlan the middle finger at the same time he moved the receiver away from his head. Their mother was inarguably voicing her displeasure, loud enough for half the town to hear. When the rant slowed and decibels lowered, Jonah moved it back to his ear.

"Seriously Ma, I don't know what Shauna told you but to be fair, she ran out of here without telling us anything ... Yeah, probably, but I have to say from what the brat's said, I'm on their side. If he's as old as they're hinting, you better hope I put him in jail before Lachlan gets his hands on him. Shauna's only sixteen no matter how old she acts ... Yes, agreed ... Okay, Ma ... I'll remind them. Bye, Ma." Jonah growled, the loud thunk of the phone sliding home into the cradle signaling the end of the call.

"Asshole, you can't just unplug the phone when you don't want to answer it."

"Ha." Lachlan pegged the ball back at Jonah's head. "That's Sheriff Asshole to you and I can unplug the phone anytime I want to. What did ma have to say anyway?"

"Urgh, she's not happy with the way Zac and Josh went about it but she won't be unhappy if they've managed to scare him off. Dad's going to keep an eye on the situation. Neither of them knew anything about a new boyfriend. She's mainly just reminding us about family dinner tonight."

"Shit." Max groaned. "Dinner with three fighting teenagers. Seriously?"

"Yup." Jonah's smile didn't look at all happy. "Could be worse."

"How?" Max dropped his head into his hands.

Yeah. Even Lachlan wanted to hear Jonah's answer to that question.

"Imagine if the other three were home from college too!"

Shit. Yeah, that would be bad. Mackenzie would no doubt be on her little sister's side but then the older twins Parker and Cooper would jump in and back their younger twin brothers on principle. Which would have led to the six of them arguing all through dinner. It wouldn't occur to any of them to stay out of it and not pick sides. It seemed Max agreed.

"Sure, okay. That's fair. Why your parents had to have eight kids, I'll never know."

"Hell yeah." Lachlan smirked. "They had perfection after their first, they should have stopped there."

This time Lachlan ducked as the stress ball came flying back at him.

"Temper, temper, little brother. Anyway," Lachlan aimed reproachful eyes at Jonah. "If you're finished with your tantrum, we still have hours until dinner. So, you two might wanna go check on Riley and Magee. They got into it again yesterday. By the end of their squabble, Magee had six stitches and was covered in pumpkin slush. I don't see him letting that go unanswered. And while you're there, check if any of the kids have stocked up on eggs or toilet paper lately. I'd rather know ahead of time if we are gonna have any issues tomorrow night."

"Yeah, sure, no worries," Jonah was already moving. "We'll even grab some lunch on the way back. Wait, where are the boys?"

"Under my desk," Lachlan gestured offhandedly.

Jonah waited a beat before walking around to his side when Lachlan didn't give him any more details. Half curled on top of each other, their two huskies were fast asleep. Super cute but a blind person could see something was a little off with the picture.

At Jonah's quizzical look, Lachlan shrugged. "Mannix scored himself a huge ass bone from the butchers. I reckon Racer smelt it and came in here to investigate. I'm guessing Mannix isn't in a sharing mood since it appears he's sleeping on top of it. Every now and then Racer will give him a nudge to see if he can dislodge Mannix enough to get his paws on the treat. Damn hard to sit at my desk when I've gotta share leg room with them. It's not like they're small."

The huskies were also brothers. Mannix was the oldest of the litter and the biggest although Jonah's husky Racer was only slightly smaller. The pups other two litter mates were also part of the family. Viper, the youngest of the four, belonged to Parker and Cooper. The second youngest belonged to Mackensie. All the dogs had great names except for Mac's pup. Somehow, Mac had lost the naming rights to her own pup and Parker had taken full advantage. PIMF which stood for 'Parker Is My Favorite.'

No one knew what Mac did to earn that name, but it must have been good. That it sounded like someone was yelling for a pimp whenever the pups name was called, was never not funny especially considering some of the looks garnered by strangers.

Lachlan had acquired the four pups when he was in Afghanistan. A newbie supply officer misunderstood the commander's request for four new Huskies and instead of ordering the tactical support vehicles, he acquired the four-legged kind. To be fair, at the time, huskies had just started becoming popular in the country.

Seeing an opportunity, Lachlan used his contacts and called in a couple of IOUs to get ownership and deal with the paperwork to get them back to America and through customs. So, after discussions with his siblings and all names being sorted, he and a teammate had spent months training them before bringing them back to the US.

But, at fourteen months, Mannix and Racer were still young. So, it was strange for them to remove themselves from drama instead of diving in amongst it but then again, a huge meaty bone was likely much more tempting.

"Well?" Jonah bent closer to the dogs. "Either of you coming with me and Max?"

Both dogs opened their eyes but only one made to move, albeit slowly. Racer was in no hurry to leave. His huff, making it known he wasn't happy. Mannix managed a yawn before lazily stretching his legs out, claiming even more room, and promptly going back to sleep.

"Oh my God, look at that face. Okay already, we'll stop and get you your own bone on the way back. Geez!" Jonah rolled his eyes and walked out, the now smug looking pup prancing at his heels. Lachlan would swear the pup had understood every damn word.

"That dog so has your number." Max dodged Jonah's elbow but Lachlan couldn't stop his smile, his baby brother hadn't liked that comment even though it was the truth.

"Shut up, Max."

As soon as the station door closed, Mannix jumped to his feet and maneuvered himself into the most optimum position to start gnawing his bone.

"Did you have to lie on it?" Lachlan groused, his faithful and very awake pup not even pretending to care. Someone was getting a bath tonight.

Silence. Opening her eyes, the need to move was overpowering. Her body rebelled, too sluggish and uncoordinated to follow the commands. She lifted her head, but it was too heavy. As the side of her face hit the ground, she heard a clang and something cold dug into her neck.

Renewed panic tore through her, shaking hands searched only to encounter a metal collar, an O-ring attached the collar to a heavy chain. Tracing the chain back to the end, led to the wall. As clarity around her situation dawned, it all came flooding back. "Mary!" she cried out. "Where is my baby?"

Dinner together was often a noisy affair. The family home was located a couple of streets from Main Street. A charming double story, with wooden shutters, a veranda that encircled the entire house, and the cliché traditional white picket fence. Upstairs was full of bedrooms and bathrooms with a huge kitchen and open living space commanding the downstairs area. Attached to the kitchen was a makeshift clinic where Claire Michaels had doctored most of the town at some point.

While the practice she shared with Doc Steven's was on Main Street, it quickly became apparent a lot of incidents happened when she wasn't on the clock. Having a clinic at home saved time and occasionally, lives. Although for many a year it was her own children that provided most of the business and even now her youngest twins were regular attendees.

Claire smiled as she studied the table. It was nice to have everyone over for a meal. She longed for her middle sons, Parker and Cooper, and oldest daughter Mackenzie, to come back from college so the whole family could be together. The younger twins still lived at home, as did Shauna, but it would only be a couple of years before she would also leave for college.

Jonah and Max's house was one road over, between them and Main Street. As far as Claire was concerned, Max was also hers. The two boys had been inseparable since they were four years old.

Unbeknown to the two men, they had been the subject of many passionate discussions over the years. Claire had a growing suspicion that she was on the wrong side of the family betting pool. Unfortunately, it was too late to change sides. The stakes were long set. Time would tell.

Despite the age of her eldest boys, she had to admit she might be waiting a while for grandchildren. None of her offspring looked like settling down anytime soon, especially her eldest.

Lachlan had built a giant house a couple of streets back from the station on the other side of Main Street. The maddening part was that the construction workers had spent three years on the project before Lachlan came home and no one in town had known who the owner was. Claire was still upset with the mayor for keeping that knowledge from her.

It had been the topic of much gossip as the construction workers were tight-lipped when it came to divulging any information about their employer. The security was even tighter. Many of the town's teenagers, including her own if Claire hazarded a guess, had tried to sneak in, but none had ever been successful. It wasn't until Lachlan came home that everyone found out he had bought the land and commissioned the build.

Claire still didn't know why construction took so long, but she, like everyone else in town, assumed the builders took advantage considering the landlord wasn't there to supervise.

Lachlan had always liked his privacy, and this was no different.

He had picked land well segregated from other properties, backing straight onto the woods leading out of town.

What Claire found the most frustrating was despite Lachlan having been home for months. He had yet to invite any of the family inside, stating that the house was still under construction. Understanding his desire to show them the finished product, Sam and Claire had discussed it and decided to be patient, but all this time later, they were still no closer to seeing inside.

They trusted their son; they were immensely proud of their eldest. It was wonderful that Lachlan could afford to buy such a large piece of land and build the massive house, but they knew damn well something was wrong.

Her boy always seemed distracted.

Even when he was smiling and laughing with them, it was like he was somewhere else. Lachlan had returned with a harder edge. More mature and not just in years. His wicked sense of humor and cheekiness that had never been far from the surface, now seldom seen.

Many of the town's residents claimed Lachlan had come back a completely different person. One who was now always so serious. But with family, he let his guard lower a little. Although it was when he was on the phone with his ex-navy teammates that she would get glimpses of the old Lachie.

Claire would give anything to see the mirth in his eyes that had always warned that her genius of a son was about to use his brains for mischief and tom foolery, usually wreaking havoc on whoever had garnered his attention.

Lachlan was one of the most eligible bachelors in Forest Haven. But, had he taken advantage of it? No. Despite multiple offers and some damn right predatory behavior in one case, he hadn't dated. Not that Claire wanted Lou-Ellen to succeed. Claire or Sam would step in if it ever looked like Lou-Ellen was wearing Lachlan down. But if Claire didn't know better, she would think he was avoiding all the single women in town on purpose.

Claire didn't like the thought that Lachlan was keeping to

himself even more than what she once knew his normal to be. Alone in such a big house, it appeared he was just erecting more barriers to keep people out. Until they broke through them, she'd continue to nag him into eating and spending time with the family. A sure-fire way to keep an eye on him. It was a mother's job.

Although her oldest sons lived only a few streets away, she missed having them constantly underfoot. Nine children—including Max—had meant a noisy house and darn it if it wasn't too quiet with only three left living at home, even if the three left were indeed the loudest, most troublesome of the lot.

Shauna and the twins were still arguing.

Sam sat at the head of the table, listening to Jonah and Max's account of their fishing trip while watching Lachlan. If Sam hadn't had a smirk on his face, Claire would have missed that Lachlan was slipping more food to the dogs than he was eating.

"Lachlan, I did not slave away at the stove all afternoon for you to give it all to the dogs. Despite how they're acting, I made sure to feed Manix and Racer before we sat down to eat."

If Claire didn't know better, she'd swear the dogs understood her words since both plopped on their butts and aimed big, soulful puppy eyes at her.

"Busted, huh?" Lachie flashed her a quick smile. "I mean, seriously Ma, there was more food on my plate than a yeti could eat. How could I let such great food go to waste? Besides, you were the one that taught me to share."

And there it was.

For a moment, that smile changed his whole demeanor. He was handsome without his smile, but downright gorgeous with it. With deep-blue eyes, Lachlan was a striking man, his blond hair still in a military-style buzz cut, his body lean and taut with muscles in his six-foot frame.

It was inconceivable that, out of all her children, she now worried about him the most. Well, him and Cooper, but that was another story.

"Huh," Claire grunted. "I suppose you think that'll work on me, do you?" Lachie grinned at her. They both knew flattery worked on her and that he was smart enough not to say so. "Shauna, Zachariah, Joshua, stop bickering this minute. Is it too much to ask to have a pleasant family dinner? And don't even think about back chatting me, Zachariah."

"Yes, ma'am," Zac grumbled. Claire had heard Zac's complaint many times that he always got the blame even when there were three of them involved, but whether Zac liked it or not, he was the one that took delight in upping the ante of all their arguments. The boy just refused to admit it.

"Now, let's…" Claire froze. All conversations halted and dread filled her as an annoying albeit catchy ringtone sucked the energy out of the room.

"Baby Shark, doo-doo, doo-doo, doo-doo. Baby Shark, doo-doo, doo-doo, doo-doo." The Baby Shark song hung in the air like a swarm of bees preparing to attack. Any cell calls Lachlan received made Claire and the rest of the family anxious because they didn't know what it would lead to. Only that he often left on the back of them and didn't tell them where he was going or for how long.

Whether the ringtone was something innocuous like the Baby Shark song or more menacing, like the Imperial March, they all knew the call was unlikely to be about his role as sheriff. Claire doubted Lachlan would bother assigning ringtones to any of the townsfolk.

Besides, most of the locals hadn't worked out Lachlan took cell calls without any issues. It was interesting how he somehow managed to have better cell coverage than anyone else in the small town. The rest of the family had noted that their cell reception had also improved. They didn't discuss it, but enjoyed the benefit.

Locals didn't tend to use mobile phones often because the reception was highly unreliable. So, they stuck to the landlines unless something was urgent, but even then, they were more likely to use the CB and radio in for help, especially the older generations. Plus, the gossip grapevine was in full force in this town, so it was likely everyone knew the boys were at their house for dinner tonight.

Lachlan stood and mouthed sorry to Claire. All eyes were on Lachlan as he moved across the room to take his call in some measure of privacy.

"Michaels." As they watched, Lachlan stiffened, his voice lost all congeniality. "No." Concern raced through Claire, Lachlan's eyes narrowed to tiny slits before he abruptly turned his back on them, focused solely on the caller.

Lachlan gave a final growl. "Give me ten" before ending the call and turning back to face them. "I need to go. Thanks for dinner, Ma."

Claire risked a quick glance at Sam, only for him to shrug his shoulders before he turned toward their oldest son.

"Is everything all right?"

"Yeah," Jonah jumped in and gestured at Max. "Do you need us?"

Claire couldn't miss Jonah's unspoken plea, but she noted Lachlan's demeanor. He wouldn't be offering them an excuse to leave.

"Nah, all good, just got some personal things to attend to." Lachlan leaned over and kissed Claire goodbye before striding out the door, Mannix hot on his heels.

She had drifted off again, the fight to stay conscious, a losing battle. Desperate for her eyes to adjust to the dark, she rubbed her hands over the cold metal fastened around her neck.

Driving. She remembered driving, heading toward a new town, a fresh start, back to the man of her dreams to restart a life together, the five of them.

Five of them, oh Mary, oh Mary—her baby. What happened to her baby? As she thought of the approaching winter and her baby girl left in the back seat of her car, she lowered her head and uttered a plea to the universe. "Please, let someone have found my baby in time."

Lachlan paced back and forth inside his bedroom, a freshly washed Mannix watched on from the foot of his bed. He had tried to go to sleep, but the call and subsequent calls had unsettled him. His 2IC hadn't bothered with niceties. The initial call had been blunt.

"Michaels"

"It's Anderson. Do you have a secure line?" That he identified himself as Anderson and not Nate immediately put Lachlan on alert.

"No."

"Call me back when you do. Atrophy."

"Give me ten."

Atrophy was one of their code words. It could be used in different contexts, but all drilled down to one thing. This is serious. I'm not playing around. Pay attention.

Eight minutes later, he was through his front door, hitting the call button on his phone even as he ran for their secure base command center, also referred to as the control room. One call had led to another. He'd been on the phone for hours before he finally admitted there was nothing else to do but wait. There were too many unknowns. They had a plan and running off half-cocked would do nothing but disperse his restfulness.

His team was coming here to Forest Haven, to him. He needed to stay calm and act like nothing was wrong until they got here. Easier said than done, considering the conversations that had taken place.

Damit to hell, Lachlan wanted to rant, he needed to act or at least hit something. His family was in danger. There was no way he was sitting back and taking this, considering everything they'd already been through.

Cold chills ran down his spine as he replayed everything again in his mind. Tomorrow, his team would descend upon the town with a package. One of the most important and precious packages ever.

Waiting was the hard part. And the why. Figuring out the why was going to make for a long, sleepless night.

———

She came too, a strange sound having penetrated her dreams. Frantic to locate where the noise had come from, her eyes fell upon the mound of blankets across the room. A strangled cry escaped her throat when the blankets moved. Without thinking, she used her hands and feet to scurry back, closer to the wall furthest away, keeping her eyes on the moving pile. The chain around her neck clanged against the floor as she scurried. With a sudden burst of clarity, she realized she had been wrong—incredibly wrong—she wasn't alone!

The sound that had emitted from the mound of blankets was inhuman. As it moved again, a blanket dislodged, revealing what she could finally make out as a silhouette of an emaciated woman.

"Hello, are you okay?" Her voice came out soft and timid. Garnering her courage, she carefully made her way toward the woman who she had mistakenly thought to be a small mound of blankets.

"My name is—"

"November," the woman interrupted. "Your name is November," her voice cracked, "and soon my hell will be over, but yours will have just begun."

What the hell? With those few words, panic raced through her body. Muscles tensed; shivers ran down her spine and her heart pounded even as she fought to draw breath. Her next words came out loud, rambling and high-pitched.

"Soon your hell will be over. What do you mean? How will it be over? Are you getting out of here? Please. I'm scared. I need to understand what's happening."

Dull brown eyes stared back. Assessing. It was mere moments, but it felt like time had slowed. A jerky nod, the only acknowledgement before the woman managed to lift her head in slow jolting movements. Next, her right index finger joined the upward motion, pointing three quarters up the wall, to the left of the door. "The blanket."

Newly named November, she made her way over and tugged. Red light blared out. The room abruptly swamped with an artificial dull-red glow. But that wasn't what caused her hair to stand on its end. On the wall, an electronic sign was counting down the time in large red numbers.

DAYS	HOURS	MINUTES	SECONDS
001	02	:07	:28

"What happens when it hits zero?" she stuttered, struggling to ask the question, half afraid the woman would answer.

"October is over, he will kill me, and then, November, your countdown begins. Trust me, you are lucky to be November."

"What?" *Is she nuts!* "Why am I lucky? How the hell can I be lucky in any of this?"

"There are only thirty days in November, as October I had to suffer through thirty-one."

THREE

TUESDAY 31ˢᵀ OCTOBER—HALLOWEEN

By 0700hrs Jonah was ready to head out. Max wouldn't be far behind him, but they'd decided Jonah would go on ahead. Both he and Max were worried but getting Lachlan to talk if he didn't want to, was nearly impossible. They were hoping Lachlan might confide in Jonah if they were alone. Plus, Jonah missed Racer.

Unlike most mornings, his energetic pup hadn't woken him wanting to be let outside. Instead, Jonah concerningly woke to find a short text from his big brother.

'Taken dogs for a run. See U @ work.'

That wasn't the issue. Jonah and Max only ran a couple of times a week so Lachlan would sometimes take Racer along with him. Lachlan had a spare key and Jonah's permission to use it for this purpose.

No, the issue was that the text was sent at 0323hrs. Jonah was unsure if having his phone on Do Not Disturb had been a good thing or not.

Leaving the car for Max, Jonah walked across the street to the station and headed for the front of the building. Living so close was handy. Seeing the office lights on and knowing it could only be Lachlan, Jonah felt a rush of relief. A small part of him had worried that Lachlan wouldn't be there. Running through the mountains at zero ass o'clock in the morning didn't exactly lend to safety.

Knowing a sweet tooth was something he and his brother had in common, Jonah detoured to the bakery for a few delicious bribes. Less than ten minutes later, laden with various baked goodies, Jonah found his brother behind his desk, buried in a pile of paperwork.

Sprawled in the middle of the floor, the dog's tongues lolled out of their mouths.

Racer opened an eye at his master's presence but swiftly closed it again with a long-suffering sigh. The smell of baked goods, not enough to rouse either of the dogs. Normally they'd both be dancing around his feet, begging for a treat.

"We went for a run," Lachlan stated as Jonah stared at the dogs.

"They don't normally look like that after a run." Jonah's eyes still hadn't left the sight of the two dogs lying on the floor even as he pitched the statement-veiled question to his brother.

"Well, I had already planned on a long run and then about three quarters of the way through, these two geniuses heard something and took off. So, by the time I caught them, they'd lost the cat or whatever they'd heard and added another eight miles to the run."

Jonah nodded and moved to drop one of the boxes of bakery treats on Lachlan's desk. Nothing said 'fun' like chasing two dogs across the lower mountains in the pitch black of early morning. Next time, Lachlan might be inclined to hold out until at least dawn before going for a run. Dumbass!

"Thanks." Lachlan nodded at the pastry box before continuing. "Oh, and by the way, you and Max are doing any leg work today."

"Huh, fair enough." Jonah mused, turning to take Lachlan in. His brother looked tired, black bags prominent under his guarded eyes. Those same eyes were staring back at him waiting for Jonah to make his move.

There had been other phone calls in the few months his brother had been back, many of which had resulted in Lachlan dropping everything and leaving town without explanation. His brother had secrets. Something was going on, and he knew his parents were also worried. Jonah had learned years ago if he wanted to get inside Lachlan's head, he needed to be the annoying younger brother and start a good old-fashioned fight.

Jonah's every instinct demanded to know what was going on, but everything about Lachlan's current demeanor told him to back off. So, he did. Unfortunately, this wasn't the time or the place for a fight. Besides, he was still here; so, it couldn't be all that bad.

"You wanna give me half that paperwork? Hopefully, we can have it knocked off by lunchtime?"

"Take it all. That sounds like Max. I have other things to attend to." Lachlan stood, tension bled from his profile as he grabbed the pile of paperwork, dropped it into Jonah's arms, and pushed him out of his office. The door was shut behind him before Jonah could find his footing enough to turn around and glare at his big brother. Asshole.

"Is he okay?" Max asked.

"Yeah, okay enough to dump all the paperwork on us, says he's got other stuff to do," Jonah grumbled as he placed half the pile on Max's desk.

"Hmmm, one day he might tell us what he does when he's locked himself in there. Your dad never spent so much time on the computer with the door shut."

Max and Jonah often debated what Lachlan could be doing. It wasn't as if Lachlan passed off the workload to them, then sat and did nothing. If anything, it was the opposite. Even with the door closed, the sound of pounding keys and frustrated murmurs drifted through. Nothing ever clear enough to make out, but even when Max and Jonah had left for the day, sometimes locals reported Lachlan was still at it late into the night. Whatever was going down was big, and Jonah wasn't going to wait much longer before confronting the man.

"Anyway, guess we better start on all this paperwork. I'll get the coffee." Shaking off his melancholy thoughts, Jonah watched as Max headed toward the kitchen before stopping short at the dogs lying sprawled on the floor in front of Lachie's office door. "Should I even ask?"

"Probably not." Jonah smirked at Max's nod. His partner continued his quest for coffee without another word.

Lachlan pushed away from his desk in disgust and moved to stare out his office window after ending another call. It was something he did most days. Watching people go about their normal lives was usually comforting, but today it brought no solace.

He needed to get back to his search. Frustrated or not, there was nothing he could do about last night's calls, until his team got there. They couldn't afford the distraction. Little lives were depending on him, but his mind couldn't settle enough to focus. The other issue… How did he know this wasn't all connected?

Tempted to go for another run, Lachlan started pacing. He needed to get rid of this built-up energy, but the dogs were already exhausted, and he had assured his team he would go nowhere without Mannix, if they weren't with him. Lachlan didn't always adhere to that rule, not that he'd tell them that. If one of his team caught him, he'd be in deep shit. But there was a difference between walking the main streets of town alone and running into the mountains by himself.

Especially when they were under threat.

And right now, they were under threat.

He didn't know what they were heading into, only that it wasn't good. Lachlan figured he was going to need his strength. With that thought, he decided to go check on Magee himself. Yesterday, he'd sent Max and Jonah, but it wouldn't hurt for another follow-up to ensure Magee knew he was serious.

Born in Ireland, Magee's family had moved to Forest Haven

when he was only young and bought the general store. Many years later, Magee was the only remaining family member in town, yet he still possessed a strong Irish accent. On the short, pudgy side, Magee was an amicable sort of fella who got on with all the towns-folk—everyone, except for Riley.

Riley was also Irish and short. Unlike Magee, Riley had only moved to Forest Haven five years ago, so the town still considered him an outsider. The man had replaced Doc Rainah as the town's dentist. He hadn't acclimatized as well as Doc Stevens, but the town consensus deemed him nice enough—for an outsider.

No one knew what had started the feud between Riley and Magee. Nor could anyone understand them once they got going. Their accents, thickening and distorting further with anger, didn't help the cause.

Whatever the case, there was no end in sight. There would inevitably be a fight whenever they met. Other business owners had had enough, going so far as to deny entry if the other was already inside. Lachlan had no clue how Riley got groceries, since Magee ran the only general store in town.

Lachlan gave his deputies a heads-up on his intended where-abouts and set off on foot, leaving an exhausted Mannix behind. Magee didn't like Mannix in the store anyway—something about hygiene—although Lachlan figured it was more about fear than anything else. The young pup was quite large.

The walk along Main Street didn't help his mood. Having to smile and participate in polite conversation with anyone that engaged him on the way just pissed him off even more. He was the sheriff, not a sideshow clown. Lachlan couldn't wait to hand the sheriff's duties back to his dad. The next three months couldn't go fast enough.

Already on edge, Lachlan zeroed in on another time bomb and quickly corrected course—ducking behind another civilian—before she could see him. Lou-Ellen had been standing at the counter in the hairdressers, putting her purse in her handbag, which meant she'd be heading out onto the sidewalk within moments. Lachlan quickened his pace and continued to duck and weave around other townsfolk to hide himself from her view as he made a beeline for Magee's store. He needed to get in there before she saw him. Savior only feet away, a laughing but familiar voice stopped him in his tracks.

"Seriously Lachlan, you're still hiding from that poor girl?"

"Ha, ha Sanders. If you're not careful I'll send her older sister your way. I'll tell her you like them younger."

No one in town would ever associate the words 'poor girl' with Lou-Ellen and Sanders knew it. Smart ass.

"Shit, that's not funny. She's half my age. You used to have a sense of humor!"

"Yeah, well, misery shared is vengeance achieved."

"Now what the heck does that even mean?"

"You work it out. I gotta get inside before she sees me."

Lachlan rounded the stumped Sanders and hurried into the store. He might have been in war zones, but Lou-Ellen terrified him.

To Lachlan's despair, Lou-Ellen was one of the *many* single girls in town that thought she would like Lachlan as a husband. Some hadn't been backward in coming forward. Nor had some of their mothers on their behalf. But Lou Ellen was poisonous. She wasn't a nice person full stop. Even Mannix disliked her. She reminded Lachlan of a rattlesnake. He wouldn't be surprised if she swallowed small children whole for dinner and he dared anyone to tell him different.

Lachlan had never been good at declining women's advances. Being a man of few words when not around his teammates and family, he preferred to avoid them. Less drama that way, but easier said than done in a small town. Unlike the others that had reluctantly backed off, whether or not they believed Lachlan had a partner. Lou-Ellen seemed hellbent on getting her fangs into him and Lachlan wasn't going to passively standby and let that happen.

Luckily for Lachlan, he had great security.

Lou-Ellen had appeared on his doorstep multiple times, but

Lachlan had never acknowledged he was home. Lights could not be seen inside his house from the front and his sound proofing was awesome. He could fire a Glock into the floor, and no one outside would be any the wiser. Lachlan had only learned the importance of that requirement a few weeks earlier. But answering the associated questions that came after law enforcement received multiple reports of gunshots, well that had been tedious.

It was handy that people couldn't tell if anyone was home or not, since Lachlan hadn't been there as much as everyone assumed. For as many times as Lou-Ellen had sullied his doorstep when the house had been occupied, there had been many more times when the townspeople all thought he was home, when he wasn't.

The bell above the door signaled his arrival and Magee appeared from the back of the store. His welcoming face changed instantly upon seeing Lachlan.

"Look at this, Sheriff, look at what he did ta my head. What are ye going ta do about him? I want him locked up, throw away da key, kick him out of town, anything! Get rid of him once and fa all. I'm sick of this. If ye ain't going ta do something about him, I will!"

Magee's bellowed words ensured everyone walking past the store slowed to watch the show, which included his fellow town board member, the annoyingly peppy town gossip, Mrs. Hayworth.

Great, all he needed now was for Principal Mullins to magically appear. Gesturing the nosy townsfolk to move along, Lachlan fought the temptation to yell back at the infuriating man. Although shooting the motherfucker in the knee would be even more satisfying, and considering his mood, he was more tempted than he should be.

"Put a lid on it, Magee. For fuck's sake, you're a grown man. We've already been through this. You hit your head on the sidewalk after you fell trying to take a swing at him with a shovel. Assault charges ain't gonna stick. In fact, he has more on you than you have on him."

Why the asshole even had a shovel at the time, Lachlan didn't want to know.

"Baloney, ye can't trust a word dat fecker says."

"I don't need to, Magee. You had this fight right here on Main Street. I have half a dozen witnesses who saw it happen. You need to let it go. Because I'm telling you right now. If I catch the two of you arguing in Main Street again, or any public area, for that matter. I'll not only throw you both in jail, but I'll also shoot you both in the foot and chuck you in the same cell! Do you understand me?"

"Are ye telling that fecker the same thing, 'cause he's da one that started it?"

Lachlan shook his head.

These two were acting like his baby brothers. Surely it was wrong for two middle-aged men to carry on like this.

"I'm warning you Magee—do not go after him again! Now, tell me if you understand me?" Lachlan commanded in a quiet voice.

"Aye, aye, I hear ye, naw need ta get ye knickers in a knot. Now, ye want something or ye just here ta threaten a good, law-abiding citizen?"

"Yeah, I'll leave that one well alone. Law-abiding citizen! Seriously?"

"Aye, that I am. Anything ye heard to the contrary is lies, all lies. Now, I got ye order dropped off ta ye house this morning. Left it in the cold box by the door as per usual. Not sure ye ma would be happy if she knew how much junk food ye eating though," Magee added, unable to hide his blatant curiosity.

Magee had been unnerving in his focus on Lachlan's grocery order, having straight out called it adolescent. While Lachlan agreed, it hadn't been consistent with other orders over the last few months. He didn't understand what Magee's problem was. Why was he so fixated on it? Lachlan had all the basics needed for winter now. Why the hell couldn't he have some fun stuff too?

Besides, sugary foods weren't only for kids. Magee had initially queried if the twins had tampered with his list without Lachlan's knowledge as some sort of prank. So, Lachlan had rechecked the list because yes, he wouldn't put it past his baby brothers, either. But in this case, Lachlan confirmed the order was correct.

"Thanks," Lachlan called over his shoulder as he headed out, "but if my ma finds out I'll know exactly who told her."

And that, he thought to himself, was a threat!

Sam Michaels knew his town. He knew his people. And he knew the surrounding woods better than most, but what Sam didn't know was his two youngest sons. The two of them found trouble wherever they went.

At five foot nine, Sam was more solid than any of his boys. His face had aged over the years, but town gossip was great for his ego. Sam wholeheartedly agreed with them, he was still ruggedly handsome, thank you very much. And yes, those baby-blue eyes of his could certainly work wonders on his wife if they had to. But they most definitely did not work on the twins' school principal.

Summoned to the principal's office. Sam had sat there listening to his boys' latest escapades, wondering how the hell they concocted these schemes. It was telling that a pool of sweat had formed at the base of his spine. Even after all these years, the school principal was still someone who invoked fear.

Although, it didn't feel that long ago when he himself had been sitting there in that same office with his own father by his side. At least he had never been in this principal's office as an errant student. She was a damn scary woman and anyone who said different was lying through their front teeth.

Sam drove the brat's home in utter silence. Once inside, he sent them to their room and went off to find his wife. He was impressed he'd been able to keep a sober if not stern face as he had recounted what the boys had done. Leaving his fuming wife to deal with the twins, Sam headed for the safety and manly surroundings of the station house. At least there he would find three of his sons that he did understand.

Walking into the station, felt like coming home. Six months was a long time. With three months still to go, Sam was already looking forward to coming back to work. If it were solely about him, he would have been back on duty last week. The injury had healed much quicker than anticipated but both he and his wife were enjoying having Lachlan home. He just had to work out how to keep his oldest son from leaving again. That Lachlan now had a house and seemed to be settling in was comforting but his boy was keeping secrets and God only knew what work his son would find to occupy him in this small town. A bored Lachlan was a danger to all and sundry.

Earlier that morning, Jonah had sent word that Lachlan was in, but had run the dogs hard before the sun was even a thought on the horizon. But as he entered the station, he figured Jonah must have been exaggerating. Both Mannix and Racer bounded over to meet him, no doubt more excited at the prospect of the treats in Sam's pockets than seeing him.

Allowing a tremendous sigh to escape, Sam gave the dogs their treats and rubbed his hands over their heads. Ignoring Max and Jonah's meerkat impressions as they watched from their desks, he took the opportunity to wallow for a few moments.

"Hmmm. You two could be my sons. Change your names to Zac and Josh. Claire would acclimatize after a while—you'd be a hell of a lot less trouble."

"Don't bet on it," Lachlan retorted as he came in to join them.

Sam faced the three men, all of whom he considered his sons, the two younger ones already smiling in anticipation.

"Come on, Dad, what did they do now?" Jonah asked.

Instead of answering, Sam walked straight into the kitchenette, opened the small cupboard above the fridge and groped around until his hand rested on a bottle of whisky. Moaning in relief, Sam grabbed the bottle, found a clean glass, and wandered back into the bullpen where his sons still waited.

"I don't know how they devise these things. How am I supposed to discipline them when part of me is so damn proud?"

Sam poured three fingers and swallowed before continuing. "I swear they'll be the death of me. Felt like a nervous teenager sitting in the principal's office listening to their latest tricks. By God, she is one scary woman, that one. No chance we'll have to worry about her softening with age. You remember Mr. Davey?"

"Sure!" Jonah answered. Sam frowned. Jonah might have answered 'sure,' but it sounded more like 'duh.' Although he couldn't blame him—Forest Haven was small enough that everyone knew everyone—he wouldn't stand for insolence. Luckily, Jonah continued in a normal tone before Sam could call him on it.

"He started our last year in. Lachlan had already left. He's the economics teacher, boring as bat shit. Kids used to play tricks on him to see how far they would have to go to get him to react. His eyes never left the book he was reading, and he would only speak in a flat monotone. It was pure torture."

Sam watched as Jonah carefully kept his eyes averted from Max's should either of them laugh and let it slip that they, too, had participated in this *hobby*. Sam wasn't dumb. He knew his boys weren't always angels when they were young, even now they had their moments.

"Well, I guess not much has changed then. Did you know Mr. Davey has four ceiling fans in his classroom and that each of those fans has three prongs?"

"Ah, no," Lachlan shrugged his shoulders. "Can't say I did. Um, what did they do exactly?"

"They went fishing!"

It was a good few minutes before they stopped chuckling after Sam recounted the story. The boys had found old man Billy passed out on the bank of the river with a few buckets of salmon next to him.

Instead of waking the drunkard, the boys seized his haul of fish. They'd been adamant the fish had been in those buckets without water and in direct sunlight for hours. The smell was too telling for there to be another explanation. Knowing the fish were already dead and now weren't safe to consume, the boys removed the temptation from the old man to try to sell them to unsuspecting folk after he woke.

But that wasn't the problem. What they did with them was. Sam painted a clear picture of salmon stuffed with rainbow colored glitter attached to each fan prong steadily twirling around the ceiling for the first half of the class. Then Zac turned the dial to full speed, sending glitter filled fish flying across the room. Chaos erupted as students tried to dodge out of the way. One salmon even knocked the glasses off Mr. Davey's head. They ended up with one broken window and a hell of a mess. Well, they got Mr. Davey's attention, and the boys were in for a hell of a clean-up. Few of the fish remained in one piece. Blood and guts had exploded wherever they hit. And as for the glitter. Those little buggers would be impossible to clean. Students would find glitter for years to come, no matter how good a job the boys did.

But the smell alone was enough to drive many of the young students out of the classroom onto the lawn, whereby they had garnered the principal's attention. No, it wasn't a pretty picture, but it was an entertaining one, and every one of them would have loved to have been there to see it. The smiles got wider when Sam admitted he had taken the boys home and dumped it all in their mother's lap.

An hour later, Sam left the station feeling content. The recounting of the twins' escapades had doubled as an opportunity to check on Lachlan. He was grateful to see his eldest son laugh, even if it was only for a few moments, before the weight of the world seemed to descend upon his shoulders once again. Sam would give it a few more days, but enough was enough.

It was time to find out what the hell was going on with his son. He just had to work out when to pounce.

FOUR

Lachlan sat at his favorite booth in Sherry's, the diner on Main Street, intent on getting an early lunch. Not bothering with the menu, he ordered his usual steak and cheese sandwich. Tinted large windows allowed him to watch people walk past without scrutiny. Knowing his body needed fuel, he'd ordered out of necessity. His early morning run had burned a lot of calories and the protein shake after, hadn't sufficed. Although the cupcakes from Jonah had taken the edge off.

Sherry, the diner's owner, had tried to cajole him into a slice of his favorite pumpkin pie, but he wasn't in the mood. Time was going too slow. He had already popped back to his house to rescue his groceries and yet he still had the best part of half an hour before he could meet his team.

If he'd thought things couldn't get worse, he was wrong. Sherry had just dropped his steak sandwich off when the click-clack of stilettos on the vinyl floor echoed loudly along with the grating, high-pitched voice that accompanied it.

"Lachlan. What a lovely surprise. It's kismet that we're here at the same time. Don't you think, darling? We can finally have our date without any distractions. Sherry," Lou-Ellen yelled across the diner, making sure everyone heard her. "I'll have my usual Greek salad. I'm joining Lachlan."

Before Lou-Ellen could slide in beside Lachlan, Mannix jumped onto the seat and laid his head on Lachlan's lap. If Lachlan didn't already love his dog with all his heart, that one action would have clinched it.

"Oh pooh. I wanted to sit there. Dog! Get off there. Seats are for humans."

Huh! Lou-Ellen was a human?! Who knew? Lachlan would have voted for an alien. Or a monster. Not sure Lou-Ellen would be happy with that classification if she ever found out how Lachlan got rid of monsters…

"Lachlan, are you going to move your dog for me?"

"Nope." Lachlan shoved his steak sandwich in his mouth and took a bite as he scrambled for a reason to escape. He knew if he tried to walk out now, she would follow him, and Lachlan couldn't afford to let that happen.

"Here." Sherry dumped Lou-Ellen's Greek salad in front of the empty seat across from Lachlan.

Weird.

Sherry shouldn't have been able to serve Lou-Ellen her fancy ass Greek salad that quickly. It wouldn't surprise Lachlan if Sherry had acquired those pre-made bag mixes instead of making them fresh. Especially since Lou-Ellen was the only one in town that ate it and had demanded Sherry supply it just for her. Lachlan would have to ask later, but the thought that the pretentious bitch was eating a budget premix bagged salad and paying a premium price made Lachlan laugh internally.

"Leave Mannix alone. Lachlan, hurry and finish your lunch, if your late for your budget meeting with the mayor again, he said he'd sick your ma on you."

Damn, Lachlan was in love. If he wasn't already married… Sherry was the best, and the wink she gave him before she turned and fled back to the kitchen told Lachlan she damn well knew the mayor had canceled the budget meeting.

"Oh pooh. Seriously? Lachlan, you need to make time for me, honey. Surely the mayor can wait. I'll call mama and get her to handle him for you. I'm sure he'll agree our relationship is more important than a silly budget meeting."

Oh hell, no.

Lachlan wasn't sitting here listening to her grating voice for a second longer than he had to.

Decision made, he swallowed his bite, opened what was remaining of his sandwich, scraped out the onion and handed it to Mannix. His boy had certainly earned it. One scoff and the whole thing was gone. The look of disgust on Lou-Ellen's face was clear as day. If she thought Lachlan would get with someone who didn't love his dog as much as she loved him, she was plain stupid. Well, that was a given anyway.

"Sorry Lou-Ellen, I gotta go. Besides, I've told you I'm taken. Just because you haven't seen her doesn't mean she doesn't exist. I wouldn't cross her if I were you. She has a bit of a temper when women try to impede on her territory."

"Seriously, this crap again. No one believes you, Lachlan, and it's getting pathetic. Playing hard to get is the role of the woman, not the man."

"Whatever Lou-Ellen. Don't say I didn't warn you. Mannix, let's go, boy. We have work to do. Good day all. Thanks for lunch Sherry." Lachlan yelled out as he strode for the door. Escape was in sight.

With an even stride, Lachlan headed straight for the town hall. Keeping up appearances, he went inside for a few minutes in case Lou-Ellen skipped her fancy Greek salad and followed.

When enough time had passed, Lachlan went out the back entrance, through the courthouse, and out into the parking lot. Out of sight of Main Street and prying eyes.

Twenty yards later, Lachlan was in the park. With Mannix at his side, they strolled toward the river at the edge of town and the prearranged meeting point.

Tense and on full alert, he focused on the surrounding environment, aware that missing even a small detail could unravel their plans. Normally, they would have met at Lachlan's house. But if they had a tail, going through the woods to get to the back door would put them in danger. They didn't know how many they were up against.

By meeting here, they weren't directly leading anyone straight to Lachlan. And if a confrontation happened, they wanted it out in the open where Jonah, Max and his dad could get to them quickly. Prewarned or not, if a fight broke out, the three of them would descend within minutes and would help keep the package safe.

At the park, if anyone came upon them, they could easily say the guys were visiting from the next town over, which was technically the truth. If they were engaged. They had more room to separate off and take cover in the mountains before reconvening somewhere else. They were being over cautious but that was better than getting dead.

The park sat on the bank of the river where it leveled out and made for a popular swimming hole. After a petition from the parents' group, the town board had built the playground and fenced it in for the smaller children so parents could relax and use the picnic tables and public BBQs yet keep an eye on the little ones.

The picnic tables were far enough away for small families to have their own space and close enough that big groups could spread themselves out without feeling isolated from each other.

In a few days, the park and surrounding grounds would be full of people enjoying the annual Winter Festival. At some point the town board might get around to changing the name to the Autumn Festival. Few could remember the last time the town held the festival in winter. It was usually too cold by December even if the snow hadn't arrived yet.

Lachlan headed toward the picnic table furthest away from the street. It was impossible to see from outside the park which was why he picked it. Halfway there, Lachlan paused as Mannix stopped next to him and lifted his head.

"I know, buddy, they're all here, but there are two uninvited guests we have to get rid of first."

Lachlan lifted his hands to cup his mouth and called out at the top of his lungs, "Zac, Josh, get your ass's front and center. What the hell are you two doing hiding over there?" Brats! How the hell had they gotten past their Ma?

"Man. How did he know we were here?" Zac's voice carried over to Lachlan. If that boy, thought he was whispering… Mary, help them all. "There's no way Ma knows we're gone yet, she's normally on the phone at least an hour when Grandma rings."

"I dunno. He knows everything, maybe Dad came home and found our room empty. The first thing he'd do is call Lachlan. Either way, we better go. If we make him wait, he'll get angrier."

Lachlan allowed a brief smirk before smoothing out his expression. Trying to look bored, like he had all day, he waited for his two baby brothers to emerge from their hiding spot in the long reeds next to the river's edge, dragging their fishing rods behind them.

They'd been quick to drop and hide but not quick enough. A few minutes more and they'd have made it to the lower river and their favorite fishing spot. Idiots, it's the first place any of the family would have looked as soon as it had become known that they'd left the house.

The twins trudged their way over, every step tortured and slow before eventually stopping in front of him. Lachlan struggled to hide his mirth. Shit, you'd think they were on their way to the gallows. Finally, they met his eyes. Lachlan managed a convincing frown, raised his left eyebrow, and waited.

"What's the problem? We weren't doing anything wrong," Zac tried. When Lachlan still said nothing, he continued. "Well, it's not like we were causing any trouble. We're trying to stay out of Ma's way."

Lachlan again said nothing and watched as Josh started moving from foot to foot while Zac handled all the talking.

"Okay, okay. We're supposed to be in our bedroom. Are you

going to tell? We'll go back right now. Come on, Lachie. Say something, are you going to tell on us?"

Screw that, Lachlan didn't see the point in letting them off the hook and he knew silence worked on them better than anything else. Besides, he didn't want them to relax enough to question why he was there. Standing firm, Lachlan responded with another lift of his eyebrow.

"Fine, come on, Josh, let's go home before he gets any madder."

Shoulders slumped, both boys walked past Lachlan and headed toward town. When they turned around, Lachie was standing there, arms folded, watching them go. They didn't dare turn back again. If they were smart, they would get home fast. Ma would be spitting mad if she found out they'd sneaked out.

Lachlan waited another few minutes after he lost sight of the twins before he moved to the designated spot. Taking a last look around, satisfied they weren't any further uninvited guests, Lachlan raised his fingers to his mouth, and mimicked the sound of the bald eagle to signal it was clear.

Nate, Lachlan's best friend, was the first to emerge from the trees. He was holding the package. With a quick nod, Nate lowered the squirming package to the ground and Lachlan watched as his three-year-old daughter came running toward him as fast as her little legs would take her.

A few long strides and Lachlan had closed the gap, pulling his little girl quickly into his embrace. Her arms squeezed his neck hard as she clung to him. Lachlan inhaled the smell of her hair and closed his eyes for a moment as he tried to comfort his daughter as her tears started to flow.

"Dad-dee, Daddy!"

"It's okay, pumpkin. I have you. You're safe now. Daddy has you."

Gracie held on tight, little fingers digging into his skin. Her left hand fisted in his shirt while her head tucked into the crook of his neck. Muttering soothing words, Lachlan stroked Gracie's shoulder-length blonde hair until her crying eased. Snuggled in his arms, within a few minutes, she was out like a light.

It had been less than two days since he'd held his daughter having spent the weekend with his family in Falls View. He'd kissed his sleeping daughter and wife before leaving early yesterday morning to sneak back into town in time for the stupid town council meeting. Yet it felt like it'd been forever.

Lachlan pressed his lips to Gracie's head once more before focusing on Nate, Deeks, and Taniq. After shaking hands and quick, one-armed embraces, it was time to make plans. They needed to talk, but the park wasn't the place. All three of them looked like they needed sleep and a decent meal, and Lachlan needed to hunt.

"Any issues getting here?"

"Nope. All good so far." Nate reported. "Hardest part was getting Gracie to wait quietly when she could see you were so close. Despite having practiced this, I don't think she would have lasted much longer considering what happened yesterday."

Yeah, Lachlan could see that being a problem. Not many three-year-olds could have waited in silence for so long but they'd trained for situations like this. She knew when things were serious that she had to follow instructions for her and everyone's safety.

An incident in Afghanistan involving a child suicide bomber and a stray dog had been a near fatal lesson for both Lachlan and his young daughter.

"Okay, let's head home. Give me a twenty-minute head start so I can turn off all the alarms and then space yourselves out every ten after that."

"Sounds good!" Nate rested his hand on Lachlan's shoulder. "We weren't followed, and we made sure we weren't seen, but we'll take the extra precautions."

"Here," Taniq unzipped his coat. "Take my jacket. It might help hide her in case you run into anyone."

"Shit, yeah, I can't argue with that. We'll head on through the woods and use the back door. I'll keep the blinds closed. If the blinds are open and the porch lights are on, something's wrong, so hang back until I signal you. Stay safe."

They all locked hands and then Lachlan, holding his daughter, disappeared into the woods with Mannix at his side. The other three then separated and retreated into the trees.

Lachlan made it home without any problems. Gracie safely curled in his arms. Even in her sleep, her grip on his neck was tight. He'd tried to put her to bed with her favorite stuffie, Mr. Rambo, but that failed. Mr. Rambo. It always cracked him up that 'Mr. Rambo' was a huge pink dragon with silver accents. So, instead of fighting it, Lachlan moved round the kitchen, making a late lunch with his daughter and her large stuffie attached to him as he worked. Hmmm, he might even get to eat something this time.

Fifty-three minutes after he had left the park, the call of a bald eagle sounded nearby. Seconds later, Nate entered through the back door. He nodded at Nate, who walked straight past him to dump his duffel in his room. Twenty minutes and another two eagle calls later, Taniq and Deeks were also safely ensconced in the house.

The first agenda needed to be food. Gracie's stomach was rumbling even as she slept. Lachlan dumped platters of steak, eggs, and toast in the middle of their large, hand carved, solid square, bog oak wood dining table before plonking in his chair. Now, he just had to wake his daughter to partake.

"She wouldn't eat!" Nate cringed. "We tried everything. The only thing that finally worked was Smarties, and even then, it was a battle."

Lachlan nodded and gently disentangled Mr. Rambo from Gracie's grip before kissing the top of her head. "Wake up, baby."

"I want Mummy." Even as she said it, her little fists tightened their hold on Lachlan's back.

"I know, baby, but you have to eat."

"Don't want to."

"Tough cookies! That might work on these boys, but it doesn't work on me, young lady. Now, what will it be—steak or eggs on toast?"

Gracie looked into Lachlan's eyes. Even now, the brat was deciding how far to push. As her bottom lip quivered, Lachlan shook his head. "Don't even think about trying that with me either, young lady."

His men watched on as Gracie shrugged her shoulders. The quiver stopped as fast as it had started, and she smiled up at him. With another kiss to her head, he flipped her around to sit on his lap, facing the table.

"Egg n toat."

"Toast, baby, that's toast, not toat."

Gracie ignored him and reached for the egg with her little hand. Lachlan knew she didn't understand what was happening, but she knew something was wrong. Mummy was gone. Hell, at this point Lachlan didn't know exactly what was going on.

Nobody spoke much during lunch as everyone ate. The boys, Nate especially, looked relieved Gracie was eating something. Although it was a tossup if she ate more or wore more. Clean-up was going to be a bitch.

Lachlan wanted to debrief his team again in person. Last night, over the phone, had given him a good understanding, but Lachlan needed to rehash it to make sure he hadn't missed something. Unfortunately, that was going to have to wait until Gracie was asleep.

After finishing their food, Lachlan took one look at Gracie and sighed. Since his wife wasn't there and Lachlan didn't want to traipse the remnants of lunch throughout the house, Lachlan stood with Gracie still in his arms and squatted so Gracie could say hello to Mannix.

If it also meant that Mannix cleaned her face of food when he licked his hello, well, that was a bonus. No one could prove he did it on purpose. Gracie, Nate and Taniq thought it was funny. Deeks not so much, but Lachlan doubted he'd tell on him unless they needed a distraction of some sort.

With the bulk of the food pieces now gone, Lachlan took Gracie upstairs while the boys did the dishes. A quick wipe of her hands and face with a washcloth, a change of clothes, and a story, Gracie was ready for a nap.

If only it were that easy.

Every time he tried to tuck her into bed, she woke again. After several attempts, he brought her to his room and climbed in with her.

After another story, this time, when she slept, he was able to get out without waking her. Lachlan figured she could smell him on the bedding, so he slipped into his bathroom and grabbed his cologne. Back in the bedroom, he sprayed her pillow, hoping it would buy him a couple of hours before he would need to come back. With a flick of his hand, Mannix jumped onto the foot of his bed to keep watch over his baby girl.

Minutes ticked by. Mocking her with every number that clicked over. The clock steadily counting down. Large red numbers, getting lower and lower, the pungent stench of fear increasing with every second that ticked away.

The door opened in what seemed like slow motion. The silhouette of a large man filled the void. Once he entered, the door slammed behind him, making November jump. Without a word, he strode over to October and yanked her head off the floor, pulling her up by her hair. Holding her in a half-seated position, he kicked her in the stomach with an air of disinterest. Over the last few hours, Julie Ann had revealed her real name and had slowly confided in November. She had explained the horrors to come and his 'expectations.'

While November had a better understanding of the circumstances of her predicament, the knowledge didn't add comfort. It only terrified her more.

"Did you fill her in, October?" the man demanded of Julie Ann as he again kicked her in the stomach.

"Yes, sir. I filled her in," Julie Ann squeaked as she struggled through the pain. He'd broken Julie Ann's ribs early on. November had been so angry on her behalf when Julie Ann had explained everything. Unconsciously refusing to acknowledge that November's own story would likely mirror that of Julie Ann's.

Now there were too many pains to differentiate them unless they received a direct hit. The woman was praying for the end. Julie Ann no longer prayed for someone to save her. She wanted this to be over. She wanted to surrender to nothingness. November wondered how long it would take for her to also want death to claim her.

"Good," the man exclaimed with a fist to October's face. Fingers shaking, he lowered his zipper enough to pull himself out. Pumping his length hard, he slammed on top of her, pushing into her in one rough movement. Thick fingers covered Julie Ann's mouth as she cried out in pain. November was helpless to do anything but watch the scene unfold in front of her, the brutality and glee with which he took to his task not going unnoticed.

FIVE

Nate and the boys got comfortable in the smaller, cozier living room while they waited for Lachlan to come back downstairs after putting Gracie to bed. They left the double-seated, well-used, custom leather recliner vacant, knowing that was Lachlan's spot.

Nate claimed the long couch, his head resting on the back of his arm. Deeks sprawled on the floor by the door and Taniq had perched on the box seat in front of the window. It meant that with Lachlan taking his place, the four of them had a line of sight over the entire room. They were on guard, even though this was their home. The one place where they should be safe.

Lachie came through the doorway already speaking as he aimed for his chair. "Run it through for me again from the start. I don't understand how my wife gets kidnapped, and we jumped straight to it being a serial killer, when we have so many enemies?"

A deep breath and Nate moved his six-foot-two frame to a sitting position before he ran a hand through his brown military-cut hair.

Second in command, he was a natural leader, but this was his captain, his best friend, and his brother-in-law. There was nothing less he wanted to do than to have this conversation again. Last night had been hard enough.

"Alright. I came home around 1700hrs expecting to find everyone still packing. Instead, the house was dark, locked tight and empty of people. Everything was ready for the moving truck. I figured she'd finished packing early and hadn't been able to wait. Probably thought to surprise you. I tried ringing her cell. When she didn't answer, I got worried. I kept hitting redial while at the same time, I texted Bruce to track her phone. On the fifth attempt, the call connected, but it wasn't her."

"The FBI?"

"Yeah. They wouldn't tell me anything at first, trying to work out who I was. Multiple threats later we were getting nowhere when Jake grabbed the phone."

Jake was the sheriff in the next town. He was a decent guy, and they all got along well enough, even if Lachlan's team didn't go out of their way to interact with the man.

"He told me to come to Railings Road, a quarter mile out of town. I got there in sixteen minutes. Gracie was screaming and kicking out at the deputy holding her. I yelled her name and ran towards them. Another deputy tried to get in my way, I mean I get it, he didn't know who I was, and I was running into a crime scene, but it took a few moments to get past him." Nate blew out a breath. The whole scene still frustrated him, seeing Gracie so distraught was not something he ever wanted to see again.

"My yell got her attention. As soon as she saw me, her movements became even more frantic, and she landed a hard kick to the deputy's gut. His grip loosened enough that she slipped from his arms and ran straight for me. The bastard was lucky he didn't drop her. By then, I was only a few feet from her. As soon as I scooped her up, she stopped screaming and curled into me." Pausing, Nate waited a moment before continuing. He was used to giving verbal reports, but this was personal. His niece was three damn it and he couldn't forget his sister was missing.

"As if summoned from hell, this dour faced child services

woman stormed over, demanding to know who I was. I told her I was her uncle and asked what the hell was going on. She got all hoity and stated that the child was under her protection, but not what had happened, only that she needed to verify who I was before I could take her. Then the stupid woman grabbed Gracie's arm like she intended to pull her from me." Nate didn't mention that the woman seemed to take delight in upsetting his niece. He'd clocked her when he'd arrived standing off to the side, watching but doing nothing to try and calm Gracie when she'd been in the arms of the deputy.

"Gracie screamed, but she wasn't leaving my arms without a fight. Her little fists pummeled the woman's arm. As soon as the shrew let go of her, I stepped back out of reach and Gracie calmed. I threw the bitch my wallet at the same time Jake walked over to intervene." It was good timing on Jake's part, woman or not, Nate would have knocked her on her ass if she'd tried to touch Gracie again.

"Jake confirmed that I was Gracie's kin. The sour cow was not happy." She'd be even less when Nate put in a formal complaint about her. "But she had no recourse. My license confirmed my identity, the sheriff had backed me, and Gracie was content in my arms. That's when I found out she'd basically been screaming the whole time they'd been there. Jake then walked me over to the car and asked me to confirm it was my sister's, before finally filling me in on what they had found."

Lachlan was white. Nate had watched his best friend's face drain of any color when he heard his daughter had been screaming for the best part of an hour. They all knew that was the least of it. It was doubtful the police had stumbled upon Gracie right away. It was nearly dark when they found her. The little girl had barely spoken once Nate had hold of her and when she did, her voice had been raw. It was no surprise that Lachlan's eyes kept rising to the ceiling where his daughter slept, safe and protected by Mannix. Needing to get it all out and stop Lachlan from spiraling, Nate continued.

"Two of Jake's deputies had been returning to town. The car was sitting in the middle of the road with the driver's door wide open. Before the patrol had even stopped, they could hear Gracie's screams. When they approached, Gracie was trying to get out of her booster seat. They pulled her out but couldn't calm her. A search of the area didn't find anyone else. No signs of a struggle, but there was a smattering of blood on the road about ten feet in front of the car and two sets of footprints."

Lachlan dropped his gaze to the floor in front of him. "There is no way she would leave Gracie alone like that, not if she was conscious."

"We know, brother," Taniq spoke quietly from his perched position at the window.

"Okay, okay. So, explain how we get from kidnapped to serial killer. I thought you two were on a job in DC. We weren't expecting you back for another few days." Lachlan looked from Taniq to Deeks.

"Yeah, our bosses called us as soon as they identified Nate and it led to you. They had us jump on a helicopter. We were on another case, but under the circumstances, they figured it would be best to get us back here. Not sure if the Admiral had something to do with it or not, but this is where we needed to be."

Oozing with frustration, Lachlan's knee bounced as his eyes flicked between the ceiling and his team. Last night Lachlan had stated multiple times that he needed to come to them. Adamant they should start tracking from where they found Gracie, that he could have brought his father or brother with him to get Grace, and then they could have gone from there.

His brother-in-law hadn't been thinking straight. There was no way Gracie would have happily left with strangers whether blood relatives or not. It was only after Nate had reminded him that Lachlan's wife was his sister, his twin, that Lachlan finally understood they weren't guessing.

Deeks' voice penetrated the silence that had fallen.

"There have been similar abductions close to the border over the last two years that we know of. Some were from the same town, but there were only three towns that there hadn't been an abduction from. It took longer to catch on to than anyone would like to admit because these abductions are happening on both sides of the border. The Feds are working with Canada in a joint task force. They now believe the perp lives in one of those towns, that he is deliberately staying away from his own backyard. With this abduction, we're left with two towns. Forest Haven and Riverdale."

Riverdale was the town across the mountains to the east. The two towns shared the mountains, but there were still over a hundred miles between them, and it crossed the border.

"You think the perp is from here?" Lachlan asked.

Nate shook his head at the question. The number of times Lachlan had laughingly joked there was a serial killer or two in his hometown, now seeming more like a prophecy instead of the lunacy that sometimes came out of their captain's mouth. Ironically, they always listened to Lachlan's gut in the field. Looks like they should have extended that to their home life as well.

"No way to know for sure. But it doesn't matter. These women are disappearing every month like clockwork..." Deeks paused. It was obvious he didn't want to say the next words at all, "...and they've never found any of them. It's the same MO. We figure the mountains are the perps home territory. That's why we didn't come here by road. If the perp is a local and has any brains, he'll be watching both towns. A woman taken, a child abandoned, news will spread fast. We need to stay hidden, and this is where we need to start our search from."

"Dammit, Deeks," Lachlan's voice shook. "Those mountains are treacherous, one hundred and thirty miles straight across, hundreds more in width. We could look for a hundred years and still never find his hideout."

"No, that's bullshit, and you know it. The Feds and the Mounties are hiding out in Riverdale. They're coordinating the search from the Canadian side, but a few agents will head here as added support for us in another day or two. The profilers believe the perp is from Riverdale, they believe this abduction was too close to us here in Forest Haven. Our bosses aren't going to try and keep you away from this. You know the mountains better than most. No one is going to stop you, Lachlan. They want this guy as much as you do. All they ask is that we keep them informed and yell out if we need more feet on the ground."

"So, who exactly are you two answering to on this, me or the Feds?" Lachlan's voice dropped several decibels, the question quietly spoken but leaving no doubt as to the intent behind it.

"Lachlan!" Nate interrupted with a growl.

"No, Nate." injected Taniq with a sigh. "It's fine. He's allowed to be a dick under the circumstances. Yes, we're currently loaned to the Feds for six months, the same as you're currently playing at sheriff here. But nothing has ever come between us before, nor will it now. We're a team. Brothers. Family. We'll always come first. Of course, we'll use the resources of the Feds if we need to, but only with your approval. Our SAC knows that we're always active and that you outrank him. Your orders override his. If he ever has a problem with something, he knows to go to the Admiral. Although, previous comments suggest he doesn't think the Admiral has much control of you."

Nate choked on a laugh, there was a lot of truth to those words depending on the situation. His dad tended to give Lachlan a lot of leeway. For his part, Lachlan gave the guys a small nod of acknowledgement, seemingly content to ignore Taniq's last comment and the smirks both Taniq and Deeks didn't bother hiding. His best friend focused back on Nate.

"What does the Admiral think? I didn't get a chance to talk to him much. Luca and Xavi commandeered my focus." The Admiral wasn't only their boss. He was Nate's father. Which also made him Lachlan's father-in-law since Lachlan married Nate's twin sister. Nate loved how close their family was, but he got even more enjoyment out of watching his best friend annoy the hell out of his dad. Lachlan could drive the sanest man crazy. He had a talent.

"Yeah, I spoke to him on the way here. He's notified the hierarchy and briefed Reaper and Arrow. They're both on the tail end of ops, so he hopes to get them to us asap. No matter what, we'll get any resources and backup we need. Bruce is staying put for the moment, but DBD is already on his way. Mum and Dad will keep Luca and Xavi with them until we know it's safe. He said to call in tomorrow if you can. The boys are still not happy about going to therapy."

Nate couldn't resist another smirk as Lachlan rubbed his face with a sigh. They all knew Lachlan would have to deal with the therapy issue soon, but right now, they truly had bigger problems.

It was time to plan, so, the team relocated upstairs. Their control room was high-tech, split into two sections, the left side was flat, holding only a large conference table that could seat twenty-four people. In contrast, the right side comprised three levels, stepped down at two-foot drops, steps ran between the two sides.

The room faced a wall of screens, some of which connected to satellite feeds. Multiple workstations were set up at the lowest level. Another three workstations, the brains, sat in a triangle formation on the middle level where their IT gurus would oversee and assist in ops. Command, on the top level, held four desks where the Admiral or team leads sat looking out over the room. Small but mighty, any government agency would be jealous if they ever saw it.

Five hours later, they broke from the conference table to reheat some frozen pizza before getting back to it. Gracie had woken long enough to drink a bottle of milk. The little tyke was utterly exhausted. The boys spent another six hours going over the terrain, Reaper and Arrow joining in via phone to solidify their plans.

With that done, they headed to bed. They all needed some sleep. Nate didn't need to be a psychic to know Lachlan would spend half the night worrying about introducing Gracie to her grandparents. He had a lot of explaining to do.

If things had gone to plan, Lachlan would have been telling them today anyway, but he would've had his wife and daughter at his side for support.

Lachlan stopped short at the sight of his little girl asleep in his bed with his dog. Cuteness overload. Mannix had moved to lie lengthwise down the bed, his daughter cuddling him and her huge ass dragon. Murphy's Law reigned supreme. He'd spent weeks preparing his daughter's bedroom. Painting it in different variations of her favorite color—Smarties pink. Disney decals covered the walls. A bed any princess would be proud of under a ceiling of stars. And yet here she was, asleep in his bed. Although considering the circumstances, it was understandable.

Trying not to wake her, Lachlan climbed under the blankets and pulled his daughter into his chest. Gracie snuggled in while Lachlan's brain ticked over the day's events and tomorrows to come.

Shit!

He'd forgotten to check in with his deputies. He had no idea what state the town was in following any antics facilitated in the name of Halloween. Not much he could do about it now. Jonah or Max would have rung him if there were any major problems. Probably... Whatever the case, Lachlan needed sleep, tomorrow was going to suck.

Hours.

DAYS	HOURS	MINUTES	SECONDS
000	03	:46	:58

November sat huddled, unable to move. Her fingers, drained of blood from the strain of hugging her knees tight to her chest. She wanted to turn away. Close her eyes to the horror happening in front of her.

Hours.

DAYS	HOURS	MINUTES	SECONDS
000	02	:38	:47

Helpless, no way to make it stop. This couldn't be happening. She needed to wake from this damn nightmare.

Hours.

DAYS	HOURS	MINUTES	SECONDS
000	01	:23	:35

Fists flew as he raped October, climaxing, only to start over again in a frenzied rage. He never went soft. All the while, the clock steadily counted down. The dull red glow of the room in contrast to the bright sharp numbers. Impossible to ignore.

Minutes.

DAYS	HOURS	MINUTES	SECONDS
000	00	:10	:28

November's eyes stayed glued to the counter.

Was it in her head?

As soon as the numbers went under ten minutes, it appeared to go faster.

That couldn't be.

October's cries seemed even louder.

Surreal.

Disbelief.

Frozen.

Her mind told her to turn away, to block her ears, but she couldn't move.

And then nothing.

The sudden silence, the only thing that could have torn her gaze away from the clock.

He was glaring at her. His eyes showed no life. The smirk on his face was pure evil, accentuated by smears and smatters of October's blood.

A straight arm and a finger pointed to her and then at the electronic counter on the wall.

"Count it down!" He snarled.

"Now!"

November's eyes flew over to October. Her view was now unobstructed. She wasn't moving. Pieces of October's flesh had flown from her body at the force of his assault.

She was unrecognizable.

Warned.

Don't delay in responding. October had repeated it like a mantra. Tearing her gaze back toward the clock, she opened her mouth to do as ordered.

Too slow.

The back of his hand lashed out before she could comprehend what was happening. Pain exploded across the right side of her face.

She looked into his eyes, only to see empty black pools.

"HURRY!"

Blood trickled from her mouth as she complied.

"Six... five... four... three... two... one..."

CRACK!

The sound reverberated around the small concrete dungeon.

He shot her.

Just like that.

He shot her.

Numbness crept along her limbs.

Fog clouded her brain as November stared at the counter in disbelief.

Watching as it continued counting down as if nothing had happened.

As if nothing had changed.

DAYS	HOURS	MINUTES	SECONDS
029	23	:59	:33

He watched as it dawned on her. The knowledge easily read on her face. Eyes widened in horror, the moment she understood her life was ticking down before her.

When she finally looked back at him, he stepped over and smashed his fist into her face. Not hard enough to knock her out. Just enough to daze and ensure compliance. The bitch needed to know he wasn't playing, that he was in charge.

Riding the high of his latest kill, he fucked her for the first time. A few quick tugs of his cock, the only concession to wiping away any undried blood or pieces of October's dying flesh.

She was tight. He entered her in one hard thrust, tearing her flesh. There would be no compassion from him. Buried in her warm heat, her pussy squeezed around him. The sounds of his balls slapping her ass created a symphony in tandem with her cries, the only other sound echoing the room as he pounded into her with the still warm body of October lying next to them.

She would be a fighter. When she had time to process what had happened, the current confusion and disbelief in her eyes would turn to hate.

He looked forward to it. Nothing thrilled him more than one of his bitches fighting back, thinking they had a chance of escape. It would make conquering her all that much better.

When he finally came and pulled out, he noted with satisfaction that November's blood had joined October's on his cock.

It was always so hard waiting those last few hours to claim the next month while the dying hours of the last ticked by. But it was worth it. Heaven for his cock going from the sloppy and loose cunt of the last bitch to the tight warmth of the newest.

He'd taken advantage of her dazed shock, not bothering to secure her properly as he would going forward. Pushing himself to his knees, he waited for November's terrified eyes to meet his. Then he grabbed her hair and used it to slam her head into the concrete floor, sending her back into the oblivion she would soon desire every waking hour.

He had some cleaning to do.

In the future, he would wear condoms. The last and the first time he fucked them was the only time he went unsheathed. It was possible that some bitches he had buried would have had his spawn inside them. Possible but unlikely. He always gave them the morning after shot after the first claiming and disinfected the cunt of the dead before he buried them.

It was a job he would have rather passed off to the girls, but he had made that mistake early on. A sweet February. Wasted. He'd learned his lesson the hard way. That getting her to dispose of the body and clean the room, only then to watch the timer on her own life tick away, had been too much for her brain to handle.

She had shut down completely. It had been a long month for him. Nothing worse than screwing a corpse. She might not have been dead, but it felt the same. Been there, done that. But he learned his lesson, and luckily for him, it had been the shortest month of the year.

SIX

Lachlan woke as soon as his daughter moved. Feigning sleep, he didn't have to wait long before two index fingers and a thumb tried to pry his left eye open.

"Daddy, are you awake? Daddy?"

Lachlan wasn't sure how he could still be asleep with fingers yanking at his eye. And as it wasn't particularly comfortable, he flipped them both and started tickling.

"I am now, you little munchkin!"

With the tickles came screams of delight. Seconds later Lachlan's bedroom door burst open and all three of his men stormed through the door, guns at the ready.

Quick to take in the circumstances, the boys hid their weapons from a still squealing Gracie. Lachlan frowned and shook his head.

"Don't you know the difference between happy squeals and screams of terror?" Shrugs and grumpy grunts, the only reply from Deeks and Taniq before they both turned and walked out. Based on that display, you'd never know they'd all lived together for years.

He guessed under the current circumstances; they just weren't taking any chances.

Nate stayed hovered by the door.

"Neither you nor Mannix moved an inch."

Lachlan shrugged, still tickling his daughter.

"Mannix didn't sense any danger, and nobody would have made it in here without going through the three of you. It's unlikely that none of you would have been able to warn me."

"Daddy, stop."

"Do you give up? Say uncle."

"Uncle, Daddy, uncle."

Lachlan stopped tickling and looked at Nate, who was still watching, the small smile the only sign he was enjoying the sound of Gracie's giggles.

"How 'bout I make breakfast? What will it be?" Nate raised his hands in question.

Lachlan and Gracie looked at each other before calling out at the same time, "Pancakes!"

Nate smiled. "My specialty."

"No, Uncle Nate, Mummy says that's the only thing you can make ed table."

"Gracie, the word is edible, and your mummy is one hundred percent correct!" laughed Lachlan.

"Hey, I'm still standing right here. I can hear you," Nate lamented as he turned to head down to the kitchen. It was a long-running joke between them about Nate's inability to cook anything but pancakes. Nate kept threatening to prove them all wrong one day, but so far, that had never happened.

Lachlan gave Gracie a much-needed bath and let her play longer in the tub while he had his own shower, keeping a close eye on his active terror. As an extra precaution, Lachlan had let Mannix into the bathroom. When it came to his three-year-old, four eyes were better than two, although, much to his daughter's delight, Mannix appeared more occupied with trying to catch the bubbles his daughter was blowing into the air than keeping guard.

Twenty minutes later, Lachlan dried and dressed, stood in his daughter's room, with frustration setting in. He had picked Gracie's favorite pink dress for her to wear for the much-anticipated introduction of his parents. Gracie was not happy with his choice.

"Baby, don't you want to wear your pretty pink dress to meet your grandparents?"

"No!" Gracie held tight to the denim overalls she'd plucked from her dresser. Her face getting pinker was as good a sign as any, announcing an impending explosion. With a shrug, Lachlan gave in. At least they were clean and if his wife got upset, he could honestly say that he'd tried. Lachlan insisted on a white singlet and T-shirt underneath, and they settled on a long-sleeved pink sweater to go over the top. He had tried to point out the sweater was supposed to go under the straps but considered winning two out of three a good outcome. Besides, it looked like she was wearing jeans and a top.

After grabbing some sneakers and her fluffy pink winter jacket, Lachlan considered it a job well done. But the exchange had made him think of his wife. Last Friday, she had been telling him how determined his daughter was at deciding what she wore.

Lachlan had laughed at his wife's comment that his three-year-old was turning into a fashion diva. His wife had chastised him, knowing he was only laughing because she was the one dealing with the arguments most mornings, but Lachlan only cared that Gracie was warm enough. He had no doubt that would change in a few years. And if it was this hard when she was three with a special occasion in front of her, he shuddered to think of the battles ahead in her teenage years.

With a last thought to his beautiful wife, Lachlan swept Gracie into his arms, blowing a couple of raspberries on her cheek to make her laugh before grabbing the bag he had packed for her, they headed downstairs to breakfast. Mannix on his six.

The sooner he got this done, the sooner he could start hunting.

Lachlan had asked Grace the night before when he was trying to put her to bed if she remembered anything, but all she'd said was a bad man took mummy, and then she'd tightened her hold on him and cried into his chest.

The boys would stay in the house until 1100hrs and then make their way to the rendezvous point. They confirmed their plans as they ate, half entranced by the scene in front of them as Gracie made her pancakes swim on her plate of maple syrup.

Lachlan was too slow to stop her from throwing one of the saturated pancakes to the floor for his tail wagging dog. Mannix's focus hadn't strayed from Gracie as they ate breakfast. So, the pancake disappeared, but at least he also cleaned the floor afterwards. Bonus.

The pup then plonked his butt back down at Gracie's feet in case more offerings would be forthcoming. Shaking his head at their antics and ignoring the smiles of his men, Lachlan confirmed the boys would get the gear and food organized in his absence.

If they had any chance of having the upper hand, it was imperative no one knew that there were four of them. Part of that was staying hidden. The other part was convincing Gracie that she had to keep the secret. If anyone asked her, Daddy got her, Daddy brought her back. When in doubt, the answer was Daddy or the bad man. Lachlan didn't need that confusion getting out there.

Locked and loaded, Lachlan drove his all-terrain SUV out from the back of his property. The reason he had skipped in and out of town unseen so easily with baby seats in the back was that no one knew he had a personal vehicle.

He kept his police issue vehicle in the driveway in the front of his house, but he'd built another garage at the back of his property —although the guys argued that compound was a better descriptor —that opened into the woods. Lachlan's contractors had cleared a road to get to the outskirts of town and onto the main road out. Hidden from above, the opening on to the main road was also well concealed.

Any time one of his deputies was on call overnight, Lachlan used the back path to sneak away. Where possible, Lachlan spent most of his nights in Falls View with his family. If Jonah or Max ever cottoned on that he was out of town, he just let them believe he was out with friends. They would, of course, assume he was attempting to pick up, and the subsequent teasing was merciless. But that was better than trying to explain the truth. The time hadn't been right, and now he had no choice.

As Gracie sat buckled into her seat, babbling to Mannix, who was resting his head on her lap, Lachlan made the call to his dad.

"Hello."

"Hey, Dad, it's Lachlan."

"Hey, son, what's happening?"

"Are you home with Ma?"

"Yes, it's just us. Shauna took the boys to breakfast in Falls View before the roads close."

"I thought they were still fighting?"

"They were, but I figured young Josh was over it. I heard him threaten to tell you who it was and his age. Miraculously, seconds later, they were best friends again and wanted to go out for breakfast."

"Okay, now I'm worried. Do you know who it is?"

"No, but I'm keeping an eye out and if I need to, well, I can always get one of the twins to blab. Anyway, enough about them. What's going on with you, son?"

"Actually, I really need to speak with you and Ma."

"Well, you better come over then. I'll round up your mother. Is everything okay?"

"No, unfortunately everything is far from okay. I'll fill you in when I get there. I just need you both to know that I never meant to hurt you."

"Geez, boy. Your mother and I knew you were hiding something. Whatever this is, we will get through it together. You can always count on us. We love you." His dad stated what Lachlan had already known but had needed to hear.

"I know, Dad. See you shortly." Lachlan probably should have mentioned he was just pulling into their drive, but he wanted a moment to compose himself as well as to get Gracie out of the car before they ran out and bombarded him with questions.

She struggled to focus on his face but in the dim light she did not recognize him and for all she knew he was wearing a mask. It was hard to tell if this was the same man who had stumbled in front of her car. There had been a knife protruding from his stomach and what looked to be blood gushing everywhere.

Once they were face to face, she knew it was a setup, but it was too late. She had tried to run back to the car, back to her baby, but he was faster and yanked her to him. The last thing she remembered was a strange metallic smell and then nothing.

In horror, she looked up at the faceless man.

"Who are you? Where is my baby? Why am I here? What do you want from me?"

His only response was to walk over and hit her, sending her back into oblivion.

When Sam pulled the door open, Lachlan stood in front of them. He looked nervous and that just wouldn't do. But before Sam could yank the boy into his arms, Lachlan spoke.

"Ma, Dad. There is someone here I would like you to meet." It was then that Claire gasped and nudged Sam with her elbow. Beside Lachlan stood Mannix and there were two tiny pink-mittened hands holding on to Lachlan's thigh.

"Gracie, do you want to say hi to your grandma and grandpa?"

A little blonde head peeked around Lachlan's thigh and two piercing blue eyes peeped out at them before she quickly hid again.

"Come on, baby, you ain't that shy." Lachlan swung the little girl into his arms. Holding tight to Lachlan's neck, she tucked her head under his chin.

"Ma, Dad, this is my daughter, Grace."

It was Claire who found her voice first. Sam was glad she resisted the urge to pull them into her arms. He doubted the little tyke would welcome the move yet.

"Hello, Grace, it's lovely to meet you. Come on, let's get you both inside out of this chilly air."

Sam waited for Lachlan to pass, clapping a hand on his free shoulder in support as his boy paused to kiss Claire on the cheek. Shutting and locking the door, Sam followed them into the lounge room. Lachlan had chosen to sit with Grace on the floor in front of the fire, so Sam guided Claire toward the couch to give everyone a little space. He had a lot of questions.

"Gracie, come on now. Let's get you out of this jacket." Young Gracie let go long enough for Lachlan to unzip and remove her arms from the garment before clinging back to Lachlan's chest. A few moments later the jacket lay over the arm of the chair next to him and his son finally met his gaze.

"I guess you have some questions?"

"That, my boy, is a rather large understatement." Sam studied his eldest. Lachlan radiated tension. His face was pale, almost devoid of blood, his eyes looked haunted. Even with no idea what the hell was going on, it was clear this wasn't a happy family reunion.

It was also clear Lachlan loved his daughter. Just as obvious that his daughter loved her father, which meant they were not strangers to each other. And yet Lachlan had never once mentioned that he had a daughter.

"How old is Grace?" Claire wrung her hands together. Sam understood. He too, was itching to hug the little girl. In a matter of only a few minutes, they'd become grandparents to a toddler.

"Gracie, your grandmother wants to know how old you are."

At the same time Lachlan spoke the words, he used his left index and middle finger to deliver a single tap to Gracie's right wrist. Frowning, Sam made a mental note to ask what that was about later. Gracie peeked out from the safety of her dad's chest to look at them.

Sam knew that he especially looked like Lachlan, a slightly older version, but there was no doubt they were related. He hoped that would help ease the introduction. Then Mannix was on his feet. The pup walked over to lay his head, first on Sam's leg and then Claire's, before walking back to lie in front of the fire.

Confounded, Sam watched in amazement as the little girl's face transformed. Flashing them with a thousand-megawatt smile, now vouched for by Lachlan's dog, she held up four fingers.

"Ahem!" Lachlan cleared his throat.

Gracie swung her head to glare at her dad, who raised his right eyebrow in response. With a huff and a pout, the little girl faced them again, slowly tucking her pinky finger away so only three fingers remained. Sam didn't even attempt to hide his mirth.

"I nearly four," the little girl said with force.

Lachlan smiled and focused back on them, shaking his head slightly.

"Her birthday is August twelve. She turned three a few months ago, but she keeps telling people her birthday is nearing—although we think Luca is to blame. She likes attention, cake, and presents. The brat has worked out that if people think a birthday is coming and they might not be around for it, they'll send presents early."

Before Sam could ask who Luca was, the little sprite piped up diverting the conversation.

"I like cake."

"Well, I'm not sure Grandma has cake, but she makes the best chocolate brownies in the whole town. Maybe if you ask her nicely, she might find you a piece." Lachlan smiled at his daughter. Eyes gleaming in anticipation, the little girl bounded from Lachlan's lap and promptly climbed on to Claire's.

"I like chocolate brownies," she declared. Claire laughed and hugged the little girl tightly.

"Well then, let's go find you some."

"I'm not sure that was what I meant by asking nicely," Lachlan directed to his daughter as she walked hand in hand with his mother into the kitchen.

"Lachlan, what the hell is going on?" Sam demanded in a hushed voice.

This time when she awoke, she knew she wasn't alone. There was a single bulb in the roof that gave off a bright fluorescent light overshadowing the dim red glow from the counter.

"On your knees. NOW. Stop whimpering, you will not speak unless you're instructed to. You will come to your knees immediately every time I walk into this room. Do you understand?"

"Yes." She sobbed, the back of his hand connecting hard with her face.

"Yes, what?" he demanded.

"Yes, sir!"

"That's right, a little respect and it'll go easier on you. Now, take off your clothes!"

He glared at her as if daring her to challenge him. His eyes gleaming in anticipation. But she knew this wasn't the time to fight. Instead, she followed his commands. She had no choice and no way out.

October had indeed imparted a lot of information. Once she had started talking, November hadn't been able to stop her. In vivid detail, October had told her everything. What she'd done right and where she'd mis-stepped, along with the resulting punishments. November intended to learn from all October's mistakes, as she had every intention of ending this for herself and any future victims.

"You will undress when I enter. Re-dress after I leave. The chain around your neck gives you access to most of the room with the freedom of using your hands and your feet. There is a toilet in the far right-hand corner and a basin with a shower next to it which you can use to clean yourself when I'm not here. Make sure you don't soil yourself. I promise you won't enjoy the punishment if you do. Do you understand?"

"Yes, sir."

"Good, you learn quick. Now, fold your clothes and put them to the side."

He watched her as she followed his instructions. She noted the more she trembled, the harder he became. The look upon his face was truly evil. It was clear he wanted her aware and terrified.

"Now, sit! To your right is a cuff. Attach the open end to your right ankle. Now, reach up along the chain attached to your neck, feel for the cuffs, and lock your wrists into them.

"Good." He sneered in satisfaction when she'd followed all his instructions. She was now half sitting, half lying, naked on the floor, her hands cuffed above her head and her right ankle cuffed to the wall. From this position, she'd be unable to fight him. Exposed, completely open to him, she could do nothing as he stepped forward and tightened the cuffs before he balled his hand into a fist and smashed it into her face.

When she cried out, he rammed his fingers into her. For what seemed like the longest time, he battered his fists into her body, somehow making sure not to knock her unconscious. Red from welts and blood, with bruises already forming, he forced his way into her. Tearing even more of her flesh, he promised next time to take her ass. Before the night was out, he'd own all her holes.

Hours later, he'd kept his promise and after he'd come for the fourth time, he knocked her out.

When she came too, she was alone once more. Her wrists and ankle had been uncuffed.

Despite her unconsciousness, the timer had continued to tick her life away and yet the month had just begun …

SEVEN

Sam sat and waited for his son to speak. A couple of times Lachlan opened his mouth, but nothing came out, like he couldn't quite find the words. Finally, Sam gave up and just started asking questions.

"Where's Gracie's mother? Are you two together? You told people you were married when you first came home, but since no one ever saw this mystery woman, and you kept changing the subject we assumed you were telling porkies to keep the wolves at bay."

"Ha, not that it worked. Lou-Ellen never believed it either. Yes, we're together, legally wed," Lachlan answered as his eyes dropped to watch the flames in the fireplace.

"Okay, was Grace the reason you both got married? Was it a shotgun wedding, so to speak?"

"No, we were already engaged but the wedding didn't go as planned."

"Well, how long have you been married then? Do you even love your wife?"

Lachlan's eyes met his in an instant. The look of shock and anger clearly displayed on his face.

"Of course, I love my wife. What kind of dumbass question is that?" Lachlan demanded.

"One a father asks when his son comes home alone with his three-year-old granddaughter that he has never met, let alone heard of. I haven't seen any evidence of a wife, despite vague comments about being married. You've been home for three months, and I've never heard you speak specifically of a single woman, let alone a wife. I'd say it's a damn fair question."

"Touché! Yes. I love my wife more than anything. I would die for her."

"You didn't answer the question, Lachlan—how long have you been married?"

"Five years, sir. We've been married five years." Lachlan pulled a chain from under his shirt. On it was a thick platinum ring. His fingers started playing with it as he turned to watch the flames. "We've had our fair share of problems to overcome, but we love each other and our kids. That's never been in doubt."

Jesus, so many questions arose from that one statement. Where to start?

"What happened to separate you? Did you cheat on her? And what do you mean by kids, do you have more than Gracie?"

"What? No! Of course I've never cheated on my wife. Seriously? That's where your mind goes?"

"I've no idea what's going on Lachlan, that's the problem."

"Yeah okay. Look, we're good. Solid. We've just had a few unexpected challenges to deal with that we've needed time to come to terms with."

"Why didn't you come to us earlier? Christ, if you think your mother and I haven't noticed something hasn't been right with you, boy, you've got rocks in your head. Even Jonah and Max are worried about you, for Pete's sake."

"Yeah, I figured that when I caught them following me. But let me be clear, we're not separated! I've been traveling home most nights and any days off that I haven't been supervising contractors or working on the house myself."

"Well, I'm glad to hear that, although we would have appreciated being a part of your new family. We all love you, son."

"I know, unfortunately it wasn't that simple."

"When are things ever simple? For Christs sake we're family. We're here for you. We always will be. Lean on us. I can't believe you've been married for five years. Were you ever going to tell us? I mean, it's obvious something happened to bring this to a head now, but if it hadn't, would your mother and I ever know we had a grandchild—or is it grandchildren? Earlier you used the plural."

Lachlan could hear the hurt in his father's voice. He certainly understood it, but he didn't think that anything he was going to say to him today would ease it. If anything, it was going to make it worse.

Just as he was about to respond, his mother walked in holding Gracie's hand. From the look on her face, he had no doubt she had heard every word of their conversation. It's not like there were walls or anything. While the kitchen was in an alcove of sorts, it was still open to the lounge and dining room.

"Daddy, I had brownie." Gracie dropped his mother's hand and ran over to him plowing into his chest.

"Hmmm," Lachlan used his thumb to wipe her face and pulled her onto his lap. "I'm thinking all that chocolate around your mouth might have already told me that. Did you thank your grandma?"

"Yup. Grandma boughted you a piece too," Gracie said before adding, "I love you, Daddy!"

Lachlan laughed and tapped her on her nose with his index finger. He knew this trick.

"I love you too, pumpkin, but you ain't getting my brownie."

Taking the small plate from his mother, Lachlan watched as his little girl squirmed off his lap and made the move to her next target.

A quick caress to his hair, his ma moved over to sit with his dad, who now had his three-year-old daughter climbing on to his knee.

Gracie had picked her target well. Lachlan's dad was a pushover for little kids, especially, it seemed, those with big blue eyes. Within seconds, he'd shared his slice of brownie. Odds on his dad would be carrying sweets in his pockets now, along with his dog treats.

Everyone ate in silence for a few minutes, watching the little girl eat her brownie. It was obvious she was tired, with big yawns taking place between each bite, so it wasn't long before she was dozing, snuggled tight in her grandfather's arms. The events of the last few days had clearly taken their toll. He'd make sure his daughter got therapy after this.

Lachlan had to blink to stop tears forming at the sight of his parents with Gracie. They were quite a picture. Two grandparents in awe of the little girl, that moments ago they hadn't even known existed. So quick to love and accept her. He had kept this from them. He could only hope that once he told them everything, they would understand why and forgive him. His dad kissed his ma on the forehead before refocusing on Lachlan.

"How about you start at the beginning?"

"I'd been in the navy for a few years before we met. It was crazy how fast I fell for her. We wanted to come home and introduce everyone, but things kept getting in the way."

Lachlan couldn't miss his dad's raised eyebrow at that, so he answered his question without waiting to hear it voiced.

"Yeah, okay I've been back three months, and I still didn't say anything, but that wasn't the plan. Our last mission was a shit show. We needed time to deal with the fallout and regroup. In truth, my team and I are still active, if anything we're on a break of sorts. We're kind of, um, reservists I guess, for lack of a better word, we go when called. We've had a few rough years. After everything we'd been through, we wanted to come back to the US and work out of here as our base."

"You said team, not squad." His dad looked as though he already knew the answer but wanted Lachlan to confirm it.

"Eh, yeah. We're a special ops team. It's preferred we don't advertise who we are or what we do."

His dad nodded as he digested what Lachlan was saying. He knew his dad wouldn't hesitate to push for answers.

"The way you're talking, it's your team, you're in charge. Special ops in the navy, means Seals. You and your team are Navy Seals." It was a statement, not a question, but Lachlan answered it anyway.

"Yeah, we earned our Tridents. It's my team. We've been together in one form or another going on for seven years. They are my brothers. We're family."

"Hold on. Seven years?" His mother looked at Lachlan's dad before focusing back on him. "You've been in special ops that long?"

"Sort of. It's kind of hard to explain. It seems we were part of a pilot program; we just didn't know it. A few of us came through officer training, the others through general enlistment and a few from other arms of the military. There were twenty-four in total. But we were all approached separately and encouraged to go through pre-selection, then selection once we passed that." Lachlan shrugged, even knowing what he did now, he still didn't understand why the brass had gone about the process the way they did.

"Most of us had never met but they kept corralling us together. While other selection groups were all judged individually, no one understood why we weren't. It was weird, and everyone thought so. The training was spread out over three years. We didn't expect us all to pass, especially as we had a grumpy old guy in our group. There was a lot of tension between us early on." Lachlan allowed himself a smirk, there'd be fireworks when his team—one member in particular—was finally introduced to his family. He just needed to get out of here and find his wife first. Focusing back on his parents, Lachlan continued. He needed to give them the basics before he could take off or else they would be left vulnerable.

"Turned out, it was all part of something much bigger. After observing us during the long ass training, they nominated four of us as potential team leaders and told us to make ourselves into three teams of six."

That sounded easier than it had been. Lachlan's 2IC, his best friend, was the same rank as the other two team leaders. Nate could have had his own team but instead he opted to stay with Lachlan and was happy to be his second. That and Lachlan was pretty sure, Nate just didn't want to have to deal with his dad in that capacity all the time.

"Between us we worked together to pick our teams, focusing on skills and personalities. Final approvals still had to go through the hierarchy but once done, the six remaining candidates washed out, never knowing why."

Ha. That was a joke. It had become apparent from their last mission that at least one had guessed enough to be bitter and dangerous. But it wasn't the time to delve into that nightmare either.

"We all still had to earn our stripes along the way. Training, pre-selection and selection especially, all sucked dogs' balls. I can promise you there were a few times between us that one or more of us thought about ringing that bell." Lachlan trailed off once again, looking into the fire.

She didn't know how many times he had come in, but she knew what to expect. His routine didn't change. Every time he made her undress, he made her cuff her hands and right ankle, he would beat her, he would rape her, and then he would knock her unconscious before leaving.

Whenever she awoke, her cuffs would be hanging innocuously, leaving her only chained by the neck. She would struggle to the basin and makeshift shower to clean and dress, ready for the next time he came. He'd made good on his promise to own every inch of her. Her ass was torn, her throat raw, but she still cleaned herself as best she could.

October—it was easier to think of her as October and not as Julie Ann. Julie Ann was a person who had tried to warn her. Not long after, November had watched her murder. Shot to death in front of her, without even a flinch by the man pulling the trigger. No, it was much easier to think of her as October.

October had told her what had happened to her when she had defied him by not cleaning herself. November was not going to make that mistake. Her eyes had adjusted well to the dark. She had seen what Julie Ann had looked like before he ended her torture … it was the bright florescent light she feared now.

The door opened slowly. There was no squeaking sound, the door made no noise. She didn't know if that made it better or worse —in every horror movie she had ever seen, the door always squeaked. And at that moment, she was the star in her very own horror movie. As the opening widened, the light came on and she got to her knees. 'Christ,' she thought. 'How much longer can this go on?'

November knew she had to focus on something or else she, too, would be lost to this. So, she started to plan, and part of that was to look for a pattern. October had shown her the wall under the basin where all the girls before her had scratched in their real names and the corresponding month. She had been horrified when she had seen how many women had come before her and she was desperate to ensure it ended now, ended with her.

The wall had given her an idea. She would use it to track his appearances and the clock on the wall counting down the time worked to her benefit, not her detriment, in this respect.

Using the chain that held her captive, she scratched a single stroke on the wall for each day that passed. A stroke turned into a plus sign whenever he appeared. Each time he entered the room, she took note of the clock even as she moved into position. When she woke, she'd again search out the glaring red numbers so she could calculate the time and etch them under the cross.

It didn't take long for a pattern to emerge. Now, the question was how to take advantage of it. She let herself wonder, albeit briefly, if her family even realized she was missing yet.

Lachlan's attention was pulled back to the present by his mother's quiet words.

"How did you meet your wife?"

"One day Nate, my 2IC and best friend, walked into the small studio where we trained. He had this beautiful woman on his arm. I never believed in love at first sight, but I was a goner. Just like that. Only it wasn't that simple. So, I refused to acknowledge her. It was rude, sure. But this gorgeous woman was on my best mate's arm. There was no way it could end well." Lachlan diverted his eyes away from his mother, he did not want to get lectured about rudeness, deservedly or not...

"Everyone stood there like stunned goats while I kept on training. I'd never acted like that before. Nate didn't appear to appreciate the tactic and got in my face demanding to know what my problem was. But what do you say about that? 'Hey, bro. Sorry, but I'm head over heels in love with the girl on your arm that I haven't even met yet ...' It sounded insane to think it, let alone say it out loud, so I continued to ignore them."

The whole team could look back and laugh at it now, but it could have gone a whole different way.

"I figured Nate was about to deck me, but then the woman in question started laughing. This rich, lyrical siren call certain to entrap men far stronger than me engulfed the room. Her words were for Nate, but I felt her eyes boring into me. 'Don't worry, big brother. He's allowed to freak out. It's not often you meet the person you're going to marry, but it's a little confronting when that person is on your best friend's arm, and you haven't worked out they're siblings yet.'" A wry smile lit Lachlan's face at his mother's gasp.

"Well, that stopped me in my tracks, and it sure as hell had Nate stumped for words. I can't explain it, but one look and we both knew. With my last working brain cells, I shrugged Nate an apology of sorts. Then, I pulled his sister into my arms and kissed her like I have never kissed a woman before."

And what a kiss it had been. Damn, his wife could take his breath away. Lachlan didn't know if he could survive this world without her.

"When we surfaced for air, our mentor and the rest of my team were all trying to soothe Nate. Turned out they were twins, and he needed a little longer than we did to accept what had transpired."

Lachlan ignored his dad's scoff; he'd be lying if he said he didn't go out of his way to niggle Nate at times.

"From then on, we were always together, she even started coming to training with us. It was why Nate had brought her to the studio in the first place. His sister also led her own team, and he wanted her to have as many skills at her disposal as possible. They specialized in covert communications, spending most of their time blending in with the locals to get information on targets or movements of certain people of interest."

"So, what, the two of you became a couple, got married at some point and had Gracie all while working in war zones?" His mother sounded incredulous.

"Yes mam, that's pretty much it. She ran into trouble with one of her team which nearly destroyed us all. The aftermath was long and complicated, but we ended up in Afghanistan together, where a whole lot more shit went wrong. I'd elaborate but most of its classified and we don't really have the time anyway."

Lachlan really didn't want to go into that one. The last thing he wanted to explain was getting blown up even if that led to their shotgun marriage because that then led to his wife being taken captive by insurgents, before he then ended up in their custody for several days.

Yeah, that sounded better than being a prisoner of war but even still, his parents were not stupid.

"Let's just say, every time we tried to make it home, something invariably went wrong."

She awoke gradually, slowly focusing on the man in front of her. He had a stocky build. It was hard to tell his height as he was sitting on a wooden chair, but based on the length of his torso, she'd say he was short for a male. And while he now had a balaclava over his head, it was his eyes that drew her attention, not because they stood out as evil or anything, but because they looked strangely familiar.

How long had she been out? How long had he watched her?

At the sound of his voice, she snapped back to the present.

"Payback's a bitch, princess."

I don't understand." Lachlan lifted his gaze at his dad's words. "As far as we were told, troops left Iraq in December 2011 and around the same time they were looking to drawdown troops in Afghanistan. You've been in those two countries this whole time?"

"Yes and no. We started in the US and then in Iraq we were still finding our feet, by the end of our time there, Iraq was mainly just our home base. And yes, we left when the last troops left Iraq and ended up in Afghanistan but that also was more of a home base for us of sorts. Both countries were convenient access points to other trouble spots we were needed in. Not all our missions were contained to the two countries that housed our bases."

"So where was Grace born?"

"Oh, um. Gracie was born on a US Naval base in Italy. She has dual citizenship."

"Was that by accident or design?" Lachlan laughed at his parents' matching frowns. His mother asked a fair question.

"Design. We looked at what US Naval bases were close to us

and decided that Italy was our best choice. We transferred base there for a short time, the brass still found lots for us to do."

EIGHT

Hours later, she awoke and took stock of her body, trying to account for all the pain. He hadn't raped her, but he had hit her. Though he hadn't been particularly cruel or overly violent. No broken bones. It had felt more systematic; she was thankful she'd been able to protect her stomach, but by doing so, her exposed head had become an obvious target.

Alone, it was time to clean herself and start making plans. She was going to get out and back to her husband, back to her babies. From the way he'd treated her, she was confident her assailant didn't know she was ex-military. No, she was sure she could bide her time and escape. Her life depended on it. Clinging to the strange comfort that she'd been in a situation not too different to this before and survived.

Unable to stop, even knowing it was counterproductive, her thoughts lingered on her baby girl. Was she safe? Had someone found her in time?

For her own sanity, she had to have faith. Desperate to believe her husband had taken custody of their child.

Then what? How long had she been out? Would her little girl

still be with her husband, or had he now left her with his family to come and find her?

The thought made her pause. He had been worried about telling his family. Knowing they would be upset at everything that he'd kept from them.

His determination to protect all those close to him was one of those things she loved most about her husband. It also annoyed and frustrated her to no end. The biggest challenge for her and the team was how to deal with it when he couldn't. He'd find a way to blame himself for her kidnapping. Even though there was no way he could have seen it coming, he would still blame himself.

She knew he would come for her. No doubt her brother would be right there next to him, but it wasn't like they'd be able to drop everything and leave straight away. They had other commitments and while she expected them to come as quickly as they were able, that didn't mean she couldn't help herself, that she would sit idly by and wait for her savior.

***

He was running out of time, but he wouldn't say no to coffee. Lachlan followed his mother into the kitchen to give her a hand. He knew she habitually drank tea so while she headed towards the kettle, Lachlan aimed for the coffee machine to speed up the process.

With nothing to do but wait for the water to boil, Lachlan stepped behind her and pulled her into his arms for a long hug, swamping her petite frame.

"I'm sorry, Ma. I never meant to keep stuff from you."

"I don't really understand why you had too but I do know you wouldn't have kept this from us unless you felt you had no choice. From now on though, your father and I will be keeping a much closer eye on you."

Lachlan laughed. His mother had no clue what was about to descend on their small town. Before long, she'd be sick of Lachlan and his antics. He couldn't wait to remind her of this conversation. The whistling kettle from the stovetop intruded on the moment. Tea and coffee made, Lachlan took the tray from her and headed back into the living room just as Gracie started to squirm in her sleep. Little whimpers escaping her lips before she lurched up on a cry of 'Mummy!'

In two strides Lachlan had passed off the tray and swung Gracie into his arms, waking her in the process.

"Hey, pumpkin, you're safe. I have you. Daddy has you." Gracie held on tight. Tears streamed down her little face. She tucked her head into the crook of his neck, but even through her tears, her eyes stayed focused on Mannix, who stood at Lachlan's side head-butting her leg.

As quickly as it started, Gracie stopped crying and threw herself forward to pat Mannix on his head. Luckily, Lachlan was prepared for this move and was holding on tight, so she didn't topple right out of his arms. With Mannix patted, Gracie wiped the tears from her face and whispered to Lachlan, "I want Mummy."

"I know, baby, I miss her too." Kissing her forehead, Lachlan inhaled the smell of his daughter's hair as he held her close. His parents watched on in silence, listening to every word, but Lachlan couldn't stop himself from looking at his watch again. He had been doing it all morning, understanding that with every minute that passed, time was running out. He needed to find his wife, but he needed to tend to his daughter first.

Sam hadn't missed the number of times Lachlan had checked his watch since walking through the front door. His son was on a deadline of some sort, that little interaction they'd just witnessed made him think that Lachlan's wife was missing. If that was the case, it wasn't hard to work out what he needed from himself and Claire.

His son was getting more anxious by the minute, but Sam doubted he would leave before his daughter felt comfortable with them. Whether they got the full story today or not, they had to show Lachlan that his daughter would be happy here as well as safe.

"How 'bout you come to Grandpa for a cuddle?" Sam held out his hands for his granddaughter. With a little shrug, Gracie let go of Lachlan and happily went into Sam's arms.

"You need to go." It wasn't a question.

"Yes." Lachlan nodded. "I do."

"She is safe here with us. We will look after her."

"I know, but I have trained her—too well, in some things. I must be here to introduce her to the others or else she won't trust them and will scream if they try to touch her."

"Seriously? Son, that's a hard lot to bear for a three-year-old."

"Yes, and no. Dad, the kids have already been through a lot in their lives. This arrangement works. It settles them and makes it easy for them to know who they can and can't trust. It takes the guesswork out of it."

Again, with the plural, but before Sam could press for more, Claire interrupted with another question.

"So, if we introduce her to someone, she won't go to them at all?"

The little girl in question appeared oblivious to the conversation around her. Sitting quietly Gracie sucked her thumb, her other hand clutching Mannix's fur. The large husky was half straddling Sam's lap, trying to comfort Lachlan's little girl.

"Correct. She will only trust who her mother or I have told her she can trust. We just have to be the ones to introduce her to them." Lachlan screwed his face up.

"Look I know this seems like a lot. To be honest I don't know any other three-year-olds who could comprehend this either, but Gracie is different. Her mother was in Intelligence. She's beyond smart, but our daughter, well she got my intellect."

Oh shit. Sam couldn't stop his laugh. Lachlan fell in the top two percentile, which was mostly great. That their oldest was primarily taking college classes in his first year of high school underscored his genius title. A member of Mensa at a young age, Lachlan was often a menace growing up, especially when he was bored.

If Gracie was also at a genius level of intellect, he couldn't wait to see Lachlan experience the other side of the coin with his own daughter. Although, maybe he should be more sympathetic towards Lachlan's' mysterious wife. Sam had no doubt his son would likely get in on causing more trouble with his daughter than stopping it.

Sobering, Sam focused back on Lachlan as he explained further.

"The system has three levels. Level one means her mother and I trust them implicitly and she can be left with them. Level two is people or family we know that she can be around without worry but a level one must be nearby or supervising. Level three are strangers. Grace knows to be polite but won't accept anything from someone she doesn't know and won't go anywhere with them. If a stranger tries to hold her without permission, she'll scream and continue to scream until she's released and in the arms of someone in her trust circle."

"What level have you given to us then and the rest of the family?" Sam couldn't believe what he was hearing.

"You, Mum, Jonah and Max are level one, the others are level two."

"Well, that's definitely an interesting system."

"Yeah, but it works for us. We designed this to protect our kids." Lachlan twisted his wrist as he once again stole a glance at his watch.

"What if something happens to you and your wife?" Sam was still trying to digest what he was hearing.

"Both myself and my wife have wills that go to other people we trust. They have a code which they will use. It tells her things have changed and that they are now in charge."

Claire shook her head. "Are you seriously telling me she understands all this?"

"Yes, it's discerning how damn intelligent Gracie is. The munchkin is well ahead of her age, especially in her conversational skills. That she hadn't before the last few months spent much time around other children also would have impacted there. When people speak to her, they believe she is much older than she is. Remember she grew up in war zones with special forces teams all around her, not playing in childcare centers. She also understands the basics of three other languages. All kids are sponges but Gracie's capacity to learn is amazing. While she might only be three years old, her life hasn't been smooth sailing. This is an extra layer of security she responds to."

Sam was dumbfounded, this all sounded surreal and terrifying. "Why are Parker and your younger siblings only level two? Surely you trust them?"

"Yes, of course I do, but we made an age limit of twenty-five for level one. With our lifestyles we don't want her going off alone with too many people, especially untrained ones.

"Unbelievable," Sam shook his head. "Do Jonah and Max know about this?"

"No. They don't even know about Gracie yet. I'll fill them in when they get here. I'm sure with how close they've been sticking to me, they'll both find a reason to stumble in here well before I leave."

"They'll want to go with you. Hell, I want to go with you, and I don't even know what the story is yet."

"Yeah, I figured you would, but Dad, I need you here. If I'm leaving my daughter, it's going to be with people I trust to protect her. I can't be sure that someone won't come looking for her. You both need to promise me that no matter what happens, you won't let anyone take her from you unless you're damn sure it's safe. Screw people's egos. I don't care about offending people; I care about my kids' safety and wellbeing."

"We would never do anything to hurt you or our granddaughter," Sam stated quietly. "If she is in danger, then we promise to protect her. You can count on us, son, and we will follow your rules. I wish I had thought of this years ago. Then we might not have gone through that ordeal with Cooper when he was seven."

"Actually, that's when I devised it. I told my wife about it when she was pregnant and she laughed, told me she would not turn our child into a paranoid freak who did not trust anybody."

"I guess she changed her mind?" Claire asked.

"Yeah, the reality of our world, our life, hit us in the face a few too many times, and then suddenly she was the one assigning levels to people and giving me that look—you know, the one that says, 'Do not even think about saying I told you so!'"

"Sure, I know that look." Sam grinned as he squirmed away from his wife's elbow.

"Hadee ha, Samuel. Well, since you must wait for the others anyway, why don't you fill us in on what exactly has happened?" Claire spoke the words right out of Sam's mouth.

Lachlan sighed and reclaimed his spot in front of the fire, once again focused on the flames.

It was all about patterns. She could survive a few days of this to make sure she understood his routines. There was no other option if she wanted to escape, but luck was already on her side. He'd let her keep her clothes. If she had to guess, she figured he had too much faith in the chain secured to the collar around her neck. Locked to the wall, for many it would be inescapable.

Despite the chain, the only logical reason for letting her keep her clothes would be that he didn't want her to freeze to death even though the room seemed well insulated. She hoped that meant she was in the mountains near where she had been taken, which meant she was close to her family and in territory she had some knowledge of. If she could get out, she would survive.

"A couple of major incidences transpired that had nothing to do with any ops. It had a huge effect on both my wife and me. I lost trust in myself. We knew we needed outside help. Luckily, we have a great support base. Everyone got together and voted to move back to the States. The brass was onboard with it since our ops were becoming more and more spread out. We were also starting to stand out more in Afghanistan when troops were supposedly downsizing." Lachlan hesitated a moment when he saw Gracie wriggle in his dad's arms, but she didn't call out for him, so he continued.

"Stateside, we stayed with Nate's and my wife's parents for a bit. We wanted to give Izzy's mum a chance to spend time with Gracie. It made sense since the house here wasn't quite finished yet and while we were there, we also found a counselor. He was good. It wasn't easy and it took a lot of work from both of us, but it wasn't long before things were mostly back to normal." Lachlan couldn't stop his eyeroll. None of them had foresaw what had come next.

"We were just readying to move to Forest Haven when my team landed a major op. Not wanting Izzy and Gracie on their own in a new place, we decided to wait to move until after we returned. The mission turned into a huge clusterfuck. No other word for it. That one op impacted and changed our lives more than we ever could have conceived. As traumatic as that mission was, it helped me view things in a different light. Even though it was the worst situation we'd ever been through, the learnings and gains from it were incredible." He wouldn't change the outcome but that didn't mean accepting all that had happened was easy.

"Once we returned, we were ordered to take two months medical leave. We needed to recover and regroup. Simply put, we needed time to reacclimatize. So instead of moving into our house straight away we found a place in Falls View for two months. We figured we'd take the two months to sort ourselves out and then move here. We'd go back on ops and the guys would help me finish building the house in our downtime." Yeah right. Mary, Mary. To say that the plan had blown up spectacularly was an understatement.

"But the reality was that even after two months, some of us were still struggling. The brass wasn't sold on us going back to work yet. Then you got hurt Dad and asked me to come home. The brass jumped on that. Decided we all needed to do something else for six months. So, my team split up taking on different temporary assignments but still used the Falls View house as home base." Huffing a laugh, Lachlan paused to hug Mannix since the pup had decided he needed to come over and sit in his lap before bathing his face in doggie kisses.

"Don't get me wrong, we wanted to come here and move into our house. Unfortunately, the fallout from that one mission meant we weren't ready. We all needed more counseling and as a group we needed to focus on ensuring everyone felt secure in their place within both the team and the family before we added unfamiliar faces to the mix." Shrugging, Lachlan smothered a yawn. Shit, he was tired.

"So that's what we did. Technically, I moved here, but I spent more time in Falls View. If I was here and wasn't on duty, I focused on finishing the house. Everyone was based out of our home in Falls View, but they've all stayed here at some point whether to help with construction or to get away from the noise if everyone was home. If I was here, I was seldom alone, which is why I didn't invite anyone in. We weren't ready. Even if the guys went down to the store, people just assumed they were visiting on a day trip." They'd taken the saying, hiding in plain sight damn literally.

"We haven't been out on another official op since we returned. We've used the time to regroup and focus our energy on ourselves and a personal mission we all share."

Lachlan made sure to make eye contact with both his parents before he spoke his next words.

"I promise, I wasn't trying to hide anything from you. The last mission was an emotional overload when we were already dealing with so much. In truth, I wasn't in a place where I wanted to or could talk about it. My wife and team gave me the space and support to heal. We took our time not wanting to rush anyone, but now construction is complete and we're at a place where we all agreed it was time to move in and introduce everyone." Pausing again, Lachlan accepted more kisses from his pup. Mannix was great at picking up emotions and getting Lachlan's attention when he needed to. He could admit it was easier to keep speaking with his dog by his side, or in this case on his lap.

"In the last few weeks, we'd started boxing our things and cleaning the rental. Nate was supposed to drive over with my wife and Gracie yesterday. A quick costume change at home, and we were all coming here to meet you to explain everything. If it had gone to plan, you would have met my wife and your granddaughter last night. The plan was to go trick or treating. Your place would have been our first stop. We were hoping you'd then join us."

"What went wrong?" His dad asked.

"Remember the call I got at dinner the other night? The police had found my wife's car abandoned a couple of miles down the main road just outside of Falls View. It looked like she was going to surprise me and come early instead of waiting for Nate to get back from his trip."

His mother's gasp was soft, but Lachlan kept going. It wasn't about to get any easier.

"Gracie was trapped in her booster seat screaming for her mummy. They searched the area, but while there weren't any obvious signs of a struggle, the driver's door was open and there were a couple of drops of blood about ten feet in front of the car. Her phone and purse were still inside. Someone had taken my wife and left my three-year-old daughter alone and scared in the freezing cold in the middle of nowhere. If they hadn't found her before nightfall, she wouldn't be alive." Lachlan would murder the culprit when he got his hands on them.

"My wife is well trained, and she loves Gracie more than life itself. There is no way she would have left our child unless she was unconscious. As long as there is breath in her body, she'll be fighting to get back to us. I'm going to find her, but time isn't on my side."

His parents didn't hide their shock. Even if they'd already guessed his wife was missing, they wouldn't have been able to fathom the circumstances. Few people would leave a young child alone in the cold to fend for themselves. His dad brushed a hand over Gracie's hair for a few moments before he spoke, seemingly choosing his words carefully.

"Son, we will take care of her, you know that. What I don't understand is, if the only thing stopping you from leaving is introducing everyone personally, why didn't you stop by as soon as you had Gracie?"

"I needed to spend some time with Gracie and settle her first. Plus, that time was used to go over maps, plan, gather supplies and get as much information as possible from all the authorities involved. All evidence points to the mountains. Going out there half-cocked wouldn't have helped anyone. Once I leave here, I won't be coming back to town for any reason until I've found my wife." Sam noted the unspoken words, he could only hope that Lachlan found his daughter-in-law alive and well.

"Besides," Lachlan added. "My wife will be working on her own escape, unless she's hurt or unconscious. The woman won't be sitting back waiting for me to come save her ass.

Sam smiled; he couldn't wait to meet the woman who had claimed Lachlan's heart.

"What do the authorities think happened?"

"Honestly." Lachlan blew out a breath. "The Feds reckon there's a serial killer operating in the area. The working theory is that she's the latest victim."

"What?"

"I know Dad. None of us can know for sure but if she has been taken by this guy, then they reckon she'll still be alive. Women have been going missing around the last day of every month. The profilers believe he keeps them alive until the end of the next month when he searches out new blood. I'll get another update from them before I go, but at the very least, it gives me some hope. If this is random, whoever took her will have no idea what skills my wife possesses, he'll underestimate her." Although the alternative was that this was targeted and that didn't bear thinking about.

"But your still worried about someone taking Gracie?"

"Yes. Unfortunately, I don't know for sure who took my wife or why. Either way, nothing will stop me from going after her. I trust you both to keep my daughter safe, but I need you to keep this as quiet as possible."

"Who do we say she is? It'll only take one look at her eyes to know she is one of the family, even if she didn't look like a mini you." His mother made a fair point.

"Yeah, I get that, and I don't want you to lie. Tell everyone Gracie is your granddaughter and that you are getting to know each other while her parents work a few things out.

Although," Lachlan smirked, "try to keep her away from Lou-Ellen. Gracie has her mother's temperament and is likely to let loose with some nasty words. Her mother has been very vocal about Lou-Ellen trying to get her hands on me. The guys razzing us haven't helped."

NINE

THIS WAS IT! He hadn't hit her hard enough, and she might not get another chance. Channeling calm. She stayed still, focused on her breathing. For this to work, he had to believe he had knocked her out as intended. Waiting was the hardest part. She could feel his eyes on her, his gaze burned into her skin.

A breeze of stale air brushed her face as he turned to walk away. The sound of the door opening sent shivers of hope down her spine. As much as she wanted to see what was behind the door, she kept her eyes closed. Adrenalin pumped through her veins. She waited.

The short pattern had indicated he'd be gone at least ten hours after leaving each morning. Hopefully, it wasn't a weekend, which might change the pattern. If she had calculated correctly, it should be either Wednesday or Thursday. A scrapping sound alerted her before the door reopened.

Concentrating on her breathing, she kept as still as possible. The loud metallic clang would have startled someone with less training. Food. It was the only thing that made sense. He must have brought in a tray of food for her.

During her intelligence training in the navy, their instructors had knocked the recruit's unconscious one at a time and recorded it. As a group, they examined each unconscious classmate, learning what to look for. While there were some slight differences, there weren't many.

Afterwards, they replayed the footage several times, comparing themselves to the vision of them sleeping and under heavy sedation. Their head instructor had them focus on their facial expression, the lack of tension in their bodies, even how their breathing sounded different.

He'd explained that studying themselves and each other would also help them learn to tell if someone else was faking unconsciousness. She hadn't believed him when he had said one day it might save their lives. She'd only had to use it once before, and it had indeed saved her. A limited addition rare bottle of bourbon was a small price to pay, even if it did cost the best part of ten thousand dollars. It looked like he'd get another delivery soon.

Finally, a flurry of movement sounded upstairs. Please be leaving. That had to be a door opening and closing. What then sounded like a lock clicking in place was closely followed by the gruff burr of an engine coming to life. She thought she was alone, but as this might be her only chance, she stayed exactly as she was for another twenty long minutes.

Slowly, she started stretching her arms and legs, ensuring blood was circulating. Confident she wasn't going to fall on her face, she stood less than gracefully and moved to the basin. It was time to freshen up and make use of the facilities.

Fueling her body was the next step. There was more food than he typically left her. Fingers crossed, that meant he was going to be gone longer than usual. She ate half and packed the rest into the napkin, aware the less she would have to scavenge for food later, the better.

When she was ready, she reached into her bra and pulled out the wire from her bra cup. As an intelligence gatherer, the one skill she was proficient in was picking locks. Within seconds, she was free from the chain around her neck.

She grabbed some blankets and piled them into a log shape in the far corner near the basin, placing the end of the chain toward the top of the pile before covering it with another blanket. Expecting her to be there, he would initially believe she was cowered in the corner. It wouldn't pass muster once he got closer, however any time it would buy her might be the difference between life and death.

Satisfied she'd done what she could, it was time to move. Grabbing the food parcel wrapped in a couple of blankets, she paused momentarily to ensure there was no noise outside. Once the click sounded, signifying the lock disengaging, she forced the wire back into her bra before leaving the room and relocking the door behind her. She didn't want him to know how she had gotten out. It was likely he would believe she had used her watch. It surprised her that he hadn't taken it from her in the first place, but she would rather lose the watch than her bra.

The layout was simple. A small landing area with mud stairs led to a trapdoor. Pausing beneath the door, she again took the time to listen for any movement above. Slowly she pushed, meeting with some resistance before it gave way, but the area was strangely dark as the trapdoor lifted.

After a few moments, she shook her head. A floor rug. Geez, what a ninny. With a tug, she pulled on the material, lifting it to expose the inside of a log cabin. As quiet as possible, she crawled out, taking great care to put everything back, so it looked undisturbed.

***

"**W**hat the hell is going on?" Jonah demanded in a loud whisper as he and Max approached his parents' house where Shauna and the twins were huddled shivering outside near the garage door. They'd been about to head out to an early lunch, when his baby sister had called him in a fluster.

"I took the boys to breakfast in Falls View. You know dad's still funny about me driving too far, late in the day."

Oh yeah, and his dad wasn't the only one. Shauna had just got her intermediate license; no-one wanted her driving back from Falls View in the dark without another fully licensed driver until she was a lot more experienced.

"Anyway, we came home and went to walk in, but something was strange, it was too quiet. And we didn't know who owned that car, so we peered through the window. Ma, Dad, and Lachlan are in there, but it looks like they are all upset. We didn't know what to do, so we rang you and waited."

Max approached the window and peered in.

"Yeah. It doesn't look like they are even talking, they're just sitting there. I can't see any sign of a threat, but your parents keep looking down at your dad's lap."

Jonah had never been known for his patience and he wasn't about to start now. Striding to the door, he flung it wide open and walked on through, the rest of his siblings close behind. He stopped short in confusion creating a roadblock of sorts when he got in far enough to see what had his parents' attention. Nobody spoke for a couple of moments as they took in the scene.

Seconds later, the little girl opened her eyes and saw all the extra people in the room. She scrambled up and ran over to Lachlan's outstretched arms, calling out—Daddy???

Shit. Lachlan was a dad?!

"Hey, pumpkin, it's okay. You're safe here. These are some more of the family. Do you want to meet your uncles and your aunty?"

After a few moments, the little tyke looked up from where she'd hidden her face in Lachlan's neck. She took the time to look at each person before stretching back to whisper in Lachlan's ear. Mere seconds later his brother seemed to choke on a cough, a small smirk remained as he hugged the little girl and told her he loved her before he focused back on their mother.

"Ah, she wants to know if they have brownies."

At this, their mother smiled and made to move, but Shauna's hand on her shoulder stalled the movement.

"It's okay, Ma, I'll get them."

As Shauna headed off to the kitchen, Jonah stood frozen while the others moved around him, intent on finding a spot to sit.

Jonah's eyes stayed focused on Lachlan and the toddler on his lap. What the fuck was happening here? This little girl had just called his brother 'Daddy', and no-one was demanding explanations or volunteering them for that matter. Jonah wanted to know what the hell was going on and he had no intention of waiting for brownies, but before he could speak, his dad interceded, drawing his attention.

"Sit down, Jonah and calm your ass. You're scaring her. You'll find out what is going on soon enough."

Huh? Scaring her? Jonah snapped back to look at Lachlan and the tiny tot on his lap and sure enough, big blue eyes were staring straight at him. Flinching away from his gaze, she closed her eyes and turned into Lachlan's neck, hiding from his view.

Damn it, he wasn't trying to scare anyone, he just wanted answers. With a frustrated sigh, Jonah collapsed into the nearest vacant armchair, first having to move a tiny puffy pink jacket out of his way, and waited for somebody to explain what the hell was going on.

Racer, nowhere near as polite, didn't hesitate to bound over to the little girl and start licking her face. Giggling, she held Racer close with her right hand, her left still clung tight to Lachie.

"Daddy, look it's Racer!"

"I know, baby girl. He's grown since you last saw him."

Jonah frowned and was about to comment when Shauna re-entered the room with a tray of brownies and napkins. Shauna appeared just as intrigued by the beautiful little girl sitting on their big brother's lap but didn't go straight to her. Instead, likely trying not to scare their— niece? Shauna nodded in Jonah's direction and then moved to offer everyone else in the room a brownie first.

With the twins and their parents sorted, Shauna headed to Max next. Jonah hid his smirk as little blue eyes followed Shauna's every move. A quick detour back to Jonah, before Shauna sat on the floor in front of Lachlan, meant that he didn't miss out on his treat either. It looked like he and Max would not be getting lunch anytime soon.

"Hi, my name is Shauna. Would you like a brownie?" Shauna held out the now half empty tray. The little girl looked at Shauna, then at the brownies, before turning to look up at Lachie, who nodded. Everyone watched as fast little hands grabbed two brownies from the tray. Lachlan opened his mouth to say something, but the tiny tot twisted and raised one of the brownies, pushing it into his mouth before she focused back on his sister.

"Daddy likes brownies too."

Seemingly content for the minute with a mouth full of chocolate deliciousness, the little girl relaxed back against his brother's chest. Even as her eyes roamed over all the new inhabitants within the room.

As tempted as he was to speak and move this show along, Jonah held back, instead watching as Shauna placed the tray on the floor, grabbed a brownie for herself and got comfortable.

Everyone was focused on Lachlan, waiting. But Jonah was only growing more impatient by the second. He didn't know if Lachie was going to be able to get any damn words out. The man seemed unsure what to say, which was not normal when it came to his confident big brother. Finally, Lachie's throat moved as he made to say something before a little voice piped up.

"Daddy?"

"Yes, baby?"

Twisting slightly, the little girl raised her head to whisper in Lachlan's ear, only this time the room was so quiet everybody could hear what she said.

"Are they twins?"

Sure enough, after taking stock of the family, the one thing that had caught her attention was the two people closest to her age who had the same face.

"Yes, they are. Do you want to meet them, Gracie?"

Gracie? Thank God, Jonah finally had a name to call the child. Although he wasn't expecting her response to Lachie's question and by the gasps and badly disguised laughter in the room, no one else had either.

"No!"

"What do you mean, no?"

"No, Daddy, no more twins, Daddy, we're all fulled up on twins, no more, Daddy."

"Sweetheart, this isn't a hotel. We are not full. There is no maximum number of twins accepted into our family. Besides, they are older than both you and the boys, so they were part of this family first."

Gracie chewed her bottom lip as she thought about her dad's answer before then responding with a mischievous pout.

"No, we're fulled up, Daddy, but you can give Luca and Xavi back if you want to keep these twins, I won't mind."

Jonah had no clue what Gracie meant, but he couldn't stop his smile when a full-blown laugh escaped Lachlan. Something he hadn't seen from his brother in a very long time.

"Nice try, baby, nice try, but no, we are not giving anybody back. Now, why don't you say hello to your uncles? See the one curled into Grandma? That's Josh and the one sitting between Grandpa's legs is Zac." When Grace ducked her head back underneath Lachlan's chin, his big brother continued with the rest of the introductions.

"Gracie, that over there is your Uncle Max." An obvious tap on the underside of her wrist by her father's index and middle finger had her head instantly popping up to look directly at Max.

"Hello, Uncle Max."

Standing at full height inside the cabin, she turned to take in her surroundings. Time was limited, she had to get a move on, but she also needed supplies. Especially a puffer jacket and gloves, without them, she could very well escape only to end up dying from the elements. Winter approached early in the mountains.

In the small kitchenette, the pantry was well-stocked, allowing her to choose a couple of items, hoping their disappearance would go unnoticed. Next, she grabbed a steak knife from the cutlery drawer.

Moving toward the door, she opened the small closet. It held multiple pairs of gloves and winter jackets. Most were female, one of which was hers. Suppressing a shudder at the sheer number, she chose a few pairs of gloves and two male coats, figuring he would have worn a jacket leaving and might notice any of the female jackets missing. Especially if, as she suspected, these were his trophies.

Stepping back to close the door, something on the floor caught her attention. Bending forward, she squinted at the green canvas before reaching in to pull it out for a closer look. Blood drained from her face at the sight of the familiar duffel bag. Holding her breath, she tugged, her movements jerky as she rushed to confirm her suspicions. Tag in hand, she flipped it over to see her husband's name.

Refusing to think what it meant, she stuffed the spare jacket, gloves, food, and blankets into the duffel bag. Slipping into the jacket, she put the knife into her pocket before hauling the duffel over her shoulder. With a last look around to ensure that nothing stood overtly out of place to suggest she had escaped, she unlocked the door and exited, taking the time to relock it before heading off into the trees.

***

Max was smitten. It was written all over his face even to someone who couldn't read his partner as well as Jonah could. Jonah hid his smirk; he would have laughed his ass off, if he wasn't sure the same dopey look would likely be on his face soon enough. This beautiful little girl had conquered Max just by calling him 'uncle' and then to top it off, she looked at him with all the trust in the world. Going by the brief glare Jonah received before Max engaged with his niece, Jonah wasn't hiding his mirth.

"Hi there, Gracie. It's nice to meet you. How old are you?" Max asked in a gentle voice.

Grace looked at her father before responding. Lachlan for his part tilted his head slightly and raised an eyebrow, and with an enormous sigh Grace held up three fingers, but Jonah was quick to notice the corresponding smiles from his parents at the gesture.

His brother's head looked like it was on a swivel, his eyes were bouncing around the room watching everyone's reactions. Idiot. While they may be annoyed that Lachlan had kept this from them, she was theirs now and best of all, their mama would now get off Jonah's back about grandchildren. Not that he'd make this too easy on Lachlan, God knew what other secrets the shit was hiding.

"Grace, you've already met your Aunt Shauna, so the only one left to meet is your Uncle Jonah." With another tap on Grace's wrist, she immediately looked into Lachlan's eyes. When he nodded and tapped the inside of her wrist once again with his index and middle finger, Gracie turned to stare straight at Jonah.

Jonah didn't know what was going on, but he sensed whatever had just transpired between Lachlan and his daughter was big and how he acted now was going to make or break this relationship. Besides, he could yell at his older brother later.

"Hi, Gracie, or is it Grace?"

Jonah watched in wonder as Grace scrunched her face as she thought about the answer to his question.

"My name is Grace, but Mummy and Daddy only call me that when I'm in trouble."

"Fair enough. I think I can follow those rules. Now, what do you call Daddy when he is in trouble?"

Gracie giggled and climbed off Lachlan's lap. Moments later, she had made her way to Jonah and was climbing onto his lap before whispering the answer to his question in his ear.

Jonah laughed and held his niece tight. He'd had no clue how quickly someone, much less a little munchkin, could steal his heart and he wasn't about to let her go yet.

"Hold on!" Zac piped up. "We want to know that answer, too."

Gracie beamed as she answered, "When Mummy and me are in big trouble Daddy calls us 'young lady' but when Daddy is in trouble, we call him Yogi after the bear, 'cause Daddy gets grizzly."

While his family laughed, some of the tension bled from Lachlan and he seemed to relax a little, his shoulders noticeably dropping.

Joining in on the banter, Lachlan made a show of folding his arms and huffing before saying, "I don't get in trouble."

"Uh-uh, you're always in trouble, Daddy, like the other night when Mummy caught you dranking straight out of the juice box."

Jonah cringed at the word dranking but noticed neither Lachlan nor his parents corrected her. Relief was only brief when he reminded himself that she was only three. Because that led Jonah down another mental path. He'd be the first to admit, he hadn't been around many young children in a while, but he couldn't remember other three-year-olds speaking as well as Gracie was. Shit, Lachlan was a bonafide genius. If Gracie had inherited her father's intellect, they were all screwed. This child was much cuter than Lachlan had ever been.

"Funny, that's not how I recall it. If memory serves, you came in and saw me, then you ran and told Mummy."

Gracie didn't deny this. She was too busy laughing and rolling around on Jonah's lap to see Lachlan approach, but she sure noticed when he started tickling her.

"Admit it, you dobbed on me to Mummy, say 'Uncle' if you want me to stop."

Between giggles, Gracie finally managed to call out 'Uncle' and then to make amends as only a three-year-old could: she admitted she and Mummy got into trouble more than Daddy did.

Lachlan smiled. Jonah didn't know Lachie's wife, but he didn't think she would be pleased to hear that Gracie had told everyone that she got into as much trouble as her three-year-old, but it didn't look like Lachlan was going to contradict his daughter. His silence said he agreed that the little munchkin spoke the truth.

In an instant, Lachlan's demeanor changed, and he pushed up off the floor. He was making to leave, but like hell Jonah would let him disappear without talking to him first. Jonah needed to know what the hell was going on.

Lachlan glanced at him before he looked over at their dad, who nodded.

"Hey, pumpkin, it's time. I need to go. You'll be safe here with Grandma and Grandpa. They'll look after you."

Tears started pooling in Gracie's eyes as she hugged her father. "Are you going to get Mummy?"

"I'm going to try, baby. I promise I am going to do everything I can to bring her back to us."

Gracie nodded, her little arms flexing as she tightened her grip.

After another minute of watching them hug, his dad stood and held his arms out to Gracie, who willingly went into his embrace.

With a twitch of his head, Lachlan indicated for Jonah and Max to help him get Gracie's things out of his car and walked out the door with Mannix on his heels. He didn't need to look back to know they were following him.

Lachlan needed to go; it was time to hunt.

He wasn't waiting another moment more than he had to. His team was waiting for him. All he had to do was get Jonah and Max up to speed, then he could concentrate on finding his wife.

"What the hell?" They had barely made it out the door before Jonah started growling.

Hands in the air, signaling surrender, Lachlan turned to face his younger brother.

"Look, I know you're upset. I wish you hadn't found out like this, but it's happened now, and I can't change it. My wife is missing, and I need to move before we lose any chance of tracking her. I am trusting you and Max to help Ma and Dad look after my daughter."

"Is she in danger?" Max asked.

"Maybe," Lachlan admitted, dragging a frustrated hand through his hair. "I don't know for sure, but I ain't taking any chances."

Not wanting to waste any more time, Lachlan rushed to brief them. As their father had predicted, they both wanted to go with him. But Lachlan needed them here to oversee the town and watch out for anybody acting suspiciously. Most importantly, he wanted them to help his parents keep his daughter safe.

He didn't have time for the full background story, but their parents could fill them in. The last thing to explain was the unconditional authority they now had over his daughter. Max looked more surprised than Jonah as Lachlan outlined the system but then again, they'd all seen the pain and despair of the blame their parents had gone through when the Cooper 'incident' had happened. Lachlan had always blamed himself, even though he was only twelve at the time. He knew Jonah, while only ten, had also felt some guilt.

This system made sense and Lachlan was certain Jonah would adopt it himself when he had his own kids. With a quick hug, they grabbed the bags and went back inside for Lachlan to say a last goodbye to his family.

TEN

The first mile was painstakingly slow. She continually backtracked and changed directions to cover her trail and confuse her scent. While she hadn't seen signs of a dog, it didn't mean he didn't have one. Most people in this situation would head for the river, aiming to get down the mountain as quickly as possible. If she had simply been lost in the mountains, that would make sense. But not with an unknown assailant on her tail who would know the mountains better than she did and who had even more reason to not want her to make it.

Heading to the river would have helped mask her trail but required her to jump in and stay for several minutes. It was too obvious, and she couldn't take the chance that he'd catch up with her. Plus, with her luck, she'd catch pneumonia. So, despite her training, she followed her intuition and headed deeper into the woods, knowing she was also likely heading further away from her husband.

Stopping wasn't an option. If she'd calculated correctly, she only had another eight hours before her kidnapper would return to find she'd escaped. She hoped that taking the time to ensure she wasn't leaving an obvious trail would buy her some more precious minutes.

Not that she was stupid enough to count on it, which meant she had to continue to move for another twenty-two hours before he would have to leave to go back to work or forfeit his cover to find her. Fingers crossed, he'd go back to work, but she knew better than to rely on it. For all she knew, he didn't even have a job and only left each day to get supplies stocking up for the winter.

About an hour later she slowed when the surrounding trees started to thin considerably. With each careful step a clearing came into view. After three hours of walking, she'd come upon another cabin. It took a quick, panicked look to confirm she hadn't gone in circles.

Unable to turn away, she hunkered behind some bushes and watched the small log building from the tree line, looking for signs of life. When she was sure it was empty, she approached. The door was unlocked. Inside was dusty and covered with cobwebs, proving no one had inhabited it for a long time. However, she was taking no chances.

Lachlan drove off slowly, his family home getting smaller and smaller in the rear-view mirror. After a few minutes of driving through the streets of town, watching to make sure he hadn't picked up a tail, Lachlan headed to the meeting point north of the picnic grounds.

As soon as he stopped, the boys appeared from different directions and tossed their kits into the back before jumping in. They would only be able to drive for a couple of hours, and then it would be on foot from there. The last thing they needed was for the kidnapper to see or hear them coming.

While Lachlan had been at his parents, the boys had coordinated with the FBI and updated the Admiral on their plans. It was important to know who was on the mountain and where, to ensure they covered as much area as possible. It also lowered the chance of someone taking a bullet by friendly fire.

The team had determined the place had to be remote enough to not get any traffic. Somewhere easy to monitor comings and goings but with surrounding trees dense enough that noise wouldn't easily travel.

On the flip side, there would have to be easy access. A vehicle would make sense, as the perp would need to get bulk supplies up there and it would be hard to carry a woman too far in this terrain, especially if she were unconscious.

Logically speaking, they were looking for a cabin higher up the mountains, but still in proximity to the river. Away from any of the established tracks, but likely a hidden or long forgotten trail off from the existing well-used ones. All they had to do was find it. They had already spent hours poring over a map of the area and between them; they had identified a few areas to start.

Just short of two hours later, they pulled off the road and went off the trail further into the bush. The boys had traveled painstakingly slow to hide both their tracks and the noise of the 4WD, hoping the sound wouldn't travel up the mountain. Nate and Deeks went back to where they exited the trail to cover their tracks. While Taniq started hiding the 4WD, Lachlan removed the starter relay and shoved it into his pack along with the key. The others also each carried spares of both.

Should they get separated, whoever found his wife was to high-tail it back to the vehicle and head for the safety of town. The others would then make it back on their own.

Not that Lachlan expected this to happen. It didn't make sense that they'd be dealing with more than one or two perps at the most if what they knew was correct. This was simply a failsafe they had tweaked over the years from another of their missions when the team member with the starter relay didn't make it back to the vehicle at the predetermined time. On that op, they didn't have comms due to the nature of the extraction.

Luckily, Deeks hadn't sustained an injury, nor was he captured. But he and Taniq had had to improvise to stay safe, and that left the rest of the team waiting in a dangerous area with the package for over eighty minutes before the boys made it back to them. If they'd had a spare, two of them could have left with the package and the other two could have gone back to help them.

No matter what happened to them, the mission was first. The team would separate to get the job done, but they would always regroup later—no man left behind.

Having hidden the 4WD, the boys were back from covering the trail. Nightfall was approaching, and they wanted to be a few miles away from the vehicle before they set up camp for the night. The area would have to be well scouted beforehand. For the moment, there was to be no talking. Signals and whistles were the only means of communicating until they had the lay of the land and knew for sure they were alone.

***

Opening the door was one of the hardest things she'd ever had to do. Her movements were slow and controlled to limit any unnecessary sound. Knowing this might be a trap but unable to walk away, she paused to close it behind her.

The cabin had the same layout as the one she'd just escaped from. It wasn't safe to stay since it was close to the other one. Her kidnapper would know where all the closest cabins were located and when he found no sign of her at the river, the next logical place to look were other cabins. But, for her own peace of mind, she needed to check and see if this too had a trapdoor and a dungeon beneath.

It took seconds to locate the trapdoor, but it was pure relief that washed over her when she saw it was full of old furniture and junk. Question answered, she grabbed some much-needed matches and some more food from the pantry, again selecting only a few tins. Once sorted, with a quick look to ensure everything looked untouched, she left, covering her tracks before re-entering the tree line back into a different section of the woods.

A few hours later, she came upon another cabin. Her husband had once explained there were many scattered throughout the mountains. Owned by different townsfolk, and used for romantic getaways, fishing, or long hunting trips. The locals believed nothing cleared the head like a week in the mountains, being at one with nature. Ha! After all this, she'd be happy never to see another log cabin again.

People also liked to hike the trails. Over the years, they'd lost a few people to the harsh elements. The towns bordering the mountains got together and penned an agreement between all the owners. The cabins would be well stocked and left unlocked, so should someone get lost and find one, they would have a chance of surviving.

What spiked her adrenaline was unlike the previous cabin she had found, this one, much like the one she escaped from—was locked. Warning signs had surfaced at the sight of fresh tire tracks leading to the front of the cabin. But they disappeared at the tree line. Unlike the last cabin, there was no sign of a trail leading to the makeshift road that she had consciously moved away from. From what she could see, this cabin was even more isolated and better hidden than the one she'd been held in.

Ignoring the thudding beat of her heart pounding in her ears, she picked the lock and slowly opened the door before stepping inside and carefully closing it again behind her. There were signs of life here, dirty crockery on the sink, cigarette butts in an ashtray on the coffee table, and mud inside the doorway.

The hairs on the back of her neck were standing at attention. This did not feel right. Her instincts were screaming at her to get away from here as fast as she could, but she continued to move further into the cabin. She noted the same setup as the other cabins and felt the chill travel the length of her spine as she moved toward the rug that she was certain would conceal another trap door.

Training ensured she touched nothing as she took in her surroundings, careful to note the position of the rug and coffee table before moving them to expose the trap door. As she descended the rickety stairs, she held the steak knife in her hand, although she was shaking when she came to another locked door. Pausing, she pressed her ear to the door, trying to listen for any sounds.

The key to the lock was sitting on a hook next to the door. She removed it and inserted it into the lock, a slight, barely audible click releasing the mechanism. Inch by inch, she pushed the door open, trying to see inside. It was dark, the air smelled stale and musty. Taking a deep breath, Isabella felt for the light switch and flicked it on, a squeak of surprise escaping as she took in the scene.

"Who are you?" Isabella whispered to the woman, who kneeled before her as she took in her surroundings.

"Help me, please, help me. Are you with him?"

"No. Hell, no. I just escaped a room near identical to this one about ten hours ago. Do you know when he is due back?"

"Soon, I thought you were him."

"Shit, I've gotta go. I can't take you yet, but I'll hide close by and come for you when he leaves. You need to stay calm. If I took you now, he'd capture us both. Can you trust me to come back for you?"

The young woman looked back at her in desperation. Isabella couldn't give in. A stupid move now would cost them both. Understandably, the girl was terrified. Isabella was tall, slim, and some would say beautiful, but you couldn't tell one's personality from looks alone. She hoped something in her hazel eyes would tell the girl before her that she could trust her.

"Yes, I believe you. What is your name?"

"No. It's better you don't know my name. I'll be back. I promise. But I need to leave now."

"He knocks me unconscious before he leaves, but once he's gone, we'll have about ten hours."

Isabella shuddered. All she could think was 'same,' he did the same to her, but she didn't say it. Instead, she made herself move.

"Okay, I won't come straight away. I'll need to make sure he has left and isn't coming back for something. Do you know how long you are out for?"

"It depends how hard he hits me, but anywhere from a few minutes to an hour. Please, come back for me."

"I will, I promise. I'm not letting this bastard win."

Steeling herself to move, Isabella turned off the light and stepped back outside the door. She hated leaving her there. Hated locking the door and putting the key back on the hook. But she knew if they ran now, they wouldn't have any head start and it was too much of a coincidence that the setup she escaped from was exactly like this one.

No, the best chance they both had was to wait it out.

Isabella moved with purpose and speed. She was relocking the door when she heard an engine. It was getting louder. Sweat beaded on her forehead as she covered her footprints, moving steadily back to the tree line. No time to spare. She crawled into her hiding space as the 4WD came into view. Exhaling a soft breath she hadn't realized she was holding, Isabella willed herself not to move a muscle.

The asshole had tinted windows, so it wasn't until he climbed out of the car that she saw the man that had kidnapped the young woman. Questions ran through her mind. The most important— was he the same man who took her or were there two of them?

Isabella stayed in the same position for over an hour, focused on any movement within the cabin. She realized the risk of staying in the same place was high and meant she would lose ground on her own kidnapper, but she couldn't leave the woman here, couldn't be sure she would make it back in time. When she hadn't seen any movement within the cabin for over twenty minutes, Isabella slowly backed away further into the trees, covering her tracks as she went.

Night was falling. There was no way she could use her matches to light a fire this close to the cabin. If she were to survive the night, Isabella needed to find a hiding spot as sheltered from the elements as possible. Grabbing her duffel bag, she found a few stout bushes next to a small boulder. The trees clumped closer together than others surrounding her.

She crawled into the middle, wrapped in all but one blanket. Isabella ate some of the food and re-wrapped it in the last blanket before stashing it back in the duffel bag. The last thing she needed was wild animals sniffing out food. With the duffel bag under her head as a pillow, Isabella threw the second jacket on top of her over the other blankets, also covering her face and drifted off into a light sleep.

ELEVEN

Isabella woke to the sounds of the forest coming alive. The birds were chirping as the first rays of sunlight started to shine through the trees. With more than a little reluctance, Isabella prepared to face the day. She had lost valuable time, but the combination of sleep and food had helped to refuel her body. Carefully, Isabella repacked her duffel with the blankets and second jacket and made her way back to her previous position where she could see the cabin.

The 4WD was still there, and she could see the man moving within the cabin, so she made herself comfortable and set in for the wait. Ten minutes later, there were no further signs of movement. Isabella shuddered as she thought about what the young woman was going through and could only hope that she could hold on, that this time wouldn't be the straw that broke her.

Hope. When the woman had stepped inside her dungeon, she'd felt hope. Something told her she could trust the stranger. She had been expecting him and wasn't surprised when he arrived only minutes after the woman had left.

He'd been angry, but she did her best to act the same as always and followed his instructions. There was no way she was going to put the other woman in danger by doing something that would give the game away. Hope had her believing the other woman would come back for her. The only question was, would it be too late?

When the door opened, she moved to her knees. Last night, he had been particularly cruel. Her body still ached as bruises formed on top of older bruises. At first, she had thought he had caught the other woman. But with no evidence to confirm her worries, she instead figured he'd had a bad day. He was never as bad in the morning, and she hoped this morning would be the same.

Already a habit, she sought the time before his signature backhand would knock her out and committed it to memory. After waking, she calculated she had only been out about fifteen minutes. Moving as fast as her injuries would allow, she crossed to the basin and washed herself before redressing.

When she noted the food tray, she made herself eat half of the meal. If the woman didn't come back for her and she hadn't eaten, he'd punish her. Not that he needed an excuse. But if she had eaten the lot, he would be suspicious of why she was now fueling her body.

Eagerly, she sat watching the door. Over half an hour had passed from the time he had left her. She knew the other woman had said she wouldn't come until she was certain he had left for the day. But the waiting and the not knowing was difficult and as each minute ticked by a little more doubt seeped in.

Isabella watched him potter around the cabin for another ten minutes or so before he left after he had emerged from the basement cell. She made herself stay in her hiding spot for a full hour, figuring the twenty-minute mark on the long drive to town would be the no-turning-back point. The rest was insurance.

Once the hour hit, Isabella took one last check before making her move. Inching around the tree line to the blind side of the cabin, she carefully made her way to the locked door. Inside, she took her time to ensure she knew exactly where everything went. Last night he hadn't gone straight down to the dungeon and that half an hour would be precious time to aid in their escape.

Isabella opened the door and found the young woman on her knees. She noted the girl's body visibly relax in relief when she realized it wasn't her kidnapper coming back for her.

"Are you ready?"

"Yes, thank God you came back. I was terrified it was him and he'd somehow caught you."

"Not yet, but we have to go." Isabella moved toward her and found that the same key that unlocked the door unlocked the chain around her neck.

Helping the girl to her feet, Isabella steadied her while she found her balance.

"We have to move, don't touch anything if you can help it." The pair of them made their way out of the room. Isabella relocked the door and was about to put the key back when she decided against it.

At the young woman's questioning look, Isabella shrugged.

"If I leave the key, he is going to open the door straight away and find you gone. But, if we take the key, we may buy some time if he thinks he misplaced it, especially as everything upstairs will look untouched. Let's go."

Isabella climbed the stairs first and helped the young woman out when she reached the top. Motioning the woman to the side of the room near the kitchen, she told her to wait before moving to close the trapdoor and position the coffee table and rug back in place. A quick glance ensured it was as he had left it.

Next, Isabella headed straight to the pantry and appropriated some more food. She was careful in her choices, not wanting to make it obvious anything was missing without more than a quick glance. Passing the tins to the young woman, Isabella herded her back toward the front door, turning for a final check before nudging her outside.

Once Isabella had relocked the door, she guided the young woman to the tree line and then went back to cover their tracks. Stopping only to retrieve the duffel bag, dump the food inside, and give her new companion the second jacket. They then headed off, further up into the mountains.

"Why are we going up? The town is in the other direction?"

"True, and that would be the plan if we were just lost hikers. We'd head for the shortest route, but we're not. Our kidnappers will not want us found, they'll come looking for us. Most people would head towards the river and then down the mountain. If we do that, then we're playing into their hands. There must be two of them. Timing doesn't work for one person to have held both of us. The cabins they held us in, the set-ups, they were the same. Our kidnappers must know each other even if they're not working together. Once they realize you've escaped, they'll assume we're together." Isabella just hoped that their kidnappers hadn't yet discovered they were missing.

"It's too coincidental that both of us escaped within a day of each other. Now they'll know that I headed towards town but away from the river. Luckily, the plan was always to head to Canada. We're on good terms with the Mounties overseeing the three closest towns to the border. I had hoped that by heading down for a bit that he might stop tracking and try to jump ahead, by which time I would be further away, having long changed directions. At least there will be more cabins. We'll be able to get more food, water, and blankets." And she thought to herself, hopefully no more girls.

No, hopefully they wouldn't find any more girls, but she was determined to check every single cabin they came across. In a soft voice she continued. "When we make it over to the other side of the mountain we'll be in Canada, illegally but hopefully safe. The one thing I'm not sure we have now is time, so we gotta move. It'll be safer not to talk too much, our voices will travel so whisper if you need to say something. Keep your ears open. If you hear anything, tap my left shoulder and we'll listen. If something is wrong, tap my right shoulder."

They moved in silence, gaining much-needed distance from the two cabins with every step. Isabella was impressed with the young woman's strength and determination. She had been through hell and yet she wasn't crying or complaining. One foot in front of the other, the woman followed close behind her. It helped that she was young and fit, but Isabella knew it was a mental strength that made the difference in these circumstances and the young woman behind her had it in spades.

A full two hours passed before they came upon the next cabin. Isabella cased the whole of the area before moving approximately fifty feet past the top of the cabin, finding a suitable hidey-hole. It crossed her mind that she still didn't know the girl's name, but there wasn't time now. They could chat when they were safe.

The young woman trembled in fear when she caught on to what Isabella planned to do, her eyes wide, slowly shaking her head in disbelief before whispering one word, although it was more like a plea. "No!"

"I have to." Isabella took hold of the girl's arms and helped her settle into her hiding position behind the bush. "If I hadn't checked, you would still be in there. There might be others. I'm compelled to make sure. I couldn't live with myself if someone else died because I didn't bother to look."

"What if you are captured?"

"I won't go in if it's not safe too. If I'm not back within half an hour, then you'll know something went wrong. Stay here until tomorrow morning. The blankets and coats will keep you warm. Make sure you listen out for human sounds. Don't reveal yourself if you hear someone coming. Stay hidden. I know where you are, so I won't need help to find you. Look, they can't know for sure that we are together. They'll assume, but they won't know for sure. Do not come out, even if they threaten to kill me. Promise me that no matter what happens, you will stay hidden." At the girl's nod, Isabella continued.

"In the morning, if you think it's safe, start heading up again. By now there will be at least two Navy Seals in these mountains looking for me. If they find you, they will keep you safe. They tend to wear all black and might look a little scary. So, if you're not sure if it's them, ask them to give you the secret call sign—it's the call of a bald eagle. Do you know it?"

A flash of surprise crossed the girl's face, but she said nothing, so Isabella waited for her to nod her head. She could ponder that look later.

"Unless you are one hundred percent sure, stay hidden. You can tell the Navy Seals the truth, they'll find you, not the other way around. In the event our kidnappers recapture you, they will ask how you escaped. Tell them another man came in wearing a black balaclava. Explain how he was so focused on getting to you, he didn't notice the key drop to the floor. Not that it mattered, anyway. You'll need to make it sound like the man was careless. He didn't knock you out, instead he strode out and slammed the door so hard it bounced back open without him noticing. Here, put this key in your pocket so it backs up your story and give him this description."

Isabella rattled off a description of the man that took her and had the girl repeat it back to her. When the girl asked her why, she shrugged and explained it would cause some uncertainty and, hopefully, some trust issues.

"The other man would deny it but there would be no proof it was me and if you hadn't met me but had the description of the other kidnapper, the only way that would have happened was if he had indeed encroached on the other guy's turf. It's a gamble to buy some more time and unsettle the two of them, make them wonder if they can trust each other."

She nodded her understanding before Isabella shrugged.

"Don't worry, I will be back in no time. This is just a backup plan. The successful missions always have contingencies, and our mission is to get the hell out of here and back home."

Careful not to make noise or leave obvious tracks back to her hiding companion, Isabella's trek to the cabin was slow. It looked empty. There were no overt signs that anyone had been there in months. No tire tracks, no footprints. The windows were filthy.

Isabella decided against going in. What she could see through the dirty windows told her there was too much dust for anyone to have been inside the cabin for a long time. If she went in, she wouldn't be able to cover her tracks and her captors would know that one of them had been there. With a sigh of relief, Isabella headed back to the hidey-hole.

Knowing the girl would be tense, listening for every sound. Isabella kept her steps steady as she approached, especially since she'd only been gone a few minutes.

"It's okay, it's only me," Isabella whispered when she was a couple of feet away, hoping to ease the girl's anxiety. "The cabin's clear. No one has been there for months. I didn't go in, but we need to keep moving, anyway. Our captors won't know we can survive out in the woods and will assume we'd be holing up in different cabins overnight, so they'll be checking them. The further we are away from a cabin when we settle for the night, the better. Are you right to continue?"

"Yes, I don't like it here. I don't know why, but it feels haunted, like horrible things have happened here."

"Okay, I'm not feeling comfortable here either." Isabella swung the duffel back onto her shoulder. "Let's go."

Within the hour, the trees became even thicker and closer together. It was becoming difficult to navigate through them and if they continued, they were going to leave a trail her three-year-old could follow. But with a sweeping glance around their surroundings, Isabella knew there was no other option but to keep going.

"We're going to leave an easy trail." The girl punctuated the short, whispered sentence by pointing a finger toward the dried scrub around them.

Isabella nodded. "Yes, but we don't have a choice. Try to step in my footprints. Worst-case scenario, we might have to do some tree hopping at some point. Can you climb?"

"Yes. I'm a local. My dad and older brother used to bring us out here and make us learn survival tricks. They taught me how to climb, although that was to get away from wildlife, not maniacs trying to kill us."

"Ha, well, hopefully all the bears are hibernating like they are supposed to. I'll go first, you follow. Try not to break any branches as we pass. We don't want to leave an obvious trail if we can avoid it."

The young woman followed gracefully, ensuring to stick to the footsteps in front of her, sweeping a branch behind her, their best attempt to cover their tracks as they went. It was slow progress. Hours had ticked over as they trekked on. They didn't stop for lunch. It was necessary to use the daylight to gain as much lead on their captors as possible.

As the sun slowly set, Isabella started looking for shelter. Finding none on their current course, Isabella finally stopped and pointed up. She needed to get a view of their surroundings to find a safe spot for the night. While the girl watched on, Isabella climbed onto a lower branch of a nearby tree and competently swung onto the next branch and then the next, continuing until she was high enough to get a view of the immediate area.

Looking around, Isabella identified a spot approximately twenty feet away, previously hidden from her view, slightly down to the left that was a little open but protected by a few large rocks. Determining it would be their best bet for the night, Isabella plotted the safest way to get there and descended the tree. After indicating for the young woman to follow, Isabella led the way, conscious of leaving as small a trail as possible.

Again, it was slow going. Although it was only about twenty feet, the terrain was not conducive to moving fast even without actively trying to hide their tracks. Half an hour later, they emerged into the small clearing and set camp for the night. Taking the opportunity to rest, they grabbed some food before burrowing under their blankets and dropping off to sleep.

TWELVE

Friday 3rd November

In the morning, Isabella woke with a jerk. She hadn't meant to sleep long, intending to keep watch for most of the night. The young woman lay stiff next to her, a slight rise and fall of her chest the only sign of life. While she slept, Isabella closed her eyes and listened for any sounds that shouldn't be there.

A loud shrill call of a bald eagle sounded, jolting her eyes open. Hope filled her even as her heart pounded. Was that her husband? Her brother? How could she know for sure? It may have been her subconscious giving her what she wanted to hear, or it could have been that of a real bald eagle. The whole reason the call worked was because it was the call of an actual bird and this time, one known to the area.

Needing a distraction, Isabella instead focused on her sleeping companion. They had covered a lot of ground the day before and to continue moving through the thick scrub was going to take a lot of energy. Studying the young woman, Isabella wondered about her story. She was beautiful. Straight brown hair reached halfway down her back. Lean, even if she had recently lost some weight, she had the look of a fit and healthy young woman.

Despite her beauty, it wasn't her face, her lean frame, or her hair that Isabella had first noticed: it was her striking blue eyes. Eyes that reminded her of her husband, but she had pushed the thought aside and moved on out of necessity. Seriously. Lots of people had blue eyes. But that was before Isabella knew she was a local. In a small town…

Isabella tried to focus on something else, but then the girl in question opened those piercing blue eyes and looked straight into her own.

"What is your name?" Isabella asked.

"Mackenzie, Mackenzie Michaels, but I prefer Mac. Mackenzie makes me think I'm in trouble. What's yours?"

Shit! Mary, Mary, Mary! What were the chances? Isabella dropped her head into her trembling hands. She couldn't still them. Her whole body shook as cold ice froze her veins. Thoughts raced through her mind, but she couldn't grasp any of them.

Isabella needed to get a grip. She should have prepared herself for this likelihood. The eyes should have told her the truth, long before hearing the words.

Mackenzie scrambled to a seated position. Her head tilted to the right, a look of concern upon her face. Knowing this wasn't helping, Isabella swiped her hands across her eyes and cheeks, attempting to disperse the tears. Poor Mackenzie looked unsure of how to offer comfort or why her name would warrant the reaction it had.

"I'm Isabella and I'm married to your brother," Isabella stuttered in between shaky breaths.

Mackenzie's smile was genuine as she leaned forward to lay a gentle hand on Isabella's arm.

"You're the kind of woman I always pictured him with."

Isabella looked into Mackenzie's eyes, as her mouth dropped open in shock.

"Wait, how do you know which brother I'm married to?"

"Well, both sets of twins are too young. Also, Parker and Cooper are still in college with me. I would know if either of them got married. I'm convinced Jonah has been in a committed relationship for years, even if he doesn't know it yet. So it can only be Lachlan. Besides, he's the only one who would think he could get away with keeping this kind of secret from his family. He's gonna be in so much trouble when I get my hands on him, although I think I'll have to get in line behind Ma."

Isabella smiled at the thought of this beautiful woman tearing into Lachlan about keeping secrets.

"We didn't intend it to be a secret. Things went wrong. So many things went so incredibly wrong, and everything got away from us. Don't misunderstand me, good things, genuinely great gifts, came out of many of those situations, but they weren't things we could just shrug off and move on from. We were back on the right track and supposed to be starting over until this happened. I can only hope they found our daughter in time and that she is safe."

"Lachlan's a dad?" Mackenzie queried, her eyes widening in wonder. "That's amazing. I think he would make a great dad!"

"He is. He's a great dad and a great husband when he isn't being a child himself."

Mackenzie laughed quietly, as if she knew exactly how much of a troublemaker her big brother could be.

Isabella searched Mackenzie's eyes as tears still pooled in her own.

"She was with me. We were supposed to wait for my brother to drive us, but I was too excited to finally meet everyone. On Railings Road, a man stumbled in front of the car. He had a knife protruding from his stomach. There was blood everywhere. I didn't think, I reacted. All my training flew out the window. By the time I realized it was a trap, it was too late."

A violent shiver rocked her body, causing Isabella to pause. She wanted to stop, but Mackenzie needed to know what happened in case something happened to separate them, and Isabella didn't make it home.

"My daughter was hysterical, but he was too strong. I couldn't get away from him. I couldn't reach her. He lifted me off my feet. One arm around my waist, his other hand, held a cloth clenched over my mouth and nose. The last thing I remember was hearing my daughter's screams as he pulled me toward the trees. It wasn't long before I lost consciousness but, at that time, he hadn't stopped moving deeper into the mountains. He left her there. There's no other explanation. There wasn't time for him to have enacted anything else. I don't know if anyone found her in time. I'm so scared that they didn't. So, so scared. My daughter might be dead because I wasn't patient enough to wait for my brother."

Isabella jolted when Mackenzie pulled her into a tight embrace, holding on longer than a normal hug would entail. She took the moment of comfort. Locking away her concerns for Gracie had been necessary. Knowing she wouldn't be able to focus on escaping and getting back to her family otherwise.

But seeing Lachlan's sister here. Finding Mackenzie held in the same type of situation she was herself in. Isabella wondered if this was so much more than a simple kidnapping. If they were targeting her family, Lachlan's family, then what hope did her little girl have?

When Isabella's tears slowed, Mackenzie pulled back and looked into her eyes.

"Growing up, I always wished for an older sister. I had hoped I'd have a good relationship with whoever my older brothers married. My biggest concern was they'd meet mean people who would keep them from seeing us. Having met you, I know those fears were unfounded. I can't wait to get to know you better. I'm hoping we'll be best friends. Your actions alone, tell me you're a wonderful person. You didn't know me. You certainly didn't have to risk your safety to come back for me, but you did. And even though you desperately want to get back to your husband and daughter, you still checked every cabin we came across on the off chance someone else was in the same situation we were."

Isabella smiled. "I always wanted a sister, too. Even though we're not identical, my twin brother and I have always been close.

Everyone jokes that we're still codependent on each other. It's lucky he and Lachlan are best friends. We're never far from each other. I don't know what I'd do without him, and I don't want that to change. But it's different from having a sister. I can't wait to get to know each other better outside of these circumstances, but right now we've gotta focus on getting back to our family. God, I miss them so much and I can't wait to get back to them, even if it means Lachlan will be broody and won't let us out of his sight for days."

"Ha, yes, he tends to be protective of those he loves." This time it was Mackenzie who smiled.

"I agree. It's one of the reasons we're together. I wouldn't change a thing about him, but it doesn't stop me from trying not to get into his bad books."

"Please. I know my brother. I'm sure he manages to find himself in the bad books more than you ..."

Isabella nodded and laughed. "Oh yes, but he excels at getting himself out of trouble and making it sound like anything he did was perfectly reasonable. On that note, let's get moving. I think we have wasted enough of the daylight."

After a quick bite to eat, they packed the gear and slowly headed out. Within a few feet of the clearing, they changed direction to head where the trees had thinned out a little more, allowing them to progress a bit faster without leaving too much of an obvious trail. The trees aided in coverage. So far, they hadn't seen any signs that someone was on their tail, but Isabella knew just because you couldn't see the monster didn't mean it wasn't hiding in the shadows, ready to pounce.

The second morning on the mountain found the boys up and moving hours before the new day broke, the sun rising across the mountains normally worth the time to stop and watch the forest come alive with sounds. No one spoke, all conscious that with every minute that passed, the chances of a happy conclusion decreased.

As with the previous day, they found nothing unusual about the first cabin they came across. It was located exactly as shown on the map, with a slightly overgrown trail leading from the road to the door. The door wasn't locked. It was well stocked, albeit a little dusty, and there were no signs that anyone had been to visit in a while.

Leaving it as they found it, the team continued their search. If the map they were using was correct, there were another sixteen cabins on this side of the river to check, including the one Lachlan's grandparents owned.

There was always a chance a fire had taken one out, but it was more likely there were other unauthorized cabins among them which had never been on the damn map in the first place. As the sun set once again, Lachlan's team scouted the area before settling in for the night. They had come across and checked four cabins, to no avail. All four were close to the river, slowly zigzagging higher into the mountain but there was still a long way to go and the higher they got, the more spread out the cabins became.

Saturday 4th November

The third day crossed another five cabins off the list. They had run into no humans. The only clue had been the sound of a heavy vehicle, but it was too far away to make the direction. Neither the Feds nor the Canadian Mounties were having any more luck.

As frustrated as they were, until they got more information or something happened, the team could only continue moving, systematically crossing off each cabin as they went. They added any 'new' cabins to their map so the authorities could investigate them further later. Otherwise, they focused on searching the ground for signs of human and vehicle trails, all the while hoping next time the sound of the 4WD would be closer so they could check it out.

Instead of camping again for the night, the team continued to Lachlan's family cabin, which had been next on the list.

Max and Jonah had only been there days before, but the boys had tidied, restocked, and left the door unlocked. Knowing there were no other cabins close by, the team turned on the lights and cooked a hot meal before turning in.

Lachlan, Mannix and Nate took the bed and couch, while Deeks and Taniq went through the trapdoor to bunk in the cellar below. Hoping this would give them an advantage or at least an element of surprise if needed.

Earlier they had taken time to go over the map again, ensuring they had not missed anything and that they were covering all the ground they needed to. It was slow going, but any faster and they might miss the one clue that would bring this nightmare to an end.

Nate watched as Lachlan turned over once again. He was restless, and who could blame him? It's not like Nate had the words to offer support. This was the third night they'd been out here, and they'd found nothing. Isabella had been gone for five nights and the final blow had come only hours before from Jonah informing them Mackenzie was also missing.

They hadn't known straight off. She was supposed to be spending a couple of nights at a friend's place before heading home for the week, but she'd never made it. It looked like she'd gone missing the day before Isabella had.

The family had turned the town upside down looking for her. A search party had found nothing. Mackenzie had vanished without a trace. It looked unlikely she'd even made it to town. The only good news was Gracie was safe and happy, Lachlan's parents were doing everything to shelter her from their fear.

Were the kidnappings connected? There was nothing to prove they were, but like the saying goes, there were no such things as coincidences. Two women disappearing in the space of a couple of days, both connected to Lachlan. It could only mean it was personal. But were they after Lachlan or the whole team?

Did they know Lachlan was married to Isabella? Or did they take her to get to Nate? The connection between Mackenzie and Lachlan was clear. Were the rest of the team's families in trouble, or only Lachlan's?

Their last mission was a disaster. Summed up in one word. FUBAR. Fucked Up Beyond All Recognition. And yet, there was little they'd change even if they had the chance. The results had meant that all their suffering had been worth it. They'd believed they had taken out all the baddies involved, but what if they missed someone?

They were still searching for answers. What had started out as a simple retrieval had turned into an ongoing nightmare, bigger than any of them could have ever foreseen.

It was personal.

Every spare second, they dedicated to that search. They had people working on it twenty-four seven.

Until now, they'd thought their search was unknown to those they were hunting. Was it possible the group they had taken out had warned other cells? Did they know they were hunting them? Was this a preemptive strike against the team, against Lachlan? With that in mind, Lachlan had told Jonah to keep a close eye on Shauna. That she had been seeing an older, unknown man now was even more of a concern.

While Nate was worried about his sister, he was also worried about his best friend. They needed Lachlan to stay focused if they were going to find the girls. He couldn't imagine having your wife and sister taken within days of each other and there sure as hell were no coincidences this big. Their only hope was that they would find them, find them together and find them safe, but as every minute ticked by, their fear crept higher.

THIRTEEN

Lachlan felt like a caged tiger. Fuck them if they thought he was waiting any longer. The guys could follow later if they needed more sleep.

"Where the fuck do you think you are going? It's 0300hrs, for Mary's sake? No one is going to be moving at this stupid hour."

Lachlan swung around to meet Nate head on, fists balled at his side.

"Let me make this clear. I don't give a flying gorilla juggling monkeys what anyone else is doing. I'm leaving. If you want to come, you've got five minutes, otherwise you can catch me later."

"Fine, let me get the guys."

"We're up!" Deeks called out.

"Yeah, like any of us were going to sleep through that, although," Taniq scrunched his brow in thought, "at some stage you're gonna have to explain the gorilla juggling monkey reference because that one went way over my head."

Taniq shook his head as Lachlan went to open his mouth to

respond. "No, not yet … I wanna at least try to work it out for myself first."

"Seriously, you thought I was going to explain?" Lachlan shook his head in disbelief. "Get the fuck ready if you're coming with me. You've got four minutes. I'm taking Mannix out for a leak. Nature is calling."

***

"We have to find her, Zac."

"I know, Josh, I know, but surely, he wouldn't take her after we warned him off. Who would willingly take on Lachie, Jonah, Max, and Dad? This has gotta be a coincidence."

"But what if it's not? Jonah and Max are searching everywhere for Mackenzie, but they don't know that Shauna snuck out, and she doesn't know Mac is missing. I know we promised Shauna we wouldn't tell anyone what we know, but what if he's the one behind it? What if he took her as well? We gotta tell them!"

"If we tell them and we're wrong, Shauna will kill us!" Zac whispered back as he once again peeked out of their bedroom door.

"I don't care, Zac. Better to have her here and mad at us or even hating us than missing and dead because we kept her secret. That man's a snake. I hate him, and I don't trust him. We should have already told them. If we tell Jonah now, he'd be able to find him and make sure he doesn't have her." Josh's voice was rising higher and higher as he thought about his missing sister.

"We could search for him ourselves and follow him. If he leads us to Shauna, one of us could stay with her while the other ran for help?" Zac finally voiced what he had been thinking to his twin.

"No!" Josh yelled. Catching himself, he went back to whispering. "No, no, no. You seriously can't think we could save her? We'd only make it worse. We need to tell them Zac."

"But we promised," Zac pleaded with Josh. "Dad says a man should never go back on his word, no matter what."

"Fine, okay. I promised not to tell Mum, Dad, Lachlan, Jonah, or Max. Who did you promise not to tell?" Josh asked.

Finally, Zac smiled. He had caught on to his twin's thinking. "The same. I promised the same as you."

"Good!" Josh finally sighed in relief. "You ring Parker and I'll ring Cooper."

Within seconds, both boys had their older brothers on the phone and had made new promises to stay in the house with their parents and to help keep an eye on their little niece. Their older brothers were going to call Jonah and their dad for them, that way they weren't breaking any promises. From there, hopefully Parker and Cooper would also head back home.

***

Sam ended the call and moved over to stand behind his wife, pulling her to his chest as they stood watching their granddaughter sleep on the rug in front of the fireplace half hidden by her huge pink dragon stuffie. An animated dragon movie played in the background. There appeared to be a theme going on here and Sam had to wonder if his son had anything to do with his princess's love of dragons.

"She's so tiny, so precious." Claire wiped the tears from the corner of her eyes. "Remember when Mackenzie was that young? What will we do if we lose our daughters?"

"We won't. Hey, sweetheart, look at me," Sam turned to his wife until she faced him. "Everyone is out looking for them. Jonah and Max are tearing the town apart. Parker and Cooper are on their way here, even as we speak."

They had spoken with the youngest twins, who'd given them the name of the older man Shauna was seeing. "At least they know who they're looking for now. They've sent a message to the FBI for Lachlan, so he'll be looking for her, too. I have no doubt that we do not want to be the person standing in the way of Lachlan getting to his wife or his baby sisters. The man or men that did this are as good as dead. They just don't know it yet."

"Lachlan is out there on his own. How do we even know that he is okay?" Claire's words choked out as she cried into his chest.

"Honey, I do not believe for one second our boy is out there alone. At minimum, I would say his best friend, his wife's brother, is with him, but I'd be surprised if his whole team wasn't. Special forces teams don't leave men behind. If one's in trouble, they're all there to help, and that includes spouses."

"But he didn't say others were going with him and we didn't see anyone else!"

"No, but he didn't say he wasn't either. Didn't you wonder if it was a tight fit for him to get to the next town and back to grab his daughter? When he walked out of dinner the other night, he said he had personal issues to deal with. But he didn't appear panicked. Nor was he overtly rushing, so he had to know his daughter was in safe hands with someone or multiple someone's that he trusted. Besides, I saw him the next morning. There is no way he left Gracie at home by herself, so he couldn't have had her yet." Unless he left her there with one of his team, but Sam doubted Lachlan would leave his daughter after something so traumatic just to go to work. No, if he'd had Gracie already, that have met yesterday.

"I think he deliberately didn't tell us because he doesn't want anyone to know they're out there hunting and that they might be close. And don't forget he made a point of telling us not to give her Smarties if she asked for them as a meal. I'd say something like that would have to be a recent issue to remember it's a trigger for her. She's only recently turned three, remember?"

"Yes, you're right. That makes sense. It's hard to remember she's only three with how articulate she is. Is it wrong that I want to hold her and the twins and not let them go until this has all blown over?" Claire sniffled.

"No, I wouldn't mind doing that myself. This little one is sleeping peacefully for once though, so how 'bout you sit on the couch and watch her while I go grab our baby boys before they decide to go do something else that lands them in more hot water?"

Sam chuckled as he kissed his wife on the forehead and stepped back to head toward the twins' room. The twins hadn't been home long from their detention before everything came out about Shauna having snuck out.

Their detention had involved cleaning the classroom after their disastrous salmon prank. They had stank beyond measure when they had arrived home, so Claire had sent them straight for showers. The boys had been in good spirits, though. Happy that their homeroom teacher had been in charge. Mr. Davey had taken a few days' stress leave after the incident—which had not gone over well with Claire to think their boys had caused that—while the principal had called off the afternoon with a migraine.

Sam had barely taken a step before he had his arms full of his twins uttering an 'oomph' as they slammed into his chest.

"Well, I guess that saved me a walk."

Pulling them in close, Sam tightened his arms, taking the rare opportunity to hold his ever-growing baby boys. With a sigh, Claire joined the hug before the four of them moved to the couch. Claire tucked safely into Sam's side with the boys leaning into them, they settled in to watch the rest of the movie. Sam thanking the lord for all they had while praying for their daughters and their daughter-in-law to come home safely.

Shauna crouched behind the bushes, listening for any signs of movement. Her heart was beating so fast it sounded like drums were pounding in her chest. If she didn't regulate her breathing, her own heartbeat was going to give away her position.

And yes, the word was 'regulate.' If anyone had tried to tell her to calm down right then, she would have lost it. As far as Shauna was concerned, telling someone to calm down when they were upset was just as bad as seeing someone on the verge of tears and asking them if they were okay.

What the hell did people think was going to happen when you voiced those three innocuous words? The number of times her own brothers had looked shocked after uttering those three words and seeing her respond by bursting into tears was laughable. Although right now she would give anything to be in any of her older brothers' arms, because then she'd be safe. Hell, at this stage, she'd even settle for the baby twin brats.

Shauna held her breath as movement sounded to her right. She couldn't believe this was happening. Okay, so yes, she shouldn't have snuck out of the house. But it was so depressing. All she wanted was a little break from it. Jarrod was always so kind and loving. Shauna had been worried the twins had scared him off, but when she had landed on his uncle's doorstep, he had looked surprised before encompassing her in his arms.

It was when she leaned back and looked into his eyes that a shiver had raced through her body. He smiled down at her, but it was somehow calculated. Shauna had tried to shake it off as she followed him inside. When Jarrod had told her to take a seat while he went to make her a hot chocolate, she had complied.

He'd barely left the room when a friend texted asking where she was. Not wanting to lie, Shauna had ignored it and placed her cell upside down on the coffee table. Out of the way of temptation. She'd been starting to worry that maybe she shouldn't have kept this man a secret from her friends and family. Restless she'd jumped to her feet and started pacing. Unable to quiet her discomfort, she'd sought him out. But as she approached the entry of the kitchen, she thought she had seen Jarrod drop something into her drink. Although she couldn't be sure, she felt it. Something was wrong.

It wasn't until she started backing out of his line of sight that she saw the dried blood on his shirt and the scratches running down his arms. Shauna couldn't contain the gasp as her brain was quick to process what she was seeing—those scratches couldn't be anything other than those made by someone's fingernails.

As Jarrod spun toward her, flight or fight kicked in and she ran. He had been close behind her, but she was lean and nimble enough that she scrambled out the open window in the living room instead of heading for the door. Luckily, he was too big to follow the same path and lost precious seconds locating another route. Time enough for Shauna to make it into the bushes behind the property, but not enough to escape, and he knew it.

"Shauna. Shauna, come out now, would ya? I don't know what ya think ya saw, but I can explain. Please, baby, I wouldn't hurt ya. Come out so we can talk. I know ya can hear me. Ya couldn't have gotten that far. Please come out so we can talk this out."

But Shauna kept her mouth shut. She wasn't buying it and now wasn't the time to take a chance on being wrong. So, she kept quiet and waited even as he searched for her, and time slowly passed. It took a while, but her patience paid off. Her instincts had been right, but now the reality of her situation terrified her. His next words were made all the more chilling when he spoke them without even a hint of an Irish accent.

"For fuck's sake, you little brat. Get the hell out here. If I have to find you, you'll regret it. No one can save you now, do you hear me? Do you really think you can hide out here all night in this cold? You'll be dead by midnight and forget about trying to make it home. There is no way you'll be able to get past me. Even if you did manage to, our other partner will take that as his signal to follow you in and shoot everyone in the house. We're already watching it. It's not the plan, but we can adapt. So, what's it gonna be, princess? You gonna come inside or are you going to stay out here and freeze to death?"

Lunch felt like it was hours ago. She'd been outside in the cold most of the afternoon, but she thought it had been at least half an hour since he'd stopped shouting.

She wasn't moving. She knew better. While she couldn't hear

him, and she couldn't see him since it was getting too dark, it felt like he was still there, waiting for her to make a move.

The temptation to check her watch was overwhelming, but many a game of hide and seek with her brothers had taught her how something as small as a backlit LED on a watch face could give one's position away.

Minutes later, the trill of a mobile phone confirmed her suspicions. With an exasperated growl, Jarrod answered the call.

"What, damn it?"

"What the fuck do you mean they're both missing? ... They can't have gotten out by themselves. Someone must have helped them. ... Nah, they would be together. Even if they didn't work out who they were to each other, they wouldn't have separated. ... Damn it, this is your mess, so clean it up! ... Look, I couldn't have done this without you. You're as much a part of this as I am. So, find them now! ... Nah, I'm at your place, more isolated. I nearly had the youngest bitch, but she managed to get out to the woods behind the house. ... I know she can't make it back without going past me or falling in to one of the traps and setting the alarms off, but it's getting too dark. It's easier to leave her out here to die. Not as fun, but she won't last much longer in this weather. ... Seriously, what did you think we were going to do with them if not kill them, dumbass? Now get moving, God knows how much of a head start they already have on your fat ass."

The display of the phone going dark was all it took to tell Shauna the call had ended.

"**Shauna?** I know you can hear me. You can stay hidden. You'll be dead soon anyway. It's a pity. I wanted to fuck you. I wanted to be the first and last man to take you, I would've torn your tight little holes apart. Damn, I wish I hadn't been so gentle with you. But I figured I had more time. Too late now, though. Your body would be shivering violently in a feeble attempt to fight off the cold. Soon your organs will start shutting down. So, I'll just wait you out. May even fuck your corpse for the hell of it. I'll get some live action with your sister and your sister-in-law soon, anyway." Patrick paused, he just needed the bitch to make one little mistake and then he'd find her. He'd leave her to the elements if he had to, but he'd prefer to take care of her personally. Time just wasn't on his side.

"Don't feel bad, though. You couldn't have helped them. They may have escaped, but we will find them, if the weather doesn't kill them first. And then the great Lachlan will know what it's like to fail the women he loves. I can't wait to see his face when he realizes you're all dead. I'll come for him then but not before I take care of his little girl too. I'm going to decimate your family and there's nothing any of you can do about it." Patrick laughed. The bitch had no clue who he really was.

"You know, he was right to send me away all those years ago. I was going to kill Mac back then. Not before I raped her, of course, but I wanted her dead. I wanted to feel her life drain out of her body with my bare hands wrapped around her scrawny neck, but your fucking brother was always there. He always managed to get in the way. Don't get me wrong, I had the opportunity, but I didn't want to get caught and Lachlan always seemed to stumble upon us. Even when I had an alibi set elsewhere." That had been so fucking frustrating, but he'd learned a lot since then. Getting sent to the marines had been the best thing to happen to him even though he hadn't known that at the time. Still, that didn't mean he still wasn't going to make Lachlan pay for his interference. It was a matter of principle.

"I took the marines option because I thought I would have a chance to get away from them and double back, but they were always suspicious that I was a flight risk. Your brother may have delayed the outcome, bought Mac nine more years, but now he's gonna pay for it with interest. Sweet dreams, bitch. I reckon you'd be close to comatose by now, and while I'd love to come find you, the clock just ran out. I'm needed up the mountain. It's time to go hunt some live pussy."

With a final laugh, Patrick turned and stalked back to his uncle's house. As hiding places went, it was as safe as it could be in a small town. Shauna was the only one who knew of his relationship with the owner of this house, but she didn't know his real name.

He'd even put on a fake Irish accent for her alone, told her his name was Jarrod and that he was visiting his uncle from Ireland. Then he'd begged her to keep it secret because people were after him and the first place they'd look was with his uncle. He just never mentioned that one of the people looking for him was her own big brother.

Even if they worked out who he was, which he knew those interfering brats would eventually spill their guts on, all the paper-work led to the little house he'd rented under the name Jarrod Montgomery. They'd never connect the dots.

Ironic that the little brats would try to scare him off using his own story. He who laughs last, laughs the loudest, and soon that would be him.

A few minutes past 2200hrs, the sound of the cylinder turning as the lock clicked over vibrated through the quiet house before Parker and Cooper both stormed through the front door, Viper trailing behind. Sam's shoulders relaxed a little as he saw Cooper kiss his mother on the cheek before giving him a one-handed hug around Josh's back. Parker acknowledged his father's look with a small smile when he went in for his own hug, whispering a quiet, "I promised you I'd keep him safe, Dad."

Three of his family were missing. He was barely holding it together as it was, let alone if any more of them disappeared from under his nose. Although Sam didn't get a chance to dwell on this any further, a squeal of delight garnering everyone's attention when a wide-awake Gracie straightened and lifted her arms in the air.

"Hi, Uncle Cooper, can I have some Smarties?"

In a fluid motion, Cooper had Gracie in his arms, hugging her tightly. "Absolutely not, but Grandma makes yummy brownies."

Sam watched as Gracie's forehead scrunched adorably while she considered his answer before replying, "Okay, I spose, but Uncle Nate woulda let me have smarties."

Gracie shrieked up a storm as Cooper tickled her. Sam had forgotten how piercing toddler's screams could be. "Sure, but he ain't here. I'd let you have some M&M's though if I had some, so who's the best uncle? Huh, Gracie?"

Sam had to grin. Cooper had stopped tickling the little girl probably to let her answer him but the look on Gracie's face spelled mischief. It wasn't long until he was proven right. Young Gracie placed both hands on Cooper's face kissed his lips and whispered, "I love you, Uncle Cooper." So cute, except something was coming. My God, he'd seen that look on Lachlan many times over the years. Sam glanced to his side, sharing a quick smile with his wife. Yeah, she saw it too.

"I love you too, baby girl!" Cooper smiled back at Gracie and lowered the squirming girl to the floor. As soon as her feet hit the ground, she strained her neck back to see Cooper's face, "but M&M's are not the same and Uncle Nate is the best uncle." Then she turned, fleeing straight into Parker's arms, squealing, "Save me, Uncle Parker."

Laughing, Parker swung Gracie into his arms before Cooper could get to her. "Now why should I save you, when you just told everyone Nate is a better uncle than I am?"

Smiling, Gracie kissed Parker on his nose, "'cause, I love you too, Uncle Parker, and 'cause Uncle Nate isn't here to save me from Uncle Cooper."

Parker frowned meeting Sam's eyes. "Actually, I'm not sure I can argue with that logic."

Sam laughed; his granddaughter was a delight. "Women, son, there ain't no arguing, but there normally ain't no logic either."

Both Cooper and Parker were laughing seconds later as Sam

huffed out a breath, unable to dodge his wife's elbow seated as they were.

"I have a question." Claire held her hand in the air as everyone turned to her. "I don't understand how Smarties can be even remotely compared to M&M's?"

"Oh, you're thinking about the American brand of Smarties, which are sometimes known as Rockets, but that's a kind of tablet candy." Cooper's head bounced as he spoke. "We're talking about the Nestlé brand of Smarties. They're sold like everywhere in the western world, apart from the US. Lachlan and the guys cross over to Canada and stock up whenever they need to. Although rumor is, Lachie organized a pallet of the stuff a few months back. The Nestlé Smarties are a small chocolate covered in a candy shell. It's a little bigger than an M&M and has a slightly thicker shell. They also come in multiple colors, but more pastel than the M&M's."

Cooper finished his education piece, looking pleased to have sorted out any misconceptions. From the sounds of it, if anyone had given Gracie the American version of Smarties, the tantrum would have been epic. Thus, the problem with having a toddler who'd already visited and lived in so many countries with exposure to such a wide range of food and treats.

With Gracie still in his arms, Parker moved to sit next to Zac who was propped against Claire. Cooper plopped next to him. It took a little maneuvering since Sam had Josh on his lap, but he was as content as could be under the circumstances, holding the youngest of both sets of twins tight. They were most definitely the cuddlers of the family and right now he needed that more than he wanted to admit.

"So how is it Gracie appears to be so comfortable with you both, when, before a couple of days ago, your mother and I had never met her?"

"Oh, um." Cooper looked over at Parker for help.

Parker shrugged.

"Yeah, um, we've met her a few times. Lachlan couldn't stop himself from continually checking on us when he got back and this little one,"—Parker punctuated the words with a kiss to Gracie's forehead—"had no intention of staying hidden."

Cooper took over from there.

"Lachlan wasn't in a good place. I'm not sure what happened, but after the last mission, he was different. Nowhere like his usual self. He was quieter but hyper aware of everything going on around him, and he always had at least one team member with him. Actually… I think that was their doing, not his. Even Mannix wouldn't leave his sight, not even to play with Viper, which was weird. All he ever said was that he needed to explain everything to you and Ma himself. He wasn't ready yet and asked us to give him a bit of time. I didn't want him to go away again, so I agreed. Parker might have taken a bit more convincing, though."

"Daddy black balled Uncle Parker," Gracie announced into the silence.

The look of horror on Claire's face ensured Parker couldn't keep the laugh from escaping even though both Sam and Cooper were more successful in their attempts.

"Gracie, who told you that?" Cooper asked.

"I heard Mummy telling Daddy he shouldn't be mean to Uncle Parker. She called it black balling."

"Oh, you mean blackmailing," Sam clarified.

"Nut ah, black mailing is when Uncle Nate gives us money to stop Daddy from telling Poppy that Uncle Nate and GD blew up poppy's car. You get to cut out letters from picture books and post it to them. It's fun! Daddy lets me stick the letters down, then we buy candy." Shit, Sam didn't know whether to laugh or cringe. His son was teaching his granddaughter how to blackmail people. Charming! Sam couldn't wait to hear Claire's views on that one, luckily, Gracie wasn't finished explaining things to them.

"Daddy had Uncle Parker by the balls, so that's called black balling."

"Huh, that makes sense. Good logic, Gracie girl." Parker laughed.

"Ow! What was that for?" Cooper exclaimed, rubbing his arm where Sam had pinched him.

"Don't even think about it, Cooper."

"I don't know what you're talking about, Dad." Which would have been more believable if his boy hadn't grumbled the words and averted his gaze.

Parker laughed. They both knew exactly what Cooper had been intending to ask Gracie, but with him sitting in such proximity to his mother, he was smart enough not to ask what the female version of 'blackballing' was. Although Sam figured that would only last until he and Claire were out of earshot.

"Well then, Parker, do you want to share with the class what Lachlan had over you to allow him to facilitate this blackballing?" Claire's voice was deceivingly calm.

Parker blushed beet red before shaking his head. "Definitely not! But I reckon someone needs a lesson in listening to other people's conversations and then not repeating parts of it to others," Diversion tactics in play, his son tickled Gracie until she called out 'Uncle.'

"So, has Mackenzie met Gracie too, then? I find it hard to believe Lachlan didn't check on her as well, but I find it harder to believe that Mackenzie would keep this from us, extortion or not." Claire's gaze bounced between Cooper and Parker. Sam also wanted to know who knew what. It hurt that this was kept from them, valid reasons or not.

"Nah, Lachie knew Mac wouldn't have his back on this. He caught up with the three of us when he didn't have Grace with him, but only checked on Mac from afar when he did. We weren't meant to know either, but Gracie blew the secret, and he couldn't trust her not to do it again. He knew she would be too curious to not want to meet Mac, so he played it safe after that," Parker answered. "And just so you know, it wasn't easy keeping it from you. But we met Isabella and the guys, and we learned enough to know they needed time. Whatever happened in the last mission was bad, Ma. It shook them all, but Lachlan especially. He's different. He came back scarred. Whether they're permanent or they can be seen or not. I can't answer."

FOURTEEN

Shauna had stayed quiet during his tirade, tears pooling in her eyes that she stubbornly refused to let fall. All this time, she had been following Jarrod around like a love-sick puppy and it turned out he was responsible for her sister and sister-in-law's disappearance.

He was right, though. There was no way she would last all night out here, but he was a dumbass if he thought she was already dead and gone. The adrenalin alone had helped keep her warm, and then there was her cheeky little secret that only Mackenzie knew about.

Her beautiful big sister had been sending her boxes of 'Hot Hands' and 'Hot Feet' to aid her in keeping warm during the colder months, plus an abundance of UNIQLO heat technology tops.

Mackenzie sent the packages to Al Sanders, who not only was one of their dad's best friends, but the fire chief as well. Chief Sanders was happy to play the postman and nobody who had any brains would ever question the chief on any of his deliveries.

Shauna despised the cold but at sixteen it was more important to look good, so with Mackenzie's help no one was onto her new coping methods. Thoughts of her sister had one tear escaping before she could wipe it away.

She had heard his truck leave. The sound of his clogged muffler stood out in the cold, silent night. But was still hesitant to move in case it was another trick. With her hands in the pockets of her thin jacket, holding the 'Hot Hands' tight, Shauna tried to work out how to get away. Somehow, she needed to contact her older brothers. Her parents had to be worried sick that she was missing. If Shauna had known Mackenzie was also missing, there was no way she would have left the house. Damn, she was going to be in such big trouble—if she survived, that is.

A few minutes before midnight, Jonah walked in with Max on his heels. Sam had been dozing along with the rest of the family but the sound of the lock being disengaged had him wide awake. Watching them expectantly.

"Nothing, Dad. We went to his house, but he wasn't there. There was no sign of Shauna or that any disturbance had taken place. I've relayed the name to the Feds, who said they'd pass it on to Lachlan. For all we know, he might have run when the twins told him that Lachlan had threatened one of Mackenzie's boyfriends into enlisting. It's not like the guy would know the twins were telling stories since the guy did leave town to enlist, and it is like folklore around here."

"It's not made up," Cooper yawned, curling into his shoulder. Sam instinctively kissed Cooper's forehead before the words his boy had spoken registered. Stopping as he pulled back, Sam frowned at Jonah, who shrugged his shoulder before looking back at Cooper.

"What do you mean, it's not made up, and how do you know it's not? I mean, we've all heard the rumor, but that's more town speculation and gossip."

"Oh, it's not gossip! I was there. Lachlan didn't leave my side much back then, but he said he had to handle something, so I had to come but I had to promise to be quiet and not tell anyone what transpired." Cooper smiled at him, then at Jonah and a smirking Max, who was already shaking his head.

"He was awesome. Man, you should have seen him. I'd never seen him so mad, but he didn't touch him. Lachlan just stood there vibrating with anger and gave him two options. Jail or the Marines."

In truth, Sam shouldn't have been surprised. His son had always been protective of his siblings and in this instance had probably saved Sam from a murder wrap. He hadn't known his eleven-year-old daughter was hanging around with an eighteen-year-old until the boy had already left town. Sam had been a lot more observant of his kids after that. To the extent that he and his then deputy had started patrolling all the local kid's hangouts.

"Next thing I know, the guy had packed a bag, and we were driving him to the next town to enlist. The recruiter didn't even ask any questions, he just made the guy sign all this paperwork and then had him escorted away. As soon as they were gone, the guy burst out laughing and shoved four hundred dollars into Lachie's hand. It turned out it wasn't the first time Lachlan had done it."

Sam looked over at his wife as a chuckle escaped, not realizing she was awake. "You condone that?"

Claire laughed. "Hell yes, that's my boy and, more importantly, that's your son. You know damn well you're delighted by the notion. I'd bet the only issue you have with it is that you didn't think of it yourself because it's damn well something you would have done had you have thought of it."

They all laughed again as Sam went red, caught out as to exactly where his thoughts had gone. It was Jonah who asked the next question that was on everyone's mind. "Who else?"

"Huh?" Cooper looked back at Jonah.

"You said it wasn't the first time he did it, so who else did he do it to?"

"Oh, um …" It was Cooper's turn to flush bright red, his eyes suddenly captivated on the floor in front of his feet.

Oh boy, that was not a good sign. Sam scrambled to think of other candidates but came up short.

Claire reached over and smoothed Cooper's fringe back from his face, cupping her hand around his jaw. "It's okay, sweetie, he's not in trouble, but we would like to know who else that menace did it to!"

Cooper looked straight at Max and the pit of Sam's stomach dropped out. Shit.

"Um, well, you know that bitch that gave you a hard time and wouldn't take no for an answer and was, um, making stuff up that could've ended real nasty like?"

At Max's nod and Jonah's grunt, Cooper continued. Sam tightened his hold on Cooper and held in a breath.

"Well, we were coming around the back of the library when we heard her threatening you. Lachlan was so mad; he smashed his fist into the brick wall. Some of that stuff was already getting bandied around town and he knew you were taking heat for it. We also knew your dad hadn't reacted well to those rumors. So we followed you home. It wasn't a coincidence that we barged in seconds after you walked in the door or that Lachlan walked in right between you and your dad's raised fist."

"What?" Sam exploded. "Your sorry excuse for a father hit you and I'm only finding out about this now?" Sam couldn't believe any of his boys had kept this from him.

Shaking her head, Claire took a calmer approach. "Max, if we'd known, we would have stepped in. We wondered sometimes, but you always waylaid our fears so convincingly and I never saw any sign of bruises. Trust me, we looked for them. I wish you would have come to us. Both Sam and I despised the man your dad became after your mother passed."

Max's Adam's apple visibly moved as he looked back and forth between Sam and Claire. Had Max and Jonah ever spoken about this? He'd guessed it wasn't great after Max's mother had passed, but he hadn't expected violence from the man who was once one of his closest friends.

Sam cleared his throat. "You and Jonah were inseparable, always together. Claire and I treated you as our own even before you came to live with us. I never considered you were hiding something like that from us." He thought he'd had a good relationship with both Max and his oldest boys.

"I wasn't hiding anything, I promise." Max met Sam's eyes. "Seriously, it sounds worse than it was. He hit me one time, and I reckon it scared him more than it did me. Besides, the truth is, I hit him first. He just reacted. For a moment, I saw something in his eyes. It still haunts me because when it happened, I thought it was fear. For that split second, I thought he feared me. But I discounted it and decided it was more likely he had scared himself by hitting me back. Now I'm older, I'm not so sure. I still replay it in my mind. I was just so angry once mum died. After, I waited for it to escalate, but it didn't. Things were turning around before Stacey's lies changed everything again."

Sam nodded before turning his attention back to Cooper. He'd think more on that later.

"Cooper, what happened next?"

Cooper swallowed as he leaned back against him. His son might be twenty-two, but Sam was happy to know Cooper would still seek the comfort and safety of his embrace.

"Well, they kind of stood there glaring at each other for a bit before Max's dad suddenly dropped his fist, spun around and stormed off without a word. Lachlan then corralled us into Max's room and started packing a bag for him. Max stood there like a statue watching, he didn't speak, he didn't move. Finally, Lachlan finished packing, he then stalked over to Max and pulled him into a hug. I know he whispered something to him, but I never heard what it was."

"Brother."

"Huh?" Cooper asked.

"Brother, that's what he said. He said I was his little brother in every way that mattered and that it was his duty to protect me. When I stopped crying and started to calm down and before I could get embarrassed at what had transpired, he said he needed a favor. That he had some stuff to do and asked if I could come stay at his place, hang with Jonah, and keep an eye on Cooper until he or Parker came home." Max's eyes dropped as his words fell away.

Sam watched Jonah step into Max's personal space and lift his chin. "You were always part of this family and if it took my big brother saying the words for you to believe it, then I am eternally grateful."

Turning back to Cooper, Jonah raised his eyebrow in a sign for him to continue.

Cooper turned red before looking away. "What makes you think I know? I was home with the two of you babysitting me while Parker was off with his new girlfriend!" Cooper drawled the word girlfriend out to try to pull Parker into the conversation. Unfortunately for his boy, the tactic didn't work.

"Cooper!" Sam huffed. "Spill it!"

"Fine. He found 'the bitch.'" Cooper used his fingers to air mark the inverted comas. "His words, not mine," his boy side-eyed Claire. "Told her he had all the evidence, and that she had two choices. Hang around and live with everyone knowing she was a lying cow, or she could enlist. She was the first person he drove down to the recruitment office that I know of." Cooper looked back into Max's eyes and locked on before he spoke his next words. "Your dad was the second."

"What?"

The question loudly voiced in unison by all awake in the room, but Cooper continued to hold only Max's eyes as he continued. Damn it. Sam should have seen that coming.

"I wasn't there. Lachlan only told me some of it, so I'd keep my mouth shut. All I know is Lachlan went to see your dad. Got him so mad your dad admitted he was in over his head. It sounded like Lachlan pushed his buttons and they grappled for a bit."

Cooper kept going, despite the gasp from Claire.

"When they were finally out of breath, Lachlan told him he was doing more harm than good by trying to raise a hormonal teenager when he wasn't in a good headspace. He suggested your dad should walk away before he did any irreversible damage. So they talked it out. Half an hour later, your dad approached ours and said that he had to leave unexpectedly and asked if dad would take you in. Dad, of course, said yes, as you were already one of us and sent him to say goodbye to you. Then Lachlan drove him to the recruitment office."

Max shook his head. This information changed everyone's recollection of what had happened back then, even Sam's.

"Dad apologized, said he had done wrong by me and that he couldn't trust himself not to hurt me again. Said he was going away but that the Michaels were going to take me in. I couldn't believe it. It was like all my Christmases came at once. Shit, I always thought I'd find him dead on the floor, or that one day he might lose his temper and accidentally kill me. Best case, I'd come home and find out he'd split and left me a mess of debt. Never did I expect him to handle everything to make sure I'd be financially stable. Let alone apologize and leave me with the family I had wished were mine once Mum was gone. Shit, I can't believe Lachlan orchestrated that for me."

"I can, and I am proud of him for doing so. You know I love you like a son," Sam spoke, his voice gruff with emotion, looking back toward his wife. "We both do. You've always been an important part of our family. Although we must admit we were never sure if you would end up marrying Jonah or Mackenzie—" Sam trailed off, but he didn't bother hiding his smile when both Jonah and Max started coughing and spluttering in incredulity. It was Parker who lit the fuse again. "Please answer, we're all dying to know who wins the pool!"

"I thought you were asleep?"

"Hell, no, I wasn't missing this," Parker cackled.

"Hold on!" Max raised his hand. "What pool?"

Jonah watched, horrified, as his parents went beet red while Parker started to explain. "Lachlan, Dad, Cooper, and Josh think you'll marry Jonah. But Mum, Shauna, Zac, and I bet that it'd be Mackenzie. Jonah and Mac don't know about the pool. We've had to be more careful in the last few years, so they didn't catch on. So, which is it?"

"Hold on!" This time Jonah put his hand up to stop the flow. "How does the pool work, what … everybody in the pool 'wins' dependent on who Max ends up with?"

"No, of course not," Parker answered. "We all have certain years we believe you'll work this crap out and there is also a secondary bet on how long you keep it secret before spilling, afraid of how we will react."

"Ooh, and don't forget the third bet. If they are gay, who they tell first?" Cooper exclaimed.

At this, Jonah finally rolled his eyes. "Unbelievable, totally unbelievable!"

Max looked like a frozen statue but still managed to ask the question Jonah couldn't seem to push out of his mouth. "And you don't care whichever way it falls?"

"Hell, no! Son, your mother, and I just want all NINE of our kids to be happy, we don't care who that is with … Ah, hold on a tick, let me qualify that. We don't care if our kids are gay or straight or whatever and we won't care who it is that makes them happy. Once you are over the age of twenty-five, we are confident you can make those decisions for yourselves."

"Seriously, Dad?" Parker exclaimed.

"Huh, not so funny now, is it?" Jonah laughed in relief. He'd been worried about telling their family, even though deep down he knew they'd support him. It was still terrifying. Lachlan had called him an idiot but hadn't pushed. They did live in a small town after all.

Parked huffed out a breath before looking at Cooper. "Why don't you have a problem with any of that?"

"Meh." Cooper shrugged his shoulders. "Lachlan still does an in-depth background check on every person I meet, whether date material or not, and he has already warned me twenty-five is a deadline our parents use and that it doesn't apply to him. Oh, and before you laugh at me, what do you think happened to that girl 'Jenny' that you thought was top shit before she disappeared on you and then two months later was making a fool out of some other guy? You thought you had a close shave, but you got 'Lachie'd'."

The frown on Parker's face would have been laughable except for the next question he asked. "But how did he know? I hadn't even told you about her, let alone Lachie."

"I don't know. I figured you were the one feeding him names of people I met?"

"Nope, not once. Dad?"

"Don't look at me. I don't know how he does it, but considering the conversation tonight, I don't think anything he does will surprise me. That he pulled all that off while he was both overseas and dealing with his own crap just compounds it, so I wouldn't fight it if I were you."

"Well, of course you're going to say that. It works out great for you, fewer kids to worry about," Parker huffed.

"Ha! Your mother and I always worry about all our kids. Now, boys, what is the plan from here?" His dad redirected everyone back to Jonah.

In an instant, the mood sobered, with all thoughts turning to the missing Michaels women and Jonah sighed. He didn't have anything good to say.

"There isn't much we can do at this point. We've turned the town upside down. The Feds are here helping. They have people watching the boyfriend's house. Normally, we'd send a volunteer search party through the mountains, but that allows everyone up there, including the kidnapper, giving him free rein. Logistics say there's gotta be more than one person involved, so we can't take the chance. We'll keep watch over the town to see who comes and goes, and hope Lachlan and whoever he has with him can find the girls and bring them back home. At least Isabella is military trained, both Mac and Shauna know these mountains like the back of their hands, so they have a better chance of surviving if they are in the woods than if we give everyone license to roam free. A ban went out this evening stating no locals were to enter the mountains. Anyone found up there, they'll treat with extreme prejudice."

"Oh, but Lachlan?" His ma's voice shook slightly.

"They know Ma. No one's saying who or how many are with him, but the Feds are in regular contact with him. Everyone's tight-lipped, which is a good thing."

"So …" Max looked around the room as he found his voice, finally landing on Jonah a telltale smirk in place. "Who wins the pool, if it's this year and Jonah?"

Parker groaned out Lachlan's name. Cooper smirked while Jonah watched his parents share a small smile.

"I can live with that. What do you think, baby?" Max reached his hand out to Jonah.

"Yeah, I can live with that too." Taking Max's hand, Jonah shook his head at his family's antics. "Let's go to bed. Tomorrow will be another long day."

"Hey!" Parker called out to their retreating backs. They both paused as Parker threw out his last question. "What about the third pool?"

Jonah laughed as he started climbing the stairs, hand in hand with his partner, Racer at his heels. "Unbelievable. Just give it all to Lachlan and don't bother warning him before I get my hands on him."

"Uncle Jonah?"

Pausing in their assent, all eyes turned to the now awake little girl sitting in Parker's lap.

"Yes, pretty girl?"

"Daddy said you and Max hacking up was a secret, but if that's true, how come everyone knows?"

"Hacking?"

"Daddy said that meant living together like he and Mummy do."

"Oh, you mean 'shacking' up. Well, it looks like the cat is out of the bag now, baby girl."

"That's good."

"Huh, it is?"

"Yeah, well, you're not spose to keep cats in bags, Uncle Jonah. Everybody knows that!"

"Ah, yeah. Good point."

"So where is it?"

"Where is what, baby girl?"

"The cat, Uncle Jonah. Geez, where is the cat?"

"Ah. Will one of you stop laughing and help me with this?"

"Nope, this is gold." Cooper laughed. "Cutie pie, when did Daddy tell you Jonah and Max were 'hacking' up?"

"Kill me now!" Jonah groaned under his breath as he waited for his niece's answer.

Gracie shrugged her shoulder and wrinkled her brow as she answered. "I don't know. Mummy was laughing and told Daddy he was asking for trouble and then Daddy said it was so secret that you didn't even know about it. But that don't make sense. You gotta know when someone lives with you. And Daddy didn't know you were keeping a cat in a bag, Uncle Jonah. He woulda told you off for that. You woulda got the naughty corner, for sure."

Jonah watched helplessly as his family continued to laugh at his expense, hoping Max would come to his rescue, but not in the way he did.

"Gracie, you are one hundred percent right. I am going to take Jonah to his naughty corner right now so he can think about what he has done. We will see you in the morning. Night, night, baby girl."

"Night, Uncle Max, night, Uncle Jonah. Hey, don't forget it's a minute for every year. That's a lot of minutes, Uncle Jonah," Gracie's little face quickly turned into a frown at the laughter coming from the rest of the family. "Did I say something bad?"

"Oh no, sweetheart, not at all. Now, let's get you to bed," His mother was struggling to hide her laughter as she moved to pick Gracie up, but Jonah and Max took that as their cue to continue up the stairs, his mother's voice following them. "Say goodnight to everyone."

"Good night, everyone. Grandma?"

"Yes, sweetie?"

"Will Mummy and Daddy be home when I wake-ed?" Reaching the top of the landing, Jonah paused and tightened his grip on Max's hand. For some reason he needed to hear his mother's response.

"I don't know, honey. We will have to wait and see. Come now, it's long past your bedtime."

FIFTEEN

Shauna waited and waited in her hiding spot, unsure of her next move, wanting to run home but terrified of leaving the safety of this spot in case it was a trick. Jarrod had been right.

If she stayed here, she would die.

Not as quickly as he thought, but the result would be the same. But what if she made it home and someone was watching the house as he had threatened? She couldn't risk getting her family killed. She had to warn them somehow. How anyone could want to hurt and kill children was beyond her. This guy intended to take out everyone Lachlan loved.

Her thoughts were cut off as a hand covered her mouth. She found herself pulled back against a large, solid chest. Instinct had her fighting the hold while trying to scream through the thick fingers that muffled any sounds she tried to make.

"Shh, you're safe. Stop fighting. We don't have time for this." Shauna struggled harder, but his hold tightened further on an exasperated sigh. "Come on, Shauna, stop fighting me and listen. I'm not going to hurt you, but you need to stay still and quiet. I saw Jarrod leave but as I don't know where his partner is, we need to stay hidden. Seriously, enough! If I wanted to kill you, you'd already be dead."

Was it ironic it was the last sentence that got through to her enough to stop squirming? Taking a breath, Shauna tried to find her center. Whatever that meant, stupid yoga. But right now, she would give anything to be sitting in another class by her older sister, not that she would admit that to anyone anytime soon.

Her assailant, unaware of the direction her mind had drifted, only knew she had stopped fighting him and took that as a cue to continue talking.

"Now, I'm going to take my hand away. Then I'm going to hand you my jacket. You need to get warm. Just don't scream."

Slowly, he removed his hold on her and stepped back away from her, hands up in the universal surrender position.

"Why should I believe you?" Shauna whispered as she spun around to face him. He looked vaguely familiar, but she couldn't place him, and she was sure she had never met him before.

"Look, I know you can't know for sure that I am on your side, but if I wasn't, like I said, you'd be dead already. And I wouldn't be stupid enough to release you from my hold, especially knowing what training Lachie has given you."

"Well, duh, but who said bad guys weren't stupid?"

"Mary, it's fucken hereditary."

"Huh?"

"Can anyone in your family take a common saying, accept it for what it is, and just leave it alone? Do you all have to dissect them to decipher the logic or worse, make up your own, 'cause it's damn frustrating, especially when they only actually make sense when you work out what logic you were using at the time?"

"Oh, that. Yeah, Lachie's the worst. I am but a student of the Master." Shauna laughed. She knew it frustrated the hell out of people, which is the exact reason she found it funny and was actively pursuing the art.

"For Mary's sake! We don't have time for this. I disabled all the alarms I could find. Shocked the shit out of me when I came across the first one. I was sure he was bluffing, but he wasn't, and I can't be positive I didn't miss one or set off a silent alarm somewhere along the way, so we need to move quickly and as quietly as possible away from here. Are you right to follow?"

Shauna nodded. What else could she do? She wasn't getting a bad vibe from him. Even if he turned out to be a bad guy, she was in a better position following him out of the woods than staying and freezing to death in the one spot. Besides, he'd just done something she'd only ever heard Lachlan do before. Switching out the name 'Pete' or 'Christ,' for 'Mary' when cursing. It was still weird to hear someone say, 'For Mary's sake!' instead of saying, 'For Pete's sake!' like normal people. No one knew why Lachlan did it, but this guy using the name 'Mary' in the same way did help her decide to trust him—for now …

As an involuntary shudder went through her body, the man started to remove his jacket before passing it over to her.

"Considering that you're Lachie's kid sister, I'm assuming you know how to shoot a gun?"

"Yeah, um, Dad taught us," she whispered as she snuggled into the warmth of his jacket.

"Good, I expect nothing less. Here, take this Glock, it's fully loaded, so please don't shoot me. We need to get moving so we can get word to your family that you are safe. I'm here alone. If you see anyone else in our travels and you don't know them, treat them with prejudice."

At Shauna's questioning look, the man shrugged his shoulders before adding, "Simply put, shoot first, ask questions later. Now, stay quiet, keep behind me and try to walk in my footprints, makes it harder to track."

Without another word, he spun around and started walking deeper into the woods.

"Wait!" Shauna whispered, not moving, before he turned back around to face her. "I don't know who you are or what to call you."

"DBD, now let's go."

"Huh? What the hell kind of name is Debeedee?"

"It's mine and one I unfortunately earned, so I live with it."

"Oh, you mean like the letters D-B-D. What does it stand for?"

"Look, Shauna, we don't have time for a history lesson, and even if we did, I'm not in the mood to deliver one. You know my name, so let's go before we both freeze to death."

The grumpy man turned on his heel and started making his way through the woods, away from Jarrod's uncle's place.

"Where are we going?"

"Mary, Mary, and Mary! I don't have the patience for this. What part of we need to move quickly and quietly don't you understand exactly?"

Rude.

DBD turned back around and headed off again, albeit a little faster than the previous attempt. And if he heard her muffled 'grumpy asshole' comment, he ignored it.

All that mattered was that she was safe. Unfortunately, her family didn't know that yet, and she had no way of telling them at this moment without jeopardizing their lives. Hopefully, DBD would contact her family once they were away from here. It would also be great if DBD had a plan because, aside from getting out of here, she sure as hell didn't.

November woke abruptly from her nap, reality hitting her in the face. This wasn't a dream. Tears blurred her vision. The depravity of her situation compounded by the throbbing pains racking her body as the red glow of the numbers counting down her final days descended in front of her eyes.

How did this happen?

November remembered little about the night this horror started. Just that he had been handsome, charming, intoxicating even. He had focused solely on making her feel as if she was the most important person in the world. They had moved off to have a late dinner at a small diner a block across from the club.

She recalled eating and then feeling sick, but after that she remembered nothing until she awoke in this little room, her own little hell. But this wasn't her hell alone. There had been others before her. None had survived. November didn't see how she would either, let alone stop others from suffering the same fate.

As depression settled over her, the red numbers descended above her. November crawled over to the wall behind the door. It was time to scratch her month, year, and real name along with the others. All the while praying that someday it would reveal their horrors to the outside world.

Was anyone even looking for her? She wasn't overly close with her family, but her friends were another matter. Although, they knew she was a bit of a loner and happily accepted it when she stayed out of contact for days at a time.

Only weeks from turning twenty-seven and she was alone even before she ended up here in this hellhole. Taking a breath, wondering if this was sealing her fate, she used the chain to scratch into the wall. *November 2017—Emily Rose Duchas 11/28/1990.*

"**Well**, shit. Didn't see that coming," Max followed Jonah into his old bedroom, shaking his head as Racer jumped onto the bed. Even choosing to sleep on Lachlan's bunk, which, while bigger, wasn't even close to the size of the king they normally slept in. There was no way they would both fit comfortably, even less chance if the dog had no intention of moving. "Dibs on the bottom bunk."

"What?" Jonah spun around. "What do you mean, dibs?"

"Dibs. I mean dibs. I can't see us both fitting on the one bunk especially with Racer commandeering so much space. So, I call dibs. Besides, I'm older and the top bunk is your old bed, anyway."

"You're joking, right? Surely you have something to say…" Jonah trailed off and waved his hand about. "And you're only two months older, dickwad."

Max watched Jonah brace himself as he stalked toward him.

Jonah wasn't submissive. However, when push came to shove, Max naturally exuded more dominance. That didn't mean Jonah backed down easily, even now the stubborn man held his ground, his chin jutted out in an unspoken dare, Max was happy to answer. Toe to toe, Max met his stare, unmoving for several moments, before Jonah finally broke and looked away on a huff. Before he could storm off, Max grabbed Jonah's shoulders and took his mouth in a bruising but fast kiss.

"I hear you, Jonah, but I need time to process. So, baby cakes, get your ass in the corner. I'll let you know when your twenty-five minutes are up." Max slapped Jonah's butt and turned to reclaim the bottom bunk.

"Hilarious!" Jonah growled as he finished getting undressed.

"Hey, I'm not the one who kept the cat in the bag." Max laughed as he ducked the shoe, letting it hit the wall behind him. "What's with you two always throwing things? Come on, let's get some sleep so we can get back out there."

"Four hours, Max, that's all I'm agreeing to. Both my sisters are missing now, plus a sister-in-law I've never met. I can't even believe I agreed to this."

"Hey." Max stood and intercepted Jonah. "There is nothing we can do right now. We're both exhausted. The Feds are looking everywhere we've already looked, in case we missed something or somehow, they backtracked. Lachlan is out there searching as well and while I'm damn sure he's not alone, you can bet your ass he is still grabbing sleep where he can. We'll be no use to anyone if we're too tired to function." Max caressed Jonah's face with his thumbs as he tried to get through to his lover.

"I'm frustrated, Max. We've found nothing." Jonah dropped his forehead to his, as Max moved his arms to encircle his stubborn lover. "I can't even imagine what Lachlan is going through. Seriously, I mean, it's bad enough with just our sisters missing. It happened right under our noses. But his wife. God, if I lost you like this, I don't know if I could still function, let alone get out there to search for you. I feel so guilty not only about getting some sleep but because part of me is relieved. I'm relieved it's not you, and I'm not sure how to deal with that."

Max tightened his hold on Jonah. They had only acknowledged their feelings for each other as more than best friends a few months ago, but he knew where Jonah was coming from because he too, was relieved. But feeling guilty wouldn't help anyone. Knowing they needed sleep more than anything else, Max backed Jonah onto the bottom bunk, curling around him in the tight space, hopeful sleep wouldn't be elusive for either of them.

Monster free. It was the longest he'd left her alone. There was no food left, only water from the little basin to fill her stomach. Being alone didn't stop the clock. As much as she tried, November couldn't stop her eyes from tracking back to watch the red numbers continue to count down the seconds of her life.

She'd take the reprieve, a hundred percent certain she would rather be hungry than suffer at his hands again. As November succumbed to sleep, she prayed her monster was dead. How didn't matter. Just dead would be enough. But November had learnt long ago that prayers rarely got the results you wanted.

Only hours later, Parker woke with a start. A quick look confirmed his brother's bed was empty. His racing heart told him to get to Cooper. Knowing his brother was prone to nightmares, Parker wouldn't settle until he saw him with his own eyes. Moving quickly, Parker left his room in search of his twin. He would like to say he found Cooper in the first room he looked in, because of their twin connection, but unlike his bratty little brothers, he and Cooper weren't identical. As Lachlan would say, logic would give you the answer to most things. It was just funny that his oldest brother often made up his own.

Parker stood for a second, deciding what to do. Cooper had curled himself protectively around Gracie. It would be hard to join them without waking anyone. And the bed was only a king single, so he hesitated until the next whimpers escaped not only from Cooper but Gracie as well. Decision made, he motioned for Viper to move to the end of the bed and then he climbed in, pulling both Cooper and Gracie into his arms. Both stirred but neither woke. Best of all, the whimpers stopped.

Once Parker was sure neither Cooper nor Gracie were still suffering through nightmares, he allowed himself to doze back off.

***

Monday 6th November

It was early the next morning as Jonah stood over them that Sam entered the room. One look was all it took before he started shaking his head. "Is there any chance this family has suffered enough? How is it I can't protect my own kids from the terrors in this world, and now my granddaughter is also suffering?"

"Dad, this isn't your fault."

But Sam didn't believe his son. He and Claire had left their door open just in case Gracie had a nightmare and yet he hadn't heard anything. But standing there beating himself up wasn't going to help anyone.

"Go finish getting ready, I'll keep an ear out for them to wake."

Jonah nodded and left. Sam would have followed but Gracie chose that moment to wake. After rubbing her eyes, she leaned over and kissed both Parker and Cooper on their cheeks before lifting her arms in the universal sign for 'Grandpa, pick me up, please.'

With Gracie in his arms, Sam headed toward the kitchen, leaving the twins and Viper to get a few more hours' sleep. He could only hope Lachlan was having a better time of it out there looking for the girls.

Isabella woke with a start and swung her head to the left, needing to check that Mackenzie hadn't somehow disappeared during their sleep. Technically still nighttime, she felt like it was time to move. During the day, they had made good ground, only coming across two more cabins, which were blissfully empty. It was a slow process. In places, the trees were so thick it was hard not to leave an obvious trail. Yet she still didn't think they were out of danger. Torn between heading out while still early and letting Mackenzie sleep some more, Isabella listened out for any signs of movement.

"I'm awake." Mackenzie whispered.

Despite the time they had spent together, there had been little opportunity to talk. The need to focus on where they were going and to listen for any sounds around them that were out of place, taking priority. And while Isabella wanted to chat and try to work out who the enemy was, the bigger need was to move.

As quietly as possible, they gathered their things and continued heading for Canada. Pushing away the fear that made her want to turn back toward the direction where logic told her Lachlan and Nate would come, they continued forward.

The boys had again broken camp early that morning, keen not to lose too much time to mundane things like sleep. It was less than an hour later when they came across the first cabin that showed obvious signs of inhabitation in the past week or so. Mannix gave a low whine as they advanced, putting them all on alert. Splitting off, they surrounded the cabin to approach from four different directions, signaling to each other when they were confident their paths were clear.

With nothing to lose, Lachlan beelined for the front door, Mannix by his side. When he tried the handle, he found it locked. Letting his impatience free, he stepped back and kicked his foot out at the weakest point. Old as shit, the wood splintered and flung back against the wall, Lachlan charged through, gun in hand.

Empty, and yet, something had the hairs on the back of his neck standing to attention. Mannix went straight to the middle of the small lounge area, scratching at the rug underneath the coffee table. By the time Nate had followed him inside, Lachlan had unceremoniously pushed the table and rug out of his way. The trap door was open, and he was halfway through, lowering himself to the basement underneath.

Ignoring a muttered "Way to wait for backup, genius!" from Nate, he kept going. He felt Nate behind him rather than heard him as he stood a couple of feet in from the open doorway to the makeshift dungeon.

"She was here!"

"I'm her twin, man. If either of us was gonna sense her, don't you think it would be me?"

"I'm not sensing her, moron. She scratched a message in the wall behind the door."

"Awe man, I hate it when our parents fight," Deeks smirked as he pushed into the room, searching out the message scratched on the wall. "'I love Dutch pancakes!' What the hell does that mean?"

"It means she intends heading up and over to Canada, but will do so in a roundabout way to confuse anyone following her," Lachlan answered.

"And how exactly do you get that from 'I love Dutch pancakes?'" Deeks' eyes traveled back and forth between Lachlan and Nate.

"Pictionary," Nate answered, as if that explained everything. When Deeks continued to stare at him, Nate shrugged and walked out, heading back toward the trapdoor.

"Let's clear this place and keep moving. At least we know we're on the right track now. Lachlan!" Nate barked.

Lachlan knew what Nate was doing. He was trying to get him out of there. They had already seen enough of the room to guess some of what had transpired. Lachlan knew Nate was right. He needed to move. The last thing he needed was to stand there staring at the chains, imagining what had gone on.

"Let's go," Nate barked again.

This time, it was enough to jar Lachlan into gear. She had escaped and was heading over the mountains to Canada. That was enough to spur him on. The rest they would deal with later.

Quickly they searched the cabin, and while they found no clues about who had been staying there, they did find some clothes and jackets in the closet. But something about it made Lachlan pause and Nate noticed.

"What's wrong?"

"Um, nothing." Lachlan shook his head before he gave in to Nate's worried look and mumbled, "the clothes just look vaguely familiar, that's all."

***

November paced back and forth as far as allowable in her little dungeon. It had been a few days since he had left. She knew enough from October to know this wasn't normal, that something must have happened.

The problem now was what to do from here. She had run out of food, with only water from the basin to keep her going. There was no way he would not be trying to get back to her, so something must be stopping him, otherwise he would have left more food.

Afraid to wish him dead.

Afraid to hope.

November was unsure what was the lesser evil.

Die at his hand in twenty-four days or die sooner by starvation.

DAYS	HOURS	MINUTES	SECONDS
024	14	:32	:16

SIXTEEN

With Gracie on his hip, Sam was making toast for breakfast when the doorbell rang. Unsure of who would stop by at this hour and a little wary considering the circumstances, Sam was heading to the stairs to pass Gracie off when Jonah and Max intercepted them.

"Dad, we got this. Take Gracie to the kitchen."

"Humph, some people forget I was the sheriff round here before they were even out of diapers. Come on, Gracie, let's go grab our toast."

Sam turned back to the kitchen but kept an ear out for the situation. He doubted their enemy would come to the door and wait patiently for an invitation inside. His boys also didn't seem to comprehend the open plan concept of their house. Sure, the kitchen was in an alcove to the right, but it was still open to the rest of the living room once you were a few feet inside the house.

"Oh, man, you so haven't heard the end of that one."

"Shut it, Max."

"As entertaining as this conversation is, would one of you ding-bats kindly open the door, its f'ing cold out here." Sam swallowed his surprised half laugh, turning it into a cough.

"Did we just get insulted by someone standing on the other side of the door?" Jonah whispered. "How the hell did he hear us?"

"I've got great hearing and blue balls. Now let me in so I can get warm and introduce myself."

From the apparent safety of the kitchen, Sam watched the boys approach the door. Max stood to the side while Jonah stood in front with his gun raised. Max used his fingers to signal three, two, one and flung the door open.

In front of them stood a mountain of a man, arms folded across his chest, a deadly glare upon his face.

"Seriously, this is how you open the door. Did Lachlan teach you nothing? I could have shot straight through the damn thing and killed you without even aiming. Now move it or lose it."

The look on Jonah's face surely would have been comical if not for the situation at hand.

"I don't know who you are, but I'm considering shooting you just for being an asshole."

"Try it, Junior, but then you'd have to explain it to the captain, and he don't take kindly to his team being shot at, brother or not."

"But he's okay with you being an asshole?"

The man shrugged and walked past him into the house, but he wasn't alone. "Lachie knows who I am."

Sam barely registered that the four-legged blur of fluff that shot into the house on the heels of the stranger was Mackenzie's husky PIMF as Racer bolted over to greet his sister.

Before Jonah could throw any further accusations or questions, a high-pitched squeal sounded as Gracie ran from where she had been standing next to Sam, headed straight for the moody gigantor. Three yells of 'Gracie' intermingled with her squealing, as seconds later, the stranger had her upside down by her ankle, his arm outstretched to his side.

"Did you just run away from your grandpa, Miss Gracie?"

"Nut uh."

"Yeah? Then why does he look like he's just lost ten years of his life?"

"I wanna hug."

"I don't hug naughty girls. Besides, they don't know who I am, and Jonah could still shoot me and get you instead."

"Don't be silly, Uncle Jonah can't shoot you. You're my GD and Daddy would be mad."

"True that, but Jonah doesn't know that yet and I don't know how good a shot he is either."

Gracie giggled as she continued to hang upside down, held by one foot, when Claire walked in from the clinic and joined his side. Sam noted a small smile escaping at the antics in front of her.

"You're not scared of me or worried about the rug rat?" Gigantor frowned at Claire.

"I'm Lachlan's mother and I raised him, didn't I? Now what kind of name is Geedee?"

Shrugging, the mountain of a man flung Gracie into the air and caught her on the way down, bringing her into his chest. Sam couldn't stop himself. He, Jonah, and Max all moved slightly forward, as if to catch the little tyke, but his wife hadn't even twitched. The gigantor noticed and tipped his head toward Claire in acknowledgment before he answered her question while Gracie squeezed her little arms around his neck.

"It just the letters, ma'am, G and D, GD. My name's Justin Leeds, but the guys call me Bruce."

Claire huffed out a breath as if to say boys will be boys. "At least they tried to be subtle and didn't outright name you The Hulk."

Bruce's eyes sparkled in delight. If Sam had to guess, few people would have clued in so fast. Before Bruce could respond, the little girl in his arms commanded his attention. Hands to the sides of his cheeks, Gracie kissed him right on his lips.

"I love you, GD. Can I have some Smarties?"

"No. Absolutely, one hundred percent no. Not even if the world was ending. If Nate gave you Smarties, I'm going to brain his fool ass. In fact, when we're done here, I'm going to buy all the Smarties in the world and destroy them. Then I'm going to blow up the factory so they can't make any more."

The look on Gracie's face was of absolute horror as his words sank in. "No, GD, you can't. I love Smarties. That's not fair, and Daddy wouldn't let you, anyway."

"Huh, Daddy would be right there with me on this one, and you know it. Besides, there will still be M&M's. They're the same damn thing."

"Are not!"

"Are too!"

"Are not!"

"Are too!"

"Are not—infinity!" Gracie squealed, her proclamations getting louder at each declaration.

Before Bruce could respond, Sam stopped him with a raised hand.

"Enough, this could go on all day, and I'm sure we don't have time for it."

Sulking, Gracie curled into Bruce's chest with a muffled, "Daddy would to stop you!"

Smiling, Bruce kissed her forehead before stirring the mustard one final time. "Believe what you want, kiddo."

Pounding feet caused everyone to look up as Cooper flew down the stairs with Parker following behind and an exuberant Viper by his side, trying to get to her brother and sister.

Bruce switched Gracie fully to his left side in time for Cooper to slam into his right side, wrapping his arms around both him and Gracie as he held on tightly.

"It's okay, baby boy, I got you."

The scene mesmerized all until an expletive broke the air.

"Fuck!"

"Parker Michael Michaels, watch your language," Claire groused as Parker stood stock-still, staring at Bruce.

"Um, ma, Uncle Parker swored."

Bruce smirked at Parker.

"Worked it out, did you? I wondered how long it'd take you."

"I don't suppose you're responsible for Mary freezing me out, too?" Parker queried. "One minute she was running hot and the next I'm getting the cold shoulder."

"She was a bitch. Besides, you shouldn't trust a girl named after the virgin mother. She's never gonna live up to her parents' expectations, so is more likely to go completely the other way."

"Are you shitting me right now? I shouldn't trust girls named Mary?! No wonder you and Lachie get along so well, but that's beside the point. She was my mistake to make! You can't cock block me all the time."

Laughing, Sam relaxed as Jonah finally put his gun away. Parker was too far gone to notice his mother's arms folded over her chest, a stern frown upon her face. The boy was digging a nice big hole and none of them were above sitting back and watching the show unfold.

"I ain't cock blocking you. Gracie girl, if you ask what that is or threaten to tell your mama, I'll destroy all the cake in the world too." At Gracie's huff, he continued. "I let you be with Jessy. She was nice. Besides, you should thank me. Mary has herpes as well. Oh, and the condoms in your left-hand-side drawer are out of date. Buy new ones."

"Oh my God, I can't believe you!"

"God ain't gonna help you now. I reckon he's scared of your mother, too."

Gauging by the look in Claire's eye, the eldest of all their twins was in for a hell of a lecture as soon as she caught him alone. Rediverting the conversation, Max interrupted.

"My name's Max."

"I know who you are. Nice to meet you, sorry it's under these circumstances." Turning toward Sam and Claire, Bruce continued. "Mr. and Mrs. Michaels, it's a pleasure to meet you both. I always wanted to meet the people responsible for Lachlan. Jonah, thanks for not shooting me. Now, I'm sure you all have questions."

Introductions and makeshift handshakes made. Still holding Gracie and Cooper, Bruce made his way to the couch.

"So, who's first?"

"Me!" Jonah growled. "Gracie obviously knows you, but why is Cooper cuddled in your arms?"

Bruce shrugged and tightened his arms around Cooper before answering. "He knows he's safe there."

"Okay." Max intercepted Jonah's retort. "How about we start with something simple? If everyone calls you Bruce, why does Gracie call you GD?"

"Captain's responsible for that, needed to differentiate me from the rest of the team."

"Why, what makes you so fucken special? If anyone should stand out, you'd think it'd be her maternal uncle!" Jonah's question sounded more like an accusation, but he had the forethought to apologize to his mother before she or Gracie groused at him for swearing. "Sorry, Ma!"

Seemingly picking up on some of the tension in the room, Gracie hugged Bruce tighter as she looked straight at Jonah.

"He's my second Daddy!" His granddaughter looked proud, but her statement hadn't solved anything. Instead, it had confused the issue further. If the look of murderous intent in Jonah's eyes and the situation weren't so serious, Sam may have let Bruce goad his second eldest son further once he saw the effect of Gracie's words, but Sam at least knew where to draw the line as it seems did Bruce.

Holding his hand out to forestall any replies, Bruce took to explaining.

"Second Daddy and backup Daddy are just terms Lachlan and Isabella used to get her to understand my role. I'm her godfather. GD stands for God Daddy. Because, well, we had started with GF for godfather, but those two letters also substituted for another two words that Isabella got angry at us when we used them in front of Grace. The first time I saw the captain crack under pressure was when Gracie told him to 'get fucked,' when he told her it was naptime. Unfortunately, Isabella didn't find it as funny as we did and Gracie catches on quick, so any time after that when she didn't want to do something, she would say GF and then point to me if her mama tried to growl at her. So, GF quickly became GD."

Claire rolled her eyes at this. Sam had heard numerous times how thankful she was that they had two daughters to offset their seven sons, Max included. Sam couldn't help but grin. He could clearly picture the boys' laughter and a frustrated daughter-in-law. But those thoughts sobered quickly. Both their daughters and their daughter-in-law were missing and as the minutes ticked by, their fear for them grew.

As the mood changed, Sam decided it was time to find out exactly what the plan was from here and Bruce's role in it going forward.

"What brings you here, Bruce? I would assume you would want to be out there with your team. And how did you end up with PIMF?"

Parker, unable to stay away from Cooper for long, flung himself on the couch next to the threesome as the others finally moved to take a seat.

"He's obviously our babysitter. Anytime we went to visit Lachie, he would be there, but I hadn't worked out he was following our every move until Cooper admitted Lachie was responsible for Jenny backing away from me. Even then, I wasn't sure how until he arrived here with PIMF."

"Technically, I'm Cooper's bodyguard for six months while your normal team of guards have a well-deserved break, but yes, the understanding is I check on both you and Mackenzie when I'm sure Cooper is safe. It makes it a lot easier when the three of you are together. Since you know now, I wouldn't be surprised if Lachie had you all move in together until your schooling's finished."

"I don't need a babysitter."

"Huh, you more so than the others, kid. You and Lachie are both cut from the same cloth. The team and I step in to handle more of your shenanigans than Cooper and Mackenzie's combined."

"Well, maybe if you kept more of an eye on Mackenzie, she wouldn't be missing right now." It didn't take Cooper's sharp inhale or Claire's reprimand for Parker to look like he regretted his words as soon as they left his mouth.

"Boy, you ain't saying nothing I haven't thought myself. Mackenzie had PIMF and I still don't know how he got around her or why her roommates suddenly went away midterm. It's damn lucky I went to check on her when I did. Otherwise, we'd still be playing blind. Now I can't change the past, but I damn well can impact the future. I need to get things settled here so I can seek out some revenge. Ask anyone, they'll tell you I don't like to lose!"

Any would be response was cut off, the chorus of Keala Settle's brand-new song This Is Me, flooded the room. Sam was confused. The song was a favorite of Shauna's, she was looking forward to the movie's release in December but what he wasn't expecting was for the song to come from the phone of a tough special force's operative. Quick as lightning, Bruce handed Gracie over to Parker and disentangled Cooper from his other arm to answer the call.

"Go … Any news? … Good … No, stay there, we can't risk it … No, I just got here, I'll tell them as soon as I'm off the phone … Motherfucker! That slimy little worm tail, wait till I get my hands on him … Yeah, yeah, I know there won't be anything left if Lachie gets there first … Say what? Well, that changes things, doesn't it? … I hear ya … Okay, let's keep radio silence where possible but check in with me every four hours, I'll inform the team and pass on any further instructions … Nice work and find a comms set, we'll come on as backup as soon as things heat up … No, I'll leave that to Lachie, not sure how he and you are going to explain that one. Watch your six DBD."

Zac and Josh emerged as Bruce ended his call. From the way they walked in, it was obvious to all that the brats had been listening in for quite some time before deciding to make their presence known, although from the look on Bruce's face, he had known they were there all along.

"I have to make some calls, but I can tell you Shauna is safe."

With a last squeeze to Cooper's shoulder, Bruce stood and started to move toward the front door, but stopped when Claire separated from Sam to step into his path.

"Where is she? Can I see her? Is she hurt?"

"She's fine, ma'am, a little cold and shaken, but still maintaining an extremely high level of sass." Bruce paused to cackle. "We can't bring her here. We don't know who else is involved or what's connected to what. But I promise you she is now safe."

"Where is this Jarrod guy? Did you get him too?" Jonah's words tumbled over each other.

"No, and his name's not Jarrod, it's Mackenzie's old boyfriend Patrick John Murphy. He's the same guy Lachie 'encouraged' to enlist about a decade ago." Bruce used his fingers to highlight quotation marks around the word encouraged.

"His uncle Donald was helping him. We've confirmed that they're responsible for both Mackenzie and Isabella's disappearances. Unfortunately, they're now in the wind. I suggest you get an APB out and start looking for them. If you haven't connected the dots, I believe Uncle Donald is better known to you as Magee. Donald Liam Magee." Bruce started to walk again before abruptly stopping. "Shit, one more thing. Don't let our little miss out of sight. She's a target. He's threatened to come in and gun everyone down, but she's the target."

Accepting nods of acknowledgement from them, Bruce left the house to make his calls outside, in private.

Inside, a mixture of relief and shock had the inhabitants scrambling in different directions. Max ran up the stairs to get his and Jonah's guns from the safe. Jonah headed for the oversized closet to get their jackets, while calling the Feds to update them on the situation.

Sam watched his wife head toward the kitchen and decided to join his boys on their jumbo L shaped couch, not surprised when the youngest twins joined them, PIMF and Viper also flopping at their feet. Although Sam had to smother a smile when Racer followed Jonah into the closet. If things weren't so serious, Sam would have made a joke that it was too late for Jonah to go back into the closet. He was sure Lachlan or Parker would have had a field day with that one.

Twenty minutes later, Jonah and Max were long gone when Sam stepped out onto his porch to speak with Bruce, attracting his attention. Sam felt conflicted, part of him had wanted to cut his leave short and head out with Max and Jonah. But that would leave his family vulnerable, and he knew for now, he was of better use here than tearing the town apart.

"Everything okay, Mr. Michaels?"

"Yeah, all good. Claire herded them all into the kitchen to make sure they eat breakfast." At Bruce's nod, Sam continued.

"When do you leave to join them?"

"Them?" Bruce questioned.

"Please, you can't expect me to believe Lachlan is out there by himself and you are so clearly champing at the bit to get moving."

"I ain't confirming whether Lachlan is alone or not, but I will ask you not to repeat your suspicions to anyone else. Besides, now we know Gracie is a target. I won't be going anywhere. Hope you don't mind me sleeping on the floor."

Sam nodded. He had no intention of causing any problems for his son and the men with him. "We have a few spare beds for you to choose from. Now you spoke with Lachlan. Any news?"

"The cabin we think acted as Isabella's prison has been located. She had already escaped. Thanks to Shauna, we now know Mackenzie has escaped too. There's no sign of her yet, but we're hoping they're together like the kidnappers believe. Lachlan was *real* happy to hear Shauna was safe, although I had to tell him she was missing first. Seems we kept that piece of info from him."

"Happy, huh? I would have thought he would have been more than pissed once he found out who was behind it. In fact, if I had to lay money on it, I would have bet on him hitting a tree."

Sam noted Bruce was grinning when he answered. "Nope, no tree hitting, so happy he fell to the ground to commune with nature. Now, Mr. Michaels, do you mind keeping a close eye on the family while I do a quick perimeter check?"

"I can do that. Oh, and Bruce? Call me Sam. I want to thank you for watching my kids and for somehow stopping Lachlan from hitting a tree." With a smirk answered in return by another smirk, Sam went back inside while Bruce made his way around the perimeter.

SEVENTEEN

"Get the fuck off me!" Lachlan growled.

"Blame Nate!" Deeks hedged, the heavy bastard rolled off him and scrambled to his feet. The man hustled back out of striking range, albeit too slowly, Lachlan was quick to swipe his right foot out and take Deeks legs out from under him. Asshole.

Jumping to his feet, Lachlan focused on Nate, knowing full well he would have been behind the ambush. Hands out in front of him, Nate also backed away. "You should thank me. If I didn't tell Deeks to jump on you, you would have hit the tree and broken your knuckles again."

Nate was just lucky his phone rang again, saving him from Lachlan's response. Asshole. This time it was the Feds. Lachlan listened in silence, occasionally grunting in acknowledgement, before he ended the call and stalked off, leaving the boys to follow. "I'll deal with Bruce later." He knew the bastard had sent Nate a warning that Lachlan would not like all he would report. While he wouldn't divert lines of communication from the correct hierarchy, he would have happily sent a quick text to Nate first and knowing Bruce one word would have covered it—Incoming!

"So, are you gonna share or just sulk like a little kid that you haven't got a broken hand right this minute?"

"Next time, how 'bout I aim for your face instead of the tree?"

"Probably a lot fairer fight," Nate conceded. "The tree did nothing to deserve your wrath."

Because Lachlan was thankful he wasn't nursing a broken hand, not that he would admit it to the team, he decided to be magnanimous and drop the subject.

"Moving on. Two of the people behind Izzy and Mac's abductions have been identified and it's personal. We're ruling out your serial killer. It looks like it was coincidental timing."

"How sure are we it's not connected?" Taniq asked.

"About ninety percent. The Feds are leaving you two with me. They're still on the other side of the mountains but with no luck so far, they're steadily working their way over to us. At least this way we're boxing everyone in. From what we can surmise, besides Izzy and Mac, we're looking for a third woman. It's believed that they're two very different cases, but the Feds are adamant she's somewhere on these ranges. Apparently, she disappeared around the same time. Unfortunately, it took a few days before authorities got the notification that she was missing."

"Shit! Wait. How'd they identify the perps and who are they?" Nate demanded.

"DBD found Shauna. The perp thought she was going to die and gloated about who he was and what he was planning to do."

"Shauna's safe, and you couldn't lead with that?" Nate exploded.

"Must have slipped my mind when I hit my head on the ground," Lachie groused.

"Asshole!"

"Whatever, gump, maybe you'll think twice about holding back vital information from me, like my baby sister being missing. Anyway, the mastermind behind this is one of Mackenzie's old boyfriends. He was seven years older than her and I, ah, 'encouraged' to join the marines."

"Shit, I feel like we should ask you to define 'encouraged'…" Deeks rolled his eyes. "And what's the problem with seven years' age difference? That's nothing nowadays?"

"She was eleven, asshole, and he wanted a piece of her. I knew he would have done something to her if he had the chance."

"I take it you never gave him the chance." Nate formed it as a statement, not a question. Lachlan had only ever given the full specifics to Isabella and DBD but now that Bruce knew, Lachlan figured it wouldn't be long before his family found out, that's if Cooper hadn't already spilled what he knew. Shit, he'd worry about that later.

"Correct. I had a contact who hooked me up with some high-grade military trackers. All I had to do was attach one to Patrick's car and one to Mac's bike so I could turn up anytime they were together and spoil his party. In fairness, the town's small, and she was eleven. It was only outside of school hours during the day that I had to worry about her, and I had plenty of people willing to help me keep track of her."

"You got your hands-on high-quality trackers at what, seventeen, eighteen?" Taniq was already shaking his head. Lachlan shrugged.

"I needed him handled before I left, and my recruiter had incentive to make me happy. Different organizations had been following my progress from the moment I became a member of Mensa. The military weren't the only ones who had approached me. He knew I wasn't leaving if Mackenzie was still anywhere near that dickwad, and I had plenty of other offers that didn't take me so far from home as quickly."

"Okay, so I'm guessing he came back wanting revenge and took Mac, Shauna, and Isabella to get back at you. Who is his partner in this and are we sure it's just the two of them? It seems like it would take a lot of coordination to take three women from three separate locations around the same time," Nate surmised.

"He pretended to be interested in Shauna. We knew she was

seeing an older guy, but we thought the twins had scared him off. I didn't follow up and I'll have to live with that."

"Brother, you couldn't have known. I'm guessing Shauna was too young to remember him?"

"Yeah. Don't change how I feel. Besides, he changed his name, his appearance some, and had a residence separate from his uncle's house, so no one made the connection. His damn uncle helped him. The asshole runs the store in town—name's Magee. From here on out, anyone scared of Mannix will get a second look, no matter how long I've known the mofo. And once I get my hands on him, he won't have cause to worry about Mannix no more."

"Noted, he's all yours. Now, are we just walking around on hope here or are you following something, because this feels erratic? Wait, are those footprints?" Taniq pointed a few feet ahead where the earth had been disturbed.

"Shit, see this?" Lachlan closed the distance quickly and squatted low, but it wasn't the boot prints that had captured his attention. "That's a curve of a shoe and a tiny bit of tread but the rest of the print has been deliberately brushed away, likely by a branch. The indentations are heavier here, there's grooves scratched into the dirt so you can see it's not natural. This is where he found her trail. All these boot prints are his, knowing what we know now, I would say these are Magee's tracks."

"Can you tell how far behind we are, then?" Taniq looked ready to hit some action. Even though he was the team sniper, the man never stayed still for long if he didn't have too.

"Well, I'd say these tracks are about eighteen hours old, but we aren't as far behind because we aren't trying to hide our trail and we know which direction they're heading. Now let's pray by some miracle she's got Mac. If you think I'm handling her kidnapping badly, you should see Bruce."

"He interested in Mac in that way?" Nate asked, clearly shocked and just a tad defensively.

"Nah…" Lachlan smirked, enjoying the little dig at Nate as they changed tactics and started heading straight up the mountain, faster than what they'd previously been travelling. He knew Nate was interested in Mac but had yet to act on it, or even admit it. The man just sucked at hiding stuff.

"But it happened on his watch. So, he's furious. His focus might be on Cooper, but he keeps an eye on Mackenzie and Parker too. If he gets to the perps behind this before I do, there won't be much left of them for me. Besides, if he ever gets his head out of his ass, he might work out he's already half in love with Cooper."

"Cooper? Huh." Tilting his head to the side in thought, Nate finally nodded. "Okay, I can see that."

Lachlan took that as subject closed when Nate continued to another topic.

"Is Bruce joining us soon, then?"

"That was the plan, but Shauna told DBD that their end game is targeted at Gracie. And Cooper was there when I 'encouraged' the asshole to join the marines, which makes him a target, too. The jerk told Shauna the house was under watch and if she went back, they'd go in and shoot everyone there. The Feds are checking to see if they can see anyone lurking around, and DBD is gonna keep Shauna away from there, so they think she froze to death. Bruce wants to be with us, but even he admits he's best staying where he is. We should pray for DBD right now. That man is gonna need patience he hasn't needed in years to deal with my youngest sister."

Before anyone could make a smartass comment, Mannix scratched a tree up ahead of them and sat next to it. "Good boy, Mannix, good boy." Lachlan praised the pup, his eyes darting up to start his search. Within moments, for the first time in days, a genuine smile broke free. By continuing straight up the mountain, they were saving time, intercepting the zigzagging path of the people they tracked, counting on the knowledge that even under force, Isabella wouldn't lie in a coded message.

"They're together, Isabella has Mackenzie. Thank Mary, they're both alive. Now we need to catch up. Let's let her know we're coming."

"Hold it. Lachie, we're *real* happy they're together and alive and all that, but do you want to tell us exactly how you know that?" Deeks asked, sounding frustrated that he didn't see what Lachlan was seeing.

Lachlan helpfully waved his hand toward the other side of the tree. "The trail ends here and starts again over there. Probably climbed the tree to try to scout the area better. Dad trained all us kids in these woods and taught us to leave little signs behind like a trail. Even if someone is tracking them, unless they are exceptionally skilled trackers, they'd be unlikely to find them. Let alone know what they meant. Both the girls left signs. Look there at the second branch. Between the first two leaves, there are two markings. That's them letting me know they're together."

"Okay, I see two scratches, but how can you know Mackenzie left one of them?" Taniq asked this time, but Nate had started laughing before Lachlan could answer.

"You're a control freak, you know that, right?" Looking at Deeks and Taniq, Nate explained. "As soon as he could, Lachlan had me learning the trails. How to track and when to seek higher ground if in trouble, or to minimize your trail if someone was following you. He taught me to scratch in a certain mark on the second lowest branch of an oak, sycamore or maple tree between the first two leaves or off-branches, dependent on the tree, but my mark is different to those two marks, so I can only assume Lachlan here has assigned everyone a different mark so he can determine who he's following."

Lachlan shrugged. He wasn't apologizing, considering it had just proven helpful. It's not like every tree was climbable. If he only had to look out for three types of trees and ones with branches low enough to grab, well, it made his life easier. He could now get word home that Mac was with Isabella.

Fingers to his lips, Lachlan, along with Nate, Deeks, and Taniq let loose with their trademark signal, hoping the girls would answer with the calls he had taught them.

Prayers sometimes were answered and within seconds a red-tailed hawk sounded, followed closely by a great horned owl. One by one, the boys sounded off again in response and to let them know how many were coming for them. Then Lachlan cupped his mouth to project two loud calls of a crow, the caws should let them know he believed there were two perps on their tail ahead of them. Acknowledged, they continued their way up. Nate put a quick call through to Bruce to update both him and the family on the news and to tell him and DBD to plug in.

The girls took the opportunity for a quick hug and hid behind some shrubs to regroup. Isabella had felt a tug of hope at the first bald eagle call which turned to joy as the calls continued. Four of the team, including Lachie and Nate, were on their way to them. They had thought someone might be behind them, but now they knew both their kidnappers stood between them and the boys. It was a relief to know all their cautiousness had been worthwhile. Now was not the time to drop their guard.

They'd sent a clear message. Should they run into anyone who wasn't part of the team, treat them as the enemy. The temptation was to stay put or change direction and try to find them. But there was no way of knowing exactly where the boys were intercepting the trail and if they backtracked, they might miss them completely or land right into the hands of those who hunted them.

"Lachie's gonna kill me," Mackenzie hedged as she took the water bottle from Isabella.

"Why do you say that?"

"I knew my kidnapper. He was my boyfriend when I was eleven. Rumor was Lachlan scared him off. Made him join the marines, but I didn't believe that. All I knew was that he'd left me." Mackenzie scoffed and shook her head.

"Even at eleven, I should have known better. Anyway, we bumped into each other at a mall a few months ago and started dating. It was new but we'd often laugh over how Lachlan couldn't have an issue with our age difference now that I was in college. Every time he came over, he asked me to put PIMF in the bathroom. Said, he feared dogs after receiving a bite from one when he was a child. What's the saying, 'Hindsight is twenty-twenty?'" Mac paused so Isabella nodded to encourage her to continue. Her husband was going to lose his shit when he found out who was behind this. Lachlan had indeed told Isabella all about Patrick Murphy and it didn't matter how old Mackenzie now was, he wouldn't want her anywhere near the man. He hated Patrick.

"So, the other night I said how since we were getting serious, I'd have to tell Lachlan the next time we talked. I figured he'd get a kick out of it, especially considering all the rumors. Next thing I knew, my cheek exploded in pain. He'd hit me. Before I fully understood what was happening, he'd grabbed my hair and yanked me up, so I was staring at him. The look on his face was terrifying. 'That won't be happening, darling. I got plans for him and giving him a heads-up ain't part of it.'" Isabella pulled Mackenzie into another hug, but this time didn't let go. Small shivers were vibrating through the young woman, and Isabella knew it had nothing to do with the cold.

"When I woke, I was in that dungeon. He came in spewing vile words that didn't make sense and forced himself on me. It was confusing. I mean, we were seeing each other, we'd had consensual, even loving sex before, but this was so different. Violent. Cruel. I could see the hate in his eyes as he took me." Isabella leaned out of the embrace as Mackenzie paused. The girl was staring off, tears running a steady trail down her cheeks. With no tissues handy, Isabella gently cupped Mackenzie's face and wiped the tears with her gloved thumbs.

"It's going to be okay, Mackenzie. We're going to get away from here. Lachlan will find us." What Isabella didn't say was that there'd likely be a trail of dead bodies behind him. Anyone getting in his way wouldn't survive this. Patrick was a dead man; he just didn't know it yet. Although, it appeared Mac knew her brother well and hadn't needed the words to be spoken out loud.

At Mackenzie's scoff, Isabella tucked her back into her side so she could continue. The scrubs they were hiding behind were full and bushy, but they still needed to be careful not to move too much or talk too loudly and give away their position.

"Yeah, that scares me too. I don't want Lachlan to go to jail for killing someone because of me."

"Mackenzie, I can promise you that even if he wanted too, Lachlan wouldn't kill someone in cold blood. If Patrick surrendered, Lachlan would hand him over to the authorities. I mean he wouldn't like it, but he'd do it." Isabella didn't believe this Patrick guy would be the type to surrender but she decided not to mention that.

"What happened next?"

"Everything was kind of foggy. My thoughts shifted from blurry to sharp and back again. It was like I'd lost time. Looking back, I guess I was in shock. He'd come and go but there'd be hours in between, the waiting was worse. The first few times, I tried to tell myself it wasn't rape, but then I couldn't justify it anymore. He'd taken me from my home, away from my friends and family, even my dog. Chained to a wall, he beat and raped me at his will. The fogginess grew stronger and stayed longer as the days went by." Mackenzie turned to look Isabella straight in the eyes.

"It was eating me, swallowing me whole. I was losing myself. Then a conversation I'd had with Lachlan a couple of months ago floated through my mind. It was like he was there encouraging me to fight, like he'd already been through something like this and survived. Shit!" Mackensie's mouth dropped open before she continued in a panicked rush. "I mean, not that Lachlan has ever been raped, I'm just saying that discussion helped me."

Isabella gave Mackenzie a weak smile. She'd never betray her husband, but Mackenzie would likely never know how wrong her words were.

"It's okay, I understand what you're saying. Go on."

"Well, I decided I wasn't going to let him win. He might kill me, but I wasn't going to give up. Everything became about survival.

He bragged that he was going to break me, use me up before slicing my neck open and sending me back to Lachlan in pieces. I still didn't understand why this was happening, what it had to do with Lachlan. Until he started ranting about how Lachlan had run him out of town all those years ago."

Mackenzie shuddered and looked away from Isabella, before scoffing.

"Patrick laughed; he told me Lachlan had been right to send him away. The plan had always been to rape and kill me. Lachlan had bought me nine more years, but it was now going to cost him in interest. Then he was crowing about another young girl he had started seeing. Shauna."

"Fuck." Isabella whispered as Mackenzie turned and nodded.

"Yeah, the bastard had gotten his hands on my baby sister, and it was all my fault. He knocked me out and the next time I woke, there was this stocky little guy in my room wearing a balaclava. The man didn't speak, but his eyes looked familiar. For ages, he stared before finally he said, 'Payback's a bitch, princess!' and then he knocked me out." Rubbing a hand over her face, a small chuckle escaped Mackenzie.

"You know what the funny thing is? Even though the guy admitted to planning to rape and murder me when I was eleven, I was still kind of mad at Lachlan for interfering. Until he said he had Shauna and then I realized I would do anything to protect her, even if it meant she wouldn't talk to me again for the rest of my life. Messed up much, huh?"

Isabella smiled and tightened her hold for a moment before answering.

"Lachlan is a unique man. It's what makes him so special. I know all about Patrick. He told me what had happened. In fact, Patrick wasn't the only one he ran out of town. Your brother made quite some spending money before he left for the navy. The menace had a cash deal going with the recruiter. Managed to up the ante from three hundred dollars a pop to five hundred by the end of his reign." It was Isabella's turn to laugh.

"I doubt anyone knows how many people he 'encouraged' or 'helped' join the service, as he likes to put it. He admitted the number to me was eight, but who can be sure? I think if he thought the person wanted to join, he didn't count them in the equation. Anyway, only three caused him any worry and they were the ones connected to both you and Max. Lachlan knew he did the right thing in his heart, but he's petrified you and Max won't forgive him if you ever found out what he did."

"Max? Oh, I bet I know—his father? Wow, no, don't answer that, it's gotta be. Wow, okay. Hmmm, you know what? I'm all for that. I was still young, but even I saw how much happier Max was after he left. No one suspected Lachlan had anything to do with it. Who were the others?"

"Not for me to name," Isabella snickered. "You'll have to ask Lachlan when you see him."

"Oh, I will. After I hit him for keeping you a secret."

Isabella's smile dropped.

"We had our reasons. It wasn't our intention to hurt anyone, but we had a lot to deal with and we needed to do that before we tried to explain everything to everyone else. At different points, neither of us could adequately articulate how we were feeling. It was easier with the team because they lived with us. They were there when everything happened, so they had the knowledge without having to hear the actual words."

Mackenzie nodded. "I can understand that, but there's no going back. You now have more family than you could have ever asked for."

"Ha. You have no idea what's coming, that goes both ways. Besides, we've met Cooper and Parker. Lachlan can't seem to stay away from them for too long, since they are living out of town."

"Yeah, he always blamed himself for what happened to Cooper. Between our parents, Lachlan, Jonah and Parker, there's a lot of unwarranted guilt. None of them were at fault. It's doesn't surprise me that he kept a close eye on them, and I can understand Cooper keeping the secret, but Parker not so much."

"Yeah, well. I don't know *what* he has on Parker, but let's just say there was a certain amount of blackmail involved."

"No doubt. So that behemoth that was always around when Lachlan visited, is it safe to say he was keeping an eye on me, as well as the boys?"

Suddenly, more interested in the woods surrounding them, Isabella's cheeks reddened as Mackenzie let loose with a laugh.

"It's okay, I had figured as much. One too many boys disappearing from my life then turning up, having hurt another girl somewhere else. Once it happened to Parker, the next time we met up with Lachlan and that behemoth, I worked it out. Considering what it had saved Parker from, and myself, to some extent—although *that* Jenny was a real piece of work—I figured I could live with it. And it was nice knowing he still watched out for us, even if he couldn't be there to do it himself."

"Yeah, well, I ain't confirming anything, except to say your brother loves all his siblings beyond anything else in his life. Although your baby brothers can yank his chain more than he likes to admit."

"Huh, that's good to know. They're terrified of him. Might be good payback to let that slip to them, so I can sit back and watch the show."

"Do so at your own peril. Lachlan hates to lose. The man has revenge down to a fine art. Besides, if Bruce has been keeping an eye on you, he has most definitely been reporting *everything* back to his captain."

This time it was Mackenzie's turn to turn bright red. "Well, um, maybe it's good for the twins to have at least one person to pull them into line. Should we go now, or do you want to stay here?"

"Both actually." Isabella chuckled. "I want to stay, but we should go, so let me scout some more before we move out."

With care, Isabella left their hiding place and started to climb the closest suitable tree, stopping occasionally to listen for any sign of one or both perps behind them. Seeing nothing out of the ordinary, Isabella descended again, and the girls continued their journey.

Not long after, the girls froze as singsong words rang out through the forest.

"Come out, come out wherever you are! I know you're out here. You can't hide forever. Ain't no one out here to save you. It's only a matter of time. Hand yourselves over to me and I'll take it easy on you."

Frozen to the spot, the girls tried to determine where the voice was coming from, conscious that only one was speaking, yet the boys had warned of two.

Certain they were clear for at least a few minutes, Isabella gestured for Mackenzie to climb a mature maple while she hid their duffel. As soon as Mac was out of sight, she followed.

The girls weren't the only ones to hear the singsong voice. Knowing they were close to both parties ensured the adrenalin spiked. With a nod of Lachlan's head and some quick sign language, Mannix took off straight after the voice, with Lachlan and Taniq on his tail. Screw being stealthy now, they had their target in their sight. Nate and Deeks separated twenty feet to the left and right respectively to circle around quietly as their backup, knowing the boys' noise would help cover them as they joined the assent.

EIGHTEEN

Back in town, DBD prayed for patience. The youngest Michael's woman was driving him crazy as she circled around him, intent on asking question after question. Hiding out in the house they'd just completed the build on was a no brainer. It was safer than Fort Knox. Although Lachlan technically owned both the house and land, this was to be their home as well as their base of operations. The house was massive, so they all had their own space even though they seldom sought privacy from each other. They were a family, a close one at that. DBD hadn't been completely sold on relocating to Forest Haven but then again, he'd been unanimously out voted.

Shauna had already searched every room she could access. Pouting at any she found locked. Unfortunately for her, pouting didn't work on him. She wasn't dumb though; Lachlan's kid sister had quickly worked out that Lachlan wasn't planning to live here just with his wife and Gracie. But that just led to more incessant questions. Luckily, she had yet to find the hidden doors or the lifts that led to the sublevels, although that was probably because she didn't know to look for them.

With a shake of his head, DBD made his four-hourly contact

with Bruce, not only to check in but also to plead for some help. Pride be damned.

A sudden burst of laughter drew both Sam and Claire from the kitchen. Seeing them, Bruce dropped the phone to his chest directing his attention to Claire. "Ma'am, would you be kind enough to assist us with a problem? It seems our man who is keeping Shauna safe is at his wits' end. Would you mind talking to her to reassure and help calm her a bit?"

Claire was rushing forward before Bruce had even finished the sentence. Although Sam wasn't far behind, he wanted to hear his daughter's voice too.

"DBD, put Shauna on, I'm handing over to Claire now."

"Mama?" Sam easily made out the words with Claire holding the phone flat up to both of their ears.

"Oh baby, you're safe." At Claire's sniffle, Sam maneuvered them so he could hold his wife to his chest and still both hear their youngest daughter.

"Mama, I'm so sorry I snuck out."

"It's okay, sweetheart, as long as you are safe now, although I think your father may have a few words to say to you when you get back home."

"Yay, I can't wait." Shauna sniffed, unable to keep the sass out of the conversation for long.

"I heard that, missy!" Sam spoke into the phone.

"Sorry, Daddy."

"I'm sure you are. Now stop giving that man such a tough time. He's there to help you."

"Okay. It's just, he looks so familiar, but I know I don't know him."

"Well, I can't help you with that right now, but Lachlan vouches for him and wanted me to pass on a message to you. 'Bears don't make good bees.'"

"Seriously, he's lecturing me now?"

"Well, I guess we don't have to ask if you know what that means," Sam sighed. Lachlan could confuse the smartest people with the easiest of concepts.

"He's saying, if a bear strikes out it'll be worse than a bee sting even if it still results in his death. This one mustn't have been tamed yet."

"Finally, she gets it," a soft growl Sam assumed was DBD echoed through the phone.

Ignoring the man in the background, Sam tuned back into his daughter's next words.

"Daddy, any news on Mac or Lachie's wife?"

"Yes, Lachlan sent a message through a few minutes ago. They believe they've picked up their trail. The girls are together, but one or two of the perps are close behind. Unfortunately, it's still unknown how many people are involved though. So you'll have to stay hidden with DBD. I mean it, Shauna, do not leave that man's side unless instructed to by someone on Lachie's team or one of your older brothers. Do you hear me, young lady?"

"Yes, Daddy, I promise to stay with Mr. Grumpy until told otherwise." At Sam's huff, Shauna continued. "Daddy?"

"Yes, baby girl?"

"I love you and Mama."

"We know, we love you too, sweetheart. Follow DBD's instructions and come back to us safely, please."

"Will do, Daddy."

Ending the call, his wife passed back the phone to a laughing Bruce. "You know you got the easy assignment, don't you?"

"Yes, ma'am, but some people would call it karma."

"You think DBD deserves some karma, son?" Sam was somewhat weary of what Bruce's answer would be, but he wouldn't be putting his head in the sand when it came to learning about the man currently alone with his youngest daughter. Something was afoot here, and he didn't like it one little bit.

"I'd say, most would say so, sir. I reckon even he is still trying to atone some."

Sam eyed Bruce. That sounded like a lot of round speak to him. "Shauna said he looked familiar, but that she had never met him before."

"Oh, you don't say?"

"Yeah, I do. Am I gonna recognize this man when I meet him?"

"Not for me to say, sir."

"How 'bout an easy one, then? What does DBD stand for?"

"I don't reckon that's my place either, sir."

"Whose place is it then, considering this man has my daughter?"

"I reckon it's Lachie's place, or even DBD's, but not mine. I can tell you, Lachie ain't gonna put Shauna in danger or keep her somewhere she ain't safe neither. He trusts DBD with his life. We all do. DBD once saw Lachlan diving for a grenade he had no chance of getting to. His death was imminent, but instead, DBD launched himself at it. He somehow caught it and flung it back, before it went off. Many good people died that day, many more lived because of both of their actions but Lachlan only survived because of DBD. So, I reckon that's all a man needs to know, but it's also something to think about later if emotions come to a head."

"Noted," Sam responded. He didn't like the sound of that at all, but the one person he did trust with his daughter's life was his oldest son. "Now, I reckon the house is way too quiet when you consider a precocious three-year-old and thirteen-year-old twins are running loose with two huskies. Best we check on them."

Heading toward the stairs, both started into a full run as a loud squeal sounded from above.

Gun drawn, Bruce slammed through the door first, Sam was only a couple of steps behind, but both stopped short at the sight of the youngest twins' hands-on hips with their backs to the door facing off against Gracie. The two huskies in front of her acting as her protector even though both had their tongues out, wagging their tails.

Bruce put his gun away as Sam stepped in front and asked the all-important question.

"What in sweet heaven is going on here exactly?"

"She's cheating!" Zac exclaimed.

"Am not!" Gracie called back.

"Are too!" Josh claimed.

"Nut ah, I ain't. You're just sore losers!"

"Would one of you explain what is going on here for the late-comers to class?"

"We're playing tag, but when we try to tag her, the dogs stop us from getting to her. Which is cheating."

"Nut ah, Daddy says it's not cheating if you're smarter than the enemy."

Laughing, Sam took a step to the side so Bruce could reach over and grab the munchkin. The dogs gave Bruce a slobbery tongue bath, but the man was still successful in his task, and averted World War III from starting before their eyes.

"Come on you, I'm not sure that's what Daddy meant, but I reckon it's time for a nap, anyway."

"GF, I don't want no nap." Gracie pushed against Bruce's chest, trying to dislodge herself from his grip.

"Excuse me, young lady, what did you just say to me? You and I are obviously in need of a discussion. Say goodnight to Grandpa."

"Grandpa, save me."

"Sorry, sweet pea, this here is between you and your GD, and I doubt pouting will help you. And as for you two!"

"What did we do?" Zac asked.

"I thought you were better than that? How could you possibly lose a game of tag, two against one and against a three-year-old to boot?"

Laughing at his own hilarity, Sam walked out of the room to the sound of his protesting sons behind him, passing by his grand-daughter's room where she was trying to convince Bruce that she had said GD and not GF.

Although funny, Sam didn't think suggesting Bruce needed to

get his hearing checked was her best response. The little minx. No one would ever dispute that she was Lachlan's child.

Ten minutes later, Bruce exited the room, leaving PIMF sleeping on the end of Gracie's bed, and headed into the lounge.

"She asleep?"

"Yep, the little brat. Forgot who she was dealing with, that's all. We're clear now."

"I bet," Sam's smile looked somewhat devious.

"What?"

"I know some of the others might wonder why Lachlan made you her godfather instead of Nate, or even Jonah, but I reckon it's real clear to me."

"Mind letting me in on the secret because I have no idea why he didn't choose one. Hell, any of the others over me?"

"Most people would have laughed at her antics, and she would still be in there, tormenting the twins. You're a lot like him, able to laugh at what's funny, will protect others with your life, but know when to draw the line and call her out on her behavior. He loves his daughter, but he wouldn't want her to turn into a spoiled brat. You are a little surly and perfect for the role. Plus, I reckon he's got you pegged to look after Cooper for the rest of your life."

"Thanks, sir, but I reckon you ought to know he pays me and a few guys to keep watch over Cooper and the others when I'm not there."

"Oh, son, I have no doubt about that. I also know and so would he, that you would do it for free."

With a smug smirk, Sam walked away, leaving Bruce momentarily speechless.

Initially, she'd thought hunger would be better than the alternative, but reality was not idealistic. November was starving, her body weak from lack of nutrition, water the only thing keeping her alive.

The chain around her foot clanged against the floor from the effort it took to drag herself closer to the sink. She wasn't a criminal, she'd never hung with the 'wrong' crowd, and she'd certainly never had any training on how to pick locks, but by this stage, what did she have to lose by trying?

Reciting a line from her favorite movie, *Shawshank Redemption*, "Better get started living or get started dying," November used all her strength, leveraging the basin to pull herself into a standing position.

Staring at herself in the mirror, she barely recognized the woman who gazed back. Multi-colored bruises and several small cuts decorated her face, her skin pale from the lack of sunlight and drawn from the sudden weight loss. "Best diet ever," she thought to herself. The irony that she might 'die-for-it' made her laugh out loud. Shit, she was losing it.

Who knew what was keeping him away, but if she wanted to escape, this would be her best chance. She was thankful the chain only sat around her ankle and was no longer attached to her neck. A concession made once she struggled to lift her head due to the weight, taking her too long to get into the position he wanted.

It was October who had told her of that trick. "Look weak," she'd said. "Struggle to move as if your head is holding you back, but only once enough time has gone by to make it plausible. He'll beat you for it, but he'll think you're too weak to fight back and he'll move the chain from around your neck to your ankle. Once you're in your last week, he'll remove the chains altogether, knowing there is no chance you'll have any strength left at all."

Potentially lifesaving instructions, handed down month by month. The women consistently using the latter part of day three after the beatings had begun, as a guide which made the pattern something in which he could trust. By the time each woman was passing on the information to the next, they had sadly lost hope for their own lives. Still, they all shared a dream that one month some-where down the line, the nightmare would end. That one of them would survive.

Every woman before her who passed on as much information as they could to the next helped keep that possibility alive. In their last hours, as the clock ticked away before them, they had a duty to explain to their replacement the expectations going forward. He demanded it.

And they did, but they didn't stop there. Instead, they passed on everything they knew. If they'd done something wrong, what the punishment was. If there were triggers to avoid. Trivial things that would make consciousness a little more bearable, a little less painful. Simple things like how to get the chain moved from the neck to the ankle.

Their monster had obviously gotten lax around the girls as the months dragged into years and his reign continued unchallenged. Well, it had to stop, and since no one was there to stop her from trying. Why the hell couldn't it be her? One day, maybe it would be the month 'November' that gave him nightmares.

With a last look in the mirror, November drank some water from the tap and tried to work out what she could use to pick the lock. Surely time would work on her side in this endeavor and, worst case? Well, she could always break the mirror and hack off her ankle. She might die, but at least it would be on her terms and not his. Seven years of bad luck didn't translate over to the afterlife, did it?

Sharp pain tore through his flesh seconds before Mannix knocked him to the ground. Several loud retorts of a rifle rang out, the sounds of bullets hitting trees and whizzing past filled the air. Refusing to get off Lachlan, Mannix growled softly at the unknown threat coming from the right of his position.

Lachlan stayed still, trying to search out the shooter through the foliage of the dense fall trees. As the seconds ticked by, Mannix finally moved off him, grabbing him by his backpack, his pup dragged him back from the edge of the small clearing. If it hadn't been for Mannix, Lachlan might be dead, having only just entered the clearing when the pup knocked him to the ground.

Taking a gamble at who his assailant was, Lachlan called out into the tree line.

"You missed, Magee. Should have waited until I got into the middle of the clearing. Dumb fuck. Are you seriously too afraid to take me on one on one? Why don't you man up? Come down here and face me." Lachlan screamed into the silence. Magee had to be up a tree; the bullets had been entering the clearing on a slight downward angle.

"No? Nothing to say? Oh, that's right, you kidnap women and threaten children, you're too much of a fucking coward to take me on like a man. You're just a low life piece of shit and I'll make sure everyone knows it." Lachlan's temper grew with every second that passed in silence. Who the hell did this asshole think he was!

"Does it make you feel strong to beat someone unable to fight back? Do you feel powerful when you rape someone weaker than you, to hold them against their will? Mackenzie and Shauna are just kids, you asshole. Shauna's not even legal. That makes you a fucking pedophile. You're a disgusting, filthy little old man. Were you planning to do that to my three-year-old, you sick fuck? You better hope you accidentally kill me because if I get my hands on you, you will wish you were dead."

Finally, taking the bait, the old man answered.

"I never raped naw one, ye da reason dare suffering. Ye want ta blame someone, blame yourself."

"Me. Pray tell Magee, what did I do to result in you and your nephew kidnapping three women? And it doesn't matter if you never raped them yourself. You're an accessory before, during, and after the fact. You're going down, Magee. There is nowhere you can run that will keep you safe from me," Lachlan called out, ignoring the telltale sound of a rifle being reloaded. Magee wouldn't get another shot at him.

"I won't have ta run. Soon ye and ye dog will be dead. Shauna is da only person dat knows I'm involved and she's dead now too. Don't worry, she went peacefully. Sorry, I can't say da same for ye wife and ye other sister. But they'll join ye soon enough. I can wait ere all day, eventually one of me shots will hit ye and even if ye did manage ta make it past me, ye won't win against him. He's gonna make ye pay."

"You think I'm afraid of pedophiles, asshole?"

"I ain't met dat little girl of ye, but I ain't naw pedophile. She was never in da plans. I only found out about da wee lass da other day."

"Looks like you don't know everything, asshole. He's keeping secrets from you. Do you seriously think a sixteen-year-old girl doesn't have a cell phone with her twenty-four seven nowadays, whether the service is reliable or not? The whole town knows you're involved, they're all hunting you, you've got nothing to return to. And by my reckoning, you help him kidnap a three-year-old baby to rape and kill. That makes you just as bad. I'll make sure it's on your gravestone, 'Here lies Magee. *Pedophile and Rapist, but otherwise impotent. A coward with a small dick but large fists.*'" Lachlan neglected to mention that Shauna was alive and that her phone had been found in Magee's house. He had no way of knowing who else was listening.

"Shut up! They'll never believe ye. Shauna's dead. Da lass froze ta death. Anything she said will be written off as mutterings of a lass not in her right mind. Naw one will believe I had anything ta do with dis. Not willingly, at least. And not dat it matters ta ye, as dead is dead, but I won't let him rape da wee wean first. Dare are some lines dat shouldn't be crossed."

"Wow. You're even more stupid than I thought. Do you honestly think you have a say in what he does? That you're in charge here? He ain't going to listen to you. At the end of this, if you're still alive, you are a liability. He'll kill you himself."

"Liar! Ye must be so scared ta tell such lies! Ye shouldn't have come alone, now you're going ta die along with ye mangy mutt. Ye should have left all well alone all dem years ago and den none of dis would be happening."

"Seriously? He was going to kill her, Magee. She was eleven! He was going to rape and kill an eleven-year-old girl. He even admitted it to Shauna! Are you such a crazy fuck that you believe it's fair game to rape and kill an eleven-year-old?"

"Fuck ye, Lachlan! Dis is all ye fault. Ye should have stayed out of it. Kids are kids. He was just a boy himself. If something had a happened back den, so be it. She wasn't important, still isn't. Just another whore, plenty more where she came from. So many more women in da world, more than men. If dare not dare for male enjoyment, what's dare purpose? Procreation? It's naw like women can only have one wee wean each. Instead ye interfered, messed with things dat didn't concern ye. All fa what? Ya little sister? She was over ten, old enough to fend for herself. Yer soft Lachlan. I don't know why people think they should respect ye. Well, ye not my problem anymore. Now ye pay da price. Ye took me nephew from me fa years and I'm gonna help him take everything from ye including all da whores in ye life yer so fond of."

"Are you fucken serious?" Lachlan couldn't believe his ears. "Ten, is old enough to be raped and killed? No fucken wonder you can't get laid! Even without being impotent. You think women are just toys for sex? Does that mean you fucked your own mother? What about your sister? Is that why she's dead and you raised Patrick? Mary, Mary, how the hell did no one know this about you?"

"Me pa took care of me mam long ago. As fa me sister, she was just another whore. Naw one missed her."

"You're a sick fuck Magee. Your accent is getting thicker by the word. You scared man? You should be, you're about to meet your maker!"

"I ain't scared of naw one. I'm not the one dying ere today. And none of ye all have a damn clue bout anything bout me."

"Oh, we know lots now, you impotent fuck."

"Enough, stop ye stalling. Why don't ye quit hiding and come on out? Yer dead, ye need ta accept dat. We wasn't far behind dem, he'll have dem by now. Ye can't save dem, ye were never meant ta, ye were only meant ta last long enough ta know ye had failed them. Maybe even see their broken and bruised bodies before breathing your last breath."

"Wow, you are an absolute fucken clueless moron! You know what? I reckon I've got all I need from you. Your right, time is a-wasting. Bye Magee! Can't say it was nice knowing you, mother-fucker. Enjoy your time in hell."

"What da feck are ye talking about? Ye delusional or something?"

"Nah, maybe a tad forgetful. I forgot to point out you were wrong about something!"

"Oh, and what's dat exactly?"

"I didn't come alone asshole …"

There was a moment of silence before a single gunshot rang out and Lachlan watched as Magee fell from the treetops above to his right.

Seconds later, Taniq emerged from the tree line and approached Magee's body. After checking for a pulse, Taniq confirmed the kill.

The best thing about being in the military and FBI were the toys they got to play with. All six of the team had their earpieces in, so when shots rang out, plans were made on the fly. It didn't take long to determine Magee was on his own, his aim likely to stall Lachlan if he couldn't kill him.

At the first shot, Taniq, who had been only a few paces behind Lachlan, dropped to his belly, and elbow crawled behind denser bushes, ensuring he stayed out of view. Having taken note of the direction Lachlan was yelling, Taniq was able to backtrack around to the right to come up behind Magee, who was kind enough to assist in giving away his position by engaging Lachlan in the conversation.

Once Magee confirmed he was alone and that his nephew was

closing in on the girls, Nate and Deeks surged ahead, knowing the boys would have this situation under control. This was the closest they'd come to the girls. They wouldn't lose them now.

The open comms meant the boys all heard the conversation between Lachlan and Magee, even though they weren't in hearing distance when it happened.

"Lachlan, where were you shot? How bad is it?" Nate whispered words filtered over the comms.

"I never said I was shot."

"You didn't have to, asshole. Mannix knocked you on your ass and dragged you back out of the clearing. He would only have done that if you had taken a bullet. Stop stalling and give me a fucking sit-rep."

"Chill lax, man, it's just a scratch."

Lachlan noted the swearing coming from both Deeks and Nate before Nate turned his focus elsewhere. "Taniq, check out the stupid mofo and let us know how bad he is, pronto."

"Already on it, Nate. Lot of blood for a scratch, though." At Lachlan's growl, Taniq held his hands up in a surrender position. "Just saying, Captain! How about you let me look at it if it's such a tiny little scratch?"

Between Mannix hovering over him and the determination on Taniq's face, Lachlan knew he was not going anywhere without showing him the wound. Lachlan could argue, but that would waste too much time and create more distance between them and the rest of the team. With a put-upon sigh, Lachlan moved his hand from where it was covering his arm, allowing Taniq to check him out.

"Was a lucky shot. Bastard was shooting blind hoping to hit something."

"Yeah, well, he did, so that worked great for him. Now, stop grumbling and let Taniq patch your wound so you can catch us." Nate didn't stop there, he just had to add, "Besides, Izzy will be pissed when I tell her you got shot again and refused treatment."

"Asshole!" Lachlan geared up to say more, but a sharp pain

when Taniq started pressing on his arm distracted him. "What the fuck, man?"

"Well, stop moving and it won't hurt as much." Comms went glaringly silent for a few minutes before Taniq directed his next words to Nate and Deeks. "Looks like the shot clipped him on the outside of the back of his right arm, took a nice chunk off, but it won't kill him. I'll throw a quick bandage on it. Guessing we're about twelve minutes behind you now."

No more to be said, Taniq started to wrap Lachlan's arm as he hugged Mannix, quietly thanking the dog for pushing him backwards, knowing that if he had made it a few more steps forward, he might be dead. Lucky shot or not.

Mackenzie and Isabella clung to each other as they held their breath, too scared to move. Several gunshots had wrecked the air before a final shot had rung out, silencing everything around them.

The shots had sounded so close and so had the voice calling them out, but with the natural acoustics of the forest, it was impossible to tell for sure. Afraid to move forward and afraid to move back, the girls sat perched on a thick, sturdy branch, waiting and listening for any movement around them.

NINETEEN

Decision made. November shuffled back from the mirror. Hands fisted in front of her face, she rushed forward, bringing her fists down onto the glass. The force was not enough to break it, instead propelling her body backwards onto the floor. Determination had her pulling herself up to try again and again. But the third try garnered the same result.

Defeated, the violence of her sobbing racked her frail body as she scrabbled back to lean on the far wall. The chain twisted, caught around her other leg as she pulled her knees toward her chest to rest her cheek on top. A couple of forceful yanks untangled the chain. It took a while for her tears to stop. But it took even longer for her to comprehend what she was looking at as she focused on the floor in front of her, or rather the chained cuff lying mere inches from her feet.

Lifting her foot, she finally started laughing. After all that, she hadn't needed to break the glass. The lack of food had shrunken her foot, allowing the cuff to slip when she applied a little pressure.

Standing, November braced herself to make the trek toward the door. With all her might, she pulled. Begging any deity that would listen, that he'd left the door unlocked. November gasped in disbelief when the door opened at her pull. Unbelievable—he was that cocky he hadn't even bothered to lock the door, relying solely on the chain around her ankle to keep her in. What a moron!

Once Taniq had strapped Lachlan's arm, his teammate helped pull him to his feet, and they both went over to search Magee's body for anything that might help them. While there wasn't a comms device, they found a sat phone which hadn't survived the fall and keys which Taniq pocketed in case they might need them.

Knowing it was better if Patrick thought his Uncle Magee had succeeded, Lachlan grabbed Magee's rifle and fired a few more rounds into the air.

He waited a few minutes before firing three shots in quick succession into the ground. Anyone who knew Magee knew that when he bagged a kill, he would fire two final shots into the animal's heart and one into its head, much like an assassin would make a professional hit. Lachlan could only hope Patrick would fall for it.

The boys secured his body as best they could, hoping that wildlife wouldn't get to it before the Feds did. Then they headed off after Nate and Deeks, not wanting to lose any more time than they already had.

Bruce ended his call with the Feds as Jonah and Max walked into the kitchen. The two men had come back to update everyone on how the search of Magee's place had gone. Although they hadn't found much apart from Shauna's phone, they had come across a sketched-out timeline of planned abductions which Bruce had swiftly relayed to his team. It appeared the perps had deviated from their own plan early on.

"What's happened?" Jonah confronted Bruce.

"What makes you think anything's happened?" Bruce countered as he leaned against the bench. Stirring Lachlan's younger brother was fun.

"You zoned out. Looked like you held your breath for several seconds before remembering to exhale. Then you came straight in here to make a call. So, I know you know something, and I want to know what it is."

Bruce tilted his head as he regarded Jonah, not rushing to respond. Before Jonah could make any further demands, Bruce huffed out a laugh, muttering, "Fine, I heard ya!" under his breath.

A knowing look came across Jonah's face as he squinted at Bruce. "You're wearing comms?"

"Course I am, and your brother just called me a dickhead, so right about now I'm happy to tell you anything you want to know." Bruce pretended he didn't hear Lachlan's response. In his defense he was listening to comms and talking to Jonah at the same time.

"Sorry, Captain, what was that? Don't tell him you just took a bullet? Okay, no problems."

"What the fuck? Lachlan was shot?"

"Oh, for Mary's sake, I can't deal with both of you yelling at once. Jonah, your brother is fine, although I might not be when he gets back. I also might be deaf if he doesn't stop yelling at me." Bruce sighed before continuing.

"Jonah, Lachlan says he got a little nick in the arm, which isn't going to stop him kicking my ass when he gets back. Also, Magee is dead. That was the Feds. I had to tell them where to grab his body so you can call off your APB on him. Ah, he's also ordered me to ask you nicely not to tell your parents because he doesn't want your mother climbing the mountain to check on him. Any questions?"

"Yeah, just one. How much shit are you in if I let it slip to Mum and Dad that Lachlan managed to get himself shot? And feel free to tell Lachlan I'm not looking to make life easier on him, either. I have three words for him: 'Family Betting Pool.'"

Bruce's laughter waylaid him from even attempting to answer

Jonah, which should have told Jonah he wouldn't like his brother's response when Bruce finally caught his breath.

"First, he can hear you and I'm already in deep shit whether you 'dob' or not. Second, it's not me you'll upset, it's your mother, so that guilt you can wear on your own back. Third, Lachlan just mentioned he thinks your ma would love to organize a spring wedding for you and Max and that he would be happy to suggest it to her for you. He would now like to know if you have any other questions or if he could get on with what he was doing?"

"Fuck off, he wouldn't dare!" Jonah might not have liked the response, but Max appeared to find it hilarious.

Unfortunately, Bruce was too busy laughing to relay Lachlan's next words and it only got better when DBD took the bait. So, Bruce raised a finger to signal Jonah to wait as the banter played out over the comms.

"Oh, for fuck's sake, seriously, Lachlan, the phrase is 'Does a bear shit in the woods?' not 'Does a bear shit wherever it wants, whenever it wants?'"

"Are you saying there are no bears in captivity?" Lachlan's whispered voice was clearly heard over the comms. "What about polar bears? Are you saying that polar bears aren't bears? Or what? A forest magically appears on top of the ice whenever a polar bear needs to shit? And what about zoos, are they technically known as woods now?"

"No, of course not, but you're just being pedantic," DBD muttered. "This argument is as old as time."

"Of course it is, because I'm right and many people agree with me, yet you're still arguing the point."

"Because it's just a damn saying!"

"Yes, but it's a wrong saying that's teaching generations of kids that generalizations are okay."

"All right, I get it, you're right—not all bears shit in the woods."

"Don't hate the messenger, man."

"Oh Mary, somebody shoot me."

"Nah, where would be the fun in that?" Bruce laughed. "Give

me a minute. I gotta answer Jonah's questions before he loses his shit."

While Bruce dealt with Jonah and the boys continued following the now much more prominent trails of their quarry, DBD turned around to find Shauna studying him.

"What's the matter, DBD? You look flushed?"

"Huh, exasperated, more like it. Your brother's just been explaining to me that polar bears are bears, too. Hope to hell I haven't hurt their feelings none."

Shauna looked like she was about to ask for clarification when understanding dawned.

"Oh, I get it. You tried to tell him bears shit in the woods."

"Oh Mary, you're a female Lachlan," DBD exclaimed, amongst more laughter ringing in his ears.

"Yeah, well, but he has a point. I mean, sure, wild grizzly and brown bears shit in the woods, drop bears too, but that's about it."

"Seriously, did you just say drop bears? You think drop bears are real?"

"Well, why do you think they're not?"

"Seriously, I think they are not real BECAUSE they are not real, for Mary's sake. What is wrong with you people? Drop bears are a made-up thing that Australians use to scare the tourists and have a laugh. It's as simple as that."

"Well, are crocodiles real?"

"Yes, but what does that have to do with this?"

"Let me finish. Crocodiles are real and many a person in Australia have lost their lives to one?"

"Yes. Crocodiles are real and they have killed many people. Your point?"

"What about snakes? Does Australia not have as many deadly snakes as everyone says, and do they sometimes end up in people's backyards or even in their houses?"

"Yes, okay, Australia has lots of deadly snakes."

"How about spiders? They say there are heaps of poisonous spiders in Australia and that they can also turn up in people's homes."

"Yes, Australia has poisonous spiders. I'm still not seeing your point."

"Well, what about sharks?"

"What about them?" DBD sighed, somehow wary about where this line of questioning was heading.

"We hear about shark attacks all the time. Is that not true?"

"Of course, it's true. Everyone knows sharks exist, but that doesn't make *Sharknado* a documentary."

"And what about blue bottles? Is it true you can go for a swim in the ocean and find yourself with a long stinger wrapped multiple times around one of your limbs, and it's so painful that people pee on each other to relieve the sting?"

"Ah, fuck, blue bottles, yes—the peeing on each other, not so much. I'd ask where you got all this from, but it has Lachlan written all over it, so get to the point, please. I feel a migraine coming on."

"Well, I'm just saying, if Australians have killer crocodiles, snakes, and spiders that inhabit the land and their houses, and sharks and blue bottles that roam the sea, which must be quite limiting since Australia is an island. Why the hell would they need to make up shit about bears dropping out of trees on top of people to scare the tourists?"

"For Mary's sake! Seriously! First, because they're Australians and they like to drink. Secondly, some tourists are dumb enough to believe them, and I'm sure there is nothing funnier than watching people walk into trees because they are too busy looking at the sky waiting for these poor bears to fall out on top of them. Now, if you don't mind, I need a drink. And Nate, I suggest you keep Lachlan away from me for a while."

"Roger that, DBD," Nate managed to reply.

"Dude," Bruce interceded. "That would have been more believable if you weren't laughing like a loon."

"You can talk, Bruce. You sound like you're hyperventilating." Nate chuckled.

"Lachlan, are you even a little bit remorseful for what DBD just went through?" Taniq questioned their captain.

"Nope, they were fair points."

"You told Shauna drop bears exist?"

"No, I told them the one reason people thought they didn't exist and gave them multiple points to consider as to why they did. The rest I left for them to decide."

"You can be a cruel man, Captain, a cruel, cruel man."

DBD snarled at Deeks' response which would have sounded like he was on DBD's side had the dick been able to hide his laughter. His teammates were all assholes.

What now? Sam had briefly gone upstairs to check on the kids. Finding the twins all playing video games and the little miss still asleep, Sam had thought he would grab a coffee, find his favorite recliner and read the paper. Instead, he'd entered the kitchen to find Jonah standing with his hands on his hips hovering over Bruce. Red faced, Bruce was on the floor leaning back against the bench, breathing heavily. You'd think he'd just run a marathon. Max, for his part, was innocently sitting at the kitchen table. Well, except for the mirth shining in his eyes.

"What happened?" Sam questioned Jonah.

"Not sure Dad. We were talking then he suddenly started laughing like a hyena and only just stopped."

Okay. Sam relaxed a little. At least that wasn't something to worry about. Lachlan and his team appeared to get up to a lot of mischief, which certainly lightened the mood. Turning at the sound of footsteps on the stairs behind him, Sam waited for Claire to join them before looking to Bruce for clarification. Thankfully the man didn't need Sam to voice his question.

"DBD is a logical man, doesn't care much for the fanciful. Your Shauna has just finished explaining to him that drop bears do exist."

"Wait!" Sam raised his hand in the universal stop gesture. "Shauna thinks drop bears are real?" Turning toward Claire, he decided to have some fun of his own. "Honey, looks like you don't need to worry about Shauna going off to college after all."

"Ha, ha, Sam. This has Lachlan written all over it, and you know it."

"What did Lachlan do now?" Parker entered the kitchen, with Cooper and the younger twins in tow.

"He somehow convinced Shauna that drop bears exist." Claire sighed.

"They do exist, Ma," Josh bounced in excitement.

"Yeah, Ma, in Australia," Zac continued. "They have crocodiles and deadly snakes and poisonous spiders, so why would they need to make up a bear that falls out of trees?"

"Exactly." Josh jumped back in. "I wish we lived there. Lachlan said he heard a lot of kids' first jobs are working in the forest. They walk around trying to catch any of the bears when they fall. Gotta be better than working at the local diner."

"What's so funny?" Zac asked as he looked around the room. Josh looked just as perplexed.

Not wanting to face his wife's wrath, Sam tried to keep a straight face, he just wasn't succeeding. Claire's mouth was hanging open in shock—she looked like she didn't know if she should laugh or cry, not that it lasted for long. Everyone else in the room fell into hysterics while his youngest sons watched on.

"Bruce, please tell Lachlan that he and I will be having a discussion when he gets back."

"Um, he heard you, ma'am, but the line is compromised as all I can hear is laughter. Guys, shut it. What was that, Captain? Ah, hold up, he just suggested he might stay in Canada for a couple of years."

"Is that right?"

"Yes, ma'am, but he also asked me to say goodbye. They need to get back on task." Bruce tilted his head listening to whoever was speaking to him through the comms. Sam assumed Lachlan but couldn't be sure.

"Roger that. DBD has the first shift, four-hour rotations. DBD, I'll tag in at 1800hrs but call out if there are any issues before that. I'm out."

Lachlan and Taniq had made up some ground, but they were still about ten minutes behind the boys. Stealth was important once more if they were to convince Patrick that Magee was still alive, and Lachlan was dead.

Wanting to warn the girls but not give away that anything was amiss to Patrick, Lachlan instructed Taniq to mimic the caw of a crow. Even without their bald eagle calls first, Lachlan hoped that the girls would understand they were trying to tell them that there was only one predator left.

"What do we do?" Isabella hesitated at Mac's question. Instead turning to survey the woods below them. She understood what Mac was asking. It was so tempting to descend the tree and make a run for it. They knew the boys were close, but what if they ran into Patrick or the other guy instead?

Was it gut instinct that the boys were trying to tell her that one of the perps was dead? Or was it a real crow and wishful thinking on their part? If there was only one assailant left and the girls separated to head down the mountain, one of them would be safe, if not both. Just because someone was out there didn't mean they would run into them. But, if it were Mackenzie who ran into their kidnapper, how would she ever face Lachlan or his family again?

"Let me go and scout the area again. If I don't come back or you hear a commotion, wait until it's safe and run for help. Do not come out if he calls you. He can suspect we're together, but he still can't know for sure. Promise me that you won't come out of hiding, even if he threatens my life."

Isabella could tell Mac wanted to argue, but before she could repeat her request, Mac agreed. At Isabella's questioning look, Mac shrugged.

"Lachie would kill me if I handed myself over. Besides, you're right. If he gets both of us, we're dead. But, if he only gets one of us, he's gotta keep you alive as leverage. Anyway, Lachlan isn't far. I'm sure he or Mannix would catch me quickly if I started running down the mountain calling for him."

"Okay, I can't argue with that. So, on that note, I'll be back. Stay safe and should anything happen to me, please make sure they know I love them, that I was doing everything I could to make it back to them."

"I won't have to. They'll know, besides we're both going to see them again. I'm too young to die and you're too stubborn."

Laughing quietly, Isabella shook her head. "That's what Lachie says." Taking a calming breath, Isabella checked the area below before carefully navigating across multiple trees, far away from Mackenzie before making her descent.

***

Walking back into the living room, Bruce headed for the couch to lay down and stretch out. A few hours' nap would be bliss, but not likely to happen anytime soon. Snapping back into a sitting position, swinging his feet to the floor, Bruce pinned his eyes on Gracie. Mary only knew how long she'd been up; he should have checked on her himself. Bruce doubted any of Lachlan's family would ever have suspected her of faking sleep. Damn, sometimes he wanted to ring Lachlan's neck.

"Grace Michelle Michaels, what did your father say about riding the dogs?"

Gracie lifted her head at the sound of Bruce's growl as the household seemed to freeze for a moment. Then there was mass-movement, with family coming from all directions at the stern calling of Grace's full name. With a smirk, the little brat answered, "Not to ride Mannix!"

Sticking her tongue out at him, defiant. She continued to traverse the stairs.

"Wrong answer, little girl."

"Nope, that's what Daddy said, and he's not here to say different."

"Oh wow, you just stuffed up, little girl. I'm sure you got that from your papa, but you seem to have forgotten what happens when we are all separated but still working. Let me give you a hint. Daddy just growled in my ear."

It was almost comical how Grace scrunched her little face as she worked out what he meant, but a few seconds later she slid off Viper's back onto the step. With folded arms, Gracie stomped her little foot while glaring at Bruce. "You set me up …"

"Do not finish that line. I cannot believe Nate lets you watch *Hellraiser* with him."

"It's a comedy," Nate whispered back.

"It is not a comedy. And as for you, Gracie girl, did I put you on Viper's back? Did I then tell you to descend the stairs? Then I did not set you up. Now why did Daddy tell you not to ride Mannix?"

Still pouting, Gracie slid her foot out in front of her, moving it side to side as she answered.

"He said I was too big, and it might hurt him."

"Oh, so it is not okay to hurt Mannix, but you think your daddy would be okay with you hurting Viper?"

"No." The tears started for real now as Grace followed the conversation.

"Are huskies made for riding?"

"No, Daddy says they like to pull."

"Correct." Before Bruce could continue, he caught movement out of the corner of his eye. "Grandparents cease and desist. Coddling her won't improve her behavior."

Once satisfied that Claire and Sam wouldn't intervene to comfort their granddaughter before their discussion was over, Bruce turned back to the crying little girl in front of him.

"Hold on, Captain, I hear you. Let me get my phone."

Seconds later, Bruce pulled his comms piece out of his ear and connected it to his phone.

"Lines open, Captain. You should be on speaker."

"Grace Michelle Michaels, you get your little behind into that corner right now. I can't believe you would disobey me like this. Once you've done your time, you will apologize for your behavior. Do you understand me?"

"Yes, Daddy." Grace was openly bawling now as she finished her descent and made her way into the closest corner.

"Bruce, start the timer and if she moves from that spot or even as much as turns around, you let me know."

"Will do, Captain."

"And Bruce, check Viper for me."

"On it, Captain. She looks fine, but I'll give her a once-over."

"Good, let me know. I'm out."

Bruce separated the comms from his phone and popped it back into his ear before calling Viper over to him. Both Cooper and Parker joined him on the couch, concern written all over their faces. He figured it would have been a long time since they had heard Lachlan get cross and the fact it was at Gracie over their dog, well Bruce could understand that would be unsettling. Not waiting for them to ask, Bruce explained that huskies were strong and made for pulling, but as with any big dogs, you had to be careful they didn't displace their hips. Putting weight on their backs was bad enough, but then making them descend stairs was a recipe for disaster.

"Gracie, that's time. You can come away from the corner now."

Still sobbing, Gracie slowly turned around. Taking a few hesitant steps, she made her way to Viper and gently put her arms around the dog's neck. Crying into the dog's fur, Gracie apologized to the dog.

"One question?" Max asked. "I thought you signed off. So how did Lachlan hear that?"

"Technically, I signed out. We don't turn the comms off. We take turns monitoring, but we can all still hear each other. Right now, it's DBD's turn to be the main backup. This way, if something goes wrong, I'll hear it and join in without having to catch up, otherwise it's like background noise. Lachlan was focusing on what he was doing, but he couldn't tune out my tone when I groused at Grace, even if he tried. Which he wouldn't 'cause he's a control freak … Right back at you, mofo. Ah, sorry, not you. That was Lachie putting his two cents in."

"Is it possible you boys can go twenty minutes without razzing each other?" Claire asked as she lifted Gracie before kissing her head and handing the crying child over to Bruce.

"Only when we're sleeping, ma'am. Hoping to grab a few minutes now if that's okay?" When Claire nodded and headed back to the kitchen, Bruce kicked Cooper and Parker off his side of the couch. Lying back with Grace on his chest, he took the opportunity to close his eyes, not letting sleep take him until Grace's breathing had evened out.

TWENTY

November counted the stairs. Twelve in total. One step at a time. Anxiety and lack of food combined to make it a slow trek. However, the fear of staying and waiting to die of starvation or for the monster to come back was a great motivator to keep going. Getting to the top, she opened a thick wooden door and found herself in a tiny, empty corridor.

Another door stood a few feet in front of her. Pushing it open, she gasped as she found herself outside the back of a small cabin. Infront of her was approximately ten feet of clearing before huge trees captivated the landscape as far as her eyes could see. She was in the mountains, the dungeon she'd been kept was hidden underneath what looked to be a small wooden cabin. Was it weird that the entrance was from the outside of the cabin and not inside like most basements would be?

She shivered; the cold breeze felt harsh enough to break her brittle bones. The sun wasn't too high in the sky. If she had to guess, it was likely mid to late afternoon, but it didn't matter. November knew she needed food and to get away from here before anyone came along to find her.

Walking to the front of the cabin, she found the door unlocked.

Inside, the cabin was covered in layers of dust. So much dust. It was obvious that no one had entered this cabin in a long, long time. While she knew it would be impossible to cover her tracks, she needed food. Without it, she had no chance.

Desperation propelled her toward the kitchen, where she found the shelves stocked with non-perishables. Tears of joy streamed down her face as her eyes feasted on the baked bean cans, noting they had a pull top and did not require a can opener. She wasn't convinced she had the strength to operate one at this point. It took November a few tries to get the can open enough to get to the contents. A quarter of the can tasted amazing, but only moments later she was empty again. Funnily enough, the beans didn't taste anywhere near as good coming back up. Luckily, she was next to the sink. Determined to try again, November rinsed her mouth and found a teaspoon forcing herself to stop after one spoonful.

A few minutes, November took another spoonful and slowly repeated the process until she emptied the can. With some fuel in her belly, November headed toward the closet, looking for a jacket and something to carry some food and water. Finding both, November grabbed what she could and headed out, hoping she had enough time to get far away before her monster came back to find her.

Once Isabella had descended the tree, she paused to check her surroundings. The girls had covered a lot of ground over the last few days, only taking to the trees to scout the area when the ground was too dense to cover without making an obvious trail. Her gut was yelling that danger was close by, but she was still unsure how to proceed.

When she heard the crack of a branch snapping, as if someone had stepped on it much closer than she would have thought, she instinctively knew it would not be the man she hoped for. Spurred into action, Isabella took off as fast as she could, doubling back under Mackenzie as she ran, hoping the perp would assume she was leading away from her and not directly past her.

With one look behind her, she saw a man hot on her trail. Dressed in camo, she recognized the man from outside the cabin where she'd found Mackenzie. Patrick. Mackenzie had said it was Patrick that had kidnapped her and now he was after Isabella. Giving into fear, she gave a quick squeal before changing direction to run full pelt down the mountain, hoping to intersect with the boys. The need to look back behind her was too strong to deny so while she didn't see the fallen tree that sent her flying, she saw her attacker leap before he connected with her back, landing on top of her as she connected with the ground.

Winded, Isabella wasn't quick enough to offer an offensive before his gun was pressed against the side of her head.

"Try it, bitch. One wrong move and I end it here and now."

"What do you want?"

"To see him suffer, of course. He was always so smug. Now. Get up, slowly. My understanding is Lachlan is already dead, but I just can't dismiss the fact that my dear uncle hasn't checked in, even after announcing his kill with his signature triple tap."

He was not dead.

He was not dead.

He was not dead.

Isabella couldn't stop the mantra inside her mind even if she wanted to, but she needed to focus and stay alert. To do that, she had to believe that her husband was alive and close by.

She wanted desperately to believe the single caw of a crow she had heard earlier had come from Lachlan. But doubts seeped in. It could just as easily have been a real crow.

And then, even if it was Lachlan, there hadn't been any other signals, none to say that there were still four of his team behind them. For all she knew, this man's partner could have taken them all out. Lachlan might have managed to end him and send out the warning before succumbing to his injuries—or maybe the call wasn't from Lachlan at all.

"Move!" the man yelled. "We need to get out of here, but first we have to go find Mackenzie."

"Who?"

"Don't bother trying to lie to me. Do you really think I can't track well enough to see that there were two sets of tracks for most of this climb. Now where is she? I haven't finished with her yet!"

Before Isabella could answer, a low growl sounded behind her. Isabella swung her head in time to watch Mannix edge out from behind the nearest bushes. The pup slowly made his way toward them. Relief was palpable. If Lachlan were alive, he would be close. Mannix wouldn't leave Lachlan's side unless he was dead. Shuddering at the thought, Isabella tensed as the arm around her neck tightened, the gun pushing harder against her temple.

Tiredness and stress meant she was weaker than usual. But she had still been able to get food into her body over the last few days and her training relied on skill, not strength. All she needed was for him to shift the gun slightly away from her head and she would make her move. All thoughts fled, however, seconds later when Lachlan stumbled out from behind a tree. Covered in blood, some even dripped from his eyes. He smiled at Isabella before acknowledging her assailant.

"Well, well, well. Look what the mutt dragged in? You're not looking too good there, old Lachlan boy. I'm guessing by the looks of you, my uncle is dead, but not before he got a piece of you, huh? Shame, I wanted to be the one to do him in."

Her husband didn't reply. Isabella could only watch helplessly as blood trickled down Lachlan's face.

"What, nothing to say? No complaints or pleading to spare your wife's life? You surely can't think you'll come out on top here. Look at you, you're basically already dead. Now the question is, should I finish you first or Isabella here? Shauna is already dead. I have to say it is a relief not having to put that stupid accent on anymore. Poor, poor simple Shauna. So naïve and willing to please. But that's the least of your problems, both you and Isabella will also be dead in a few minutes. That leaves me all the time in the world to find Mackenzie and then go back for little Gracie."

At the mention of Gracie, Isabella stiffened grabbing Patrick's attention.

He leant in, specks of saliva wet her ear and cheek as he aimed his harshly whispered words at her.

"Ha. I should have known that Gracie would be the weakness. I was hoping she'd be found alive. It will make it even more heartbreaking when I come back and take her from under everyone's noses. Hmmm, maybe I'll keep you alive, whore. You can watch me kill your husband before I tear into your little girl. She'll be screaming for you to help her, unable to understand why you just sit there and watch her suffer. And I'd make her suffer, while you watch every moment of it. I'll rip her apart before I kill her and then it'll be you're turn."

The hateful man focused his next words back on Lachlan.

"Bloody ironic, that I've been planning this for years. Dreamed about how I would destroy the great Lachlan Michaels, and then my damn uncle did it for me. I'm surprised that you're still standing but at least I'll get to finish the job. I'm going to decimate your family, and it'll all come back to you, not minding your own fucking business. Any last words?"

"Yeah, actually. You're a sick motherfucker and I hope you spend eternity being railed by old butch women wearing spiked Strap-Ons, infused with ginger while gagging on old men's wrinkled, unwashed cocks. You're lucky we're on American soil with the Feds close by. You don't want to know what I usually do to pedophiles. Just know on your dying breath that you lost. Every one of my family survived you and we'll thrive without you. Now, as Bruce Willis would say, Yippee-ki-yay, motherfucker!"

Lachlan hadn't even finished speaking when he launched the knife he'd been holding behind his back straight into Patrick's left eye. At the same time a shot rang out, knocking the gun away from Isabella's head. Patrick screamed and stumbled back a few steps dragging Isabella with him. His arm across her chest had loosened but she was still trapped in his hold. Somehow, he'd managed to keep hold of his gun. Isabella looked back at her husband just in time to see him wink at her, less than a second later Lachlan fired his Glock at the man holding her. One shot and the man was falling taking her to the ground with him.

Unceremoniously, Isabella was yanked off Patrick's body straight into her husband's arms. Taniq appeared from behind her and rolled Patrick over checking for signs of life.

"Hey, baby, you okay?"

"Lachlan, oh my Mary, all this blood. Taniq, we've gotta get him help, quick."

"Baby, relax, I'm okay. It was just a distraction."

Pushing on his chest to be released, Isabella stepped back and folded her arms assessing her stubborn husband. She was not in the mood for any of his shit right now.

"Lachlan Michael Michaels, are you telling me that blood isn't real?"

"Busted!" Taniq coughed into his hand, although he retreated quickly when Isabella whirled to face him and went back to covering Patrick's body in plastic. Isabella seldom used Lachlan's middle and last name when yelling at him so the guys should have known not to mess with her right then. Seconds later, she was pulled back into Lachlan's chest as his arms once again wrapped her in a comforting embrace.

"Relax, sweetie. I'm fine. No need for middle names or scaring the guys. What we need to do is check you for injuries and find Mackenzie."

"Mackenzie, oh shit. I left her in a large sycamore tree. We've gotta go back and find her."

"Shush!" Lachlan tightened his hold. "Nate and Deeks went ahead. They'll find her and bring her to us. Here, pop this ear bud in. Nate won't believe you're okay until he can talk to you himself."

Leaning into Lachlan, Isabella put the earpiece in before closing her eyes and taking a deep breath. "Nate?"

"Izzy, hey, sis, you scared the crap out of me."

And that was all it took. Finally safe in her husband's arms and with her twin's voice in her ear, Isabella broke, uncontrollable sobs tearing through her body.

"I'm sorry, I'm so sorry."

Lachlan lifted Isabella off the ground, her legs moving to cling around his waist.

"It's okay, everyone is okay. Gracie is with her grandparents, the boys are still with your dad, and Shauna is safe with DBD, although I'm not sure he is safe with her." That garnered a small laugh from the guys as a muttered 'asshole' filtered through the comms piece. "Nate and Deeks will have Mac any second now, and we'll all go home."

"But if I hadn't of left early, he wouldn't have gotten a hold of me. I put Gracie in danger."

"Actually, that's not true. Jonah and Max found notes at Magee's. They were planning to take you and Gracie when you went into his shop. It was never meant to be just you. For some reason he diverted from their plan, we can only assume it was a split-second decision to take you on Railings Road. But it also meant he couldn't take Gracie, she would have been too hard to handle on top of you, so in this instance, you heading off early actually saved our baby from further trauma. He was gunning for us, anyway. This is on me, not you."

Isabella frowned at her husband's words, not liking what she was hearing but luckily DBD spoke up for all of them. "Cut the crap, Lachlan. Mac wouldn't be alive if you hadn't stepped in all those years ago. Any way you look at it, a confrontation was going to happen. At least this way, everyone had a fighting chance."

Before her husband could respond with any more nonsense, Nate's voice filled the comms. "Mackenzie, my name is Nate, and this here is Deeks. I'm not sure if you remember us, but we're friends of your brother from the navy. I'm also Isabella's twin brother. The older, smarter twin." Nate broke off to laugh at Isabella's response.

"Bullshit!"

"Hush, Isabella, you wouldn't use that language in front of Gracie. Now, where was I? Oh, so Lachlan has Isabella and since Magee managed to shoot his ass, I would prefer we take you to him rather than making him climb any further up this damn mountain."

"Ouch. Fuck, Izzy, why the hell did you hit me?" Lachlan dropped Izzy back to her feet and stepped back as she marched forward, meeting him step for step, drilling her finger into his chest.

"You told me you were fine. At which point were you going to mention that you had managed to get shot again?"

"Baby, I'm fine, it's just a nick. The rest of this was just a distraction." Lachlan waved at his blood covered face. "No big deal. I promise that I'm okay."

Arms folded, Isabella raised an eyebrow, followed by one word. "Nate?"

"I don't know, sis. He refused medical treatment at first. Once I threatened to tell you that, he let Taniq look, but I haven't seen it for myself." Nate might have been laughing as he dumped Lachlan in it, but no-one missed the 'asshole' comment thrown his way or the actual threat her husband attached to it. But Isabella noted how quickly everyone quietened when a small voice sounded through their comms.

"Lachlan was shot?"

"He's fine, I'm stirring, he's been a pain in all our ass's this last week worrying about getting to you and Izzy, so a little payback seemed appropriate. Please, come down, you're safe now."

"Tell her Amalthaea!" Her husband spoke with a serious expression that even Isabella didn't know if he was joking or not.

"What? Are you insane? Why the hell would I want to blurt out Amalthaea for no apparent reason? That's weird, man! What the hell does it even mean?"

Seconds later an 'oof' sounded across the comms. Hearing the magical word, Mac had scrambled out of the tree and jumped right into his arms, sobbing softly in his ear. Deeks had been polite enough to add commentary, so Isabella and the guys knew what was happening.

"Hey there, hey now. It's okay. Here, pop this earpiece in and you can speak with Lachlan."

"Lachlan?"

"Hey, beautiful. I am so proud of you! You did so well out here."

"But it was all my fault. I locked PIMF in the bathroom and let him into my house."

"Hey, hey. It's okay. PIMF is fine, although I would suggest going forward if someone doesn't like your dog, then they are not for you—sound fair?"

"Yep, totally. He said he killed Shauna."

"Nope, Shauna is fine. Everyone else is at the house, so how 'bout you make your way to us so we can all go home and have this family reunion? Bruce?"

"Yeah, Captain?"

"Can you put the comms on speaker again? I think a few people would benefit from hearing Isabella and Mac speak in person."

"Will do."

"Lachlan?"

"Yeah, DBD?"

"You want me to do the same here?"

"No, I reckon we better wait until I get home to bring Shauna back. They're gonna want to meet you and that's gonna take a bit of explaining."

"Agreed. I'll take the reprieve for as long as it lasts. What do I tell her?"

"Tell her we have them and that they are safe, but we haven't confirmed that all perps have been accounted for yet. That'll be the story for everyone until we get home. Besides, you never know, he hinted at a third. Let's not let our guard down yet. Hooyah!"

"Hooyah!" echoed out as each member followed their leader's exclamation.

As the loud 'Hooyah' echoed throughout the Michaels' house, all family members descended upon Bruce.

Bruce smiled as questions flew at him. After plugging his comms piece into his phone for the second time that day, he grabbed Gracie and whispered into her ear, watching with a smile as the little girl's face lit up.

"Mummy?!"

"Gracie, baby, oh my Mary, Gracie, how's my baby girl?"

"Mummy, can you come home now? GD's being mean."

Laughter. Isabella was laughing and Bruce couldn't blame her. Life and death, the woman must have been petrified of finding out what had happened to her baby and the first thing out of the precocious child's mouth was, 'Come home. GD's being mean.' They all heard Isabella force a deep breath before she answered as soberly as possible.

"Oh, Gracie, what did GD do, baby girl?"

"He said he was gonna blow up all the Smarties in the world and that Daddy would let him."

"Sweetie, they're just being silly. Isn't that right, Daddy?" Bruce imagined Isabella pinning Lachlan with a raised eyebrow.

"Gracie, your mummy is correct. I wouldn't let GD blow up all the Smarties in the world by himself. I would be there right next to him to help."

"Lachlan, not helping."

"What?" Lachlan's smile came through his voice. "You told me never to lie to her."

"See, Mummy."

"It's okay, baby. Sometimes we've gotta remember you're not the only one that acts like a baby, even if you are the only one with a reason to. Bruce, is anyone else there? I think Mackenzie would like to say hi to her parents."

At Claire's gasp, Bruce watched Sam pull his wife into his arms before turning his attention to Bruce's phone.

"Mackenzie, are you there?"

"Hi, Daddy."

All at once, the silence turned to chaos. Cheers, sighs, sobs, yells of joy, and laughter rang out through the room. Both Isabella and Mackenzie were safe. The tension that had been weighing upon the family lifted with two simple words.

"Hey, sweetheart. Are you okay?"

"Yes, Daddy. I'm with Nate and—"

"And Isabella is with me." Lachlan cut Mac off. While this situation might be over, Lachlan would not chance outing his team if other perps were still out there. "Guys, listen up, would you?"

When that didn't work, Bruce figured Lachlan was about to blow a gasket. But then Izzy stepped in using his full name for the second time in mere minutes.

"Lachlan Michael Michaels don't even think about it. We can get everyone's attention without you blowing your top and, considering you're nursing a bullet wound, you should save your strength."

"Halt!" Sam lifted his hand to go along with his words, quietening the room as Isabella's words sunk in around them. Wisely, Bruce hid his smirk. This would be fun. "Lachlan, did I hear correctly? Have you been shot?"

Bruce could practically hear the scowl in Lachlan's grumbled response. He could only imagine what retribution he'd seek against his wife for letting that slip. Life was never boring, that was for sure.

"Look, a bullet grazed my arm. It is not bad but if you wanted to be 'technical' then I guess the answer would be yes. However, we don't have time for this, so I need you all to listen. We are going to hole up tonight and make our way to town tomorrow. I need you all to stay vigilant, as I cannot guarantee there isn't a third perp. The Feds are staking out the house tonight in case, as threatened, there is someone we've missed. They'll do another run through town in the morning. If they are happy the threat has been contained, they'll let you know. Now, before anyone starts in on me." There was silence as everyone waited for Lachlan to take a breath and continue.

"Yes, I know the winter fair starts tomorrow. Why it starts on a damn Tuesday, I'll never understand. Jonah and Max will need to be there for work, but I also know most of you have been looking forward to it, as has Gracie, so if you get the all-clear from the Feds you can go. However, at no stage is anyone to be left alone and anyone under the age of twenty-five will need a chaperon. Don't forget there is still a missing woman out there and we know these two were not responsible for taking her. Am I understood?"

"So what? Bruce has gotta babysit five of us now?" Parker grumbled.

"Parker, buddy, just stay away from anyone named Mary and Bruce won't cause you any troubles."

Everyone may have laughed, but Lachlan wasn't fast enough to avoid Isabella's wrath if the corresponding grunt was any indication.

"Hey, babe, no fair. One minute you're complaining about me getting shot and the next you're using excessive force. You can't have it both ways."

Shaking his head, Bruce laughed as Lachlan signed off. "We're going to make a move. See you all tomorrow."

"Lachlan, wait. What about Shauna?" Claire asked.

"She's safe with DBD for now. Until we know if there is a third perp or not, I don't want to risk it."

"Okay, Lachlan. We will leave it there for the moment, but I have a feeling you and I will be having words when you get back." Sam ended the conversation making sure Lachlan and everyone else knew he felt his son was hiding something.

"Roger that." Lachlan's sigh was the last thing they heard before Bruce detached his comms from the phone and put it back in his ear.

The message had been well and truly received.

Idiot.

He was so surprised he had stumbled onto the woman that he took his next step without looking and inadvertently announced to all and sundry that he was there. He'd been ahead of Magee's nephew but not by much, so he faded into the background, hoping Patrick would hear the noise of her retreat and make chase, to which he did.

If one of the women was here, he had to assume the other would be nearby. For now, he had two questions. How many men did Lachlan have with him? And how far away were the Feds? Without the answers, he was stuck. Unable to risk heading back to the cabin, back to his November. He couldn't take the chance. The wrong move could ruin everything.

The Feds banning all locals from the mountains had caused him multiple issues. Sneaking up here had been dangerous. If anyone recognized him, there would be no way of explaining his presence. At first, he'd hoped to make it to the cabin, but now he only hoped to make it out of here without being seen.

After all, he was confident nothing in the cabin would lead to him. Even if someone did stumble upon November. Besides, what were the chances November was still alive? She'd have long run out of food by now.

Those damn Irish idiots. He knew they were up to no good. Fuck, he should have stepped in and ended them before they started in with their stupid little plans for revenge. Now he had a mess on his hands, and he was going to need help to clean it up.

Blending into the background, he retreated as quietly as possible. The best outcome here was that Lachlan would find his sister and wife. Damn! Who knew the sneaky man had that up his sleeve —and then get the hell off his mountain.

He could only hope the Feds left with them. The concern that they were here for him and not the Michaels women persisted in the back of his mind, but now was not the time to worry. Besides, he'd know if he'd made a mistake. That was one thing of which, he was sure.

TWENTY-ONE

THE TEAM DECIDED NOT to waste daylight. Lachlan took the lead, with Mannix on his heel, the men flanked the women on all sides. It was still a slow process, unwilling to take any chances until they'd debriefed and answered all questions, no matter how small.

As the sun set, they headed toward the nearest cabin, still miles away from their hidden 4WD. Mackenzie flinched, her gasp of horror loud, even without the comms piece in everyone's ears, when she realized the plan for the night. Halting their progress, Lachlan stepped in and kissed Isabella's cheek before swinging Mac into his arms. Continuing to the cabin, he whispered assurances of her safety into her ear as she held on, much like Gracie had only days before.

Stopping at the perimeter of the cabin clearing, Lachlan still holding Mac, held out his free hand for Izzy, thankful when she grabbed it and lent into him while they waited for Nate, Deeks, and Taniq to check for any threats or nasty surprises. With the all-clear given, they went inside. Lachlan guided Izzy toward the couch. Safe in his arms, it wasn't long until exhaustion had both Izzy and Mac dozing off.

A bottle of water in hand, Nate perched his ass on the coffee table between the couches in front of him.

"Water?"

"Nah, I'm good for now. What was below? Storage or another dungeon?"

Nate shook his head. "Just storage, man, just storage. Now, before you say anything, hear me out, okay?"

Raising his right eyebrow, Lachlan sunk back deeper into the couch cushions, taking the girls with him as he waited for Nate to continue. He had no doubt he was currently speaking with Commander Nathanial Anderson and not Nate, his best friend.

"Deeks is cooking some grub. Taniq is on watch for now. Once we eat, we'll go to three-hour watches. Only when I say 'we,' I mean Deeks, Taniq, and I will round-robin throughout the night."

"Oh, and why is my 2IC taking me off the rotation, exactly?"

"A few reasons. First, while Izzy will settle with me, she won't be as comfortable without you. Plus, Mac won't settle for anyone but you, and you know it. You could order Mannix to stay with her, but there is no way Mannix will stay calm if he isn't at your side. Second, despite thinking you are Superman, that bullet took a chunk out of your arm, and you lost a shitload of blood—you need rest if you are going to take point tomorrow, unless you want me to call Bruce or DBD up here? Thirdly, you've had minimal sleep. Even before the bullet wound, you were starting to lag. You're no good to anyone running on empty."

"Fine. What's for dinner then?"

"What? Hold up." Lachlan cursed at Nate's response; damn it, he'd overplayed his hand but shit he was tired and sore. If his team had been in the same room right then, he had no doubt it would have been obvious that they had all frozen, waiting quietly to hear the rest of the interaction between him and their commander. "Just 'fine,' just like that? No arguments, no threats, no growling, just 'fine'? What the fuck have you done with our captain? And more to the point, exactly how bad were you hurt?"

"Lay off, dickwad. I agree with everything you said. I am

running on fumes and, to be frank, I don't want to leave these two alone for the moment, even if I will be nearby. So how 'bout you help Deeks serve us some dinner so the girls and I can get some sleep and then you and the boys can keep watch to your little hearts' merry content?"

Lachlan flinched when Nate abruptly stood and stormed over to Taniq. This could get messy.

"Seriously, you let us believe it wasn't bad. Now tell me the fucken truth because there is no way he just backed down from guard duty without a fight unless it's much worse than you led me to believe. Tell me why you fucken lied to me when I asked for a sit rep? Are you gonna stand there now and tell me it's a fucken scratch?"

"Wait, Commander." Taniq took two steps back in the face of Nate's anger. "First, I didn't say it was a scratch. He did. I said it had taken a nice chunk out of his arm, but he'd live. We all know damn well he wasn't going to sit out of this no matter how bad the wound was. I've already grabbed the first aid gear from Deeks' kit and dropped it by the couch so Deeks can check his wound after we eat, and the girls are asleep. Besides, picking up Mac and carrying her here wouldn't have helped."

"Seriously, man, they have comms in. The last thing we need is for Mac to hear that, you mofo."

"Enough, both of you. I think you'll find I'm still in charge here and besides, I took Mac and Isabella's comms out when they fell asleep. They can put them back in when they wake up." Lachlan gestured to the arm of the couch where two comms sets sat. "Now, Deeks is serving dinner, so how 'bout you both calm your ass's and grab some food? Hopefully, that'll put you in a better mood. The girls are safe. You should be happy, not screaming at each other like banshees."

"You're an asshole, Lachie!"

"Whatever, Nate, maybe you need a nap to un-bunch your panties."

"Do NOT kill him, Nate." DBD's voice rang out through the

comms. "He's trying to get a rise, so you'll forget he needs treatment."

"Fuck off, DBD. I thought this was Bruce's shift?"

"It is, Captain," Bruce interceded. "But none of us could ignore that pile of shit. Nate, you want me to hand Grace over to Jonah and make my way to you?"

"Hell, no, you stay with my daughter, asshole!"

"Wasn't asking you, Captain. If you're as bad as it sounds, Nate takes leadership of the team."

"Fuck you. I'm a little tired, not brain dead."

"Nate, I can drop Shauna off to Bruce and make my way to you if you want Bruce to stay with Gracie?"

"Bullshit, DBD. Even Nate knows that idea is self-serving."

"Screw you, Lachlan. Nate, what's your call?" DBD asked.

"Hold your positions. We'll have something to eat and then Lachlan will voluntarily let Deeks check him out or I'll wake Izzy and let her have her say."

"Roger that," DBD and Bruce both acknowledged.

"Assholes!"

Bruce's smirk at Lachlan's last insult died quickly when he saw Parker leading an upset Cooper down the stairs toward him. "Parker, Cooper, what's wrong? Cooper, come here. Why are you crying?"

The dead silence in his ear told him that every one of his teammates was waiting to hear what the problem was, but it was Parker that spoke.

"He's got himself worked up thinking Lachie's hurt much worse than he's let on. Any chance Lachie can speak to him?"

Within seconds, Lachlan's voice came through the comms loud and clear. "Put him on."

Bruce walked over to intercept them. As soon as he was close enough, he pulled Cooper into his arms and held him tight before corralling both boys over to the couch.

With a quick wiggle, Bruce pulled out an additional two comm pieces and popped them into the twins' ears. Parker's brow furrowed at the sight of the spare comms set, but quickly relented at Bruce's narrowed eyes. Having non-military personnel listening in when they were working was not going to happen. Shit, imagine if the family had been listening in when Lachlan had been shot, Claire would have been halfway up the mountain before they'd dealt with Magee.

"Comms up both Parker and Cooper," Bruce grunted and side eyed Viper. The pup had jumped up and maneuvered himself across their laps, but the position wasn't exactly comfortable.

"Lachlan?"

"Hey, baby boy, you know I don't like it when you're upset," Lachlan murmured into the comms.

"But..."

"I'm okay Coop. I promise. And to prove it, I'll get it looked at again after dinner."

"You will?"

"Sure, you can't be too careful and I'm happy to get it double checked if it'll make you feel better!"

"You promise?"

"Cooper, this is Nate. How 'bout I promise you no matter what, after dinner I will get his wound checked? I'll even jump on him and hold him down if I need to or, even worse, I'll wake Isabella? That way you don't have to worry about Lachlan placating you since I'm the one that promised."

"Okay, I guess."

"Coop, I promise I'm fine. A little tired. Nothing, a hot meal, and some rest won't fix. Okay?"

"Yeah, okay. I'm sorry for bugging you."

"Don't apologize, Coop," Nate interrupted. "We know what he's like. Lachlan is your brother, but he's ours too. We're family, we protect each other, and we'll always watch out for him and your family by extension. Parker will tell you what that's like. I'm so bummed I never got to meet this Mary girl."

"Assholes." Parker muttered under his breath making Bruce smile. "I'm going to make it my mission to find a nice girl called Mary to marry just to prove all you mofo's wrong."

Amid quiet laughter and a chorus of 'good luck's,' Parker wished the team goodnight before taking his and Cooper's comms out. Bruce held out his hand for them and nodded his own good-night as he watched Parker pull Cooper off the couch and guide him back towards the stairs. Viper once again at their heels.

"Wow, Captain," DBD lamented. "So thoughtful of you to think of getting your wound checked out to reassure Cooper! I can't believe no-one else thought of that."

Asshole. Sometimes his team forgot who was in charge.

"Hey, DBD? Feel free not to wait for me if you'd like to go intro-duce yourself to my family without my backup."

"Asshole!"

"Ditto!"

Before they could throw any further insults, his beautiful wife's voice broke through. Groans of despair sounded from him and his team as it became clear that at some point not only had his wife woken up and reinserted her comms, but she had overheard enough of the conversation going on around her to have worked up a nice mad. In a deceptively calm voice that would only fool an idiot, Isabella continued.

"So, let me get this straight. You've worked out he's hurt worse than first thought. But instead of checking out how badly, you're all sitting here arguing like children. And then, your solution is to eat dinner first and wait for the womenfolk to fall asleep. Is that seri-ously your plan?"

"Baby, it's not ..."

"No, Lachlan, do not 'baby' me. I am tired, hungry, sore, and emotional. But what I don't need is to be worried that my husband is going to die because he's a class A idiot. And the rest of you can stop laughing too. You're all acting like imbeciles. So, this is what is going to happen. Nate, take Mac and lay her on one of the beds please. Mannix — Schützen!" Isabella pointed at Mac, telling the pup who to protect. The pups had all been taught certain commands in German which were only ever used to indicate that they were deadly serious. Somehow, Lachlan had found himself in the proverbial doghouse.

"Deeks grab the first aid kit and get over here. Taniq, pop dinner back in the oven to keep warm. Nate, you can take over the watch if you feel it's necessary. Now, any questions?"

Mumbles of 'No ma'am' rang out from the guys as everyone jumped to follow Isabella's orders. She might not be their leader, but retired or not, she was still a captain. They weren't stupid enough to defy her in this instance, especially considering her orders made perfect sense whether anyone would admit it or not.

Well, the only one tempted to defy was Lachlan, but he was currently weighing his options and he could tell Isabella was ready to pounce if he even thought about saying or doing something stupid.

With a heartfelt put-upon sigh, Lachlan moved his wife to cuddle back into him on the couch before claiming her lips in a heated kiss.

"Mary, Mary, I missed you, baby." Releasing his hold, Lachlan moved to the edge of the seat to allow Deeks better access. "But get this straight. Once Deeks checks me out, you and Mac are next—no arguments!"

"Baby, I'm not about to fight you on that, considering what's happened the last few days. He didn't rape me. I was lucky in that regard, but we both know I'll still need to see my doctor once I get back. She'll need to run some tests before we can breathe freely."

If the team hadn't been so focused on their conversation, they might have missed the small hitch in Izzy's breath as she fought to get those last few words out. But they couldn't have missed how fast Lachlan reacted as he pulled his wife back into his arms, disrupting Deeks from his task of taking the makeshift bandage off Lachlan's arm. For a moment Lachlan expected Deeks to yell at him but instead the man looked up and asked the question everyone else was probably thinking. His men weren't stupid either, but this was not the way they'd wanted them to find out.

"How far along are you, Isabella?"

Isabella lifted her head from his chest to meet Deeks' eyes, but Lachlan answered instead. Her unshed tears were killing him.

"Twenty-two weeks. We were going to announce the pending birth of our son at the BBQ on Sunday after the winter fair. We didn't think Gracie or the boys could keep it a secret much longer, but we wanted to tell you all at the same time. This wasn't quite how we pictured it."

With nothing further to say, everyone went back to what they were doing. Isabella loosened her hold enough that Lachlan was able to adjust her, so she was plastered to his side, which allowed his torturer access to his injured arm. He wished he could tell her it was all going to work out fine. But if he was honest, nothing ever worked out true to plan for them, so whatever happened, they would face it together. They would survive and get through it. Their families, both blood and those bound through experiences, would be there to support them, but it didn't mean it wouldn't tear out even more of their souls.

November huddled into herself, pulling the jacket around her as tight as possible. She was freezing, tired, and plain terrified. Wanting to sleep but afraid to stop, November kept willing herself to continue trekking through the dark.

But only minutes later, she tripped over another risen tree root. Sprawled in the dirt, November realized she was more likely to do real damage and call attention to herself, stumbling along in the dark rather than stopping to rest until daylight. So far, she'd been lucky not to have seen any large predators. Was it too much to hope for, that large cats weren't native to these mountains?

Surveying her surroundings with the help of a few little rays of moonlight shining through the dense treetops, November made out a cluster of bushes. Pushing to her feet, November brushed the loose dirt and debris off and went about hiding herself, sheltering her body as best she could from the elements.

All said and done, she would rather die out here alone, looking into what little sky she could see, than be back in that cabin. Although convinced she'd be too afraid to sleep, her body had other ideas and within minutes, exhaustion lulled her into unconsciousness.

"Fuck you, asshole!"

"Shit! How bad is it, Deeks?" Bruce jumped in as Deeks let rip. Once again, all the attention turned back to Lachlan's arm.

Dammit. Deeks regretted his outburst before he'd even finished yelling the words. He'd wanted an opportunity to check his captain's arm without all eyes drilling into him while he did so. But the words had left his mouth as soon as he'd unfurled the last of the bandage to expose the wound.

When Taniq had stated the bullet had taken a 'nice chunk' out of Lachlan's arm, Deeks had pictured a gash an inch long, a quarter of an inch wide. But the reality was a lot bigger. The bullet had ripped off a good portion of the man's right tricep.

Looking at the trajectory, Deeks figured the bullet would have grazed his back against the bulletproof vest at best. At worst, it may have missed the vest and inserted itself into the edge of his back. Which would explain his captain's easy acquiescence to sit out of guard duty.

Exhaling heavily, Deeks looked at his 2IC and started issuing orders. He might only be third in charge but, when it came to medical, he had a full purview.

"Get his vest and shirt off, now."

With a growl, Deeks focused on Lachlan daring the man to say anything. One single word and he'd tear him to shreds. But Lachlan wasn't stupid, he had to know he was on the back foot here. Proving he had some brains left, the man said nothing as the siblings jumped into action, working together to follow Deeks' instructions.

Deeks knew Lachlan hadn't seen the wound. But did the man have an inkling that the pain was a little more than the bullet having had grazed his vest? Well, yes, Deeks was betting the answer to that was a fuck yes.

Was the asshole going to admit it?

No way in hell.

Especially considering the deathly silence over the comms and the angry looks Lachlan was getting from both Nate and Izzy. With a slight pause at the blood and tear in his shirt, Deeks helped them remove it from Lachlan's torso, making sure it didn't stick to his wound. But what it exposed only resulted in making him even madder.

"Motherfucker! You dumb shit! Get him on the other bed face down. The bullet's in his back. I'm going to have to dig it out."

Taniq swore but the man jumped in to help Nate move Lachlan.

"Shit, I swear I didn't know. I could only see his arm from the position he was in."

Nate's face immediately flushed dark red at Taniq's statement. They'd all seen that look before. The explosion would be epic.

Deeks was damn happy he wasn't the target.

It was a shock when the huge breath Nate took expelled in a ragged sigh instead of screamed words of rage.

"It's not your fault. You're not the medic. I should have sent Deeks back. We all know full well the asshole would have lied and played down any injury to stay in the game. If anything, I should have asked for clarification on what size the word 'fair' constituted."

Taniq nodded and moved out of the way.

"Well, the wound was fair compared to the size of his whole body, but I guess if I compared the wound to the size of his arm, it would have been more indicative of the situation."

It was Isabella who stood, shaking her head.

"It's no one's fault but his. He's your team leader. He knew exactly what he was doing and how to play it to get his own way. Besides, he only overplayed it when acceding so quickly to Nate's wishes. That was his downfall, but I assume he figured we were safe, and the pain would have skyrocketed as the adrenalin had worn off."

Deeks knew Izzy was right. That Lachlan wisely kept his mouth shut as Isabella finished her rant said it all. It looked like the stubborn idiot had tuned out and only realized his mistake in closing his eyes and taking his focus off them when Deeks slid the needle into his arm. Lachlan had tried to turn and block, but it was too late.

"Assholes, make sure you cover my back. Don't want Mac to see it."

"Fucker, like we'd let anyone see his back when he's unconscious, we'd never do that to him. He's out. Let's get this done." Deeks held out his hand as Nate started handing him the tools he needed to remove the bullet and clean out the wound.

DBD's chuckle came through the comms.

"I can't believe he thought you were going to dig it out of him while he was awake. What a dumb ass."

"Yeah, well, I don't think he was thinking much at all these last few hours. His arm is a mess. But the bullet's lodged in his back. All the scar tissue is going to make it difficult to get it out."

The scars on Lachlan's back were courtesy of their last mission, one they'd never forget. Many still resembled angry, red welts as they slowly healed. Removing the bullet would not help the healing process along.

"It looks like the bullet entered through the side opening of his vest and would have exited straight out the back on a slight angle, but hit his vest instead, or maybe the scar tissue. Unfortunately, it didn't break the skin trying to exit.

"It's not bad, but he must have known. There's no way the vest wouldn't have rubbed against it with every step. Once it's out, he'll have another scar, but it shouldn't cause any significant issues. The arm, though, that's going to be a bitch. Whose turn is it to babysit him through physio this time?"

"Bruce!" echoed throughout the comms, followed by laughter as the man himself growled at the synchronized call of his name from his teammates. The golden rule was the last person shot had to babysit the next one through physio. Bruce and Lachlan had been alternating that honor the last few times which in truth only caused more chaos. Alone and bored those two were a nightmare of unmitigated mischief.

In their second to last mission, the first they'd gone on after returning from Afghanistan, Bruce had taken a bullet to his calf when a vicious cat had gotten in his way.

The amount of 'meows' their teammate had suffered through from everyone once they knew the extent of the wound—that it wasn't life threatening—was extreme and would have continued if Bruce hadn't had threatened to kill the next cat they saw if they didn't cut the crap. He wouldn't have—probably—but the boys decided they didn't need to push him and find out. Much like Lachlan, Bruce could be unpredictable at times.

Unfortunately, for Bruce that didn't help him now. They were all alpha men, which translated to them all being assholes and big babies when injured. Their captain was the biggest alpha of them, which meant he was the biggest asshole and least likely to follow doctor's instructions.

It was a challenge to get any of them to do physio, but Lachlan took the cake in stubbornness. And no one wanted the responsibility of making him go. That included Bruce. Knowing the rules were hard to change, Deeks smirked as Bruce threw out his only lifeline, accepting that his only way out of this was to sink another teammate.

"That's not fair. His wound might not have been so bad if he had been treated properly at the time. Taniq covered for Lachlan. He should have to babysit this time."

DBD and Deeks laughed as they recognized Bruce's attempt to save himself, the sudden silence telling as Nate glared at Taniq, who looked like he wanted to be anywhere other than where he was. Nate opened his mouth to respond, but was cut off by Lachlan's groggy words. Shit, Deeks should have given him a higher dose of sedative. Damn stubborn idiot.

"Let him be. I ordered him to play it down. He was in a no-win situation, and you all know it. If anything, you should have noticed that the comms went down for a couple of minutes. Bruce, you're off the hook too. I don't need a damn babysitter. Between my wife, mother, and sisters, I'll never have any peace again. Ouch, will you stop hitting me, woman?"

"That's for pulling rank and putting Taniq in that position, and that,"—Isabella punched Lachlan again in his non injured arm—"is for insinuating your mother, sisters, or I have any control over what you do when you're being a stubborn ass."

Swinging around, Isabella addressed the team.

"Bruce, you will honor the team rules and take the lead. It's not like you won't be there watching over Gracie and Cooper at any rate. The rest of you can stop laughing. It's a moot point. You will all help as required when you're around. This is no different to any other time. Taniq and Deeks may get a reprieve if they're called out for work. And while I assume once DBD meets the family, he will be champing at the bit for an excuse to get out of town, it's not going to happen. So, while all this arguing is fun and all, it's a waste of time. Now, can we please eat so that some of us might get some well-earned sleep?"

Deeks kept an eye on Lachlan, happy their captain slept through dinner only rousing slightly when Mackenzie flicked his forehead in annoyance once she found out, he'd been hiding the severity of his wound. Luckily the guys had wrangled Lachlan back into a shirt since Lachlan had reacted by grabbing Mackenzie's wrist and tugging her down onto the bed with him before tucking her into his side.

Not long after, Isabella made the mistake of wandering over to kiss Lachlan's cheek. Deeks' loud laugh earned him a scorching look from Izzy, but she'd been well and truly captured. Injured or not, conscious, or not, there was no way Lachlan would let either of those women move without waking. The soft look on Nate's face had Deeks smiling, Izzy had relaxed in Lachlan's hold and quickly drifted off to sleep. No doubt feeling safe in her husband's arms for the first time in days. Now, Deeks just had to argue that as the oldest he should get the other bed.

Fuck, he was stuck. He was so close to getting back to the cabin, to his November. Fucking Feds. Earlier, he'd spotted them, but had managed to stay out of sight. Now they were in his path again. With no way to get past without drawing attention to himself, he had to take a page out of the women's book and climb a damn tree.

The indignity, he wasn't a fucken monkey for god's sake. He'd had to hide like a petty criminal. All because two Irish twats took on the royal family of Forest Haven, bringing the heat down on his own kingdom, and the Feds straight to his door.

Pondering all the torturous ways to kill them, he hunkered down to wait out the night. Hold on, November. My sweet, sweet November. I'm coming for you.

TWENTY-TWO

Bruce hadn't meant to spend the whole night on the couch, but it was comfortable. And with one of the guys checking in on the comms every three hours, it was easier to nap on the couch than risk waking anyone if he had to communicate back in anything more than a whisper.

He'd felt his presence rather than heard him, his body attuned to him more than he liked to admit, more than he was ready to admit. So, when Cooper sunk onto the couch next to him, Bruce didn't react except to open one eye and raise an eyebrow in question. Well, shit, it worked for Lachie.

Immune Cooper shrugged and closed his eyes, outright refusing to engage. With a sigh of defeat, Bruce gave in and pulled Cooper into his chest. Once Viper settled on the floor in front of them, he let himself drift back off to the land of nod.

An hour later, he opened his eyes to find Parker standing on the stairs watching them. With a nod of acknowledgement, Parker turned and headed back to his room.

At 0600hrs, Bruce untangled himself from Cooper's arms to head into the kitchen. Coffee first on his agenda, taking over from DBD a somewhat close second.

"Everything okay there, DBD?"

"God, Bruce, she's a mini-Lachlan, only with fucked-up hormones. It's terrifying. One minute she's sarcastic, and in your face, fucking up quotes to mess with me. So much so it's like Lachie's right here, egging her on. The next second, she's a little girl all crying and vulnerable, like when Gracie thought there was a monster in her closet. I'm not equipped for this, man!"

"Huh, can't wait to tell Lachie you think he's a vulnerable, crying little girl sometimes."

"Asshole, you know that's not what I meant. Lachlan doesn't do vulnerable. Don't you remember how he handled the monster-in-the-closet incident?"

"Hey, assholes, what was wrong with the way I handled that? It worked, didn't it?"

"Lachlan, what are you doing on comms? I thought you were asleep?" DBD groused, echoing Bruce's own sentiments.

The guy couldn't follow instructions. Luckily for him, as their captain, he mostly only had to issue them.

"What's your problem, DBD, my baby sister too much for you?"

"Answer the question, fucktard," Bruce growled, keeping his voice as low as possible.

After several seconds and with a huge sigh, Lachlan finally deigned to answer them.

"I took over watch an hour ago. They're all buggered, and before you start, I feel fine. All that sleep did me a world of good. Now answer my question. What was wrong with how I handled the monster-in-the-closet incident?"

"You're kidding, right? Bruce, tell me he's kidding!"

Bruce was still laughing as Sam and Claire walked into the kitchen, staring at him from above as he sat on the floor, leaning against the kitchen bench.

"For Pete's sake, what now?" Claire headed for the coffee Bruce had started on before getting side-tracked.

"Wait." Reaching into his pocket, Bruce pulled out the spare comms and handed one to each of Lachlan's parents.

"Sam and Claire online. Now, to catch you up, DBD was about to tell Lachlan what was wrong with how he handled Gracie's monster-in-the-closet incident."

But before DBD could speak, Isabella inserted herself into the conversation with a barely restrained yell.

"What the hell do you mean you don't know what was wrong with how you handled that? Your baby girl screams for you, sobbing hysterically. You run in, gun drawn, looking for the bad guy, only to find no assailant. Finally, you stop to ask our baby what's wrong, whereby you then stalk over to her closet, fling the door wide open, and unload your Glock into her unsuspecting shoes. Then you slam the door shut, tell our daughter the monster is dead, there'll be a funeral in the morning, kiss her on the forehead, and tell her to go back to sleep before striding back out of the room with Bruce on your six who had obviously gotten there only seconds after you. You both stalked straight past DBD and I as we stood there with our mouths hanging wide open, and you want to know what was wrong with how you handled that? By that stage, I was only surprised Bruce hadn't unloaded his Glock as well." Wow, Isabella was mad, that had been delivered all in one breath and yet Lachlan still walked into the breach.

"Well, yeah. I mean, I killed the monster, she fell back asleep, and we never had another sighting again. I can't see the issue. Besides, Jake was all understanding when he came to investigate the report of gunshots. And Bruce didn't unload his Glock because if she then said there was a monster under the bed, we wouldn't have had any bullets left. It's not like we ran in with spare mags on us."

"Oh my God, who the hell let you two geniuses have guns, and I'm supposed to trust you two to look after our kids in my absence?"

Claire did not look impressed. But while she stood there shaking her head, Sam had sunk to the floor right next to Bruce, laughing as hard as he was. The look Claire was giving Bruce was all knowing and somewhat dampened his mirth. He wasn't innocent in this, and Bruce suspected Claire knew it.

The thing was that while Lachlan was a certified genius, in some things he could be totally clueless. And this was one of those times. Lachlan truly didn't see an issue with the way he'd handled it. But Bruce did know better. It was just more fun doing things Lachlan's way, besides no one got hurt.

Could he have encouraged Lachlan to handle the problem another way? Sure, but why would he have? Bruce would always be happy to follow in his captain's footsteps. Seriously, who wouldn't? It was a green light to cause havoc. The two of them together were madness.

His captain could switch from their dedicated leader to a prankish child in moments, which kept life hilarious, and Bruce was going to stick along for the ride. Right next to his captain's side.

Although Bruce was smart enough not to answer the unspoken appraisal and diverted his eyes. He'd have to watch out for Claire, Lachlan's mother saw too much. It was only fun if you didn't get into trouble for any so-called antics and up until now, Lachlan had always ended up wearing the blame by himself, no matter who else had been involved.

"I am so sorry, Isabella. I thought I raised Lachlan better than that. However, considering his father is on the floor laughing along with Bruce, I can see now, I never had a chance."

"I don't get it. It's not like we had a bullet shortage or anything," Lachlan grumbled as more laughter sounded through the comms.

"Urgh! I give up! Seventeen bullets he unloaded into his daughter's shoes, and he doesn't get why I'm upset. Don't think I didn't notice Gracie's white shoes with the buckles you hated got the worst damage. And why the hell are you up doing guard duty? You're supposed to be resting?"

Before Isabella could launch into any more questions, Bruce heard an oof. From the sounds of it, Lachlan had pulled her into his arms.

"I'm fine, babe, plenty rested. The guys needed sleep and if I didn't pull a shift, it would have meant Deeks would be up next instead of Nate."

"So?"

"So... I mean, do you really want Nate on breakfast duty? Because as leader of this team, it's kind of my responsibility to keep everyone alive."

Four 'Hooyah's' followed and one muttered comment that sounded like 'You're all a bunch of assholes,' which only started the boys laughing again.

Isabella stared into her husband's twinkling eyes and sighed. Why did she think she would win an argument even when logic and common sense were on her side?

With a kiss to his lips, which only encouraged Lachlan to take it deeper, his tongue pushed for entrance and swept into her mouth, taking hers in a slow and thorough show of dominance. She finally stepped back and conceded, ignoring the cat calls and whistles filtering through the open door.

"Fine, you're right. No one wants Nate cooking."

"Seriously, and from my own sister! Them," Isabella turned to see Nate wave his hand through the air, "I can understand, but you, my own twin. Next time you get kidnapped, you can save your own ass."

With a look at the sky, Isabella left her laughing husband by the door and stepped back into the cabin, looking to placate her twin. It took but a glance to see that he was smirking at her. Knowing she'd once again been played, she hit him on the arm as she headed toward the kitchen to make everyone breakfast.

"Ma?"

"Yes, Mackenzie?"

"I thought the twins and Shauna were bad, but they have nothing on these guys."

"Yes, well, I expect the elevated levels of stress and adrenalin build up and when the pressure eases, it bursts, and this is the result. I don't know how Isabella copes with them all by herself."

Various exclamations came through then, but Isabella ignored them and joined the women in their laughter.

Before anyone could sign off, the sound of her daughter crying came across over the comms.

"I want my mummy!"

"Hold on." Bruce's calm voice sounded. "She's fine, Parker has her. Let me grab the earpieces off Sam and Claire, and I'll sync one with my phone. Aright, Speaker on, go for Izzy."

"Hey, baby, what's wrong?"

"Mummy, when you coming home?"

"Soon, baby, not long now. I can't wait to see you. Why are you crying, sweetheart? Did you have a bad dream?"

"I dreameded they blew up all da Smarties factories with Taniq's TNT."

"Oh, sweetheart, they wouldn't do that. Your daddy and Bruce are naughty for threatening you with such nonsense, but they wouldn't do it for real."

Frowning, Isabella turned to Lachlan.

"I don't understand why out of all your threats she takes this one so much to heart and she's so specific. Why would she think you would use Taniq's TNT? I mean, DBD is the demolitions expert and I know Taniq has a secret stash of old TNT somewhere at the house, but she doesn't know that?"

Isabella may have been focused on Gracie, but she still noted the sudden extreme quiet of all the team on comms. She also didn't miss the red tinge working its way through Taniq's cheeks, or

Deeks' head drop as the study of his feet became all compelling. Her brother's Adam's apple moving in a large gulp was also a big giveaway, but it was her daughter's next words, that she reacted too, even if it took her a moment to decipher their meaning.

"Baby, can you please repeat that for Mummy? Freeze! Don't you imbeciles move a muscle! Now, sweetheart, what did you say again?"

"Abort!"

The cry coming from Lachlan and Nate at the same time echoed loudly into the cabin.

"Bruce, you touch that speaker, and I will kick your ass from here to Timbuktu. Gracie, what did you say?"

"I said, they already blew one up, Mummy, but I don't want them to blow up anymore."

"Lachlan! Enough! You and your men need to grow a pair and explain this to me now."

"Baby, how could we get away with blowing up an entire factory? Surely it would have made the news?"

"But,"

"But nothing. She's young and has a great imagination, but imagination or not, you know we couldn't blow up a whole Smarties factory and it not make the news, even in a foreign country. Google it if you must."

"Then why do you all look and sound so guilty?"

"Um… Nate fed her Smarties for meals to get her to eat when you were gone before they got to me."

"What? Nate! What the hell, you know better than that?"

"Crap, sis, she wouldn't eat. What did you want me to do, let her starve?"

"Okay, I think it's time we signed off. Come to GD sweetheart. Say bye-bye, Mummy."

"Bye-bye, Mummy."

Bruce didn't wait for a response. Isabella was yelling at Nate and the best course of action was to cut comms before she worked out Nate had been served up as a sacrificial lamb. No one wanted her to decide there might be more to the story.

Noting Claire's narrowed eyes, and Sam's smirk, Bruce decided now was the perfect time to take Grace upstairs to get her dressed for the day. Grabbing his coffee, Bruce made his escape, taking the devil child with him.

November woke to the sights and sounds of the approaching dawn. Huddled under the blanket, she watched as the sky lightened, a hybrid of pinks and purples before orange overtook them, leaving a blue sky behind. Birds chirped and bushes rustled. The forest was coming alive around her.

Unable to enjoy it, November listened intently for any signs that she wasn't alone with nature. She knew she had to move, but she also needed to eat. Taking the opportunity while she was still ensconced in the bushes, November started in on a tin of baked beans.

Within half an hour of waking, November headed off, down and to the left, toward what sounded like a river. Fingers crossed, if she could get to it, she'd be able to follow it to civilization and savior, and not straight back into her captor's arms.

After breakfast, Bruce wrangled Gracie upstairs. The little miss would need to be cleaned up and changed again, her shirt now looked like a Jackson Pollock's masterpiece. Things were quiet over the comms, everyone somewhat patiently waiting while Lachlan checked in with the Feds. That phone call would determine how the day's events played out.

"Okay, listen up." Their captain commanded everyone's attention. "As far as the Feds are concerned, the threat is over. There's no sign that the house was, is or ever has been under surveillance. They've combed through both Magee and Patrick's properties, and they're convinced they were acting alone."

Finally, some good news.

"Therefore, we're going to split into two groups. Nate, Isabella, myself and Mac, will head for the 4WD and get back to town. Taniq and Deeks will re-join their federal counterparts to assist in the search for the other missing woman. Once everyone is home safe, the rest of us will come back up and rendezvous with Taniq and Deeks."

With a final order from their captain to leave their comms in, the parties separated, intent on making their new destinations as quickly as possible. Bruce couldn't wait to finally get in on some action.

"Lachie. Lachie! What's up, man? You're a million miles away." Only minutes later Nate's voice filtered through the comms.

"Yeah, yeah, I'm fine. There's just something that's been niggling at me, and no matter what way I look at it, I can't make it fit."

"Shit, that's never good!" Bruce paused in his task of drying off a now clean Gracie. After the washcloth failed to make a difference, he'd ended up putting her in the shower fully clothed.

DBD grunted in agreement.

"What is it, Lachie?"

"Well. Where'd Magee and Patrick get the chloroform from? I mean, nothing in their background indicates either of them were qualified as a doctor or vet. It's a controlled substance. Even buying on the dark web is a stretch for them. Plus, the Feds didn't find a stash. So, it begs the question, where did it come from?"

"Shit!" DBD groaned. "There's a third party, either directly or indirectly, but there's gotta be someone else in play. Fuck."

"Agreed!" Nate echoed DBD's sentiments. "Everyone keep your eyes open. Check in for all parties every hour on the half. Deeks, you and Taniq wanna fill in your counterparts?"

"Yeah Nate, will do. Can't wait to throw this at the bosses—not. Watch your six."

"You too. You're the most vulnerable for now. At least there are four of us."

"Copy that."

"Sorry for throwing an extra nut in the works, boys," Lachlan added.

"No, no, no, Lachlan. The saying is 'to throw a spanner in the works' not 'an extra nut in the works,' for fuck's sake."

Bruce smiled as he caught a giggle from Izzy before she covered it. Sure, as if Bruce were standing in front of Lachlan, he was positive Lachlan's eyes were glowing as he prepared to volley DBD's serve back to him.

"DBD, don't be daft. A spanner is something you use to loosen or tighten nuts. Either way, it fixes a problem, an extra nut causes problems. We thought we'd fixed this problem, but now we know there is someone we missed, an extra nut, a nut bag because you gotta be crazy to mess with us, so my apology stands. I'm sorry for throwing an extra nut in the works."

"Don't do it, DBD, you'll regret it," Deeks added as he and Taniq got further away from the team. That Taniq's muffled laughter was soft didn't change the fact they all knew full well Deeks' plea would be ignored.

"Nut bag! What the hell is a nut bag? Do you mean a nut case?"

"No, I mean what I said, nut bag. You gotta have crazy ass big balls to mess with us."

"What, you couldn't have said ball sac?"

"No, nut bag gets across both meanings, duh."

"Duh, he says, duh. Like everyone else followed his logic. Why are you assholes laughing? There's no way you got that without him explaining it."

"Actually, I did," chimed in Isabella.

"Me too," echoed Bruce.

"And me," Nate replied through their laughter.

"If I was with you right now, I don't think I could stop myself from shooting you assholes."

"I think you finally broke him, Captain," Bruce replied.

"Nope, it was you assholes agreeing with me that did it."

"It's not our fault we've been around you so much that we understand your language," Nate added.

"Sure, it is." Lachlan chortled in glee. "Taniq and Deeks have held out."

"That's because, like DBD, they try to use actual logic to see where you are coming from, instead of just accepting it's how your brain works."

Finally dry, Bruce focused back on getting Gracie ready. The interlude was over. Lachlan had done it again. He wasn't sure if the boys had worked it out or not, but any time a mission went FUBAR or had the potential to, their captain created a diversion, enabling them to release some tension before continuing.

Okay, so maybe it didn't work on DBD, but it did for the rest of them, and DBD worked best when he was riled up. So, it was a win-win for everyone. Although one day, the man was going to have a heart attack if he didn't learn to chillax a little. Thinking back to the drop bear episode, Bruce had a huge smile on his face as he re-entered the kitchen with Gracie in tow.

Fucked! This was so fucked it was unbelievable. How the hell had this gotten so out of hand? The idea had been to move to a small idyllic town where he could enjoy the slow pace and put his past mistakes behind him.

He knew, of course, his past may catch up with him one day, but he had thought he'd have had more time. Especially considering he had moved into a town populated with only six hundred odd people. That his belief was crushed was one thing, but for it to have been crushed so quickly after moving into town, that was unfathomable.

He'd had less than a week before his world had once again crumbled around him and while he did what he had to do to survive. It only got worse once that busybody had cottoned on that his drug supplies were coming in a lot faster than warranted in such a small town. But did the busybody report him? Call the sheriff, taking it out of his hands and finally ending this?

No. Instead, he used the information to turn around and extort him too. Two different blackmailers, two different intents, one far more sinister than the other, but both with deadly connotations.

Dammed if he did and dammed if he didn't. He'd thought about confessing everything to the sheriff multiple times. But how could he admit he had stood back and done nothing, his own fears dictating his actions? Both Sam and Lachlan were good men. There was no way they would have stood by and submitted to such horrific circumstances no matter the personal cost.

It had been easier to stand on the sidelines and ignore what was happening when all he'd had to do was supply the drugs to his blackmailer or do an occasional supply drop. But then everything changed. That busybody idiot Magee and his nephew had messed with the sheriff and his family. Now his original blackmailer was calling in lifelines. The mess those two idiots had created was wreaking havoc in his life.

The mountains were swarming with Feds and with every day, more Feds turned up on this side of the mountain. The weird thing was they were descending as if they'd come up and over from the Canadian side. His blackmailer had tried to get back to the girl but hadn't made it.

So now here he was traipsing through the woods by himself, trying to get to a girl who might already be dead while somehow avoiding Lachlan and the Feds.

This was suddenly all too real.

It was one thing to order more drugs than needed and hand off the excess, but it was another to actively participate.

What was he to do?

Could he look into that poor woman's eyes and not want to free her from this nightmare? Or was he about to become another monster for her to fear?

Noise to his left made him stop.

The river was close enough to hear the flowing water, but not loud enough to cover the movement. Someone was near and making their way toward the river, the only question now, was it friend or foe, and how the hell did he know the answer to that if he didn't even know if he was going to turn out to be the good guy or the cowardly villain?

TWENTY-THREE

WHEN BRUCE ENTERED the kitchen with Gracie, he had found everyone waiting and ready to go. Despite the events of the last week, there was an excited air of anticipation. Everyone was looking forward to attending the winter fair.

"Okay, listen up. Before we go, let's remind everyone what the number one rule is today. Nobody goes off by themselves and everyone under twenty-five has a chaperone over twenty-five. Are we all clear on that?"

While there were a few murmurs and clear yeses, one non-answer stood out. Bruce folded his arms across his chest and leaned against the counter, his eyes drilling into Parker's, waiting for him to agree to the stipulation. If he thought Bruce was anything but a patient man, he would be thoroughly disappointed.

With a huff, Parker grumbled 'yes' before heading for his jacket, but it was Bruce's next words that struck the match.

"Don't worry, Parker, I did some research for you. With all the cute girls in town, there are none called Mary, so I won't get in your way." The expletive that came from Parker's mouth would have egged Bruce on even more if Lachlan hadn't taken the opportunity to throw him his own curveball.

"Huh? Wait! Lachlan, how'd you know that? I didn't come across that in my research!"

Laughter flooded the comms as the team cracked up. Okay, so Bruce was pissed that Lachlan had caught something he hadn't. They could laugh but they'd be annoyed too.

With a huff reminiscent of Parker's moments before and with his teammates' laughter in his ear, Bruce turned back to Parker.

"Second thoughts, revise that. Stay away from Genevieve and I won't get in your way."

"Why, what's wrong with Genevieve?"

Before Bruce could answer Parker, Max chimed in. "Yeah, I thought she was a nice girl!"

"Lachlan says she is, but she trusted the wrong guy. Now she's preggers and looking for a baby daddy and would, at this stage, settle for a nice guy, even if he wasn't the right guy."

"That doesn't make sense then. Why is Lachlan worried about Parker falling into that trap? Who is going to call Parker a nice guy?"

Bruce stood by and watched as Parker lunged for his younger sibling. He wasn't quick enough to grab Zac before he got behind Sam, having thrown out his taunt, but the look Parker gave his baby brother promised retribution later. Although, considering the smirk on Zac's face as he stood in relative safety behind Sam's back, the twerp obviously wasn't afraid of his older brother.

"GD."

"Yes, Gracie?"

"Have you finished busting Uncle Parker's balls? Can we go now?"

While there was some muffled laughter, one growl stood out clearly.

"Wow, nicely done, Gracie girl. I haven't heard your mother growl like that since the last time she found out Lou-Ellen had bailed your daddy up."

"You got ears in?"

"Yep," Bruce smirked back at her, knowing what was coming.

"You set me up …"

"Do not finish that!" rang out throughout the room and the comms. Bruce laughed. It looked like some of the family had taken the time to search out the movie and work out what the rest of the quote was.

If he could see Nate now, he was sure his 2IC would be preening like a proud peacock. Although, not for long, based on the grunt that echoed over the comms. He couldn't be sure whether it was Lachlan or Izzy that hit him, but he knew it would have been one of them, whoever was the closest.

"Hey! Geez, Louise! It's just a comedy, for Mary's sake."

"It's not a comedy!" sounded in stereo, again making Bruce laugh.

Before Grace could get them into any more trouble, he figured it was time to move everybody along.

They had decided DBD would join them at the winter festival, so Shauna could join the family and the festivities. That DBD would rather face the rest of the family without Lachlan by his side rather than hang with Shauna alone for a few more hours, said more than any words could have. Although he knew that as soon as Shauna was with the family, DBD would fade into the background, hopefully before any confrontations could occur.

This was one situation where all the team members were happy to leave it in the hands of Lachlan and DBD. Not to say they wouldn't watch the show. But they'd do it safely—from a long distance away.

***

As the sound came closer, he held his breath, still unsure of what action he would take. Then, without conscious thought, he moved. A scream cut through the air as he pulled the woman into his arms, the gun he held to her head silencing her before she could take a breath to scream again.

He didn't know how far he was from any of the others. But he knew her scream would've been heard, which meant he didn't have much time before he had company.

With barely a chance to tell the woman to hush, he flung himself and the woman around as Lachlan, Mackenzie and two others ran with Lachlan's massive dog leading the way into the small clearing.

"Riley, what the hell?" Lachlan shook his head, like he was trying to process what he was seeing. "Well, I guess now we know where Magee got the drugs from."

"He was extorting me. I had no choice," Riley argued, desperation clear in his voice.

"Oh, no choice, you say?! Tell me, who is making you hold a gun to that young woman's head now then? Magee's dead, so it ain't him."

No doubt expecting him to argue, Lachlan looked surprised when Riley agreed with him.

"No, he only wanted the drugs and to lord it over me, my other blackmailer is the problem. He's the evil one. Pure evil. Way worse than Magee could have ever been."

It was the other male in the group that responded to his comment. All four of them, including Mackenzie and the other woman, had their guns pointed at his head. Riley didn't know if they would take the shot while he was holding the girl or not. Unfortunately, he was likely to find out the answer to that question sooner than he would like.

"Who is it? Who could you fear so much that you would do this to an innocent young woman?"

"No, no. It wasn't me. Truly. I never touched them. All I did was give him the drugs when he needed them or, in rare instances, took up supplies. But I never touched them, I swear!"

"Are you serious? You sick fuck! You knew about this and did nothing. You thought this was okay because you didn't touch them? And what happened to your accent, asshole?" Lachlan was going to tear the gutless piece of shit to shreds.

But Riley never got the chance to respond, either to defend himself or name his blackmailer. A loud retort sounded milliseconds before Riley's head blew apart in front of them. Lachlan and Nate were quick to shield the girls with their bodies, but they were too far away to get to the other woman.

Not that there had been time.

Before Riley's body even hit the ground, someone had stepped up behind him to grab the woman, disgust clear on his face.

"Damn stupid man, he was about to stand here and blurt it all out. That's the problem with this world when people who are placid in being blackmailed for years, suddenly grow a conscience!"

At Mackenzie's soft gasp, Lachlan narrowed his eyes at the new threat standing before him. Disheveled, the man looked like he hadn't bathed in days. Lachlan couldn't hide his surprise as he slowly recognized his foe.

"You're fucking kidding me! Mr. Davey?"

"The one and only. A damn near perfect cover. Who would have thought that the boring economics teacher was kidnapping women, torturing them, and killing them each month like clockwork? Quite a wonderful hobby, in truth. Pulled the wool over your eyes, didn't I? The great Sheriff Lachlan Michaels, and your father, for that matter. Although, I guess some consideration might be appropriate, considering you've only been back a few months and you've obviously had other things on your mind. Even so, it has been great for the ego, made putting up with all those sniveling little shits worthwhile. And while I would love to stand around and gloat some more, I'm sure the Feds heard that shot and if I and the lovely November here are going to escape to spend some more quality time together, we must be moving along."

November whimpered at those words. No. No more. She would rather die than spend any more time with this monster. Fearing it was the last thing she would do, November drew upon all her strength and stomped on her monster's foot, she threw her elbow into his gut, and as his grip eased, likely more from surprise than pain, she turned around to knee him in the balls. Yelling and shots rent the air as November ran from the clearing, heading straight for the river.

November knew the other four were there to help her, but her fear of the monster made it seem like they stood no chance against him. It felt like he was on top of her. She couldn't help but chance a look back to see he was only a few feet behind her.

He was facing the way they had come, firing towards the others who had been in the clearing. Counter shots sounded, but not as often as she would have thought. November turned back in time to see the river and the huge rock. But it was too late, she stumbled and fell into the water, to a death she welcomed.

This was a cluster fuck. Lachlan raced forward with the others close on his heels. He and Nate were firing when they had the chance, but opportunities were few. They couldn't risk shooting the woman who was clearly running for her life. So, he could do nothing but watch in horror when she went headfirst into the river. The large jacket acting more as an anchor than a floating device.

Isabella and Mac immediately changed course, toward the river-bank. Lachlan and Nate providing cover while also gradually closing the distance between them and their quarry.

With no one now between them, Nate amped up his barrage drawing Mr. Davey's focus, which allowed Lachlan to duck behind some bushes and come up on the man from his side. Out of bullets, just as Mr. Davey swung toward him, Lachlan tackled the teacher midbody, taking them both into the icy water.

The current was strong and dragged them swiftly downstream.

Lachlan could see Isabella holding on to the woman, trying to keep both their heads above the rapids as she fought to rid herself of the jacket.

Mackenzie was just managing to keep pace with them running down the bank, seemingly trying to keep an eye on everyone at once. He was positive she was communicating to his other team members what was happening, even though the noise of the water meant he could barely hear them.

Nate swam toward him as he struggled with Mr. Davey, both fighting for the upper hand over the gun between their bodies. While he wouldn't have said no to the help under any other circumstances, he could see the women were struggling to stay afloat.

Fearing if they didn't get help soon, they would succumb to their exhaustion and thus the water. He shook his head to indicate that he had it under control and gestured for him to bypass him and aim for the women.

Paying for the distraction, Lachlan felt the vibration of the gunshot as a bullet passed into his side. Pain shot through his gut, like hot blades straight from a fire's flames slicing and burning his skin, taking his breath with him. Water swamped his mouth, choking him as it pulled him under. But he refused to lose this. Not to some hack, women murdering schoolteacher. With everything he had Lachlan tightened his hold on the gun with his left hand and using the rapids, pushed it away from his body.

Psychotic laughter filled his ears alongside a dull buzzing sound. Mr. Davey thought he was going to win. Hell no. Enough was enough. The current was strong, fighting to drag them down, churning them in the rapids. This time the water dragged them under with Lachlan on top. Taking advantage of the roll, Lachlan used his right arm to push down on Mr. Davey's shoulder. With what felt like herculean effort, as the rapids pushed them back to the surface,

Lachlan raised his cold waterlogged body out of water, and slammed his head down onto his opponent's nose, knocking him out cold.

Holding on to the unconscious Mr. Davey, and with a now soaked backpack attached to his back, Lachlan fought to keep them both afloat while he wrestled to free himself from the bag. His arms were aching, his body convulsed under violent shivers, the pain in his gut now numbed by the freezing water but movements were hard won and slow. Yet, Lachlan couldn't help the smile that crossed his face when he saw Mannix swimming toward him.

Focusing forward, Lachlan saw that Nate had reached the women and was trying to keep everyone's heads above the surface. Isabella seemed in a better state than the other woman, requiring less help, although by now they'd all be dangerously cold and losing strength. Nate must have ditched his backpack before he joined them in the river.

Relief swamped his body as he pulled his arm free from his own heavy bag. The issue now was that there was no way clear of the rapids. They would have to ride this to the bottom and hope like hell they had the strength to get out when the opportunity presented, hopefully before the twenty-foot drop to the swimming hole. While the drop was survivable, it had taken a few lives over the years and none of them would be in the best physical condition by the time they got there.

Lachlan heard the calls come through his comms piece before his eyes translated what he was seeing. Out of nowhere, Taniq and Deeks had appeared along the riverbank, racing along its edge.

Sizing up the situation in an instant, they nodded to Lachlan as they ran past him, jumping into the fray, heading for Nate, Isabella, and Emily.

Emily. Her name was Emily. He remembered now, a brief mention when it became clear, Isabella wasn't the only woman missing. But he had been so focused on finding his wife and sister, he hadn't taken the time to absorb it.

The woman had been through hell. Likely, even more so than

his wife and sisters, but he was adamant his team would save her. And if he neglected to let anyone know that he had taken another bullet? Well, the freezing water would stop him from bleeding out and they could yell at him later.

Mac was still running along the bank, slowly losing pace with them. He could hear her communicating with DBD and Bruce. Taniq and Deeks throwing in the occasional comment, but the words sounded muffled to his ears. None made any sense to him. Lachlan released the breath he was holding when he saw Taniq grab Isabella. Deeks reached out and grabbed at Emily and Nate, seconds after they reappeared, having slid under the water for a moment.

Arms tiring, his legs weak from the effort of holding himself and the unconscious man above the water, Lachlan struggled to keep his own fight.

He could have hung on, if only that log hadn't appeared from nowhere and hit him on the back of the head. Lachlan felt Mannix's jaws clamp around his bicep. The last thing he saw before his eyes closed was the log racing down the river, Mr. Davey's body churning alongside it through the rapids.

Sam and the family had barely had time to see a few stalls before it all went to hell. They'd been walking around on the higher flatter portion of the park that normally catered for the town's sports fields, overlooking the picnic tables and playground that was at the bottom of the small waterfall.

Out of nowhere, Bruce propelled Gracie into Sam's arms and took off, racing toward the water, yelling at people to move.

Another shout saw a second man fly past them as Shauna was pushed into their fold. It only made sense that this man was the mysterious DBD. As the man flew past the fire truck, he yelled, by name, for Sanders to lower the fire truck ladder across the river.

Sam thought he recognized the voice, but it wasn't until he saw Max's face that he knew for certain who it was.

As Max mouthed the word 'Dad,' they watched as the man in question glanced over his shoulder as he continued sprinting after Bruce.

"I'm sorry, Max, I truly am sorry!"

Focusing forward again, Sam watched in horror as it became clear why the two men had taken off at such speed.

Passing Grace off to Parker, he, Max, and Jonah pushed into a sprint, following the other men, heading straight toward the bank. Fire chief Sanders had gotten over his shock and was indeed following Max's dad's instructions, lowering the ladder across the water, aiming for the other bank. It wasn't the first time the fire truck had been used for this type of rescue, the truck and ladder had been customized for this very reason.

There was nothing they could do but watch as Bruce and Max's dad raced up the side before peeling off and diving in at different points.

Seven people were getting tossed around in the wild waters. Bruce had run past the first group of five, two of whom looked unconscious, before diving in. Apparently aiming to make his way across and use the rapids to catch them.

Yet, Max's dad continued further up the bank passing two more people separated by several feet before he too dived into the raging waters. Neither looked to be conscious, one of whom Mannix had clamped in his jaws.

Knowing the strength of the rapids, Sam sprinted up behind the fire chief, and along with Max and Jonah, they pulled themselves across the ladder. They would assist in pulling them out and not just hope they would have the strength to grab the ladder as they went past. Well, the unconscious ones were going to need help at any rate.

The river tapered into a pool at the bottom near the playground and BBQ area. It wasn't that easy though. No, because before that there was a sharp twenty-foot drop that cascaded onto sporadic groupings of large rocks. If they couldn't grab them as they passed the ladder, the drop could possibly kill them, if they were still alive at that point.

Other men, including the town's three firefighters, made a line along the water's edge, ready to help pass the bodies up the bank to safety and care. As the rapids brought the inhabitants closer, Sam got a clear picture of who was who, and while there were a few he didn't know, he knew his own son wasn't amongst the first group, which meant he was one of the two unconscious men further up.

He watched as Max's dad swam toward the furthest unconscious man, grabbing hold, and could only pray it was Lachlan he had saved, hoping that Mannix was saving his master and not some unknown person.

It was callous, but something told him that if the other guy were innocent, they would have gone to him first, team member needing help or not.

***

Max watched as a man and Isabella—he had seen enough pictures by now to know her by sight—came hurling toward him and Jonah. At once, they both grabbed for them as the water tried to take them past. The force jolted Max's arm, but he held on.

Out of his peripheral vision, he noted that between them they'd somehow managed to grab all five people before the river could take them further downstream. It helped that three of the men were still conscious although just barely in one case.

Hanging on to their arms, they all belly crawled back across the ladder until they could pass them off to those on the bank. It was only when Max stood; he saw it was men dressed in black military gear who took them from their holds.

He watched as others rushed past him before diving into the water. On the grassy bank, three massive helicopters sat waiting. Max turned back towards the river even as he noted a regal-looking man heading towards them, not realizing he was aiming for him and Jonah specifically, until a hand fell onto each of their shoulders.

"Thanks boys. My men will take over from here. I believe your family could use some comfort." The man indicated for them to turn as Mackenzie came stumbling toward them, sobbing heavily as she navigated the bumpy terrain.

Jonah took off toward his younger sister, and Max didn't hesitate to follow. Wrapping her in his arms, Jonah picked her up and swung her around as they both held on for dear life. Max listened, while Mac tried to tell Jonah what had happened. He learned that Lachlan had stopped communicating and then had slipped under the water. A log had hit him from behind.

Looking further up the river. He could see his father held Lachlan in his arms with Mannix at their side. Their heads bobbled barely out of the water. Two other men were powering through the water towards them, even as the rapids hurtled all its occupants down toward the ladder still lying across the banks. Max didn't know what was going on or how Lachlan and his father had ended up together, but he prayed they would both survive. Besides, he couldn't kick their asses if they were dead.

Crunching stones and sliding rocks announced new arrivals, and Max turned to see Sam and Claire—now holding Grace—Shauna, and both sets of twins appear at their sides. Mackenzie quickly enveloped into their arms. Huddled together, they focused on the unforgiving river, watching in horror as his father, the man they called DBD and Lachlan, dropped beneath the waterline.

The rapids teasingly spat them both back up momentarily before trying to drag them back under again.

Relief was palpable when the men in black reached his dad and Lachlan before they disappeared again. Between the three of them they swam Lachlan toward the bank. More men were in line to help pull them out.

Turning, Max watched the man in charge approach their group, walking past his men who rushed Lachlan and his dad straight to the waiting helicopter. A small nod, the only indication information had been communicated between them.

"Good morning Mr. and Mrs. Michaels. It is a pleasure to meet you."

Instead of a civil response, gasps sounded, Max's included as Gracie launched herself from Claire's arms into the strangers.

"Poppy!"

"Hello, beautiful. Now, hasn't your daddy and Bruce spoken to you numerous times about throwing yourself into people's arms?"

With a frown forming on her forehead, Gracie shook her head. "Nut ah." At the raised eyebrow, she must have decided to rethink her position, then asked, "Poppy, what does numous mean?"

At his chuckle, tension left the little girl's body and she relaxed into her poppy's hold.

"Now, where were we? Ah, yes. My name is Admiral Mark Anderson. I would also be Nate and Isabella's father and this one's Poppy. As well as the man in charge of all the seals that were here, including Lachlan's team." The Admiral paused as the noise of one of the choppers taking off echoed loudly around them. "Now, I'm sure you have lots of questions and I, for one, would love to answer them. However, I need to get my people to the hospital. I would offer to bring you, but unfortunately, I don't have the room. If you would consent to exchanging numbers, I'll call and update you a little later."

"Of course." Sam stepped forward to shake the Admiral's hand. Max had long ago stopped calling Jonah's dad Mr. Michaels. It wasn't practical as an adult, especially when he worked under Sam in the sheriff's office. "It's a pleasure to meet you, although I would have preferred different circumstances."

"You're taking Gracie too." Max swung his head to look at Jonah at Claire's statement. It hadn't been a question, despite Claire ending the sentence on a higher octave. The Admiral's body language said it all. Should they allow it though? Max along with Jonah and Lachlan's parents had promised Lachlan that they wouldn't allow anyone to take her away from them.

"Yes, I am. I know you have done a wonderful job of looking after her and would be happy to do so until we return. Unfortunately, our children need hospitalization. Lachlan was in the first bird to leave. He appears to have failed to tell the team he'd been shot. Again. Which may have changed the outcome should they have known, but that's done now, and I know both Isabella and the boys will yell at him later. Isabella is, however, now conscious and refusing to leave without her daughter. She was in the water too long and needs treatment asap. The woman gets her stubbornness from her mother so you can see my reluctance to fight it. I can promise you Grace will be fine, and we will return as soon as we get medical clearance." The Admiral paused and looked at Max. "And I mean all of us."

With a nod of his head, after reclaiming the comms earpiece from Mackenzie, the Admiral bid farewell and turned to walk back to the last remaining helicopter, Gracie waving madly at them over her Poppy's shoulder.

"Admiral, wait."

"Yes, Shauna?" The General paused his steps to turn and face her.

"What does DBD stand for?"

Max wasn't sure the Admiral was going to answer but after a few seconds, he met Max's eyes.

"My understanding is that DBD stood for Dead Beat Dad. Although there doesn't appear to be any animosity between the men. As you saw today, they would die for each other and have proved it more times than I can count. I have a sneaking suspicion there is another meaning that your father doesn't know about because I'll be damned if I believe Isabella would let them or her daughter call him that to his face after all these years, no matter what mistakes he made in his past."

With that, the Admiral turned and walked back to the last waiting chopper. Max and the Michaels family watched in shock as the helicopter took off.

"He said he earned it."

Max turned to Shauna as she wiped a tear from her eye.

"I asked him what kind of name DBD was, and he said it was one he earned, so he lives with it. He was grumpy, and he growled especially when I pushed his buttons on purpose. But he never yelled. He saved me. I felt so safe with him. I'm sorry, Max."

"Hey, stop. Why are you sorry? That man is my father and yes, he made some crappy choices when Mum died, but you know what? I have good memories of before that, and even after there were good times, it wasn't all bad. And don't forget, in the end, he did right by me. Whether Lachlan pushed him or not, it was still his decision to let me stay with you and, by the looks of it, he got his act together. I figure it's gotta take a hell of a strong man to admit his faults and come back from it." Max stopped to smirk at the youngest Michaels female.

"Plus, it makes me happy to know that he and Lachlan had each other's backs over there. That's not to say I won't kick both their ass's when I get hold of them though!" Max added a wink as he released Shauna from his embrace.

"Now, how 'bout we enjoy what's left of this winter fair? I reckon there is a lot we don't know about what happened today. And I don't think we're going to find out until they sort through everything, so let's ignore them and go about our day. I, for one, could go a hot cocoa."

Max kept the 'with whiskey' part silent. His arm was a little wet from pulling Isabella out of the water, but he was more in shock from seeing his father than anything else. A shot or two of whiskey in a hot drink sounded like bliss. Sam and Claire nodded their heads in agreement. The area was swarming with Feds and even though Sam was technically the town sheriff whether on leave or not and Jonah and Max were his deputies, it was clear everyone was going to have to wait for answers.

Later that night, the Admiral rang Sam and gave an update on how everybody was. The doctors had treated everyone for various degrees of hypothermia. Bruce and DBD had come off much better than the others, as they had spent less time in the water. The other seals who had come to their rescue had also been properly attired, so had suffered no consequences.

Nate was still unconscious, but the prognosis was good. Isabella was doing well, as was the baby. Although the doctors had ordered bed rest for a couple more days. Sam didn't mention that he and his wife hadn't known Isabella was expecting again, but couldn't contain his smile at the news.

Lachlan had flown through the surgery without issue, but they were keeping him in an induced coma for a couple of days to allow his body to recover and something about protecting the hospital staff. Sam got the feeling it was an understatement to say his son was not the best of patients. The team wouldn't leave to come back until they could all come back together, but Bruce had demanded the Admiral enquire about his charges. Sam had chuckled at the Admiral's phrasing of Bruce's request.

The Admiral also confirmed that Mr. Davey and his victim Emily were both in a serious condition, but the hope was they would survive. They should have a better idea by morning. Sam hoped Emily was a strong woman mentally, as she would have a long recovery.

Before ending the call, the Admiral had asked Grace if she wanted to say hello, but the little minx appeared to be arguing with some little boys in the background and wasn't about to tear herself away to talk to her grandparents. Although she did deem to throw a shout of 'hello' toward the phone, that made Sam laugh. Their family had grown, and he couldn't wait until they were all safely at home.

TWENTY-FOUR

Lachlan woke to the sound of bickering and an annoying beep. He quickly registered his location and contemplated pretending he was still asleep. The problem was, he didn't know how long he'd been out and the one thing he knew was the longer he stayed out, the longer they would try to keep him in the damned hospital.

With a put-upon sigh, he opened his eyes and aimed them at the little munchkins sitting on top of him, arguing over who should get to lie where.

"Seriously, there is enough room for all three of you, so please stop arguing."

The fighting gave way to three shouts of 'Daddy' as they threw themselves on top of him, all wanting to hug him at once. While the 'oof' of pain didn't get through to the children, it got through to DBD and Bruce, who both jumped in to intervene, grabbing the rug rats before they could do any real damage.

Shit, three rug rats. He had neglected to tell his family about the other two. What were the chances that someone else did it for him?

"Not a chance, brother. We left that little surprise for you." Bruce grinned, somehow zeroing in on his exact thoughts.

A glance to his right showed his wife in the bed next to him, sleeping, while across the room Nate was also unconscious, as was Emily. The Admiral was napping in one armchair as Taniq and Deeks watched him from the other loungers, not having deemed to get up when the rug rats had attacked him.

A raise of his eyebrow had Deeks standing to give him a sit-rep on the status of his wife and team, including both Nate and Emily who had both woken a few times over the past two days and a still unconscious Mr. Davey, as well as the ensuing investigations.

While another nap was tempting, he couldn't stand the look of fear on his youngest son's face as he sucked his thumb, perched in DBD's arms.

"Come here, baby boy. Daddy needs a hug."

DBD lowered Xavi onto his bed, murmuring in his little boy's ears to be gentle. It wasn't necessary with this one, it was the other two who were rambunctious and unaware of the power of their limbs.

Xavi was his cuddle bug, always content to nestle in for the long haul. If allowed, Xavi would happily stay in his arms until the doctors released him from hospital. In fact, getting him to leave Lachlan for even a small amount of time might prove impossible.

Lachlan felt Xavi relax in his embrace as he eyed his other two children. Gracie was looking between him and Bruce. He knew without a doubt what was coming next and so, it seemed, did Luca.

"No, you can't have any Smarties, duh. Like they're going to give you Smarties while they're all in the hospital and if you haven't noticed, the only one stupid enough to fall for that is still asleep."

That got several laughs. Although DBD was still quick enough to put his hand up to intercept and stop Grace from hitting her brother.

"Gracie, you don't get to hit your brothers, even if you don't like what they say. And Luca, who exactly are you calling stupid?"

Lachlan grinned at his oldest son. DBD, having also noticed what Lachlan had, shook his head at his antics. Nate was starting to stir, and Luca was going to fall straight into his trap.

"Uncle Nate, of course. Who else gives her Smarties when they shouldn't?"

"You wanna come over here and say that to my face, mister?" Nate asked from across the room.

With a quick look of surprise at Nate, Luca turned back to Lachlan.

"Hey! No fair! You set me up …"

Laughter filled the room, as the Admiral's bellowed, 'Don't say it!' came too late, Gracie finishing the saying for her brother.

Kids, just when you thought they were fighting, they would turn around and have each other's backs. The laughter got louder when the Admiral turned to growl at Nate, who put on his own puppy dog eyes trying to look as innocent as possible. A mumbled 'It's a comedy, Dad' falling well short of its mark. It got even better when the Admiral tried to tell Gracie that we didn't use words like that. His little angel's response...

"Poppy, Mummy uses much worser words than that when she talks about Lou-Ellen." Ha, that one wasn't even on him.

Needing to hold his other kids just as much as they needed to be held, going by the fact both had their thumbs in their mouths, which was not a normal circumstance for his oldest and youngest, Lachlan gestured for the guys to lower them onto the bed.

Luca quickly cuddled under his right arm, his little head rested on his shoulder, as he pulled his sister in front of him, allowing her to rest her head on Lachlan's chest. Within moments, all three were asleep, with only Xavi still sucking on his thumb.

Feeling eyes on him, Lachlan turned to face his wife, who was smiling at the puppy pile. Before he could speak, Isabella was quick to quell any delusions that he was not in the doghouse.

"Don't say a word, mister. We don't want to hear any nonsense from you. If you think we don't know that you knew you were in trouble before you sent Taniq and Deeks to help us, you're deluded. Even if you couldn't hear them, you knew damn well they could hear you. So, husband dearest. The only question we have is, were you adorning another bullet hole before you turned Nate away?"

Lachlan shook his head.

Despite their grousing, he knew they all cared, and he would never lie to them. He was, however, relieved that this was not only the true answer, but it was also the correct answer.

"Lucky man, 'cause if you had been shot before you turned me away, you'd be in the doghouse for years!" Nate groused at him.

Lachlan groaned, saved only from responding as his wife redirected his attention.

"You are in so much trouble, Lachlan Michaels. While you're here, you will behave and follow all instructions from the hospital staff. If I hear you've given any of them a tough time, I'll ensure you're confined to bed rest for another day. Every time you complain or defy instructions, we'll extend your stay here. Am I clear, darling?"

Lachlan chanced glancing at his teammates and even the Admiral, but it was clear they were all on the same page, so with little choice, he nodded. He would work around this somehow. Like it or not, he might have to play their game for a day or two, but he would win in the end. He always did.

Movement from the munchkins on his chest silenced the room. Gracie stretched a huge yawn before calling for her mother. After she gave him a gentle pat on his face, Lachlan kissed her cheek before Bruce transferred her over to her mother's bed.

Luca snuggled in closer, and Lachlan started to drift, content his family was safe. The only concern was how to drop the other bomb, that of Luca and Xavi, onto his parents and siblings.

He'd been hoping the Admiral would do it for him, but having noticed the displeasure on the Admiral's face at the discussion of another bullet hole, Lachlan was going to assume he was going to have to face the music on his own.

Surely his parents would understand there wasn't enough time to delve into that story when he needed to get out of there to find his children's mother. Shit, most of it was classified anyway...

Fighting sleep, Lachlan reopened his eyes and forced himself to focus on the Admiral. His father-in-law accommodated him by moving closer with a raised eyebrow in question.

"Emily?" Lachlan nodded his head toward her bed. "Where's her family? Why is she alone?"

Admiral Mark Anderson sighed and glanced around the room before settling his eyes back on Lachlan. Of course, half out of his mind on medication, and he would still notice and worry that the young woman was alone.

"She's not exactly close to her family. Her friends are the ones who notified the authorities she was missing, but even that was a few days after the fact."

"Okay, so she's one of us now. Cool, we'll take care of her. Welcome her to the family when she wakes up. I'm gonna have a nap."

And that was it. Mark shook his head even as his daughter and the team of men around him smiled. The one thing most people didn't see when they looked at Lachlan was how big his heart was. It was huge and all-encompassing.

Lachlan didn't think twice about adding a woman who, a few days ago, had been unknown to them, into their family. Whether she wanted to see them all again or not, she now had a huge family who would always fight to protect her and not one of them in the room was surprised. It wasn't like it was the first time it had happened.

"Dad?"

"Yes, Nate?"

"Where's Mum?"

"Ah, well, she left after you and Isabella fell asleep again. She needed to go home to pack and finalize some paperwork."

"Pack?"

"Yes, for some reason, she doesn't trust me to get the job done right."

Neither Nate nor Isabella bothered to contain their smirks at this, but it was Isabella who took over the questioning from her brother.

"Why is she packing, and what paperwork?"

"Ah, well. Um. Your mother and I planned to talk to you together, but I suppose she won't mind if I tell you without her here. We're, ah, selling the house. We decided to move, and we bought some properties elsewhere. Happened all kind of fast, but there you have it."

A glance around the room told him his answer hadn't helped. Everybody who was awake looked to be frowning.

"Poppy?"

"Yes, Luca?"

"You suck at ex pan nations."

"Yes, well, you learn too much crap from your dad. But what I was trying to say is we decided we didn't want to be so far from our kids, the teams, and our grandchildren. We knew you were all planning to settle in Lachlan and Isabella's house again or use it as a home base as needed if on the road, so we started looking into properties. With everything that's just transpired, we may have jumped onto some opportunities and, well, we, ah, bought Riley's house and Magee's general store. Mother and I are going to take over the store as a future retirement plan of sorts for her and, well, it also means we can keep track of what is coming into town—less surprises that way and fewer questions when it's armory and so forth for our teams."

Silence. You'd think he's just said something crazy. Feeling a red tinge color his cheeks, Mark waited for their reactions to the news. Luckily it didn't take long.

"Oh my God, that's great. I can't believe you'd move to be with us!" Isabella managed to smile even as tears pooled in her eyes. "It'll be great to have all our family around us. Kids, doesn't that sound good?"

While Gracie nodded, it was Luca's answer that shocked the group.

"No!"

"Luca, what do you mean, no?" Isabella exclaimed, clearly as surprised as Mark was by the answer.

"Xavi, Gracie, and I aren't staying with Poppy and Nanna again until they learn how to get rid of monsters properly!"

Ignoring the loud groans that filled the room, Mark focused on his daughter.

"Honestly, I still don't know where we went wrong. We woke to the boy's screams, scared the crap out of us. But we jumped out of bed and got to them within a minute. Your mother gathered them in her arms, and once they told us there was a monster in the closet, I opened the door to check and showed them it was empty. I even checked under the bed, but they wouldn't settle. We ended up taking them back to our room and all they would say is that I should call Daddy or Bruce to take care of it."

"I'm going to kill him," Isabella muttered. "And where do you think you're going, Bruce?"

"Um …" Bruce stopped his backward progress to the door.

"Poppy, don't you know monsters are see-through?" Gracie sat shaking her head, sitting beside her mother on top of the bed.

"Oh, they are, huh? Ah, did you mean invisible?" At Gracie's nod and Luca's 'Duh,' Mark pushed on even though it felt like he was on shaky ground. "Well, no, I guess I didn't know that. So how am I supposed to get rid of invisible monsters from the closet if we can't see them?"

Mark was beyond frustrated. He had a feeling he was in a no-win situation here and damned if he and his wife didn't enjoy having their grandkids stay over occasionally, but at what price?

Isabella was fuming. His daughter would never be a good poker player. DBD was rubbing his temple as if trying to dispel a migraine of epic proportions. While Taniq, Deeks, and Nate were failing to hide their laughter. Bruce was looking for an escape, the man continued to inch slowly toward the door, but it was the look of bewilderment on a newly woken Lachlan's face that clinched the deal.

"I don't get what the big deal is!" Lachlan mumbled, no doubt purposely avoiding his wife's eyes.

"Don't be sad, Poppy, it's okay. Daddy's teaching us how to shoot."

"Gracie! That was a surprise, idiot."

"Don't call your sister an idiot, Luca, and trust me, I'm surprised. Look at my face—see surprised."

"Oh, um, Mummy, you look more mad than surprised. But it's okay, Poppy. We can come stay with you in a couple of years when we have our own guns. We'll take care of our own monsters and Gracie's if she's still too young."

"Lachlan! Are you teaching our babies to shoot?"

"Geez, you make it sound bad. It's not like I'm using real bullets."

"Bruce, sit the hell down." Mark growled. "Lachlan, why do my grandchildren think they need a gun to deal with monsters in the closet?"

"Daddy?"

Lachlan turned to face Xavi, "I thought Poppy was smart, but he didn't know you have to unload your Glock into the closet to kill the monster."

"Perfect terminology, son. I'm so proud."

"Dad, can you please shoot my husband?"

"Isabella, right this second, I'm damned tempted. However, I might leave that for his parents once he tells them there are two other 'surprises'—or should I say four?—he's kept from them! But in the meantime. *Son*—are you telling me the only way to have reassured my grandchildren the other night would have been to shoot up the floor of their closet?"

"Why are you both so angry?" Lachlan threw his hands up jostling the twins. "We tell our kids that we go out and shoot monsters all the time. These two have lived it. Of course, they are going to expect that we do the same if there is one in the closet. I still don't see the problem here!"

"See, Dad, see what I'm dealing with, and now he's teaching your three-year-old granddaughter and four-year-old grandsons to shoot."

Before Mark could respond, laughter choked out from the other side of the room. As one, all turned to Emily, who was sitting up in the bed holding her stomach as she laughed and tried to explain herself in between gulps of air and gasps of pain. The young woman was so thin, covered in cuts and bruises, she also had multiple broken bones so to see her smile. Well...

"Oh, my God. I'm sorry but... He seriously doesn't see a problem with shooting up a child's closet to scare away monsters, and now he's teaching them to shoot. He's got to be the coolest dad ever."

Mark watched as Emily looked around the room a small smile on her face dropped away quickly with everybody's focus now on her, reality intruding on the moment. The young woman focused on Lachlan.

"Thank you! I've already thanked everyone else, but it doesn't seem like enough! I didn't think I'd survive, let alone ever laugh again. You saved me. Even when I had lost all hope, you all risked your lives to save me. I will never forget you."

Once the proper introductions were made between Lachlan and Emily, Emily sat back to watch the antics of the team. Although she looked anything but relaxed, Mark hoped once she got to know the team, she would feel safe with them. He understood it would take time. Her gaze flicked around the room but routinely bounced back to the doorway. Wide eyed, her fingers twisted and scrunched the sheet covering her, while her right foot bounced side to side underneath the blanket at a frantic pace. The poor girl was terrified but tried to hide it behind a smile on her face.

Mark knew his team would distract her as much as possible. Little moments of relief, where the smile was genuine before she tensed and remembered why she was there. They wouldn't even have to do anything but be themselves.

His men were often funny and razzed the hell out of each other, which admittedly had gotten much worse once their captain, the ringleader, had woken. They had undoubtedly been worried for him, but it was clear they were a strong unit, one that cared for each other beyond measure.

But the look on Lachlan's face when Mark put the phone on speaker with Lachlan's whole family on the other line was worth it. Priceless. He would not admit to taking some small satisfaction in seeing Lachlan's demeanor. Lachlan drove him nuts on purpose most of the time, so small paybacks had to be savored. It was time to pay the piper. The fact that DBD was also uncomfortable at that moment was for good reason.

TWENTY-FIVE

"UM, hi, everyone, you're on speaker. The gangs all here," Lachlan would get his father-in-law back for this. There was no way this call had to happen this quickly, nor on speaker with everyone listening.

A chorus of hellos or versions thereof filled the room. With a quick glance at his morphine drip, he caught Bruce smirking at him, aware of the temptation to press the button and knock himself out.

As the voices finally quietened, it was his dad that started the conversation.

"Son, is everyone well?"

"Yep."

"Uh huh, well, that's informative," His dad continued as chuckles filled the air. "Let me guess, there is something else you haven't told us and you're wondering how to say it?"

"Yep."

"And are you going to tell us or make us guess?" Lachlan would have picked neither but after a few seconds of contemplation, his dad sighed and made the decision for him.

"Okay, guess number one. Is it that Isabella is pregnant?"

"No, but she is, and the baby's fine."

"That's great, honey. We're delighted for the both of you." His mother inserted, bringing a smile to his face. She'd been vocal about wanting grandkids for a while. The poor woman had no clue her wishes had been filled multiple times over.

"Okay, guess number two. You plan to move your entire team into your house and live together for the rest of your lives?"

"No, that's not it, but yeah, they're all moving in. It's what we do. Even Emily, if she wants to, but I don't think we asked her yet." Lachlan took in Emily's reaction. "Yeah, she looks surprised. How did you know?"

"Shauna explored your house when, under Daniel's protection, said there were a number of rooms specifically decorated, so I made the leap, especially since it sounded like you all lived together previously."

"Daniel?"

"Yes, Daniel! I refuse to call him DBD since we've been informed what it means unless you'd like to tell me differently?"

Shit. Lachlan winced and shook his head, not that his dad could see him.

"Um?" Emily raised her hand like she was back in grade school. "What do they think DBD means?"

Feeling a burn that no doubt meant his face had reddened, Lachlan met her eyes to reply. "I'll assume Dead Beat Dad."

"But it doesn't?" Emily asked, looking between him and DBD.

"No!"

"Yes!"

Both Lachlan and DBD answered at the same time.

"DBD, what's your middle and last name?"

"Davidson and I don't have a middle name." But DBD stared at her a moment before continuing. "Although these idiots used to say it was Bernie because they thought I looked like the dead guy from that stupid movie… you… you assholes!"

His team burst into laughter.

All this time, DBD had stood for Daniel Bernie Davidson, and he'd finally worked it out.

"Wow, they're just like my third graders, only taller."

His traitorous wife laughed as she agreed with Emily. "Yep, and what's worse, they give them guns and set them loose on the world at large. It's terrifying."

Ha, ha. Lachlan poked his tongue out at Isabella.

"Okay, well, I guess we're up to guess number three then, unless someone would just like to tell us straight?" At the sudden and complete silence, Lachlan practically heard his father's eyes roll.

"Okay, I guess not. Would this have anything to do with Xavi and Luca?"

"Maybe—kind of—yes? How you know those names?"

"Son, you are driving me insane here. I already told you that Shauna had explored your house. She saw the bedroom with their names on the door. Gracie also mentioned their names a couple of times, and you also referenced the term 'kids' several times. I even asked you about it, but you nicely dodged my questions. Plus, when I spoke to Mark last night, he was trying to get Gracie to say hello, but she was too busy arguing with what sounded like two little boys. So, we figured at some stage you would fill us in. Now, are they Gracie's cousins?"

"No."

"Lachlan!" His dad groaned.

"Daddy, you suck at this. Grandpa? I'm Luca. I'm five."

"Hold it right there Mr. and back that train right up! You want to try that again Luca?" Lachlan mock growled at his oldest son who was currently wearing his Mr. Stubborn Pants face.

"No."

"Luca!"

"Fine!" Luca huffed. "Grandpa, my name is Luca. I spose if you want to be tech-e-call, I'm four but I'm still the oldest so that makes me the bestest. Daddy and Mummy adopted us 'cause we were borned in

Portugal. It's a secret, but we're legal, Daddy said so. Whatever that means." Lachlan hid his smile when Luca looked at his brother and shrugged but didn't stop his narrative. He should have known his oldest had ulterior motives when he'd willingly spoken up.

"Gracie said that Grandma gave her lots of brownies, but she didn't bring any back to share. That was mean. Mummy says we're spose to share."

"Well, hello, Luca, great to meet you." His dad may have been chuckling, but it was his mother's sigh of exasperation that echoed through the line. "I'm sorry we didn't send any brownies. It seems we're a little out of the loop. We'll make sure you get some when you come home. There is never a shortage of those here. So, if you're four, how old is Xavi?"

"He's four too, but I'm still the oldest."

"Of course, you're twins. That explains so much."

"No, they're not, Grandpa."

"Gracie, of course they're twins. We've been through this before. How is it you accept that Uncle Nate and I are twins, and that Parker and Cooper are twins, but you won't accept that Luca and Xavi are twins?"

"Zac and Josh are twins too, Mummy. They denical."

"Identical, honey, and yes, that's the same as Luca and Xavi, they're identical twins too."

"No, they're not, Mummy, we're fulled up on twins. They're just Peter's."

"Lachlan! Why are you laughing?"

"Um." Shit, was he still in the doghouse? This could be bad.

"And who is Peter? Isn't that their therapist, Dr. Peter? And I still don't get why the kids call him Dr. Peter. His name is Dr. Hank Shepard. What am I missing here?"

"Um." Funny how no one in his team jumped in to help him. Assholes.

"It's PITA not Peter, stupido, and you're the PITA."

"That's what I said, dung bat."

"Lachlan!"

"Yes, dear?"

"You know what? Forget it. Xavi? Please tell me what your siblings are squabbling about?"

"Mummy, I'm Daddy's favorite and the smartest. Answering your question seems counterproductive to my status."

Lachlan didn't miss the look his wife cast him at Xavi's correct use of the word counterproductive. It wasn't his fault their youngest son was smart and didn't like to be away from him. Although maybe he should stop taking him into the control room for a while...

"Xavi, you are exceptionally smart, but Daddy does not have a favorite."

"Yes, he does, and it's you, Xavi."

"Lachlan!" "Daddy!"

"What?"

"You cannot say you have a favorite."

"Sure, I can. I love them all, but Xavi's my favorite. He doesn't dob on me to Mummy if he catches me drinking out of the juice box." Lachlan paused to poke his tongue out at his daughter. "Nor does he spell it out for Mummy when I teach them how to call each other and their doctor names without calling attention to themselves." This time he poked his tongue out at Luca.

Seconds later, Gracie had somehow joined her brothers on Lachlan's bed. Squeals of delight echoed through the room as Lachlan tickled all three of his children at once.

"Seriously, Lachlan. For Mary's sake. Xavi, what does Peter stand for?"

"PITA not Peter, P – I – T – A. Pain In The Ass."

"Huh, you're no longer my favorite!" Traitor!

"Daddy!"

"Nope, too late. My new favorite is in Mummy's tummy."

"Daddy?"

"Yes, Gracie girl?"

"How is the baby going to get out of Mummy's tummy?"

"Huh, hadn't thought that one through. Tell you what, why

don't you ask Mummy that question and then let me know what the answer is?"

"Okay, Daddy."

"Claire, would you like your oldest son back?"

"Sorry, Isabella dear. Going on the laughter in this room. I seem to have enough on my hands. Best of luck though. Samuel?"

"Crap, the whole first name, huh? Um, son, we're going to sign off here. We'll see you when you get home. Can't wait to meet the boys. Try to stay out of trouble for a little while, though."

"Sure, Dad, no problem. Um, just one thing. I wasn't hiding the twins from you. Their story is complicated. The boys didn't come into play until one of our first missions once we had relocated state side. There, ah, may have been a couple of months' gap between us returning to the US and me returning home to become sheriff …"

"Understood, Lachlan. I believe we have a lot to talk through once you're all back. I suggest you call Max later though and then have Daniel do the same. I don't believe those conversations need to be a group exercise, but there will be no hiding from them by either of you. Am I understood?"

Urgh! "Yes, sir, understood. See you all later."

"One last thing son, Mayor Lewinski wants you to get in touch, something about an influx of several families looking to relocate to our small town. They've used your name as a reference."

"Yeah, okay Dad. I'll call him later. They're all good people, a lot of them have skills the town will benefit from. If I remember correctly, one's a teacher. Huh, actually… I think one's a dentist too. Geez, if I didn't know the background, I'd think it was too coincidental."

"Another interesting story, no doubt. Talk soon son!"

Lachlan signed off to DBD's groan, which of course made everyone laugh.

With a final chuckle, Lachlan beamed over at his wife, who couldn't hide her smile any longer. The kids had settled into a puppy pile on top of him. Everyone was safe. Soon they would all be able to go home.

Lachlan would have happily drifted off for a nap, except for the evil smirk the Admiral was aiming his way. Judging by the look on the Admiral's face, Lachlan was positive he shouldn't ask his father-in-law what the smirk was about. Unfortunately, the man was happy to tell him unprompted.

"So, boy, now the only thing you're hiding from them is CRONUS plus Maia and Ryan, of course."

"Mary, Mary, Mary!" Lachlan groaned ignoring the laughter from the peanut gallery.

"What's CRONUS?" Emily asked quietly as the chuckles morphed to smirks, matching that of the Admiral's.

"CRONUS is the code name of a group of three specialist black operations teams, Zeus, Poseidon, and Hades, which report to me. These teams work both domestically and internationally. Although this team is currently on a hiatus from any major or international operations unfortunately, they still seem to get into and find more trouble than the other two teams combined."

Harsh! But yeah, the original plan had been to relocate the base back to the states and continue ops as per normal while they settled in. Instead, one mission went haywire and then they needed time to recover. After two months of straight rest, recovery and bonding, taking six-month temporary roles or assignments had been meant to stop them getting into too much trouble. Although considering, the last week or so, Lachlan figured next time they should all just go on a damn holiday.

Lachlan tuned back into his father-in-law's response to Emily, a little surprised that the Admiral was giving her so much information. Very few people knew the truth, most thought them to be three Navy special ops teams. No more, no less.

"CRONUS sits above and across all arms of the military under the United Nations banner. In fact, we report to the UN, but the Vice President of the United States oversees us. The teams can arrest anyone, anywhere. American citizen or not. Even in a foreign country. We have diplomatic powers many would kill for. It gives us the freedom to do whatever we need to get the job done, although we try to get in and out unannounced, much like any other special ops team. Even so, most of our work focuses on US interests since the UN has four other groups just like us, based in other parts of the world. One for each of the five original members. We're called when no one else can do it but we also take on more mundane ops when other teams are all tied up. It helps with maintaining our cover." The Admiral paused for a breath before finishing his spiel.

"No other teams have the powers we do across all the military arms. All paperwork will confirm us as Navy Seal teams and salaries are paid via the Navy. As most of the guys were Seals first, that's not too much of an issue. It's the few Green Berets who are always grumbling that they're not frogmen. And to be clear. Emily, you're currently amongst the members of team Zeus. Although Poseidon and Hades were all there to pull you out of the river."

"Holy mackerel! And Lachlan's family doesn't know this?"

"No, not only does Lachlan's family not know anything about this. I believe he told them they were, for the lack of a better word, 'Reservists.'"

"Damn it. I didn't have the time to get into it with them. It was the easiest descriptor. Maybe they won't notice!"

"Seriously, Lachlan!" Isabella looked at him like he had lost his mind. His family knew nearly everything now, and he had to admit they'd taken it better than a camel's foot in the ass. But Lachlan didn't like awkward conversations and they all knew if he could avoid it, he would.

"Exactly, Isabella." The Admiral rolled his eyes at him. Rude much! "Besides, you don't think they're going to notice an influx of men into the town who look and act a hell of a lot like you and your team? They will not believe you're all reservists. Or did you think I didn't notice the large parcels of land on either side of your monstrosity had been cleared ready for construction?" Oh boy, the Admiral was working up steam.

"Once your dad and brothers get inside your house, they're going to work out the space doesn't fit the dimensions, and that you've built a bloody compound. As soon as the other two houses go up on either side of yours, they're going to cotton on damn quick, so I suggest you have the conversation with them first. Just like you, Zeke and Liam should have told me your damn plans upfront."

Lachlan kept quiet for a few moments as he tried to work out how upset the Admiral was. Zeke, better known as Reaper, and Liam, nicknamed Arrow, were the team leaders of Poseidon and Hades, respectively. They were both commanders, the same rank as Nate.

After that particularly bad mission before Lachlan took on the role of sheriff, the guys had decided they all wanted to stay close to each other, like they had been when located on various bases around the world.

CRONUS had only been fully green lit three years ago, the teams having to learn their craft and pay their dues first, even though it had been the plan from the start. Now they were both feared and revered by those that knew of them.

When Zeke and Liam had approached Lachlan with the idea of living together, he had been ecstatic. It was rare that all three teams were on ops at the same time, so it meant his family would always be protected.

He knew his parents—and the town—would adopt everyone. They also figured if they were all together, the Admiral and his wife would have more reason to move to the town as they would be close to not only their kids and grandkids but the rest of CRONUS as well.

"Okay, I can see why you would think that we should have told you. But we had our reasons. We only just got the building permits passed through the town council. I had a hell of a time getting Mayor Lewinski to agree to keep my name anonymous, after he copped so much backlash from ma for keeping the secret last time round."

For some reason, it had become a game and the whole town had been actively trying to get the mayor to reveal who had bought the land. In a small town, everyone's gotta know everything.

Ma had never let the man live it down when she found out it was her son coming home to roost and he had kept it from her. He still appeared terrified of the petite woman.

"Ah, can I ask when you decided to move, was it before or after you saw the blocks cleared?"

TWENTY-SIX

Admiral Mark Anderson wasn't sure what was going on. But Lachlan had a gleam in his eye and was now not as worried about the fact the three team leaders had made major plans without telling him, as he was about the answer to the question of when the decision was made.

Suddenly wary of walking into more of Lachlan's antics. The feeling solidified by the narrowing of Isabella's eyes and that of most of Lachlan's team's; Mark stepped off the metaphoric ledge and answered the question. Albeit reluctantly.

By the looks of it, his team didn't know about the plans either, although he knew they would be happy with the announcement.

"Mother and I had been discussing it, but yes, when I saw the two plots on either side of your house cleared and I surmised what you were up to, that was the deal clincher."

Lachlan's face lit up in the biggest, most genuine smile Mark had seen for quite some time and he wasn't the only one that noticed.

Through all the crap that was the last several months, it felt like they finally had the old Lachlan back and Mark would happily deal with the fallout of his antics to keep it that way, not that he'd let

Lachlan know that. The pure joy on Isabella's and the kids' faces at seeing Lachlan's smile was worth any inconvenience.

"Where's my phone? I need my phone asap!" Lachlan started looking around the room.

Deeks didn't make him wait too long before approaching the bed to hand Lachlan his phone. They all knew something was afoot.

"Here you go, Boss Man!"

Lachlan threw a distracted 'thanks' Deeks' way, already punching the screen. The sound of ringing coming through on speaker reverberated throughout the whole room.

"Lachlan, you're alive, ya bastard! Everything okay?"

"Hold up, Reaper, just connecting Arrow." Another click sounded before Arrow's voice came through the speaker.

"Lachlan, you good?"

"Yeah, yeah, listen up. You're on speaker. Everyone's here. The Admiral just blew our surprise. You bastards lost, pay up, losers!"

"No way!"

"Fuck off!"

Lachlan was cackling, about to respond, when Xavi interrupted.

"Daddy, Zeke swored at you."

"Yes, he did Xavi, what a bad man and a sore loser!"

"Xavi? I'm sorry for swearing, buddy, but your dad's an asshole. Lachlan, are you seriously trying to convince us the Admiral has decided to relocate based on Liam and I moving our teams there and not because that's where Izzy, Nate, and the grandkids will be?"

"Yep, losers! They were discussing it but didn't make the jump until they saw the plots next to mine cleared, although he assumed we were building your team's houses on them and not that you were taking over the already built sublevels below the main house. Bonus though, they already bought a house so we no longer have to build them one, we can use that money to build the other training compound we talked about with the additional space for Mad Dog, Boomer, and Bruce to blow things up."

Mad Dog was the explosives expert in team Poseidon and Boomer for team Hades. Ironically, DBD was the explosives expert for team Zeus. It was—against stereotype—that their IT expert/hacker, Bruce, was more likely to join Mad Dog and Boomer in blowing things up for fun.

"Hold up." Mark's voice boomed throughout the room. "Are you telling me the reasons for not including me in your plans to move to the same town was because you had a damn bet going?"

"Shit, my connection's a bit iffy."

"Arrow, if you hang up, I'll have you and your team doing maneuvers at 0200hrs in your skivvies every morning for the next month. I believe snow is imminent."

"Roger that, sir, connection just stabilized."

"Dude, even Gracie doesn't believe that," Luca piped up, causing a barrage of cough-covered laughs throughout the room in deference to the anger emanating from Mark.

"Way to have my back, little man!"

"Daddy told me to call it like I see it!"

"That's my boy!" Lachlan high-fived his oldest.

"You've got my bank details. I expect to see the money by the end of the week."

"Crap." Zeke came back across the line. "Whose stupid idea was this bet again?"

"That's what I want to know." Mark's tone made it clear he still wasn't a happy man.

"Can't remember, sir!"

"No idea, sir!"

"Bullshit!" Mark was not happy, it's not like everyone didn't know his two team leaders were lying through their teeth.

Glaring at Lachlan didn't help either, the man was happily ignoring him all the while rubbing his hands with glee. You'd think he was a cartoon villain or something.

"Lachlan?" Reaper called out.

"What?"

"Is your team happy with us all moving there and living together?"

"Why wouldn't they be?"

"Who the hell knows, did you ask them, asshole?"

"When the fuck would I have asked them? They only just found out now, dickhead."

"You're such an asshole sometimes," Reaper groaned, although with Arrow mumbling in the background, it was a little hard to make out the words.

"Whatever." Lachlan responded, somehow ignorant of all the groans and curses directed his way.

"GD, GD?" Luca yelled out, gaining everyone's attention.

"Yeah, buddy, what's up?"

"Can you please take Gracie, me and Xavi over to Mummy?"

"Um, sure, but can I ask why, little man?"

"Duh, we don't want to be next to Daddy when the lightning hits him."

"Um, why would lightning strike your daddy? We're not in a church. Even he's not that stupid?"

"Mummy said that the 'God of lightning,'" Luca pointed at Lachlan in case anyone was unsure who Izzy had been referring to, "would himself get struck down one day if his games upset Poppy too much. And looking at Poppy, he's gonna blow."

"You can't get hit by lightning inside, stupido. Besides, if Daddy is Zeus, he controls the lightning, not Poppy." Xavi didn't move or open his eyes to deliver his diatribe to his older brother.

"You're stupido. Daddy said that CRONUS is Zeus's daddy. That makes him the boss. Poppy is in charge of CRONUS and Daddy, Zeus, so Poppy would control the lightning, duh!"

"Enough. No one is getting hit by lightning, no matter how tempting. Lachlan, I'd suggest you ease up unless you want to be tortured through your rehab."

"Geez, such sore losers. If they couldn't handle the heat, they shouldn't have made the bet."

Mark narrowed his eyes as the cursing continued from the other end of the call. Lachlan's team remained silent, apparently having cottoned on to something else being at play. Damn it!

"Don't tell me there are more bets!"

"No, sir!" Lachlan's reply was giddy with happiness. "Technically, only multi parts to the same wager. I had to keep it from the team. If they found out before you, I lost. You had to decide to move because they were coming and not only to be closer to the grandkids. If not, I lost. My team had to be happy the other two teams were relocating, or I lost. Though that one was pretty much guaranteed, anyway. But if I could manage everything coming out at once, the bet was to be paid in double. Poseidon and Hades will now be buying each member of my team the latest ATV of their choice."

The cheers from Lachlan's team were loud, but not as loud as the curse Mark himself let loose. Dammit! He was so screwed.

"Dad, what's wrong?" Isabella asked in the sudden silence that had surrounded them. There would be no hiding from this.

"Your husband is sitting there gloating, not only because he just won the bet with Zeke and Liam, but because, by doing so, he also won the bet he had with me."

"Uh oh, Poppy, you said you'd never bet against Daddy again, you even promised Nanna!" Xavi was wide-eyed as he announced this to the room.

"Poppy is in big trouble!" Gracie agreed solemnly with her big brother.

"She's going to kill me! To be fair, there was no way he should have won the bet."

"Seriously, you're acting like you've never met my husband before. What was the bet?"

"He said he could make Poseidon and Hades buy each member of his team an ATV. I said he was nuts, knowing how much they go for, and told him if he could make it happen within three months, I'd buy you and the kids one each as well."

"Well, what can I say, Dad, except for thank you! The kids and I will enjoy them immensely, but yes, Mama is so going to kill you. Um, what would you have won if he had lost?"

"Hey, wait a sec!" Lachlan interrupted, glaring at his wife. "You should thank me, not him. Without my strategic prowess, none of you would get an ATV."

Isabella looked at her husband's grumpy face and laughed, but the gleam in his eye let Mark know there was more at play here than mere ATVs. The man was a genius, but he often used his powers for evil by way of driving his team and family nuts.

It's not like all his men weren't rich. Their jobs paid extremely well. Plus, Lachlan was a generous man who invested in the stock market for everyone. No, the money wasn't the point. Rich or not, losing bets sucked. The ribbing from the smug winners wasn't fun either. Why buy expensive toys for another team when you could buy them for yourselves or your own team?

"Okay, yes, we all do need to thank you, but I still want to know what Poppy would have won should you have lost, and was that the whole of the bet?"

Since Mark was onboard with that, Lachan's bets were never cut and dried, he answered his daughter's question.

"Fine, yes, all right. I bet him he would have to behave whenever in hospital, to follow doctors' instructions, and not try to escape. To do any physio fully and without complaint. If I lost, I wouldn't gang up on him with you to keep him in hospital longer than he deemed necessary. In my defense, who would have thought he could get the other team leaders to buy everyone on his team an ATV? It should have been an easy win!"

"Oh, my Mary, are you insane? He's going to be a nightmare now. Look how smug he is—XAVI, stop! Why'd you hit your brother?"

"I told him not to make the bet, Mummy!"

"What is happening right now? Bruce, bring me Luca, please," Isabella demanded. Mark cringed, he hated seeing his grandkids cry, especially the twins considering what they'd been through.

"Baby, why are you crying? Is it because Xavi hit you or did you make a bet with Daddy?" Isabella cuddled Luca close to her chest as they all waited for his response. His daughter was also glaring over at her husband who, along with Gracie, was rubbing Xavi's back trying to comfort him.

"I bet Daddy. Daddy said he could get everyone a brand-new ATV without paying anything himself. He said Poppy would buy ours. I even asked Poppy if he would ever buy us all an ATV, and he said no. It's not fair!"

Oh crap. Mark remembered that conversation but to be fair he hadn't been lying. He'd just forgotten about the bet and even if he hadn't, Mark would never have thought he'd lose.

"Hmmm, okay. Daddy's being awfully quiet over there, so before I say anything else, how about you tell me what you bet him?"

"We didn't want to go to therapy no more, so we bet that we wouldn't have to, but we lost and now we have to go to therapy until we're twenty-five without making a big deal about it."

"Ah, I see. Well, baby, I have to say I would have been furious with Daddy if he lost that bet. You need to go to therapy, but on the bright side, you'll now have an ATV of your own to go out on in between times." Isabella rubbed Luca's back as she looked over at her husband, who smirked and shrugged.

"They bet, they lost. They'll learn or not!"

More groans coming through the phone Lachlan was holding again caught everyone's attention. It was Emily that started giggling. The sound was great to hear, considering all she had been through.

"There's another part of the bet, isn't there?"

"Reaper? Arrow? Is there another part of the bet?" Mark knew asking was probably the wrong thing to do, but he clearly wasn't the only curious cat in the room.

"Yeah, yeah. Of course, there's another part of the bet, isn't there always? The suck-ass part is that if we didn't have integrity, we could easily deny he's won the third part."

Arrow jumped in before Mark could ask Reaper what the bet was.

"Exactly. I hate my mother for installing morals on me right now."

"Okay, enough. One of you spit it out before you give DBD a migraine."

"Too late, Admiral!" DBD held his hands up in surrender. He might be happy to be getting a brand-new ATV, but the man hated playing games.

"Fine. Look, if at the end of all this we were somehow happy we had lost the bet, then Lachlan would win the overall bet. Of course, we couldn't have predicted we would be happy to lose. Seriously, why would we be happy to buy his whole team ATVs? And Admiral, just to be clear now we've lost everything, the bet was Arrow's idea!"

"Not my fault. This should have been a sure thing!"

"Arrow!"

"Okay, okay. The bet doesn't matter. We lost because Zeke and I would have happily bought everybody a brand-new ATV if it meant the twins would stop fighting everyone and keep going to therapy. So yes, unbelievably, we're happy we lost, if it's the difference between them not going and going. If it weren't for our integrity, we could have bluffed our way out of that one, but that's not how we play. What you should have asked was what Lachlan would have owed us if Zeke and I had won!"

"Okay, I'll bite." Groaning, Mark looked to the ceiling before continuing. "What would you and Zeke have won?"

"Lachlan would have had to facilitate all disciplinary discussions, personally oversee punishments, and handle all the paperwork for any of the crap Mad Dog, Boomer, and Bruce got into over the next five years."

"Holy hell!" DBD blew out a long breath. "To be honest Admiral, even I would have taken that bet on." Yeah okay, that was fair. Mark noticed the rest of team Zeus, including Bruce, funnily enough, were all nodding their heads in the affirmative.

"Yeah," Zeke lamented. "The odds of him winning were so low, we were already crowing in victory. Remind me not to bet against him ever again."

"Ah, Commander? As a soon to be proud owner of a brand-new ATV, I can honestly say I wouldn't willingly remind you not to make bets with our Captain. Especially when his bets normally benefit the entire team."

The chants of 'Hooyah!' that rang out proved Bruce's words stood for the whole of team Zeus.

"All right, look, I think everyone needs to get some rest, but I am not okay with Lachlan having something over the heads of the two other team leaders that I don't know about, so one of you needs to tell me what he won, private or not."

Mark waited for Zeke or Liam to respond, watching as Lachlan alternated between tickling Xavi and Gracie and blowing raspberries all over their little faces. Luca, safely tucked in his mother's arms, didn't wake despite their happy squeals.

"I'm waiting, boys!" He pushed again when no answer was forthcoming.

"Fine, Lachlan gets free babysitting for a full year as soon as the baby is born!" Arrow stated, as the occupants of the hospital room all looked at each other in confusion.

"That doesn't make sense," Nate pointed out. "A, you didn't know Izzy was pregnant and B, any of us would happily babysit whenever he asked, whether team Zeus, Poseidon, or Hades, irrespectively."

"I agree with my son on that one, Liam, and considering all the grandparents, uncles, and aunts just added to the mix, I think you've left something 'major' out."

"Shit, I guess there's no way around this. Okay, this all starts at the birth of his next child, whenever that was to be. Which we now know is sooner than later. Oh, and congratulations Izzy! So, Lachlan will receive a bottle of liquor of his choice, up to the value of five thousand dollars, each month until the child turns one. Isabella gets twelve vouchers for her favorite spa retreat to be used at her convenience. We'll take Luca and Xavi to twelve Minnesota Twins baseball games and Gracie to the same number of children's entertainment concerts, whether in the US or Canada—Smarties were also to be a consideration. Plus, Lachlan can ring us at any time, day, or night, to come and change the baby's diaper. If the asshole times it well, he and Isabella will never have to change a diaper for the whole first year of their child's life. Happy now?"

The silence was deafening but short-lived before the room erupted in laughter.

The idea that Lachlan had two active Commanders of the United States Navy, and leaders of CRONUS special ops teams at that, on call to change his baby's dirty diaper anytime he wanted for a full year, was hilarious.

That he had also sought thoughtful acts for his family was telling of the kind of man he was. Whether a bet or not, Lachlan was making sure his older kids didn't feel left out or that the new baby was usurping them.

Everybody knew Zeke and Liam would have multiple willing bodies to accompany them to take the kids to baseball matches and kids' concerts alike. By making it a bet, Lachlan was ensuring that someone responsible would be there. Without a leader around, sometimes the boys could make poor decisions. It was the diapers that were the killing blow.

Suddenly, feeling fine with losing his own bet, Mark took the phone from Lachlan's hand, saying goodbye and ending the call in one swift movement.

A second later, he pushed the button on Lachlan's morphine drip. The fact that it knocked him straight out told them all just how much pain he'd been in.

With Lachlan out, it wouldn't be long before the rest of the room settled. Laughter was good for recovery, but so was rest, and that was something they all needed, whether they wanted to admit it or not.

EPILOGUE

Emily kept her eyes closed for a few extra seconds as she slowly woke from yet another nap.

Was it over?

For real?

Was she safe now?

Or was this another trap, waiting to be sprung?

Even with the men being as big and take-charge as they were, she felt safe with them. Especially the one called Deeks, who stuck close to her bedside. He made her feel safe, even with the huge scar running down his face, but could she trust her instincts?

She had willingly gone to dinner with the guy who kidnapped her, and he turned out to be a serial killer.

Looking around the room, Emily decided she was seeing things too because surely there couldn't be a huge husky lying under Lachlan's hospital bed, and if there was, wouldn't she have noticed earlier? No. Dogs weren't allowed inside hospitals. If she was not already crazy, she must be well on the way.

Despite everything, Emily still couldn't stop looking at the clock.

What day was it?

Was he out there waiting?

Was this an elaborate part of his plan to make her think she escaped and at the last moment come back to finish the job just as the month of November would tick over into December?

How in the world would she last the remaining couple of weeks of the month, watching the clock, waiting for her monster to reappear?

"Did you mean it?" Emily looked between Lachlan, Deeks, and Isabella. "You'd want me to come back to live with you all?"

"Yes, if you'd like to, that is." Isabela smiled at Emily. "We would love to have you. There is plenty of room. You'll be safe with us, and there will always be someone around should you need to talk or have someone shoot up your closet. It's your decision. The offer is there, but we would never force you."

Emily nodded and closed her eyes to think. It was a lifeline that she wanted to take, but again, there was that niggle. Could she trust herself, trust in her instincts at this point? Although what was the alternative? If she went back to living by herself, wouldn't she make an easier target?

Night was falling when Emily woke next. A blanket of dread had settled back over her. Emily knew she would have to answer questions about what had happened. She wasn't looking forward to having to relive the nightmare, but she had a question that she wanted, no, needed, an answer to.

As if thinking of being questioned conjured them. Two suits walked into the room, introducing themselves as Feds. They had tried to clear the room, but had fallen on deaf ears, scowls, and a series of quick barks. Yep, there truly was a large husky lying under Lachlan's bed. When that failed, they pointed to the children, who promptly had noise canceling headsets put over their ears.

Deeks sat to her left and held her hand while Taniq stood behind him. It turned out they were also federal agents. The two strangers stood to her right. Instead of peppering her with questions, they wanted her to tell them what had happened in her own words. The room was quiet as she told her story uninterrupted.

While she'd expected follow-up questions, it was their answers that were horrific.

They had found the cabin where they'd all been held. As well as the wall where they had scratched their names one by one. They'd also found the graves where the other women had all ended up. Well, except for her. Thirty-four women, she would have made thirty-five. That this had been going on for nearly three years was terrifying.

They told her the man that supplied the drugs was dead, but she had been there for that. Although she didn't remember ever having seen him before.

The Feds also explained that the man behind it, the economics teacher, Mr. Randwick Davey, was in an induced coma, but they hoped to bring him out soon enough. Since he'd been charged federally, he would face the death penalty for what he had done.

It was Lachlan who realized she was expecting to hear more, silencing the room when he asked his question.

"Emily, what have we missed?"

Ignoring the grunts and murmurs from the other agents, she focused on Lachlan.

"They didn't say. I mean. What about the other guy? The bigger one? The one who always wore a condom. He, he was the meaner of the two. I always thought he was the one in charge."

"Go!"

With just one word from Lachlan—Bruce, Taniq, and DBD flew from the room, the other Feds hot on their heels.

When they got to Mr. Davey's room, it was too late. His throat had been slit, arterial spray highlighting the white wall behind him.

Leaving the Feds to the scene, Bruce, Taniq, and DBD returned to the room to brief the rest of the team.

Bruce grabbed his laptop and hacked into the security feed. The Admiral didn't even pretend to ignore what he was doing. As soon as he found the footage they needed to view, Bruce froze the screen and turned it to show Lachlan.

"Fucken son of a bitch. Are you kidding me?"

No one answered. They all knew it was rhetorical. The screen was clear as day. Principal Mullins stood waving at the camera, 'her' Adam's apple in full view, the scarf she routinely wore around her throat, nowhere in sight. Later, they would find it around the neck of the officer who was supposed to be keeping guard. He had been strangled and stuffed into a small closet.

They watched as the principal slit Mr. Davey's throat and then used his blood to write a message on the back of the pillow, holding it up to the camera before turning it over and once again placing it under Mr. Davey's partially severed head.

"November, my sweet. One day, I will be back for you!"

ALSO BY ASHER ZANDS

Cronus: Team Zeus Series:

Thirty Days Has November

6 Days Missing

ABOUT THE AUTHOR

Asher Zands has always been an avid reader, having traveled to many places around the world, Asher is a walking contradiction. An introverted self-confessed hermit, happy to hunker down and not leave the house for days yet quick to jump at any opportunity to travel by air or sea. Asher has a normal fulltime job, so for now, writing is only a hobby. A wannabe writer, Asher hopes to one day turn this hobby into a career. This is Asher Zands first published novel. The second in the series is already written having taken much less time and is heading for the editors. If given a choice, Asher would write and someone else would worry about all the editing, marketing and other varied decisions that go hand in hand in the self-publishing process. Asher loves humor and tends to stay away from too much angst. Life is too stressful to not enjoy happier endings.

ACKNOWLEDGMENTS

To everyone that helped me get here.

From my friends who read the first versions of this story, found errors and gave me wonderful feedback, including the stubborn one that was adamant that I couldn't fire licorice bullets or jellybeans out of a Glock 17, fiction or not.

To those closest to me that encouraged me to keep going. Other writers who offered much advice and a shoulder to lean on.

And finally, to the editors along the way, especially Sarah Williams and her team at Serenade Publishing who got a lot more than they bargained for.

It's been a long road, but without you, this would never have been published.

Thank you!